EROT

Tom came to his senses as the noise from next door reached a crescendo. The sound of Eve's excitement was a familiar one but this was even more intense than usual. What was she up to?

He stepped into the room, expecting to find Eve pleasuring herself and intending to lend a hand. He did not expect to see another woman in her arms on the bed, the two of them stark naked, their loins dancing in tandem. Tom saw the dark hair tangled in Eve's blonde mane, the slim arm around her neck and the scarlet-painted toes scrabbling against the bed sheet: Petra, his ever-efficient office colleague. He'd always imagined she kept a clipboard between her legs. From here it was plain there was something more interesting in that location.

Tom knew it was rude – an inexcusable breach of sexual etiquette – but without announcing his presence he approached the bed . . .

Omnibus editions available from Headline Delta

Eroticon Thrills
Eroticon Dreams
Eroticon Desires
Eroticon Secrets
The Eros Collection
Erotica Italian Style
Follies of the Flesh
Forbidden Escapades
The Forbidden Texts of Cremorne
Habits of the Flesh
Hidden Pleasures, Secret Vices
Insatiable Lusts
Illicit Desires
Lascivious Ladies
The Mysteries of Women
The Power of Lust
The Ultimate Eros
Wanton Excess

Eroticon Fever

Anonymous

Edited and Introduced by
J-P Spencer

Copyright © 1995 J-P Spencer

The right of J-P Spencer to be identified as the Author of
the Work has been asserted by him in accordance with
the Copyright, Designs and Patents Act 1988.

First published in this omnibus edition in 1996 by
HEADLINE BOOK PUBLISHING

A HEADLINE DELTA paperback

10 9 8 7 6 5 4 3 2

All rights reserved. No part of this publication may be
reproduced, stored in a retrieval system, or transmitted,
in any form or by any means without the prior written
permission of the publisher, nor be otherwise circulated
in any form of binding or cover other than that in which
it is published and without a similar condition being
imposed on the subsequent purchaser.

All characters in this publication are fictitious and any
resemblance to real persons, living or dead, is
purely coincidental.

ISBN 0 7472 4921 0

Typeset by Avon Dataset Ltd, Bidford-on-Avon, Warks

Printed and bound in Great Britain by
Caledonian International Book Manufacturing Ltd, Glasgow

HEADLINE BOOK PUBLISHING
A division of Hodder Headline PLC
338 Euston Road
London NW1 3BH

Contents

Lust Under Licence	1
The Secret Diary of Mata Hari	29
Lena's Story	51
Crazy Time	79
The Adventures of a Schoolboy	105
Jazz Baby	135
The Devil's Advocate	165
Betsy Thoughtless	199
With Open Mouth	215
The Carefree Courtesan	237
Madeleine, A Lady of Quality	255
Lust at Large	277
My Secret Life	307

Lust Under Licence

Business tycoon Tom Glass is suffering from memory loss following a fall from his penthouse balcony. At the same time he is under investigation by the Sex Police, a crew of jackbooted female officials determined to expose his rampant depravity to the world. Unbeknown to him, his recovery is being accelerated by drugs which trigger off memories of past sexual encounters.

While Tom languishes in a strictly guarded private hospital, his closest colleague, Petra Rosewater, struggles with the pressures of a revolutionary fitness regime designed to promote health through orgasm.

This is an excerpt from the third of Noel Amos's *Lust* sagas. Prepare for a ride on a train heading way off the rails . . .

Whatever the rumours, and the tabloids were full of them, Tom Glass had not come off his trolley — though sometimes he felt as if he were about to. It was nearly a month now since he had fallen into the street and lost control of his life. And though he was getting back to normal he knew the whole process was taking too long. He was still unable to run his business empire and he was the subject of some kind of crazy prosecution by the fanatic females of the Sex Police.

Thank God for Eve, he thought for the umpteenth time as he sipped his afternoon tea on the patio of Spilling Grange. She had devoted herself to him completely since his accident, sleeping by his side at the hospital in London and accompanying him to this luxurious nursing home in the Leicestershire countryside.

In front of him stretched a green expanse of lawn laid out with croquet hoops, beyond lay a meadow full of grazing sheep where bunnies romped at twilight. Around the old house curved a rippling trout stream which meandered away into thick woods criss-crossed with sun-dappled paths ideal for the strolling convalescent with a few hours to kill. It was idyllic but Tom wasn't fooled. Sooner or later each path came to a halt at the fence, ten foot high and topped with barbed wire. Guards with dogs patrolled at night. Every visitor was checked in and out at a security barrier. This was Spandau Spilling and Tom was Rudolf Hess.

So thank God for Eve, he said to himself again as he watched her walk across the lawn, a spray of freshly gathered wild flowers in her hand. She was a tall, sturdy girl and she looked good in a country setting. The starched white blouse of her nurse's uniform was stretched tight across her jiggling bust and her strong firm thighs undulated beneath the navy blue of her skirt as she strode towards him. He knew, from the memories that had returned to him, that he wouldn't have fancied her in his past life. He would have dismissed her as too big and gauche, not 'sophisticated' enough for him. But now he knew better. He appreciated every glorious inch.

Of course it was all bound up in his recollections. The process of reclaiming his past was somehow all about sex. Each snapshot of his personal history framed a woman in his bed or on the floor or in the garden or, well, almost anywhere. And not just one woman, either. There had been many, in all sorts of combinations. And each of these encounters had plunged him back in time as if on some erotic Tardis. The dreams had seemed more real than the first time around – if that were possible. He didn't understand it. He found it frightening. Particularly because he didn't much like the person who was revealed to him this way. He told Eve as much, each time he woke from a trip into his past. He'd cling to her and confess and she'd absolve him with her understanding words, her loving smile and her magnificent, opulent body. Thank God indeed for Eve.

'Oh Tom,' she said as she arranged her posy of flowers amongst the tea-time crockery. 'Look at you!'

He realised she was looking at his crotch. He grinned a sheepish grin. His cock was sticking out of the fly of his pyjamas, the stalk stiff, the helmet gleaming red.

'You've been thinking about your old girlfriends again, haven't you?'

'No,' he said truthfully. 'I've been thinking about you. Come here.'

'Oh no, Tom, not now,' she protested even as she stepped close enough to his chair for him to slide his hand up her smooth thigh.

'You're not wearing any knickers,' he said, parting the fluffy hair of her bush with his fingers and exploring the frill of her labia.

'You asked me not to.' She gave a little moan as his fingers circled her clitoris.

'Why not?' He lifted the hem of her skirt with his other hand so he could see her pussy as he toyed with it.

'So you could feel me any time, you said.'

Her cunt was like a flower, he thought, lifting its head to the sun and opening its petals. Her fragrance filled his nostrils.

'You're not wearing a bra either, are you?'

'You know I'm not. You forbade me. So you can watch my tits bounce, you said.' His fingers were sticky with her juice now. They made a squidgy sound as he slipped them in and out of her slick vagina.

'I was watching them sway as you walked towards me across the field. They seem to move about of their own accord. As if they've got a life of their own.'

'They're too big.' She was rocking backwards and forwards from the hips, as if trying to capture his entire hand in her snatch. He held his fingers still and watched her movements quicken.

'Take them out,' he said. 'Take off your blouse so I can see them properly.'

'Oh no, Tom, please. Someone might be watching.' Despite her protests her fingers were already unfastening the buttons. She slipped the blouse from her shoulders and dropped it on the floor. 'There. Satisfied?'

They probably were too big, Tom reflected, even for her substantial build. The huge white globes quivered in the sunlight, slung halfway to her waist. What made them seem even larger was the smallness of her nipples, tiny rose-pink buttons thrusting out from the centre of the dimpled saucers of her areolae.

'I think they're magnificent,' said Tom, his voice hoarse with desire. 'Play with them for me.'

'Tom!'

'Lift them up and squeeze them. Wobble them around. You know what I like, Eve.'

She did indeed. Her cheeks flushed bright pink but she did as she was told. She shivered her shoulders and set the great tits dancing from side to side. She took a breast in each hand, cupping them, lifting the weight of flesh upwards and then letting them fall in a pink and white shimmer. Without being asked, she lifted first one breast, then the other to her mouth, bending her head so that she could suck and tease the tiny nipple into a scarlet point. And all the while her pelvis thrust back and forth as she humped shamelessly on Tom's fingers.

'God, Tom Glass, you're a beast,' she hissed, pinching her nipples with her fingers. 'You really bring out the tart in me.'

Her bottom lip was swollen and her eyes were half shut. Her thick fair hair had come loose from its ponytail and now danced around her head in a blonde cloud.

'You're no tart,' he said. 'You're a magnificent, horny woman. You do it because you love it, don't you?'

'Oh yes,' she cried as he leant forward and placed his lips over her vagina. She thrust her loins onto his mouth. A plump buttock in each hand, he lapped at her eager cunt. She ground herself to ecstasy on his face, moaning, 'Oh yes indeed oh gosh oh Christ YES!!'

The orgasm slowly drained away leaving her weak and delirious. She rested her weight on his shoulders, his head still buried beneath her skirt. She felt exhausted and lightheaded – especially as she knew she'd have little time to recover before he'd want to bury his burning erection somewhere in her tingling body.

She supposed he was right, she did love it. But she knew she was indeed a tart. After all, someone – not Tom – was paying for her services.

'They're at it like rabbits down there, guv,' said Sergeant Amy Tooth as she looked towards the rear of Spilling Grange from a window in the west wing.

Inspector Claire Quartermain stood up from her seat across

the desk from Dr Madeleine Flint and joined her junior colleague.

'My, my,' she said as she took in the sight of Nurse Eve Biscuit wriggling half naked on the fingers of patient Tom Glass, 'they don't care, do they?'

'They think they're on their own,' said Dr Flint.

'Obviously,' said Claire.

'Cor, look at those knockers swing,' enthused Amy. 'If she belts him round the head with those he'll never get his memory back.'

'That'll do,' said Claire administering a severe pinch to her subordinate's left buttock out of Madeleine's sight. 'Though that would be a nasty setback, wouldn't it, doctor? All of this is taking long enough as it is.'

The doctor's mouth compressed to a thin line. 'As you know, inspector, you cannot accelerate the healing process.'

'Can't you?' The policewoman turned to face her. 'I thought that's exactly what you were doing. You said you could speed up his recovery with your wonder drug. You promised me you'd slip him some extra.'

Madeleine Flint sighed. 'I did increase the dosage, it's true, but I'm not sure the result isn't counterproductive.'

'What do you mean?'

'I mean that the more he takes, the more he remembers. Instead of just recalling the significant sexual moments of his life and using them as stepping stones to recovery, he's now reliving many insignificant encounters as well.'

Claire Quartermain cursed. 'You mean he now remembers every time he got his leg over with one of his pop singers fifteen years ago?'

'Not every time.'

'Just as well, eh, guv?' said Amy. 'We'll be drawing our pensions by the time he's finished otherwise.'

Claire shot her a look of pure venom. It was all very well for Amy to laugh, she didn't have Gossamer Hawk breathing down her neck. Yesterday's meeting with the Prosecutor was too fresh an encounter for Claire to find the present situation amusing.

Gossamer had laid matters on the line. The recently established Primrose Court had not found universal favour – which wasn't much of a surprise in Claire's opinion, though she did not venture it. Too many of its victims had been non-entities: middle managers with wandering palms, dinosaurs on the verge of retirement who weren't worth reforming, and so on. What was required, according to Gossamer, was the public villification of a youthful captain of industry. Put a man like Glass in the dock, she had said, and you put The Primrose Court on the map.

As things stood they could probably stitch Glass up with no problems. However there was no point in bringing to book a politically incorrect business mogul when he had no memory of his crimes. 'We're not Stalinists,' Gossamer had said when Claire had ventured to suggest that it didn't matter what Glass remembered. 'We must expose the whole man in all his ghastly chauvinism and force him to recant. Then we'll make a real impact on the male bastions of power.'

This kind of talk made Claire uncomfortable. She was just a pragmatic policewoman and she'd go a long way to avoid starry-eyed idealists like Gossamer. Unfortunately Gossamer had a lot of clout. A zealot with power – just who you didn't want for a boss. And right now she was demanding Tom Glass's nuts on a platter.

'So how much does he remember now?' said Claire to Madeleine.

The doctor consulted her notes. 'He's just taken over Chas Cross's company, Euphoria, and become a millionaire at the age of twenty-four.'

'Blimey,' said Amy, 'how did he manage that?'

'Shani and the Shagbags had six number ones in a year and two platinum albums. Euphoria had been in trouble and the company had such desperate cash-flow problems they couldn't pay Glass his royalties on time. Cross let Glass buy him out.'

'With his own money?' said Claire.

'Basically, yes. The real story was that Cross suddenly lost his grip. He became besotted with one of the Shagbags and his business went to pot. Glass took advantage. Here's Nurse Biscuit's report.' Madeleine pushed a folder across the desk. 'You could also look at the videos.'

'What videos?' said Amy.

'We've got recording equipment in his room. So far there's about five hundred hours of material. We can use it to corroborate Nurse Biscuit's testimony and vice versa.'

'I wouldn't mind looking at some of those videos,' said Claire.

'I see no objection provided they are logged out.' Madeleine pointed to a bookcase overflowing with cassettes. 'They're completely unedited. You'll have to fast forward through a lot of, er, activity between Glass and Nurse Biscuit.'

'Of course,' said Claire. 'We'll ignore all that, won't we, Amy? It's of absolutely no interest to us at all.'

Downstairs, in Tom Glass's room, Nurse Eve Biscuit was oiling her big breasts unaware that a concealed camera was watching her every move.

Tom was watching too as she slowly poured aromatic flower essence onto the upturned jellies of her chest and smoothed the lotion into every pore. Tom stood by the bed, breathing hard, his cock twitching in impatience as Eve's little fingers teased her nipples to firm peaks and smoothed under and over the big rounds, setting the flesh wobbling deliciously.

'Now you,' she said, beckoning him closer and slicking the lubricant up and down the broad spear of his distended penis.

He straddled her chest and laid his cock in the valley

between her pink and glistening mountains. She grasped one in each hand and folded the warm flesh over his aching member, squeezing her bosom in from the sides until his big barrel was completely enveloped. He braced himself on his hands and began to shaft up and down that delightful passage. On the upthrust his empurpled glans speared up from her cleavage and she bobbed her head to lick the gaping eye in the shiny helmet before it slid back down her slippery valley.

The ritual of the tit-fuck was well established between the pair of them.

As they amused each other in this fashion they talked. It wasn't uplifting conversation – in a general sense, that is – though they found it stimulating. It concerned the pleasure they took in each other's body – the shape, the size, the feel and so forth. Comparisons were made with others and, in particular, their suitability for the precise activity in which they were engaged. Dr Madeleine Flint, it was agreed, would be too slender of bosom to provide much comfort for a lusty tool like Tom's; and Eve's last boyfriend, so she said, had been so diminutive that his cock would have been lost forever had they ever tried to do it this way.

As ever, when discussing the matter, Tom would conclude that Eve provided the most exquisite, the most perfect and probably the most unbeatable tit-fuck in the entire world. This comment always pleased Eve and led her to greater activity with her hands and tongue. The whispered endearments became more obscene and less coherent. Soon, in fact, Tom was unable to utter anything at all beyond 'Ooh' and 'Oh yes' and finally, 'I'm coming' at which point he inundated her face and neck and chest with a river of spunk.

As always, Eve rubbed the cream from his cock lovingly into her tits, soothing the abused flesh, laughing up at him with a sparkle in her eye. And a hunger, too, for it was her turn now and she was savouring what she would have him do to her next.

And, unknown to them both, the camera in the ceiling recorded every thrilling moment.

Petra was feeling pretty good – the Honeydew fitness routine had put a spring in her step and a twinkle in her eyes. In fact, she was a real convert.

'My,' said Cassie with a sly note in her voice as she reviewed Petra's results, 'I wouldn't have thought Kelvin had it in him.'

But it was no thanks to Kelvin that Petra had achieved her orgasm target every day for a month. And there were no new names in Petra's personal organiser – unless you could count The Magic Wand. The glass dildo had put Petra to sleep every night with a smile on her lips and woken her in the morning with an urge to plunge its smooth glowing head between her thighs at least once – maybe twice – before breakfast. It was the most entrancing thing she had ever owned – the ultimate sex object. She was in love.

Truth be told, it had taken her mind off Kelvin and the sudden deterioration of their relationship. Petra felt guilty because it had started the night she had first wanked herself to exhaustion with The Wand. Kelvin had been out late, so late that when he'd returned he'd bedded down in the spare room so as not to disturb her – or so he said. He'd stayed out late the next night and the night after that. Soon the late nights and the spare room had become a pattern.

Petra thought it was funny how quickly the new regime had become established, obviously it must have suited them both. She would leave the office around ten or eleven at night and go straight to bed with a sandwich, a glass of wine – and The Wand. It would often be one or two in the morning before she fell asleep, usually with the glass tool still buried in her sated pussy. She didn't care to speculate on what Kelvin might be up to. They rarely saw each other and at weekends they found reasons not to be together. His reason, like hers, was called 'work' but she had no doubt – if she were to force the truth out of him – it might be better termed 'another woman'.

On the morning Cassie congratulated Petra on her Honeydew endeavours and made her sly remarks about Kelvin's prowess, Petra put down the phone and marched into the spare room.

It was neat – that surprised her. Like most New Men, on the domestic front Kelvin was pretty much old school and Petra did the clearing up around the flat. She had expected chaos but the bed was made, his clothes were hung tidily and folded in drawers and, on the table by the window, pencils and paper were squared away by the side of the word processor. Even the waste-paper basket was empty. This was not at all like Kelvin. As a journalist, it was an article of faith that his working papers were in unfathomable disarray.

This orderliness made it easy for Petra to spot the clues to Kelvin's new way of life. On the bookshelf above the table was a row of paperbacks with uniform luminous green spines. Petra was surprised to see that they were porn books designed for female readers. And hanging up in the wardrobe was a weird all-in-one garment of black rubber. She took the smooth membrane between thumb and forefinger – it felt like loose skin. She shivered. She noted that the article had a cutaway crotch. Kinky.

Of course she checked for the obvious things: dirty shirts with lipstick stains, love letters hidden at the back of a drawer, female trinkets under the bed – not that she really thought Kelvin would dare bring a lover back to the flat. She found nothing.

When she left she took with her one of the erotic books – maybe it would provide some clues to Kelvin's mysterious conduct. On the other hand, she wasn't holding her breath.

She looked at the book on the train up to Spilling Grange. In a tightly packed carriage full of men she would have felt embarrassed to be seen reading *Cold Stone, Warm Flesh* by Morticia Chekhov. However, she had selected her first-class accommodation with care. It contained only one other person, evidently a businesswoman like herself, dressed in a severely cut navy blue suit, making notes on a foolscap pad. Holding the book so the cover could not be seen, Petra began to read.

By the end of the first chapter the naive young heroine, Deliciosa, had fallen into the hands of the cruel but charismatic Thaddeus who took her back to the family castle. By page thirty he had introduced her to the delights of the old schoolroom and caned her bare bum, by forty-five he had flogged her in the ancestral hall and on seventy he was heating up meat skewers in the kitchen to pierce her nipples.

'Yuk,' said Petra out loud and the woman opposite looked at her keenly through her black-rimmed spectacles.

Petra found it hard to believe Kelvin was turned on by this stuff. Surely he didn't want to stick red-hot skewers into *her* nipples? Evidently not. Whatever he was sticking where these days, it wasn't into her. She flicked on through the pages.

On page ninety-five Deliciosa, now pierced, degraded and rendered multi-orgasmic, was introduced to Thaddeus's former governess, an imperious female with horn-rimmed spectacles whose first words to her were –

'Take off your knickers!'

Petra's head jerked up, she could have sworn she had actually heard the words. The woman opposite was grinning at her.

'Take off your knickers,' she repeated, 'that's what someone always says to the heroine in those books.'

'Oh,' said Petra. 'You're right.'

'Of course. And the silly girl goes around bare-arsed for the rest of the story. You can imagine what happens then.'

'Quite.' Petra nodded, not wanting to appear ignorant.

'So now you can put the book away and talk to me. If you'd like to, that is.'

Behind the spectacles the stranger's eyes were almond-shaped and hazel-hued. She had a wide curving mouth that tugged upwards at the corners. She didn't look kind but she did look interesting. Petra was surprised to find she did not resent being bullied like this. She put the book into her briefcase.

'What did you want to talk about?' she asked.

'Your pretty little cunt, of course.'

The woman's smile was still in place but Petra felt as if she had just been doused in cold water.

'You can't talk to me like that!' she spluttered.

'Why not? If you don't like it you can go and sit somewhere else.'

'I could report you.'

'You could but there's no point – who'd believe you? Anyway who's reading pornography around here? Not me. If I were a man, of course, I'd never get away with saying something like that. But then, if I were a man I wouldn't dare.'

Petra stared at her, aghast. There was no arguing with what she said.

'So, take off your knickers and hand them over,' continued the woman. 'Unless you're not wearing any.'

'Of course I'm wearing knickers.'

'What colour?'

'White.' Why did she say that?

'How sweet. Let me see.'

It was the recent encounter with Inspector Quartermain, Petra later reasoned, that caused her to comply. That all-too-vivid scene had been replayed frequently on nights she had cuddled up with only The Wand for company. The woman opposite her had the same mocking arrogance of the inspector and the same confidence that her will would prevail.

Petra stood unsteadily, supporting herself with one hand as the train rushed on. With the other she raised the skirt of her short summer dress.

'Oh yes,' said the woman, leaning forward to gaze at

Petra's bare white thighs, 'you're quite a curvy little thing, aren't you?'

The hem of Petra's skirt had now reached the vee of her pantied crotch and her hand shook as she lifted it the last few inches to reveal herself.

'White indeed,' said the woman, 'I rather hoped you'd be lying so I could punish you. Never mind, I'll find some other reason.'

'What?' Petra couldn't believe she was doing this.

'Take them off quickly.' The voice was harsh. 'Show me your cunt, slut, and hurry up.'

The words hit Petra like blows to the face. She fumbled her panties down her thighs and fell back onto her seat to slip them over her shoes.

'Who said you could sit down? Stand up at once!' hissed her tormentor and Petra jumped to her feet, her panties now in her hand. The woman snatched them from her and pressed them to her lips.

'They're soaking wet,' she pronounced with a hoarse laugh. 'You delicious little baggage. My, are we going to have fun! Now, let me have a good look at you . . .'

And as the train rushed onwards Petra held her dress high and eased her feet apart. Maybe she was going crazy but she couldn't help herself. The woman leaned forward till her mouth was an inch from the impudent curls of the exposed pussy. Her eyes were on Petra's most intimate secrets like a torch beam at midnight and her breath caressed Petra's itching clitoris like a warm breeze off a summer sea.

'Oh God, oh God, oh God,' she moaned softly.

Though her persecutor had not even touched her, Petra knew she was about to come.

Petra knew her behaviour was shameful. Standing there on the train, holding her dress high to reveal her nude pussy mound to a complete stranger – that was shameful. Shameful and glorious. She couldn't help herself.

The dark woman simply stared at her bared pubis and Petra came. The strength melted from her legs and she hung on to the luggage rack with her free hand as her pelvis jerked convulsively. She could feel the petals of her cunt opening before the woman's penetrating gaze. She could smell the perfume of her own excitement thick in the air. And she danced like a puppet and orgasmed in the woman's face.

The sound of the carriage door sliding back broke the spell. Petra fell back onto the seat in a confused and blushing heap, pulling her skirt hastily down her thighs.

'Good morning, ladies,' came the sound of a cheerful voice. 'I trust you are enjoying the journey on this delightful morning. May I remind you there is a buffet car on this service, providing a variety of delicacies – though I would recommend from personal experience that you steer clear of the croissants.'

Petra stared at the tall youth in the uniform as though he were a man from Mars. The intrusion of everyday reality into this fantasy journey was hard for her to take. Her companion, on the other hand, was not fazed for a moment.

'I suppose you'd like to see my ticket, inspector.'

'I would indeed, madam, though I'd prefer to be called Phil. We're user-friendly these days, especially to attractive ladies travelling in first class.'

The woman flashed Phil a smile as she flashed her ticket. She looked positively flirtatious.

Petra reached for her handbag but the dark woman suddenly grasped her hand, preventing her from opening it.

'It's all right, darling,' she said to Petra, 'I've got yours here.' And she held out her other hand to the railway inspector.

Phil looked bemused as he took the white scrap of material from her. Petra froze, rigid with panic. She knew what he held in his hand.

'Bloody hell,' he said as he unfolded Petra's tiny panties. Then, bonhomie instantly replaced by suspicion, he demanded: 'What's your game then?'

'Just a little user-friendly fun,' said the woman. 'My friend's lost her ticket but she can show you something else instead.'

Petra said nothing, the other woman was in control. She could feel the juice seeping out of her onto the seat beneath her bare buttocks.

Phil was turning the panties over in his hand. He fingered the damp gusset.

'Wet, aren't they?' said the woman. 'She can't help having such a juicy quim. Would you like to look at it?'

Phil was speechless now but the bulge in the grey serge of his trousers was unmistakable and spoke volumes.

The woman had removed Petra's bag from her lap and was looking at her. Petra knew what she was expected to do – and she did it.

'There!' cried the woman in triumph as Petra slowly pulled her skirt up her thighs. Her little black bush, framing two pink-frilled pussy lips, sprang into view. 'Isn't that a pretty sight?'

Loquacious Phil was now lost for words. Just a grunt issued from his dry throat but his appreciation of Petra's charms was obvious.

'Perhaps you'd like a closer inspection, *inspector*? Why don't you spread your legs, my dear, and let the gentleman have a good look.'

Petra did as she was told, sliding forward on the seat and parting her thighs. Both her inner and outer lips were on full view and at the top of her glistening sex furrow her impatient clitoris throbbed.

'Play with yourself,' came the order and Petra obeyed. She drew her fingers through her muff, fluffing out the silky hairs. She ran a slim index finger around the edge of her gaping hole and up to the pearl of her clit. She nudged it with her long varnished nail and her whole pelvis rippled in response. Breath hissed between her teeth. She stroked herself again.

'Put your fingers in.' She did so, one then two. Then the

whole of her hand as she rubbed the nub of her clit, ramming her knuckles into her juicy slot and moaning out loud. She couldn't have stopped herself from coming if the entire railway inspectorate had entered the carriage.

'She's a complete slut, isn't she, Phil?' said the dark woman, amusement and contempt in her voice. 'Have you seen enough yet? Or is there something else my friend can do for you?'

Petra hoped there was. Her hand was still between her legs, gently fingering her labia, keeping her raging desire on the boil. Her eyes were on Phil's flushed face – and on the swelling at his crotch. He looked as if he might burst out of his trousers at any minute.

Finally he spoke. 'By Christ, I've got to fuck her!' he growled and took a step towards Petra's enticing form.

The dark woman seized his arm and held him back. 'Don't touch her,' she hissed. 'I want to look at you first.'

To Petra's surprise, he obeyed her. At the woman's bidding he stripped down to brief blue jockey shorts that barely contained his excitement. Beneath his uniform his tall sinewy body bore the remains of a Mediterranean tan and his stomach was as flat as a board.

'My, we're in luck,' said the woman and pulled his briefs to his knees.

Petra gave an involuntary moan as his cock sprung into view. It was sparsely haired and thick, the flaming-red head gleaming with excitement. For two pins, she would have sunk it between her legs at once. But that was not permitted. Yet.

'Not bad,' said the orchestrator of this bizarre occasion. She peered closely at the bobbing organ through her spectacles and, taking a pencil from her jacket pocket, she used it to lift his heavy scrotum. 'Turn around,' she commanded and the two women surveyed his bronzed back and the tight white moons of his buttocks.

'Do you want him?' the woman said to Petra.

She nodded, her eyes bright.

'Very well. But you'll both have to do what I say.'

She made Petra take off her dress and allowed Phil to fill his hands with her small swaying breasts. She positioned their bodies to her liking, with him standing and Petra in his arms, her legs scissored round his waist, her hands holding on to the luggage rack. Thus, wrapped around each other in a hurtling train, the two of them made intimate acquaintance.

The dark woman took charge of their genitals, pressing the plum of his stiff tool into the hungry vagina suspended above it. And then feeding the fat length of him inside her.

The weight of Petra's body drove her down onto Phil's broad penis. He stretched her wide and she howled as she sat on him, bumping and shifting with the rush of the train. His mouth was on her upturned breasts and his hands held her up by her arse cheeks, his fingers curling into the crack of her behind. Petra felt helpless, suspended in midair, balancing on a stranger's cock, hanging on to the rail above her lest he should be thrown off his feet by a sudden jolt.

It was incredible. Every judder and shake of the train rubbed their sex membranes together and sent electric thrills jolting down to their nerve ends.

Below them, the choreographer of this erotic *pas de deux* sat making notes. Petra looked down in amazement to see the woman peering intently at their writhing bodies and jotting things on her pad. What the hell was she doing?

But Petra was no longer capable of rational thought. Her body was one mass of sensation. The difficulty of sustaining the position had delayed her satisfaction long enough – and she guessed her partner felt the same way too. He thrust up into her with carnal intent and bit down on her nipple. As a finger pushed at the dimple of her anus and then sank in to the second knuckle she squealed and rubbed her belly furiously against his. If only he would reach round and diddle her clit . . .

And then she felt something hard and slim nose into the gap between their lunging loins. With remarkable accuracy it approached the hood of her clitoris and applied the exact point of pressure that she required. Petra looked down and saw the dark-haired women leaning close to their lunging bodies. With one hand she appeared to be groping between Phil's legs – fondling his balls maybe from the way he was now bucking into her. And with the other she was poking the top of a pencil onto Petra's aching, yearning clit.

'AAH!' Petra's squeal of ecstasy was drowned in a shout from Phil that reverberated throughout the carriage. 'Oh God!' he yelled again as he emptied his balls into her and the two of them collapsed onto the floor. At that precise moment, the train began to slow down.

'Oh shit, I'm late!' cried Phil as he disentangled himself and scrabbled frantically for his clothes. 'You're two wild women, I've got to say that,' he added, grinning from ear to ear and hopping into his trousers. Suddenly he grabbed Petra's hand, 'Just tell me one thing, darling – did the train move for you?' And he backed out of the door laughing, his good humour quite restored.

On arrival at Spilling Grange, Petra accepted the offer of a drink with alacrity. The ice shook in the tumbler as she gulped a generous gin and tonic poured for her by the ever-solicitous Nurse Biscuit.

'Is there a problem, Petra?' asked Tom. 'You look a bit frazzled this morning.' He himself looked a picture of health, lounging in a deck chair on the sun-dappled lawn.

'No problem, Tom,' said Petra as emphatically as she could. What else could she say?

The truth was that she had just experienced the train ride of her life and she was still in shock at her own behaviour. She had never done anything quite so outrageous before as fucking a total stranger on a train. But it wasn't so much the hip-hugging pelvic dance on Phil's thick cock that disturbed her, it was the way she had allowed the dark-haired woman to manipulate her. The fact that she had positively gloried in handing over to another person the responsibility for her own insatiable libido.

Well, at least she had solved one mystery about her erotic companion. Her identity. And that was as bizarre a coincidence as any she had ever come across. As they parted the woman had handed Petra a business card with a sardonic smile. It read: Morticia Chekhov, Author and Purveyor of the Erotic Arts. So now Petra was the proud possessor of an authentically autographed and spunk-stained pornographic novel. She intended to put it back on Kelvin's shelf as soon as possible. Let him work it out.

'Another drink, Petra? You look as if you're about to eat the glass.'

'Perhaps you'd like a shower,' suggested Eve Biscuit.

'Oh yes,' Petra said at once. The expression 'travel worn' hardly covered how she felt.

Under the splash of warm water she began to feel better. But her mind was still in turmoil and two quick gins hadn't helped. She stepped out of the shower stall and felt giddy. She subsided onto a stool and buried her head in a towel.

'Are you all right, Miss Rosewater?' Nurse Biscuit was at the door, concern on her pretty face.

Petra opened her mouth to say, 'I'm fine' but nothing came out.

The nurse took over, gently towelling her dry, providing a bathrobe and producing a hairdryer. In seconds, it seemed, Petra found herself sitting in front of a dressing table. The small room also contained an easy chair, a portable television and a bed. As Eve dried her hair she said, 'This is where I sleep. It's right next to Mr Glass so I can keep an eye on him at night.'

Petra glanced quizzically at the voluptuous blonde nurse.

Who was she kidding? She spent most of her nights in Tom's bed, it was well known.

The bathrobe was open almost to Petra's nipples and Eve's eyes in the mirror were on her breasts. More specifically, they were on the raw marks of Phil's ardent attentions. The nurse put down the hairdryer to examine them.

'That looks sore,' she said. 'How did you do it?'

Petra was caught by surprise. 'My boyfriend,' she said hastily, 'he's very passionate.'

'I can see that,' said Eve, opening a jar of ointment. 'The marks are very recent.'

'Yes. They are.'

There was a silence as Eve began to rub the cream into Petra's abraded tits. Her fingers were soothing and supple. The bathrobe fell to Petra's waist as Eve sought and found further sore spots. Her nipples were red and swollen. There were bite marks on the undercurves of her high pointed breasts.

'Ooh,' cried Petra.

'Did that hurt?'

'No, not exactly.' It was the opposite, in fact. Petra's flesh was singing, her nerves still jangling from her adventures on the train, from ceaseless application of The Wand, from her constant search for orgasmic release in the cause of Honeydew heaven . . .

'Oh yes,' she moaned between closed lips as Eve found a sensitive spot on the back of her neck.

'Stand up,' said the nurse and Petra obeyed without a thought, presenting herself nude, every square inch of her sensitive flesh alert to Eve's ministrations.

The nurse found the marks of rough fingers on Petra's bottom cheeks. She saw the fresh bruises on her inner thighs. She noted that her labia were puffed and swollen. 'I can guess what you've been up to, Miss Rosewater,' she said. 'You took a lover on the train, didn't you?'

Petra nodded. Eve was rubbing cream into her bum now

and she found herself pushing her arse cheeks back onto the girl's hand. She couldn't help it. It felt delicious.

'I suspected something like that when you turned up all wobbly at the knees, with your hair messed up,' said Eve. 'But I knew for sure when I picked up your clothes while you were in the shower.'

Petra looked at her blankly.

'There were no knickers.'

'He must have kept them,' said Petra.

'How romantic. Was he handsome?'

'Very.' It was true. Phil had been a hunk. She'd been lucky. The mood she'd been in she'd have shagged Quasimodo.

'Are you going to see him again?'

'I hope not,' said Petra, aghast at the thought.

'You're a bit stiff across the shoulders,' said Eve. 'Would you like me to massage you? I know what I'm doing.'

Petra had no doubt of that. As she lay face down on the bed, Eve busied around fetching what she needed and soon those strong knowing fingers were working their magic across Petra's shoulders. She felt as if she were in a dream. So it was a few moments before she identified the weighty kiss of flesh across her back that was not generated by Eve Biscuit's hands. She turned her head to look at Eve and her heart thudded in shock. The nurse was bending over her stark naked. Petra was in receipt of a double massage, from Eve's hands and from the biggest pair of breasts she had ever seen.

'My God, Eve, do you ever massage men?'

'Only the ones I really like.'

'I bet they like it too.'

Eve giggled and smacked Petra on the rump. 'Turn over, Miss Rosewater, and let me do the other side.'

Petra had never before contemplated the fleshy opulence of one of her own gender. Until recently she had not taken any interest in women in a sexual sense. But from Claire

Quartermain to the woman on the train, the next step was obviously meant to be someone like Eve Biscuit.

As the curvaceous nurse stood over her, massaging her limbs, Petra felt she understood for the first time the lure of a woman's body. Watching all that glorious nude flesh on the move, the thrust and swing of the girl's big bosom, the curve of the hip and the dome of the belly as it sloped down to the mystery of her pubic delta, Petra reacted as she imagined a man might. First she wanted to explore all that tumbling creaminess – to roam those big bouncing hills, to explore the winding curves, to lose herself in the secret nooks and crannies of Eve's generous flesh. And then, if only she had The Wand to hand, she'd fuck her stupid.

'Oh, Eve,' she breathed as the nurse worked on her upper thigh, the little finger of her left hand a millimetre away from the pouting lips of her yearning pussy. 'That's so good!'

Nurse Biscuit smiled. 'Would you like a body hug, Miss Rosewater? It's my speciality.'

Petra nodded. She'd have agreed to anything.

The nurse mounted the bed and straddled Petra's thighs. For a moment she loomed over the supine woman, the cloud of her fair hair and the rounded mass of her sumptuous body blocking out the light from the window. Then she slowly lowered herself on top of Petra. She covered her like a silky blanket of warm flesh: the big breasts crushing against the smaller woman's chest, the firm columns of her thighs capturing Petra's slim ones, her entire body cleaving to Petra in an incredible all-over embrace.

'My God,' whispered Petra, her arms automatically folding around the other woman's back, accepting the soft weight. 'Oh Eve,' she muttered into the nurse's neck as she felt, for the first time, the pressure of another woman's belly on hers.

Eve was wriggling now, searching for the right connection between their forms, taking the weight off Petra's chest but increasing it on her pubic bone until – 'Oh!' cried Petra in surprise – their vaginal slits were joined in an open-mouthed kiss.

Petra swooned. It was too much – the heat, the gin, the incredible body rub. And now this, the feel of another woman between her thighs, pressing her cunt into hers, their clits rubbing together, rushing them both towards an orgasm of unique intensity. What a day for Honeydew, she thought as her loins rippled to the first thrill.

She found she was kissing Eve Biscuit like a lustful male, her tongue halfway down her throat, her hands palming and stroking the silky globes of the other's swollen teats where they stuck out between their heaving bodies. 'Oh Eve, oh Eve,' she muttered over and over like a mantra, as her lips flicked over the sweet curve of the other's neck and her hands found the girl's nipples – big and fat and rubbery in her fingers.

Eve had set up a masterful rhythm now: rolling her pelvis down and across Petra's, driving their hungry pussies together, marching them to the summit of their first come. A high-pitched squeal rose from both throats as they reached their destination together.

Outside, on the lawn, a discordant yet thrilling sound roused Tom Glass from sun-baked slumber. These days, the once nervy hard-edged business tycoon tended to drift off into a sensuous reverie in any spare moment – and, between shagging his delicious medical attendant, there were plenty of those.

He came to his senses fast, the noise from the room next to his reaching a crescendo. He knew at once what it was, though he could hardly believe his ears. The sound of Eve's excitement was a familiar one but this was even more intense than usual. What was she up to?

Tom stepped slyly into Eve's room, expecting to find her pleasuring herself and fully intending to give her a helping hand. What he did not expect to see was another woman in her arms on the small bed, the two of them stark naked, their loins dancing in tandem as the insistent cries of female orgasm echoed around the small space. Tom had quite forgotten about his visitor but now, as he took in the implications of the dark hair tangled in Eve's blonde mane, the slim arm clasped tightly around her neck and the small feet with their wriggling, scarlet-painted toes scrabbling against the bed sheet, Tom remembered Petra.

He had been erect already, of course. But if it had been anatomically possible, this realisation would have put another six inches on his straining, throbbing tool. Petra, his petite and curvy chief executive, with her air of ever-vigilant efficiency, who gave the impression she kept a clipboard between her legs – he couldn't believe it! And yet here she was in a position that clearly revealed she kept something much more interesting in that location.

The two women had not noticed him, their pleasure was too exclusive. He approached the bed as if sleep-walking, his eyes fixed on the apex of their splayed legs where the rivers of their gratification mingled. Above were the pale swollen moons of Eve's shaking arse cheeks, the deep shadow bisecting the smooth spheres pointing down to the brown-tufted maw he knew so well. And beneath that, winking and gaping, thrusting upwards like a thirsty mouth at a water fountain, was the pretty pussy slit of Petra Rosewater, framed by the succulent flesh of her trim but well-rounded thighs and buttocks.

The line that ran from the base of the blonde girl's spine down to the bedsheet, encompassing two arseholes, two cunts and a myriad of dizzying possibilities, hypnotised Tom. He fell to his knees and leant forward as close as he could. The scent of female excitement was overwhelming and the proximity of their abandon intoxicating. He could see their labia rubbing together, the slippery folds of skin clinging and sucking as they kissed. And, deeper, in the heart of their connection, he could glimpse the two clitorises – Eve's small and pink, Petra's long, redder – glued together, keeping the women on a never-ending roundabout of sensual pleasure.

Tom knew it was rude – an inexcusable breach of sexual etiquette – but without previously announcing his presence he thrust his face into the double-cunted fissure of flesh in front of him and began to slake his thirst.

Later, when the afternoon had come and gone and the two women were lying in Tom's arms, Petra said, 'That's the most enjoyable business meeting I've ever attended.'

Eve rolled over onto her back and stretched. The three of them were sprawled across two mattresses on the floor – hospital beds not being wide enough for the afternoon's activities. 'Is that what happens at business meetings?' she said. 'I've often wondered.'

Tom said nothing, he was still in a reverie of sexual intoxication. The impact of these two different but equally delicious women had rendered him incapable of idle speech. He still savoured in particular the look of horror and of expectation on Petra's face when she had finally registered his presence – and that had not been for some while after he had begun lapping her delicious cunt. Since then he had been forced to revise his opinion of his colleague. She was a perfectionist at everything she did and she did much more than he had suspected.

'I came up here for a reason,' she was saying.

Tom nodded and idly stroked her silky smooth hip.

'I don't think the police are interested in finding out about your accident,' she continued. 'Quartermain just wants to nail you for sex crimes. It's up to us to find out who pushed you off the balcony.'

'We've talked about this before, Petra.'

'I know.' She was sitting up now, her face earnest, her pouting breasts shaking as she made her point. 'But now you remember so much more of your life, can you think of anyone who might want to kill you?'

'No.' Really those little tits were quite delicious.

'But you must have made enemies. People in your past who might bear a grudge.'

'No.' He'd never have imagined he was still capable but his cock was suddenly at full stretch. Again.

'Don't be stupid, Tom,' said Eve. 'Present company excepted, what about every woman you've ever slept with?'

Tom gave it some thought. By God, she was right!

Suddenly his erection had melted like a snowflake in the summer sun.

The Secret Diary of Mata Hari

The real Mata Hari was a Dutch dancer with a liking for military men. Her life was tempestuous, including a disastrous marriage to a Scots alcoholic, the mysterious death of her small son in the Dutch East Indies and subsequent fame and notoriety in Paris as an exotic dancer. Almost everything said about her can be disputed: whether she was truly beautiful, whether she was much of a dancer – whether or not she was really a spy . . . What is not in contention is that she cast an erotic spell over her audiences and had many lovers. And that the French executed her for spying in November 1917. Whatever the facts, Mata Hari is now a creature of myth and fair game for movie-makers and writers and those keen to exploit her scandalous reputation.

The *Secret Diary* explores the sensual side of the legendary voluptuous dancer. It is not a historical document, as can be seen from the following extract. On the other hand it *is* good rude fun . . .

Paris, 19**

In the beginning I liked the milieu I found at Madam Desiree's place very much; her clients consisted mainly of members of the middle class. She had, as she proudly assured me, an exceptionally 'fine' class of customers. 'They are all very well brought up; yes, most of them have had a good education.

'In my establishment you will not find those Apaches that scare a lady and trick her out of a few nickels, entirely aside from the fact that they try to use the material for free, and not only that, they work it too hard. Whenever such a man sleeps with a girl, the poor thing can't be used again for at least twenty-four hours . . .'

These prospects did not deter me in the least, on the contrary I would enjoy being worked over rather well. But the greatest attraction for me was being able to 'work' in Madam Desiree's house with my face hidden behind a mask. Madam Desiree insisted upon it, because she realised full well that this little 'trick' had its own special added attraction. Moreover I worked very cheaply. Anyhow, the set-up was cheaper than a piquant gown or real silk stockings. However, she did not object when the ladies used their own fineries when the overall effect would be enhanced by them. And after all, she was the one who made the largest profits from them.

Whenever I arrived I would slip through the side entrance of a small cafe which was connected with a secret door to Madam Desiree's house. Drinks and other orders were also delivered through this door and the Madam of this fairly reputable, well-managed bordello made a good profit from them also. Once arrived, I would climb the small and very narrow spiral staircase till I reached my own little apartment on the second floor. It was my very own, tiny little bedroom with an even tinier little toilet. Both rooms were very clean and decorated according to the typical taste which one might expect in these small hidden shrines dedicated to the services of lustful Venus.

The moment I reached my room, I must admit that I quickly and happily divested myself of my clothes, especially my expensive lingerie. I draped a huge shawl, an exquisite piece of Turkish handwork, around my body, the long fringes clinging to my nude thighs. This shawl had the added advantage that it could be draped around my body in a thousand different ways, each one of them enticing, without ever hiding too much . . .

On other days I dressed in a tricot which consisted merely of holes; I mean that my flesh showed through a net whose mazes were almost two centimetres in diameter. Obviously I never forgot to wear a pair of black stockings worked with open lace. This particular costume drew the open admiration of Madam Desiree. 'Oh, Madam,' she was always very free giving us the title Madam unless she suddenly preferred to introduce us as her co-workers, 'you really do your best for my house, but believe you me, and I always tell the other ladies exactly the same, my profits are also yours!'

The most exciting moment, at least for me, was that of the 'selection', namely that particular moment when we were put in touch for the first time with the unknown person visiting this home of carnal pleasures to feast, however shortly, his physical senses. Actually 'putting in touch' is slightly exaggerated; this moment, in which we had to stand in line, forming a parade of more or less nude female bodies, was dedicated to feasting the eyes of the visitor. To look at us was supposed to put the guest in the proper mood; to suggest to him that we were there only for his pleasure . . . all he had to do was take his pick. The only thing he had to do really was to make up his mind which one of us would be his temporary true love.

These minutes of waiting always gave me a pleasant tickling thrill – it was invariably me who was selected. And it was always my pleasure, because I had the right to look through a secret peephole at the unknown visitor and whenever I agreed to stand in line for the 'selection', it meant that his type would please me as a partner.

The more selection, the greater profit. Madam Desiree knew full well that not only did Paris have many women who were ready and willing to increase their small budgets by 'sacrificing' an occasional afternoon, but that there were many others who also had a small budget which they were more than willing to enlarge, namely the joys of the flesh – and some of them were more than willing to pay her for it.

I have spent many fabulous hours; the charm to be in a place which is dedicated to only one goal, exactly the same one for which the male visitors came to it, was in my opinion worth more than the few thousand franc notes I gave her. Even though I insisted firmly that 'my customers' handed over their money (it would have humiliated me not to be considered a good professional), I was never stingy toward my 'colleagues' or the owner of this invaluable institution.

Ah, whenever the doorbell rang, whenever a happy hubbub of naked bodies ran to and fro to pick up something to cover up, then rushed toward the narrow staircase, laughing in anticipation – maybe today there would be a real good piece of ass – tumbling into the reception room to line up in sacred tradition . . . faces expressionless, standing erect, waiting to be selected – oh, how entertaining this was for me!

And then the excitedly inspecting gentlemen would point out one of us, one who conformed to his particular ideal of eroticism, one who in his mind could give him the delights he secretly hoped for, and with an imperceptible nod of his head he would select the person with whom he intended to have a delightful sexual bout.

As I said, I was most often the one who was selected. I am not trying to brag, but I was considered the queen bee of our little group and frequently they put me in the most advantageous position. Whenever I had my gentleman it was the turn of the others; this was the established procedure. Madam Desiree never failed to congratulate my latest conquest on his good taste and excellent selection – 'The lady is a wonderful companion, but I leave the final decision up to yourself!' she used to say.

I remember one visitor in particular as an exceptionally understanding partner. In the beginning I treated him like all the others; upstairs in my little room I threw my arms around his neck and whispered into his ear: 'Well, we are going to have ourselves a good time, aren't we?'

And I would grope into his pants, trying to open his fly as quickly as possible so that I could have a good look at the most important requisite for the following ceremony.

'What's your name, darling?' I'd ask, the moment I had his rapidly growing hard-on in my hands.

Most of the time they'd murmur just about any kind of a name, but this time my opponent said quite clearly, 'Call me Mimile – my real name is Emile . . . And what's yours?' His question was polite but firm.

'My name is Lolotte, my big darling!' I tried to copy the tone of voice of the true inmates to avoid any possible detection and to prevent my partner from getting the wrong picture.

'But come on, he is so beautifully hard and I'd love to have him in me as soon as possible.' With those words I pulled him toward the bed. We almost fell down upon it; in my enthusiasm I had pulled quite hard on the incredibly stiff instrument. The next moment this strange man, whose strong build had attracted me from the first moment I laid my eyes upon him, lay between my widely spread thighs and I felt his entire weight against my bosom. Since he pushed with all his force against my body, I could not do anything but guide his powerfully swollen prick toward my yawning crotch and let him disappear into it.

The moment this fantastically hot prick discovered its entry, Mimile started to jab and hump furiously, pinning me down on the bed. Since I had one hand free, I grabbed his big balls and started to squeeze them with the same rhythm in which his hard pole was pushing up and down. I completely forgot that these organs are to a man his most sensitive possessions. Mimile seemed completely unperturbed by my counterattack and paid no attention as he doubled the force of his jolts while voluptuously groaning and moaning. It is hardly surprising that his behaviour led me into true ecstasy and the hotly desired climax came much quicker than I had expected...

'Oh, you screw splendidly... fantastic... oh, please, fuck me as wild as you can... please, don't hold back darling, quick... *quicker*... no, really, you are not hurting me... *aah*, great – more, please, please... more... I have to... please go on... yes, yes, that's it... oh, you – now... *now*... aaah... *aa-aa-aah!*'

I had made my first number. But Mimile was coming, too, and I felt his hot jism spurt into me at the exact moment that I reached my own climax.

'That's a pity,' he murmured rather dully. 'I came much faster than I had hoped – now it's all over and I just started to like you so well.' And with these words, my partner, who believed the game was over, was about to get up and put on his clothes. But he was mistaken. It was far from me to treat him like a professional trollop would have done and I had only one desire. I wanted to enjoy the pleasure he had given me with his well-proportioned pecker at least once more and, if possible, several times...

'Please, stay awhile, Mimile. Do you really want to go? Can't I play around a little bit with your big rod?' I smiled coquettishly at him and could see that he was rather bewildered by my request which is unusual in a public house.

I took a towel and started to dry off his sopping wet love arrow. I noticed that it had lost some of its attractive hardness, but it was still pretty big and I was convinced that with the proper treatment I could make it stand up all over again. My experience told me that this was one of those men who had a considerable power of recuperation. And that pleased me enormously since it was the sole reason for my being in a place like this; to find a dong capable of performing something extra special . . .

Even while I was still playing around with the half-hard rod, it started to get a new erection and when I suddenly decided to take the whole machine into my mouth it only took a few moments before it was as hard and stiff as it had been when Mimile came into my room a short while ago. It was a fantastic experience to feel how the proud man completely filled my mouth. Even though it was difficult, I succeeded in engulfing the heavy knob and licking it with my tongue, causing it to throb excitedly and making Mimile cry out: 'You are driving me wild – come on, let's make another round, I've got to come once more . . . let me . . . I have to lay you . . . you've got a . . . I have to . . . you . . . I've got to put it into your cunt quickly . . .'

There was nothing I wanted more. But the moment Mimile wanted to pin me down again, I rolled away from under him. 'No, not this way . . . wait a moment . . . I want to get fucked from behind!'

I loved this particular position. Besides, I knew that my behind, a work of art in itself – firm and round – fired every man whom I honoured this way to his greatest performance. The strength and intensity of the pushes I received in this position had convinced me of this.

It is fantastic to stick your behind freely up in the air and slowly take a prick between your legs. So I pushed myself

The Secret Diary of Mata Hari 37

back and felt his hard lance shove into my hole. Almost immediately, Mimile started to hump me thoroughly and the speed was, at least for the beginning, quite satisfactory. Slowly he pushed deeper and deeper into my body and I felt the instrument of my partner filling out my entire womb. Mimile worked without stopping. He banged with renewed vigour against my buttocks and grabbed alternately one or the other of my full, dangling breasts, squeezing them as hard as he could.

Our bodies welded together in a beautiful curve; the knees of the man nestled themselves into the back of my knees and his hairy muscular chest pressed against my back. The big mirror next to my bed reflected our picture – I looked at it and was thrilled by what I saw. It never tired me to watch the frolicking of the two bodies working together in the act.

Throughout my life I have always had a weakness for mirrors. And especially whenever the mirror shows me a second couple busy with what is most important and most pleasant: a good screwing... Is it not far more pleasant to know that there is another couple busy with the same intimate occupation right next to you? Ah, even the mute couple in the mirror caused extra excitement; if it were only possible to see those parts in action which one feels, but it is so difficult to take a good look when the straining bodies start their voluptuous convulsions.

Mimile was not entirely disinterested in these same impressions; he turned around to look in the mirror at my beautifully rounded backside – and I made it even easier for him by turning slightly sideways – to convince himself optically that I returned every one of his jolts with one of my own.

'Are you very horny, Mimile?' I asked him, so that I could enjoy the pleasures of sound as well as those of touch and sight. 'Do you like my backside – yes?... I love to be fucked from behind... so very, very much... just push a little harder... I can stand it... ah, that feels good, – that feels terribly good...! Just go deeper if you can, Mimile – *aaaah... aaaah!* You've got to come here more often... always... ask... for... me... I want to feel your prick – ever day – deep – inside me...'

Mimile banged with all his force against my ass. 'Just you wait, I'll screw you so hard that you won't know whether you're coming or going... you horny bitch... you would love to have a prick like mine in you all the time wouldn't you... It's all right with me... I'm gonna give it to you good, baby... you can have it any time you want to as long as you behave yourself... I'll fuck you all night... I – you – you...'

With these words, which had not failed to have their desired effect upon me and which made me enjoy the entire situation even more, the unfortunately independent human nature demanded its due – Mimile squirted his second load into my thirsty innards and pulled out without saying another word.

'But Mimile, please, don't do that... I haven't come yet...' I protested. 'Come on, quickly, put it back again...!'

'That was fantastic my little Lolotte – dammit, I haven't enjoyed myself so much in quite a long time... What?... You didn't come...? Really, you want to do it again...?' Mimile was quite surprised, and at the same time was very flattered that the inmate of a 'house' was begging him explicitly to be satisfied once more by him. That had never happened to him before!

'You'll have more chances during the remainder of the night, little one... I'm sure you'll come at least once more,' he tried to reassure me condescendingly.

'That's quite possible, but I want you to screw me, Mimile!' I had not yet given up hope.

'Well, you know I would love to – but look at it, you can see for yourself that I couldn't possibly bring it up!' and he looked down upon his rather droopy instrument with which we had made such beautiful music together.

'There's nothing wrong with it. It just needs a little extra excitement. Just wait, I have something for the gentleman which is guaranteed to put him in the proper mood again – yes, my dear Mimile, I have a weakness for you!' I really had a fantastic idea.

'I like you very much, too, Lolotte, and as far as I am concerned I'd never say "no", but I am afraid that for tonight . . .'

I did not listen to him. I went to the door, opened it slightly and called, 'Madam, could you please send Vivienne up to my room?'

And when I turned back to Mimile and saw his questioning expression, I explained what I had in mind. 'You will like her, little Vivienne is my younger sister, and her type is the absolute opposite of mine – if that does not excite you, my darling . . .'

Mimile perked up his ears. 'Your sister? Really? That's fantastic . . . and you both work in the same cathouse?'

I noticed that my little improvisation had the desired effect. At the same time Vivienne entered. I liked her best of all my colleagues and the two of us were quite intimate together. She was quite often my partner whenever one of the clients desired to cavort with 'two ladies at the same time', or when two couples had to be formed.

'Vivienne, may I introduce to you Mr Mimile – well, what do you say, dear friend, do you like my little sister, isn't she a real doll?' Unquestionably Vivienne's charms were very enticing; she was of medium size, very soft and she was a blonde, with that particular silvery blonde hair which one only finds in the northern parts of France and in Belgium. Her eyes were large and blue like forget-me-nots. Her most visible charms were very pointed, not-at-all-small breasts, which formed a piquant contrast to her otherwise frail figure; they bobbed up and down with every step. She forced them a little bit to do so, but the overall effect was so incredibly charming that one could easily forgive her this little mannerism. Even though she was already nineteen years old, she did not look a day over sixteen and, for this age, an incredibly oversized bosom added extra spice which the real connoisseurs in our establishment considered a first-class titbit.

'Well, my dear Mr Mimile, so you are a little lecher, one of those people who can't get their fill with only one woman,' said Vivienne, leaning against the big man. He put one arm around each of us, and looked with lustfully burning eyes from Vivienne to me and back again. Mimile seemed to be content, but I had only one desire, and that was to speed up the proceedings.

'Take off your chemise, Vivienne, and show the gentleman what you can do. I am sure that Mimile will show you in return the full impact of his virility – one favour is worth another.' I urged my little girlfriend on. Now the three of us were getting on the wide bed.

'Listen, Mimile, I will take your little brother into my mouth again and meanwhile you and Vivienne can start to get to know each other better; but when I have made him ready then you have to promise me to stick him in me again!' Said and done. The dangling thing already showed signs of getting up again. And, when I took it between my lips and at first very softly, almost superficially, then a little bit stronger and finally truly energetically started to suck on it, his erection began much quicker than I had hoped for. It stood up proud and stiff, with a hardness that promised fulfilment of my wildest desires.

I would lie if I were to claim that I did not get pleasure out of trying to drive this huge cock into my gullet. However, I was afraid that Mimile would come too soon again, otherwise I would have played around with it much longer. And I was also very excited to notice the quivers that ran through

Mimile's athletic body because of the unexpected pleasures and exciting new tricks that Vivienne played on him – aah, I knew them too, too well.

My eyes burned passionately when I looked at those two. She pressed one of her pointed breasts into his face, at the same time Mimile was using one hand to fumble around with her firm buttocks and the other to squeeze her free breast. Then, because she knew full well what a greatly desired plaything her big bosom was, she began to put one and then the other breast into his mouth, enticing him to suck the full, red and very hard nipples.

At the same moment I let the now hard and throbbing snake slide out of my mouth and decided that my time had come!

I shoved Vivienne aside and straddled Mimile's body. I took his big heavy prick in both hands and put it in position upon my crotch. As if he had waited for that signal, the sudden bucking of the man under me caused his magnificent arrow to pierce deeply into my waiting hole.

Vivienne knew exactly what I expected her to do. She threw her full weight upon Mimile's chest, pressing him down upon the bed in such a way that only his loins could move. He obliged with full force because the moistened crotch of Vivienne rested upon his lips and his wildly swinging hands had taken firm hold of my pulsating breasts. The combination of these feelings brought in me a complete frenzy. He no longer pushed against my down-pressing belly but raced up and down as if he was whipped by electrical jolts, quickly and regularly, driving his dong deeper and deeper into my sopping, longing cunt.

Vivienne was rubbing her behind across his chest and I could clearly hear the smacking of Mimile's lips as he was trying to crawl around with his tongue in Vivienne's moistened hole. I tried to put off my climax as long as I could, but I was no longer master of my nerves and was unable to dam the flood that ran through me – it kept going on and on, releasing the sweetest feelings which pushed me three, no, four times into seventh heaven . . .

The other two were also reaching their climax. Vivienne's body stretched momentarily like a steel spring, floated away from Mimile's lips, stayed up in the air for just a second and collapsed, a small frail bundle of weakened flesh, resembling the fainted body of a very young girl. Our mutual partner bucked up high for the last time, releasing an enormous load of jism against my diaphragm and also collapsed. Without moving, the powerful body under me lay there like a dead lump.

This was one of those nights in which I got my money's worth at the house of Madam Desiree . . .

Paris, 1906

I am now almost incapable of resisting this terrible urge – the wild desire to undress in front of men I hardly know, if at all. Whenever I am alone I practically tear the clothes off my body, preferably in front of a mirror, and revel voluptuously in the sight of my own naked body . . . I quite often stage it in such a manner that usually one of my male servants is about to enter the room when the last tatters of my gown drop to the floor. I almost experience a climax whenever I see the surprised, even greedy look on his face. If this strange desire overpowers me when I have a guest, be it a critic, a painter or an author, I pretend to be on the verge of fainting, or I explain that my newest dance can only be shown in the nude – then I start tearing off my clothes. The poor onlooker quite often stammers some excuse, feels somehow that he is accosting me and tries to get out as fast as he possibly can.

Not too long ago I went on one and the same day to four different painters' studios and offered myself as a nude model. The incredible sensual pleasure it gives me to undress in front of these 'artists' whose more or less lecherous eyes gaze up and down my voluptuous body! But it is especially the ceremony of undressing which causes me to reach a climax. And I truly don't know whether it is more intense when I am undressing while it is more or less expected of me or when I suddenly give in to the urge, and shock and surprise whoever happens to be with me at the time . . .

Today I visited a man and allowed him to admire my body without letting him know that this was my own greatest desire. It was the famous Doctor Milhaud. I met him not too long ago socially and since I liked him – as a male – at first sight, I decided to trick him and make an appointment to see him as a patient. Milhaud is a tall, strong man, born in the Auvergne district and even today he still has something of the powerful peasant in him. And I made no mistake; his erotic power, his ability to procreate and the tools with which to do it are simply gigantic . . .

The moment I entered his study, I took off my clothes.

He immediately perceived what troubled me. In his busy practice he may have met enough hysterical women with complexes and manias. I was tortured by the idea that I was about to gaze into the hell of unfulfilled desire which befalls many modern women who are not getting any younger . . .

'It is only functional, dear lady – mere nervousness,' he murmured while he was examining me. 'You need a good calming down. Do you want me to give you a prescription for a mild sleeping-potion?'

'I need something more solid than a sleeping-potion, Doctor. Something which really tires me out, not just makes me sleepy; I need something which will put my senses to rest – after they have been put through a thorough test . . .' I answered, giving him a significant smile.

It was not just by chance that my gaze travelled down my partner's body and came to rest at the enormous bulge in his pants. The look of this made my nipples harden and my breasts throb.

'All right, Madam, we will try a little massage of the more important nerve centres. Then you can tell me when you reach the desired state of relaxation. Would you please stretch out on this couch and close your eyes?'

I followed his directions. My body was entirely nude, except for my thin, patterned stockings, embroidered garters and tiny, high-heeled black shoes. I had stretched myself upon the couch and was eagerly awaiting things to come.

'It would be better if I bind your eyes, Madam, so that you will be fully in the dark and able to relax completely!' With these words the doctor put a black kerchief across my eyes.

'I will first caress your skin slowly and softly because I want to awaken the dormant magnetism very carefully; afterwards I will increase the pressure.'

His soft stroking unnerved me. I protested, 'But I don't feel a thing – ah, that is a little better . . .' and soon the almost imperceptible light touches were replaced by a more energetic squeezing and kneading.

'I am about to reach the origin of your restlessness, dear lady. Please, don't be afraid . . . it will do you a lot of good and it won't hurt a bit! Maybe it is not even necessary to use my probe . . .' Milhaud started to work on that spot which really could use a good working over . . .

'If you deem it necessary, Doctor, please, don't hesitate to use it – I have complete confidence in your abilities . . . *aaaah*, yes, it feels like a true liberation . . . yes . . . there . . . please . . . more . . . there, yes . . . a little bit . . . deeper, please . . . more on the inside . . . yes, there . . . oh, I feel that this is doing me a lot of good . . . yes . . . please, a little bit more pressure . . . stronger . . . deeper . . . yes, yes . . . and quicker . . . quicker . . . *aaah*, that felt . . . won-der-ful . . .'

My good Samaritan had pushed his powerful forefinger deep into my yearning vagina. Just before that he had given my shuddering clitoris a strong and long-lasting massage so that the front of my rapidly swelling love spot had become

The Secret Diary of Mata Hari

very moist. The famous neurologist used his other hand to squeeze my swelling breasts.

'I do believe that I have to introduce the probe . . . it always gives excellent results . . . or do you think that this exploratory massage is enough for today?'

That was completely contrary to my expectations, but I did not want to give myself away. 'I leave that entirely up to you, Doctor – I am only interested in getting rid of my terrible insomnia. By the way, I'm still a little bit itchy . . . right here, can you see something there? . . . Yes, ouch . . . it's more of a burning sensation . . .' The spot which I vaguely indicated with my hand was located exactly between my legs.

'Well, in that case, I'd better introduce . . .' and at the same time I felt the instrument Milhaud had alluded to, his aforementioned 'probe'. It was an instrument which seemed to be covered with a velvety soft membrane, and it felt like a rather heavy shaft. And now this wonderful apparatus slid slowly and carefully into my wide-open cleft. I had to spread my thighs. 'As high and wide as possible . . . yes, Madam, that way . . . please, open up a little more, so . . . yes . . . that's the proper posture . . . excellent . . .' And he told me to hold my legs in that position with both my hands.

The probe, which felt more like a strong penis, stuck deep into my flesh. For a while it rested there without moving, only a slight pulsating told me that it was still there; then it started to pull out very slowly, occasionally pausing, leaving more and more of my insides untouched. Finally I could no longer stand it and I cried out, 'Stop! Please don't . . . don't take it out now!' Again it sank slowly back into position; then the whole procedure was repeated, and again – for the third time. Finally it started shoving back and forth and caused such an incredibly voluptuous joy that I shortly lost all self-control and forgot all my inhibitions.

'Why don't you massage me a little bit stronger, Doctor, and quicker . . . above all, quicker . . . yes, I want to be massaged more forcefully ... please, push harder – with your probe ... I want it ... I want to be massaged strongly ... surely you know how a woman wants to be massaged ... You are a medical man ... *aaah* ... no, it does not hurt ... now! ... Yes – that's it ... it's ... so ... good ... no, no ... it won't do any damage ... please, massage some more ... yes, I – will – come – back – for – another – treatment ..., *aaah*, it feels so good ... Doctor, you are an angel ... and so well-built and heavy ... Doctor, please push your probe deeper into me ... yes, I know ... but I'm sure it will do me a lot ... of ... good ... I – *aaah*, I can feel it ... your probe ... it's pushing against my stomach ... Doctor, Doctor ... the probe ... your probe ... quick ... quicker ... I want you to hurt me with it ... Don't ... you ... have ... a ... heavier ... probe ...! It feels so wonderful ... You'll have to massage me ... every ... day ... Otherwise ... I ... couldn't ... stand ... it ... yes ... that's fine ... Ooooh, I'm beginning to feel ... so good ... good ... I ... I ... *aaaaaah!* ... *aaaah* ... now ... now ... I'm coming ... I'm coming ... *aaaaah!*' I veritably screamed these last words while I was thrashing around on the couch. Then I completely collapsed.

After I had rested for a while, I tried to lift my head but everything remained pitch black. I shivered.

'Not we can take off the bandage, my dear lady. Do you feel a bit better now?' I finally regained my senses completely. Doctor Milhaud, the great medical sage, stood in front of me, smiling and with roving eyes that did not seem to notice my nudity. 'Normally my fee is fifty francs, Madam, but you, an artiste, the famous dancer honoured by all of us ...' With these tactful words, which elegantly veiled the true reason for my visit, Doctor Milhaud showed me the way out of his office.

Berlin, 1908

I had always believed that there was no other city in the

world which could stand comparison with Paris — especially in regard to its world renown as the largest fair of carnal pleasure. But I soon had to admit that along the Spree River the goings-on were more nefarious and wicked than along the abysmal banks of the River Seine.

I had been anxious for quite some time to visit one of those infamous places which are hidden in downtown Berlin . . . I believe in the neighbourhood of the Potsdam Platz. And one night, a famous reporter who was a very good friend of mine, introduced me into the most notorious of these 'dance halls'. My friend explained to me that it was a gathering place of same sexes, a particular speciality of Berlin.

'You mean there are just men. Plain homosexuals?'

'No, both kinds; homosexual men as well as lesbians meet here, but the most interesting thing is that a third class has formed here which has a predilection for both . . .'

'And this is really true, not just fake for the sake of tourists — like it happens so often in Paris where they offer you a sixteen-year-old girl and everybody in the business knows that she is at least twenty . . .'

'In these circles you can rely upon authenticity, my dearest friend — but you can convince yourself!'

When we arrived in the dimly lit room which was filled with little tables and sofas, an infernal turmoil was going on already. After I had become used to the heavy smoke in the room I could see that the various activities, underscored by loud and lascivious music, could only be classified as a true orgy.

All the tables were occupied and the couples that were sitting around them were all engaged in various tender activities. I noticed many picturesque and beautiful women, tall and slender, but my guide explained to me that they were men. And when a Spanish dancer, a perversely supple little girl with gorgeous legs and a dazzling low-cut back, moved lithely and enchantingly to the sound of her castanets, I absolutely refused to believe that this beautiful creature was in reality a man.

'Alex, why don't you come over here and show the lady that you are really a boy!' my friend called shamelessly across the room. The little beauty approached our table and stood smilingly in front of us, all the while in the posture of a real, gracious and inimitable Carmen.

'I see you're surprised my dear woman. Well, take a good look...' and with these words the pretty creature pulled up her skirts with an incredibly vulgar gesture, high above the knees, and – between a pair of finely chiselled thighs I saw a strong, half-way hard virility framed by a mass of dark curly hair...

Nobody took notice of this slight intermezzo. They were all too accustomed to curious visitors. I did not mind this at all because now I felt much more at ease. At the table next to us two women were seated, both beautiful blondes with full busts and strong but shapely legs. They were busy kissing each other and one of them, the tallest, was groping under the skirts of her friend, which seemed to give both enormous pleasure.

'Ah, Ede, today you've got such a delicious firm grip – yes, – oh, come on... a little bit more..., no, I'm not about to come yet... I promise... you know I only do that when I can get a hold of your dong... Tell me, why don't you let me... are you really going to screw that damned twat before I can touch your peter – oooh, please, let me touch your teenie-weenie just a little bit... I want to rub that delicious thing so strongly... I promise... I'll just give you a good solid hard-on when you leave me for Paula...!'

'No, forget it – aah, there she is – well, Paula, now it's your turn!'

'Oh, really? I was afraid that you couldn't tear yourself loose from that stupid boy. And remember, baby, when you shove it up me, it better be hard and heavy... I have no use for a dangling little brother.'

What a most peculiar atmosphere! They truly had everything mixed together. Now I was watching another couple, this time they were women who were both taking up with a third trying to make the latter some sort of a mutual present for one another.

'But take him, Kate, yes, I mean it . . . really. Just make yourself good and horny with his long pole. I'm sure you will muff dive me twice as good as ever . . . All right, come on young man . . . show her that rod of yours; don't make us beg for it. Obviously we can't screw you in the ass . . . you'll have to wait for that till your boyfriend comes back. Then you can let him ream out your behind till you faint . . . but please . . . at least show it to her . . . you don't have to put out. It's only supposed to be *hors d'oeuvre*, my dear – then it's my turn and I'll give Kate's pussy something solid to look forward to . . .'

The conversation was free and easy. If one of the couples succeeded in accomplishing something truly out of the ordinary, all the other guests climbed upon their chairs to have a better look. And when the ecstasy had subsided, everyone turned again to his own partner. Upon many tables young men and young girls had spread their legs and, while they were leaning back in their chairs, received the homage paid to them by the lips of passers-by.

Lascivious dances where the partners grabbed hold of each other's sex organs, yes . . . they did not let go of them, spurring the onlookers to ever greater excitement. They drank incredible amounts, many of them sniffed cocaine and even needles for morphine were freely passed around . . .

Two girls had found a place at our table and they occupied themselves with increasing rapture with my breasts, then my thighs and finally with what I had between them. And I must admit that they gave me a rather lively impression of what lesbian love was all about. But soon I asked them to introduce me to one of their friends whom I had liked the moment I set eyes upon him. He was a singer-dancer and had one of the most beautifully proportioned bodies I had ever seen. And when he performed a few dance steps, he did it with so much grace that the artiste in me almost became jealous.

But most exciting to me – it almost killed me with unbridled desire – were his hidden charms of which I now and then could catch an all-too-short glimpse. Whenever the young man, who was dressed up as a female dancer, made a few quick whirls, his short silk skirt would lift up and show a delicious, enormously heavy phallus.

The delights which this well-hung man put at my disposal for the remainder of this unique night will forever be burned into my memory . . .

Lena's Story

It's a complicated business being a professional mistress and the life of Parisian courtesan Lena de Mauregard contains as much double-dealing as that of Mata Hari. Though she loves him passionately, Lena has separated from her husband, Stanislaus, to be kept by the wealthy Count de Clameran. It's a career move. And while she salts away the Count's money, Lena earns as much as she can on the side, often by participating in orgies with her friend Elvira for the benefit of a fat businessman, Barfleur.

As a relief from fornicating for profit, Lena cultivates a new friend, blonde minx Lucy des Etoiles who has a passion for gambling and has ruined two bankers already. But Lucy is not just a threat to the male sex, as Lena is about to discover . . .

After lunch I simply could no longer stand to be alone. I had the carriage prepared and drove to the home of Lucy des Etoiles. Her gossipy chatter always was a pleasant distraction.

When I arrived at her place, I found her in a state of fury. She was completely nude, standing in front of a full-length mirror in the middle of her room.

'Dirty swine ... you can go to hell! I despise you! You would like to be a man of the world but the horseshit in the stable is worth more than you!'

She interrupted her deluge of swear words when I walked in.

'At whom are you mad today, Lucy?'

'That son-of-a-bitch d'Obrenval! That's one I am not going to hang on to. If that pig thinks that his lousy five thousand francs will keep me glued to him, he's got a surprise coming! Shit on that! I have had better ones than him and it is easy to find myself another.'

'Calm down, my dear, calm down! Don't get so upset!'

'Oh, no! That bastard irritates the hell out of me. Imagine ... he has the gall to complain that I don't have titties. He says that I am too flat! You hear that? Too flat!! Do you see that tit I am holding in my hand? Isn't it firm and round? God knows, they are a little bit separated, the cleavage is a little bit too wide, and they point a little to the side. But, dammit, that isn't *my* fault! My other lovers did not mind at all, they drooled over them! I think that that miserable stinker wants to fuck me between my tits. Now he calls them too small only because his pecker isn't big enough to turn the trick. But I am just not in the mood to have a pig like him make fun of my tits. And this morning he really picked a fight with me. I jumped up from the table, took off my clothes and screamed at him, "Here, you filthy animal, take my tits and blow in the nipples. Maybe they will balloon to your filthy satisfaction and become as big as those of Miss Lear or Madame Lena!" Excuse me dearest, for repeating this, but he is always harping about the beautiful bosoms of the two of you.'

The idea that d'Obrenval was supposed to blow up Lucy's titties had made me laugh. Therefore, the mentioning of my rival's name escaped me. But when Lucy mentioned me, I stopped laughing.

'My bosom? And, pray tell me, when is he supposed to have seen my bosom?'

'At one of your parties, I suppose. And you can buy pictures of Miss Lear in the nude at every street corner in Montmartre.'

'Oh!'

'Yes, and do you know what that dirty pig answered? He advised me to buy a set of little bellows and have my maid pump me up every morning before I joined him for breakfast. Oh, the dirty swine . . . I could kill the bastard with my bare hands! But he did not pay for this place. I am my own boss. And tonight, good-bye . . . he'll find this door locked forever!'

'Oh, no, Lucy! You are going to be a smart girl, and you are going to forgive him.'

'Never! Never! No tits!'

'Oh, come on, Lucy . . .'

'Maybe yours are a little closer together, possibly a little bit fuller, but I do not believe that they are more charming than mine. I have known poets who would prefer mine over yours.'

'I understand, dearest. You are absolutely right. You have very charming breasts, and there is no reason on earth why you should be jealous of my full bosom. I must admit that my breasts are fairly large, but they are really not too large. It is easy to squeeze them together which makes it possible to capture the tongue of an admirer so that he cannot pull back. My husband has quite often experienced that neat little trick...'

Lucy looked at them and said, 'Only a lecher would find more pleasure with your breasts than with mine. But I just cannot stand lecherous pigs like that d'Obrenval... My, oh my, they are pretty, indeed! Here, a little kiss for each one of them as a sign of our friendship. Let's forget about d'Obrenval and my furious outbursts. Did you come over to take me out for a ride?'

'Yes, I would like to chat with you.'

'I will be ready in just a minute. Let me ring my maid to help me dress.'

'Allow me to return these friendly kisses.'

'Aah! You don't despise my breasts?'

'God forbid, no! They are divine!'

I bent over and nibbled the jutting tips of her breasts. They tasted delicious, eagerly stretched toward my moist, warm lips, and I rolled each one of them around in my mouth with flicking movements of my tongue.

Lucy threw her arms around my neck, 'You are so sweet! I said it this morning to Clameran, who had breakfast here. He went away when d'Obrenval and I began our fight.'

'The count had breakfast here?'

'Yes.'

She voluptuously stretched her arms behind her, her little breasts jutting out invitingly. I kissed them again, tenderly, licking the contours slowly. Her nipples instantly responded. I leaned back and studied her body: her beautiful, flaring hips, her marvelous slim waist and that little triangle of golden curly hairs which provocatively stood out against the alabaster-white skin. She twitched it slightly and the sight fascinated me. It had a magnetic attraction for me. She stretched out her hand to ring for the maid, but I stopped her.

I murmured, 'D'Obrenval must be out of his mind if he is not satisfied with your divine beauty.'

The poor girl did not understand the meaning of my huskily

whispered compliment, and she answered, 'Men, my love, the more a girl offers them, the more they want. I sometimes believe that those pigs only exist to plague us! Take Clameran for instance. Last night he slept with that American girl, and I told him that he is nothing but a swine, regardless of his noble title. When one possesses a woman like you, one of the most beautiful in all of Paris, when one abducts such a woman from her lawful husband, then one should spoil and love her, and one should definitely not be rutting after another girl. That's what I told him.'

She had touched an area which interested me and I answered as casually as possible, 'I have heard about his little fling.'

'Who told you about it? Oh, I bet it was Albert Tisin. He is a dear boy, but incredibly loose-lipped. I warn you about him . . . he runs after every new star, charms them, and when they have given him their favours . . . good-bye . . . he'll turn his attentions elsewhere.'

'Aha!'

'He will show up with a new item in his column, and he will try to frighten you. He always knows things that are absolutely of no importance. Clameran got carried away with that American girl but he has no intentions of leaving you. Unless, of course, you are giving him grounds. We'll talk about it when I am dressed, when we are riding through the Bois.'

'One moment, please.'

I inspected her flaring hips, the delicate rounding of her buttocks, her firm thighs, the gorgeous little golden patch between them, her delicious legs and finally, finally, she began to notice my barely concealed ecstasy. I had not yet closed my corset and my breasts were still showing. Lucy suddenly took them in her hands and said:

'Your eyes have a curious sparkle in them. Would it be possible that you could love another . . . woman?'

Her hands squeezed my breasts, and I almost fainted with delight. Lucy became ecstatic and, kissing my erect nipples, she said:

'That is marvelous! I... I... I want, I want to... Oh, please, take off your clothes. We shall make love. Let's get at it with all our fervor and passion. Do you want to become my lover? You may not believe this, but I swear by everything that's holy that you are the first one! But I promise that I will make love to you, oh, will I ever make love to you! It's driving me wild with passion and desire. You are so beautiful. Oh, God, you are so beautiful. But I also must warn you that I am very jealous. No other woman but me! I don't care how many male lovers you have, that's business, but if you want to love me, I want to be the one and only. Is that understood?'

I wanted to grab her, devour her with my hot caresses, but she slipped away from me, helping me to get out of my clothes so that we could get together quicker. And when I was as naked as she, she pulled me close to her, in front of the mirror, saying:

'Oh, we are beautiful, we are both very beautiful. Now, please, teach me what I have to do. Make love to me first, and then I will do the same to you!'

I knelt down before her, embraced her slender thighs, kissed and licked the passionately twitching blonde rug. Carefully, but insistently I inserted my tongue between the rosy lips, penetrating deeper and deeper...

She had put one leg across my shoulder and, looking in the mirror, she said:

'I can see the cleft between your buttocks. You are beautiful, oh, so beautiful, both of us are beautiful... oh... so... beautiful... please, please... don't stop... deeper... your tongue is reaching places where no man has ever been... oh, God... it... feels soooo good. Suck me harder, darling... I am coming... ooh, I am... coming... I am coming as I never have before... not in my entire life... oooh... aaah...

'What do you want... the other side? You want my behind?... here, I give it to you... lick me... ream me out... oooy... aaah... it feels so good... your warm, loving tongue, sliding up and down between my buttocks... I... I... am coming... again... oooh!

'Please... please... get up... hold me tight... let me look into your eyes. Have you ever made love to another woman before? You must have! You are sooo good at it. I came twice in a row... no man has ever been able to do that...'

She began to play with my breasts, squeezing them firmly together, rubbing a finger between the cleft.

'Has a man ever done it to you here?'

'No.'

'It is possible, you know. Push your belly against mine... give me your mouth... Tell me, have you ever loved another woman before?'

'I love you.'

'You aren't answering me.'

'What difference does it make?'

'I would like to know. What has happened won't hurt me. You had not met me. Tell me, you can tell Lucy...'

'I did have a girl friend... once...'

She pinched my arm brutally. It hurt so much that I screamed.

'You said yourself that I had not met you. But I don't like these brutalities. My love for you would cool off awfully quickly.'

'Forgive me, dearest love... I got carried away by my jealousy... I promise it will never happen again. I will make you forget it... I promise. I want to lick your behind... I want to lick your beautiful fleece, and I will make you reach a climax like you have never experienced before... Ooh, you are so beautiful... your behind is soft as velvet... your little pussy is so delightfully moist... mmmm... it tastes so good.

My tongue can feel your inside muscles twitch... Are you coming, my dearest? Quick, quick... climb on top of me... rub your cunt against mine... we are made for each other... oooh... aaah... I am dying with passion... we shall be lovers forever... I knew it, I knew it all the time...'

Our embraces became hot and passionate; our bodies rubbed against each other, sweat trickled out of every pore. Our bellies were wet, we flooded copiously. I turned around, licking her golden fleece, giving Lucy the opportunity to lick mine at the same time. It was almost as beautiful as Stan's embraces.

Afterwards we took a bath together, dressed, and went for a ride into the Bois.

Our dresses were magnificent. Lucy had embellished my costume with lace and ribbons, because she wanted to celebrate the occasion of our union. She wanted us to be the sensation of the Boulevard, the envy of our rivals.

We were just that...

It was difficult to imagine a more charming couple driving around in the Bois de Boulogne that afternoon. We leaned carelessly back in our seats and enjoyed the men on the sidewalks craning their necks to gaze at us. They literally devoured us with their eyes. And we talked, laughed and joked.

'See all those stupid asses. Rich or poor, all men are alike. Incapable of appreciating the delicacy of a woman. Tell me, Lena, do you really love me?'

'I adore you, my dearest Lucy. But we should not scorn these poor creatures that are staring at us. After all, without men, we would not be here, nor would we enjoy our luxury.'

'They make children, and they prolong misery that way. Without them, life would be an endless dream with flowers and cloudless skies...'

'Oh, silly, silly girl.'

'What man could be compared to you, Lena? Where is he,

whose forms are as smooth as silk and velvety to the touch? Is there a man alive whose curves are as soft and delicate as yours? Tell me, what do you think of me?'

'I love you, Lucy. There is not a man on earth who could compare with you. But it sometimes happens that one has the desire for a man. It refreshes one's nature.'

My eyes turned moist. Stan drove past us; he looked at me imploringly. I knew he wanted to get together with me. He had gone by and I really felt guilty. I should have gone to him for advice instead of visiting Lucy.

'We shall see each other every day. One day I'll come to visit you, and the next day you come and see me. And we are going to do it, every day to each other.'

'Yes, yes... our life will be blissful.'

'And we will drive out into the Bois daily, exchanging love talk, feeling each other's closeness. And I think I will forgive d'Obrenval for his rudeness. Well, look who is there... our American girl friend. Let's outstare her... she is our enemy, bent on stealing Clameran from you. But I won't let her, she won't succeed.'

Miss Lear drove by in a superb carriage. Her face was ideal for a sculptor's model. Her dress was dazzling. A slight sneer curled around her lips. She did not lower her eyes, and neither did we.

'That bitch,' Lucy whispered, 'just wait till I get my hands on her...'

'Leave her alone. Let's think about us.'

But suddenly I bolted upright. Stan led his horse toward the carriage of the American. He had something in his hand. We were not too far away, and I leaned forward to see what was happening. I was right. He smiled at her and handed her something.

'Oh, that's too much...' It escaped me before I could check myself. 'Not her, too!'

'What's the matter, dear?'

'Nothing...'

'Do you have secrets from your little wife?'

'Please, don't ask me. I have had enough of this driving around.'

She pouted a little but ordered the driver to turn around and go home.

Nothing in the count's behavior betrayed to me that he was unfaithful, but I felt as if I was living on a bed of nails.

It's impossible to think of seeing Stan; I hate to break my promise to him, but at this moment I must tread lightly. We will have to postpone our hotly desired happiness. I am feverish with impatience.

Lucy is like a second shadow. She is beginning to get on my nerves. She is as jealous as a tigress with kittens and I live in constant fear that she will catch me with Elvira. That's all I need... an unexpected visit from Elvira. It would be the scandal of the year, because I am sure that Lucy would give away all our intimate secrets to whoever would listen.

Going into the Bois has become sheer torture. I always seem to run into Stan. He is either on horseback or in a carriage, and he is always alone. It seems that he is trying to catch my attention every time we meet. He does not understand my silence.

Meanwhile I wrote him through Elvira. I explained that there was a sudden, unforeseen complication. I wrote him that I was in danger of losing the count's favor and, with it, the chance of a speedy reunion. He has not answered, and Elvira, too, gives not a single sign of life. I am constantly in fear of her sudden appearance.

Tisin has written a glowing article. It was called, 'Female Internationalism,' and it tells the whole story. Obviously it is slanted in my favor, and Tisin uses a lot of swollen phrases. Everything in it is grossly exaggerated. The count, who – naturally – received a copy, said after reading it, 'What the hell is the matter with these journalists? These things are none of their business. What do they want to do next? Rule the world, or something? This article, my dove, is written by a man who has been received by you three or four times, as far as I know. When you see him again, tell him to look in the mirror, and to keep his nose out of other people's business.'

'If it displeases you that I see him, I will not receive him any longer. He was introduced to me by Lucy.'

'That stupid little goose? She will never learn from experience. Maybe it would be a good idea not to see her as often as you do.'

'Who said that I should cultivate her friendship? Who has brought us together? It is terribly difficult, you know, to become friends and then, suddenly to turn cold again.'

'I'll give d'Obrenval a hint. He will see to it that you will not carry the blame.'

I did not answer. If the count could succeed in helping me decrease visits from and to Lucy, I would be overjoyed.

'That's settled then? You tone down on your provocative visits to the Bois, and I promise to talk to d'Obrenval. Don't worry your pretty little head over the details.'

He picked up his cane and hat, and left.

He must have talked to d'Obrenval. Lucy did not show up this afternoon. I went out alone. Stan followed my carriage at a discreet distance. I stopped near an out-of-the-way little footpath and told the driver to pick me up later. It did not take long before I heard Stan's footsteps.

'Irene, what has been the matter?'

'A woman wanted, and still wants, to take me away from the count. I need all my wits about me. Meanwhile I am suffering, oh Lord, I am suffering...'

'The count cannot get rid of you that easily. You can't tear a woman away from her household and then throw her back out in the streets again.'

'Oh, he won't throw me out in the street! But what is going to happen to those beautiful thousand-franc notes of which I expect to collect quite a lot?'

'Is this woman dangerous?'

'You have seen her, you have talked to her . . . I was pretty mad about that.'

'I know this woman?'

'I don't know if you know her, but not too long ago you gave her something . . . right here in the Bois.'

'Oh, the American girl!'

'Yes, Miss Lear. And what did you give her?'

'A little package. I saw it fall from her carriage, picked it up and handed it back to her. She was very kind and thanked me profusely. Who is that woman who is always riding with you?'

'Lucy des Etoiles. She is the only one of the demi-mondaines with whom I regularly go out. But she is overdoing it a little. The count has promised me to talk about it to her lover.'

'The two of you are not fooling around together?'

'Stan! No! How could you think such a thing? My heart is too sad about our continuing separation to think about frivolities. And what about you and Juana?'

'I have some good news for you. Juana got rid of Paul and I got rid of her. I live now in a little home in the Rue de la Terasse.'

'Why didn't you go back to our home?'

'I was planning to, but the gatekeeper was terribly nosy. He asks nothing but questions that, at times, are difficult to answer. I told him that we were on an extended trip, and that I was only going to be in Paris for a short time. I would only return to *our* home with you.'

'That wasn't very smart. And what about Elvira?'

'I have seen her. She, too, has a serious protector, but we managed nevertheless to amuse ourselves.'

'Has she shown it to you . . . her behind . . . so that you could kiss it, lick her pussy, and ream her asshole?'

'We didn't do much. We just talked. Mainly about you.'

'What did she have to say about me?'

'Nothing but good things. I told her that I saw you every day in the Bois with your new friend, and that it was impossible for me to get to talk to you.'

'Now what did you have to do a thing like that for?'

We walked along the footpath, and our conversation was not as pleasant as the last time. It seemed as if something cold and separating loomed between the two of us. I was horrified. I grabbed his arm, pressed myself close to him and asked coaxingly, 'Does that mean that you don't long for your loving little wife any longer?'

'I love her more than ever, but I am afraid that I would tear you away from that damned count, if I listened too much to the inner voice.'

'Oh, Stan, dear, stupid Stan. Use your brains!'

We were alone. Finally our lips met, our tongues touched. He explored my mouth. He exclaimed, 'Juana, Elvira! They are not bad . . . but they can't replace you!'

'So you still see Juana?'

'When . . . my God! I am not made out of stone! I need a woman and her door is always open for me.'

'You still have Elvira.'

'God . . . not her! Always the same old advice. I would love to see you, touch you, get to know all those secret little spots. I have almost forgotten what they look like.'

I felt intensely sorry for him. I, too, was anxious to be touched by him. Therefore I answered,

'If you promise to behave yourself, I'll let you see. But . . . don't touch. You must be satisfied with it, for the time being, and not want more than what I can give right now. Otherwise we might get ourselves in trouble.'

'Oh, yes? And what do you propose to do?'

'You boys are all alike . . . no imagination! We are all alone here, aren't we? And there are the bushes, right? Well, then, lay down on the grass, and I will show you everything.'

He quickly did as he was told, and stretched out on the grass, full length. I quickly reassured myself that we were completely alone, courageously lifted my skirts, opened my panties and crouched down as if I was going to take a leak.

Aah, what a feeling. He was the man I loved! Nobody else was capable of making me come that quickly. His face grazed my pussy and my buttocks, his fingers squeezed my thighs. A hot shudder ran through me from tip to toe and I almost plopped backward on his eagerly sniffing face. Suddenly he bit me. This brought me quickly back to reality. I stood up and straightened my clothes. Stan's face was as red as a boiled lobster; he coughed and panted and the bulge in his trousers was simply enormous!

'It's enough . . . let's go!' I whispered.

'There is nobody here . . . I have only kissed one thigh . . . please, show me the other one, let me look at it before you kneel on top of my face again.'

I have always been weak as wax under his insistence. I lifted my skirt about the waist, pulled down my panties and let him look. I even allowed him to eat my pussy for a moment. Jolting spasms went through my body. Suddenly I heard footsteps. I quickly stepped back, dropping my skirts and hiding behind the bushes.

A lonely gentleman walked by. Fortunately he did not see us. However, I could not risk that we might be seen by someone less preoccupied than the old gentleman who had just passed by.

Stan was completely distraught. Beads of sweat stood on his forehead when he dropped me off at the place where my carriage was supposed to pick me up.

Poor Stan . . . I love you so very, very much!

* * *

A letter from Elvira. Invitation for the first lunch with Barfleur. I have promised it, and I see no way out. I simply cannot refuse. Unfortunately, Lucy has sent a message that she plans to visit me this afternoon. She'll be furious when she discovers that I won't be home. But, there are ten gold pieces at stake, and I have no intention of letting them slip through my fingers.

I went, dressed in my best gown. Barfleur had never seen me so elegant and beautiful. He was already there when I arrived. Elvira met me at the door. She immediately asked:

'Who is that little girl friend about whom your husband has told me so much?'

'Oh, she is simply terrible. She hangs onto me like a leech and I can't shake her. She drives me to distraction but her lover is a very important man. It's impossible for me to send her away. Fortunately, the count has already offered to intervene.'

'The idea that she has stolen you from me makes me furious.'

'Living proof of the contrary stands before you, my dear. You needed me and I hastened to come to your aid.'

'You won't believe Barfleur. He has become so tame, he's almost eating out of my hand.'

She let me enter the salon. Our man was sitting there, reading the newspaper. He got up when I entered, shook hands and exclaimed joyfully, 'Ah, my little dove! You have kept your word! Now I am truly happy!'

I allowed him to embrace me, and offered my lips. He pressed them hotly against his own fat lips, trying to squirm his tongue between my clenched teeth. I answered.

'I always keep a promise, especially when I know that I can do a favor to my best girl friend and a gentleman I prize highly.'

'Oh, yes . . . and we are good friends, are we not? Elvira and I get along splendidly. She has decided to accept my offer. And I, too, am a man of my word. See, this is for you, my little angel. The fee we agreed to and a little diamond which, I am sure, you won't refuse to accept.'

'You're a little darling. I am deeply indebted to you, and I promise to obey your every whim.'

'Isn't this little piggy delectable in her beautiful dress? How about it, Elvira, why don't the two of you play one of your girlie-games?'

'No, not yet! After dinner. Otherwise we will get too involved, and the food would be spoiled.'

'Oh, you soulful woman. Come here, so that I can thrash your little behind. You have made me mad at you.'

'Wait, wait, Barfleur. You don't have a good view. Here, now it is in full light. But don't hit me too hard!'

'Lena, quick ... your behind, too. Hold it against hers.'

'But I am still wearing my panties.'

'Take 'em off ... you can't take those things off too soon!'

'It's done!'

'Fine ... ooh, as beautiful as ever!'

'Now what do you want to do with it?'

'I want you to thrash Elvira's buttocks with your behind.'

'Like this?'

'No ... harder ... much harder. Oh ... look at those delicious butts, viciously slamming against one another. Come on, come on, Lena!'

Elvira butted against my ass, and our buttocks slapped together. We had lifted our skirts high, and our behinds flattened under the continually increasing collisions. This exercise was fun ... we both became hot. Our buttocks reddened, and Barfleur, his tool in hand, was our umpire. He called the shots, so to speak.

'One, two, three, four ... Lena's ass is quicker, it pushes better; one, two, three, four ... aaah, now Elvira's buttocks are taking their revenge. Lena's ass is in retreat; three, four ... Lena's buttocks have come to a standstill, they have begun to resist the onslaught of Elvira's delectable globes; one, two ...

it now seems as if the behinds are in firm embrace, they have interlocked like gigantic suction cups and are squeezed so tight together that the pussies are touching; three, four ... the buttocks are separating, ready for renewed attack; one, two, three ... aaah, now Elvira's buns are ready for counterattack, the vicious slam into Lena's derriere almost topples the hapless owner; one, four ...'

(Barfleur had become so excited that he could no longer count straight.)

'Lena is down on her knees, that was a shove hitting the bull's eye; four, two ... good, good, she is standing up again, Lena's ass has flattened the behind of Elvira ... the ladies are panting and sweating ... another vicious slam ... the buttocks are red ... what is that? The ladies have turned around and are embracing ... they are now slamming their cunts together ... six, seven ... I can see the moisture dripping ... they are fondling each other ... Elvira's dainty finger is slowly disappearing in Lena's little asshole ... Lena has her thumb up Elvira's little fleece ... ten, eleven ... ladies, ladies ... stop, stop it!'

Unfortunately, Barfleur was the one who paid for the entertainment. Elvira and I did not want to stop at all. We were about to reach our climax.

But finally Barfleur succeeded in separating us. He put his tool back in his trousers, we straightened our skirts, and then we sat down to dinner.

Dinner was splendid. The most exclusive restaurant in Paris was the caterer. We served ourselves, because we wanted to be intimately alone. We had worked up a good appetite and devoted our complete attention to the food. We did not fool around, as usual, because it seemed a shame to mix two different pleasures.

I must admit that I love this way of life. It really seems to fit me. It is not bad at all to give my body now to this one and then to another. On the contrary, I like it! I have learned to dress and undress quickly, and even the most complicated gown gives me no trouble ... none of my temporary lovers loses out with the time I have allotted them.

During dinner we laughed and joked, and my heart and soul were filled with happiness. Yes, I thought about my husband a lot, but my conscience was clear. I did it for him, too. I worked as much for his future happiness as I did for my own. No dark shadows spoiled the outbursts of happiness in my joyful nature. I was greatly amused by the admiration with which Barfleur showered me. Up to this moment – I was sure – he had taken me for an ordinary whore, despite the things Elvira had told him about me.

Now he was finally convinced that I was a married woman, kept in riches by one of the outstanding members of our nobility. Barfleur saw to it that we would not tire ourselves, and he served us. Besides, I was still fully dressed and had no intention of spoiling my dress with a possible mishap. Barfleur liked my gown. It was black with golden buttons. He looked at it with naive admiration. We had to laugh about it.

During dessert he said, 'Elvira, did you tell your friend the big news, yet?'

'The big news?'

'Yes,' Elvira said, 'I have some news for you. I haven't had the chance to tell you.'

'What is it? Are you going to get married?'

'Are you out of your mind? Single life agrees with me. Since you will never guess, I may as well tell you. I am going to become an actress and singer.'

'You are going to be a what?'

'An actress-singer! I am going to make my debut at the Boulevardier. One night I sang a song for Barfleur which I had heard in the Alcazar and he made the decision for me. He maintains that I have a marvelous voice and great acting talent. I have received lessons and he introduced me to a good friend of his, the director of the Boulevardier. That man was simply ecstatic about my singing, hired me on the spot, and gave me those three songs over there on the table. They seem to be made for me. I studied them, sang them, and the conductor was very happy. My starting salary is not too great, but Barfleur insists that after my debut, I will be covered with gold. Meanwhile, Barfleur is now the lover of the diva... that's what he calls me now.'

She began to laugh and petted our friend on the cheeks. He was glowing with pride, devouring her with his eyes. He no longer looked at my divine gown. He embraced Elvira to kiss her lips, and she did not refuse him.

'The diva's lover,' he said. 'She will go far in this world and I, Barfleur, discovered her. It was criminal not to have thought about it much sooner.'

'I have never heard you,' I said.

'You will soon,' he said, 'and you will have the same opinion about her as I have. And you will have one advantage over her audience, because she is going to be as naked as the day she was born when she is singing for us!'

Elvira's eyes were big and dreamy. It seemed as if she was listening to an invisible lover who whispered sweet nothings in her ear. Her face had an ecstatic expression. I whispered to her.

'Oh, yes, my love... you have the soul of an artist and, even though I have not yet heard you, I am sure that Barfleur is right.'

'To her triumph!' Barfleur exclaimed, lifting his glass.

'We shall applaud you,' I said, finishing my drink. 'We are going to attend your debut.'

'Naturally! I'll reserve a loge for you and... your friend, large enough to bring a few other guests!'

We had finished our champagne. Barfleur took Elvira upon his lap, opened her morning robe, and began to stroke her belly and her breasts. Then he said to me:

Lena's Story

'Take off your dress, Lena, and eat our diva's beautiful pussy.'

'Oh, no!' Elvira exclaimed. 'If you want me to sing, then this will have to wait. I wouldn't have a voice left after Lena is through diving my muff!'

'You are right. But you can begin with that beautiful song, what's its name?'

' "Dissatisfied" . . .'

'Oh, yes! And, while you are singing that beautiful song, you and Lena can undress each other so that I can admire the two of you.'

'All right, wait for us.'

'Please, hurry! Or may I come with you?'

'Of course you may. And you may even fool around a little with Lena while I am taking off my clothes. Why don't you undress at the same time?'

'My love, you are right, as always.'

We retired into Elvira's bedroom and, each of us in a corner, took off our clothes. Then we returned, completely nude, into the salon and Elvira, naked, sang 'Dissatisfied' for us.

It was a rather ordinary song, describing the suffering of a woman who cannot be loved enough. A catcher of souls who uses up an endless stream of male and female lovers but who, nevertheless, has never been able to reach a climax.

But Elvira gave the song a certain twist. Her throaty voice, her precise timing, her suggestive movements, her marvelous facial expression and, especially, the suffering she knew how to put into her delivery, lifted the ordinary, dull material out of its drabness. The rather stupid words were transformed into a beautiful work of art.

She sang the song naked, her voice only a whisper, and we became so hot that my hand automatically reached for Barfleur's erect prick. He pulled me upon his lap and began to squeeze my breasts. Meanwhile, I tickled his balls and was riding his erection.

Elvira sang her last few lines with a smile of satisfaction on her lips. She walked toward us, put her head between ours, throatily whispering the last words.

'The universe is yours, oh woman!'

'Oh, you sweet little animals, you . . . oh, you little licking pussies,' Barfleur whispered hoarsely, and Elvira, who had knelt down between my legs, was sucking my clitoris.

He was twirling my nipples between his fat little fingers, kissing my shoulders, nibbling the back of my neck. He asked me to stick my tongue into his mouth, which I did. Suddenly he exclaimed:

'You know, Lena, I have never fucked you! Today I shall take you . . . right away!'

Elvira got up and asked, 'Do you want me to make the bed?'

'Yes, yes . . . we'll go to bed!'

'Then, come along . . .'

He lifted me up and carried me in his arms, the same way one carries a little child. Meanwhile, Elvira had taken the coverlet off the bed. He put me down. Elvira looked at me, and Barfleur said:

'Dearest, why don't you give me a tongue bath, while I grope Lena.'

She knelt before him and did as he had told her. He touched my entire body. His hands fluttered everywhere. He tickled me between my thighs and in the cleft of my behind. He gave himself plenty of time, and it was obvious that he did not intend to hurry matters. But I, however, had become tremendously excited; the meal had been spicy, the song has been touching, and now the tickling of his feverish hands. I died of desire . . . I wanted to be taken! I realized that I had to distract his attention from Elvira's tongue bath, if I were to forestall his climax. I tried something which I remembered from parties we used to have a long time ago. It never failed to work with a man.

His hand was groping my buttocks. Slowly I put my hand upon his and guided his index finger toward my twat. As soon as his finger touched the outer lips, I lifted my behind, groaned voluptuously and lolled my head upon the pillow. He correctly construed this as an invitation to penetrate me, shoved Elvira out of the way, and climbed on top of me. I quickly embraced him in my waiting arms.

'Ooh,' he sighed, 'this party will be over quickly!'

'Oh, no it won't,' I smiled seductively. 'A little rest, and we shall start all over again.'

Elvira was standing next to the bed. She stroked his spine and his buttocks. He slipped into me up to the hilt as I pushed myself up toward him, whispering hoarsely:

'Oh, lover, lover . . . take me . . . take all of me. Did you know that you are making me cheat on the man who pays me richly, and on the husband I adore. But I don't care . . . I don't care . . . I have wanted you for so long . . . I know that I am going to come quickly . . . you are sooo good . . . aaaah!' and I let my head loll upon the pillow from left to right, right to left.

I knew that nothing makes a man so horny as the idea that he is cheating another man out of his woman. Basically they are traitors by nature. However, the thought of Stan made me, too, hornier than ever and I was thoroughly enjoying the idea of being flooded with a considerable amount of semen. Right in my belly, the part of my body which had been bought by the count, and which he considered his personal property.

Barfleur was pretty good for a man of his weight. I clamped my legs around his heavy waist and he pumped his tool mightily into my body. He came suddenly, with a deep sigh.

Elvira helped us dress, and she invited us to table for a cup of coffee and a cigarette.

'Bravo!' Barfleur exclaimed. 'You know exactly what a man needs in between bouts. Long live the good life!'

'And women . . .' we exclaimed.

'Amen . . . especially women!'

'You have possessed me for the first time,' I said, 'and I swear to you by all that is holy that you are the first one besides my lawful husband, and my official lover.'

His vanity was tremendously pleased. I had not been mistaken. He made me a compliment.

'You are beautiful and you are also too smart to save it all for only one man. Ah, your willingness is nectar and ambrosia.'

I felt I had to give him another compliment.

'With a prong like yours, and the expertness with which you know how to handle it between a woman's thighs, you fully deserve the willingness of a good . . . pussy.'

We went into the dining room. Elvira was already smoking a cigarette. However, when I wanted to light one, she held me back.

'Dearest,' she said, 'you have made Barfleur very happy . . . now, please, do it to me!' She pointed at her behind.

I hastened myself to satisfy her. She stood up, I knelt behind her, took her buttocks in my hands and began softly to knead them. I regaled her with the most tender caresses I could think of, and she spasmed and whimpered. Still smoking, she turned toward Barfleur, played with her clitoris, making faces at him. Good old Barfleur. He was surprised at himself . . . he had another erection! Staring at Elvira who was playing with herself while I was tonguing her asshole, Barfleur began to jerk off. And, oh miracle of miracles . . . he came again, squirting in the handkerchief which Elvira had tossed him just in time . . .

The second part of our party began. To amuse Barfleur we modeled before him in various poses. We climbed up on the furniture, lay down on the table, and, in general, tried to outdo each other in lascivious poses.

The afternoon was a complete success, and after dinner I went home, deeply satisfied . . .

* * *

Lena's Story 75

Oh, if I had known the consequences of my little afternoon visit to Elvira.

Lucy had arrived just after I had left and she had gone in a terribly foul mood. For some reason I cannot fathom, my servants had told her that I had gone to lunch with one of my best girl friends. She had left the message that she would pick me up tomorrow for a trip through the Bois de Boulogne, and she had stomped out of the house.

I was all dressed for our little trip, and just about to put on my hat, because I had heard her carriage drive up in front of the house. I still had my hat in hand, and the maid had not had time to announce Lucy's arrival, when she barged into my room, closed the door behind her and roughly asked,

'Where were you yesterday?'
'I had lunch in town.'
'With one of your girl friends?'
'With the count.'
'Filthy liar!'

She suddenly boxed my ears. I almost fainted. I also became furious.

'Filthy liar, pig, whore, dirty streetwalker, lesbian... there... here... here! Aah, you think that you can cheat on me, do you? Making fun of me, telling me how much you love me, while you are rutting after another girl's cunt. I know everything... and I don't like it... here... here... and here... Do you understand me, you treacherous lesbian whore? I don't like it! You belong to me, and I belong to you... I eat your pussy and you lick my cunt... that is how you promised it, and that is how I want it... And I don't like it when you are diving someone else's muff, or when someone else is eating your cunt... It's me, me, me, or nobody at all!'

She was livid! She had grabbed me around the neck and was shaking me like a leaf. Her fists rained down upon my shoulders, my head and face. She threw me down upon the floor without any thought about my beautiful riding costume, she kicked me and then let herself fall on top of me. I was helpless, powerless, destroyed . . .

I almost lot consciousness. I barely had a chance to cover my face, protecting it from Lucy's vicious attacks, and to roll over on my stomach. Brusquely, Lucy lifted my skirts, tore off my panties, and she began to hit my poor buttocks with the flat of her hands.

'You stinking, lousy whore, rotten skunk, filthy piece of shit . . . aaah, till now you have only known my caresses . . . this time you shall get to know my fangs and claws! I will teach you not to play with me. When a lover bores me, I am the one who leaves, and never the one who is being left . . .'

She viciously pulled a few pubic hairs from my lower belly, then wriggled her whole hand into my maligned little cunny. I spasmed, she boxed my ears, I grunted, she pulled another hair, I screamed and lost consciousness. A peaceful blackness fell over me.

When I woke up, everything had changed.

I was in bed, fully undressed, the pillows were fluffed comfortably, and the blanket was snug and warm. I sighed deeply and opened one eye. To my horror I saw that Lucy was sitting next to the bed, and slowly the things that had happened came back to me. I quickly closed my eye again, and began to moan softly. Lucy bent over me, fearfully.

'Oh, please, please, forgive me. I must have been out of my mind! But I love you so much – oh, I love you so much.'

Her voice trembled. I carefully opened my eyes and saw that she was crying.

'Where am I?' I asked feebly.

'I put you in bed, my poor dear. Your breathing had almost stopped. Oh, darling, darling, I was so afraid. I was afraid that I might have killed you. Oh, I could not have lived without you any longer. I would have driven home and shot myself.'

'Ouch! Ouch! I am hurting all over . . .'

'It's nothing, it's nothing, dearest. Here, stay in bed. I will give you a calming medicine. They told me to give you a teaspoon every half-hour. Tomorrow you will be fine again. I will sit up with you and watch over you. The count said that it was all right.'

My eyes opened wide. She was amused that it was fear.

'Please, don't be afraid, my little darling. I will never do it again! Never, I swear it! And to prove to you that I mean what I am saying, you can go to any girl friend you choose. I know that it will make me suffer, but I will have to get used to it. You can command me to do anything you please, and I will do it! I will be as obedient as a little lap dog. I swear that you will never be able to find a truer friend than me. And, if you ever get yourself a real lover, and you don't know where or how to meet him, you can tell me, and I will find a way for you. Oh, please, please, dearest . . . tell me that you have forgiven me . . .'

'A real lover?!'

'Do you have one?'

'No.'

'That's not good. Everyone should have a real lover. I am going to let you into a secret. I have Paul Solencourt. He is my consolation for all those pigs who pay me. But I love you more than him, and ever since you and I have been making love, he hasn't had a thing from me. Oh, the poor boy . . . he is eating his heart out, but I stood firm!'

'Solencourt is your real lover?'

'You mean, you never suspected? Say, do you want Albert Tisin? He is absolutely crazy about you . . . I know that from a very reliable source. And if, I would advise you, he is kept at a little distance, he will literally eat out of your hand.'

' A real lover!'

I sat up, leaning back in the pillows with a groan when Lucy looked at me. An idea was forming in my mind.

'Do you want to write Paul? He will bring Tisin right here.'

'No, no!'

'Have you forgiven me?'

To forgive her! Wouldn't it have been terrible of me not to forgive her? Of course, I would forgive her. Through Lucy it would become possible to meet Stan again! Stan!

Tearfully, Lucy repeated her question.

'Lena, Lena, dearest Lena . . . name any punishment you want, but please, please, forgive your loving Lucy . . .'

'You are forgiven, Lucy.' The words came feebly and haltingly. 'But don't do it again. I am not used to such treatment. And, though I may not have the strength, I have friends who would take a terrible revenge.'

'Don't be afraid, my dove, don't be afraid and drink your medicine. Please, rest some more. You have forgiven me. I will wake with you like a mother watching her sick child. I have sent a message to d'Obrenval. Did you know that d'Obrenval, too, is crazy about you? If you'd ever decide to leave the count, it would be child's play for you to steal d'Obrenval away from me. Oh, I would gladly give you d'Obrenval. He is at least as rich as the count, and quite probably he would give you more than he has ever given me . . .'

'Oh, no . . . I couldn't do that . . .'

'It is not difficult to satisfy him. He has a crazy passion, and I don't like it at all. He calls it "praying to the moon," and it takes him at least a half-hour. It's boring as hell, though. He wants you to bend over, then he lifts your skirts, pulls down your panties and he begins to lick your buttocks, poking his fingers and tongue in your asshole. But, dearest, why don't you go to sleep . . .'

I had taken some of the medicine, and closed my eyes to go to sleep. An idea was born. Lucy was going to be the means to bring about a rendezvous between me and Stan.

I fell asleep, a smile on my face and a finger up my quim . . .

Crazy Time

They say every cloud has a silver lining. And when that cloud is marital infidelity, the silver often lines a private investigator's purse. Private Eye Raymond Fielding has a sharp eye for a business opportunity and right now he is maximising the potential of adultery. Why waste time? he tells his clients. If you think your guy's a rat, flash a piece of cheese under his nose and see if he bites. The cheese, of course, being a mouthwatering babe in a short skirt perched on a barstool near your husband – with a tape-recorder running to catch all his boozy indiscretions. Some might call it entrapment, Fielding like to think of it as a fidelity test. And whether a guy passes or fails, it doesn't hurt the books.

There's just one snag from the investigator's point of view. Given the combustible elements of such an operation – jealous wife, horny husband and wired-up sex bomb on the loose – how the hell does an operator stay in charge? Ray Fielding says so far things have never got out of hand. Not yet . . .

I'm waiting in my office just this side of midnight with my feet up on the desk. I've got sparkling lights in my peripheral vision due to an unwise selection of cocktails earlier in the evening and a numb right ear on account of the extended phone conversation I am engaged in. It is a one-sided exchange of views. My client, Mrs Marilyn Mountjoy, is not a happy woman. She's not happy in general because she thinks her husband is fooling around. And right now she's not happy in particular because someone has fucked up the operation to catch him. In her opinion that someone is me.

'Everything's cool, Marilyn,' I say to her. 'I'm sure there's a good reason Bella is a little late. Give her another ten minutes. She's gonna come walking through the door with all the evidence we need.'

'And if she doesn't?' Marilyn says, and I blather a bit because, to be honest, there's nothing I can do. We're both in the hands of some ditzy Italian broad with legs up to here and tits out to there and brains nowhere – probably. But we mustn't prejudge the issue. That's what I say to Mrs Mountjoy. Fuck you, Raymond Fielding, is what she says to me, I wish I never saw you on TV. And hangs up.

Which is all part of the job, I remind myself. There's the glamour side – the TV stuff and the *Hammondsville Clarion* profile – and the other side. Which includes hiding in a garbage bag while one of my assistants tries to break into a man's bedroom wearing nothing but a black lace teddy and six-inch spike heels. When she falls off the ladder we both end up at the local hospital. Me with a broken rib. I laughed till I cried, as they say.

I told that story on the Winona Walsingham TV show and the studio audience cracked up. Afterwards Winona took my card and said she'd tack it to her kitchen noticeboard so her husband could see it over breakfast and think twice the next time he came on to some fluff bunny in a hotel bar. The way she said it I half expected to pick up a little business in that direction but not so far.

However, I did get Marilyn Mountjoy who is an over-groomed blonde with well-oiled hips and pouty lips that go all tight when she talks about her husband, Clyde. Clyde has the kind of job that entails lots of trips to lunch and planning sessions round the pool and breakfast meetings in cities a plane-ride away. At the same time, his role as a key trouble-shooting exec means his working hours are apt to be extended at short notice. He can never be relied on to fit into Marilyn's extensive social calendar. He can't guarantee that, ten minutes into the opera or the Rockerheim cocktail party or the Guild fund-raiser, his bleeper won't summon him to do something very important somewhere else. In short, Marilyn can't ever count on the shmuck to be around.

When she first came to see me it was obvious this state of affairs was eating her alive. There were worry lines tugging down her mouth and furrowing up her smooth brow. They put years on her which, of course, was making her worry more.

'I'm sure he's seeing someone. More than one, maybe. He's never home, he could be porking half of Hammondsville for all I know. You catch him, Mr Fielding, like you said on TV. You dangle some babe in front of him and get it all on tape. Then I'll chase the asshole through the divorce court till I've got enough to buy my own stable of live-in studs.'

'Are you sure you want to do this, Mrs Mountjoy? Sometimes it can be best not to know the truth. If you and your husband have a comfortable modus vivendi—'

'Modus what? Don't talk crap, Fielding. Do you want to make some money or not?'

Well, of course I did. As badly as she wanted to find out if Clyde was a rat, one way or another. We shook hands on the deal.

Which is why I'm sitting here, wondering what in hell has happened to Bella.

Bella is without doubt the horniest woman I've ever been in the same room with. She oozes pussy. Which is not a delicate way of putting it but it's true.

Every little thing about her you could look at on its own and say it's not perfect. She's got thick honey-brown curls that hang in a tangle, like she can never be bothered to find a hairbrush. Her eyes bug out slightly they're so big and one's not quite the same shade of burnt sugar as the other, it's got flecks in it. Her nose is probably too long and her lips too thick and her tits are definitely too heavy for such a slender build. But . . .

But she looks half the time like she's just climbed out of bed with a lover and the other half like she can't wait to climb back in with a new one. You. The first time I met her, she tripped at the door and I caught her arm. She had this tiny dress, a flimsy summer thing with straps, and I found myself holding her bare arm up high with the back of my hand in the hair of her armpit. The smell of her was in my face, part perfume, part woman smell – ripe peaches, bare skin, scented sweat.

I'm used to American females, every square inch of them exfoliated, deodorised and sanitised. Suddenly I had my hands on a real woman not a Barbie doll. I pulled my hand from her armpit like I'd accidentally touched her snatch.

Though I knew I was going to use her, even if only to make sure I was going to meet up with her again, I had misgivings. I wasn't convinced she understood everything I said about my procedures and there were things every other girl I used always picked up on and she never did. Like the money. I told her what I'd pay her, with a bonus if it all worked out, and she never blinked or pulled a face or said you gotta be kidding, like most of them did.

Mrs Mountjoy – Marilyn by now because we'd had lots of tearful should-I-shouldn't-I? conversations and I was up there in her pantheon of father confessors along with her shrink and her gynaecologist – Marilyn had said Clyde was a sucker for European women and big breasts. So, despite my worries about Bella – her lack of experience in the world of subterfuge and surveillance etc – I decided to hire her. After all, I thought, she may not know a damn thing about the divorce laws or how to bug a phone but I'd bet a doughnut to a diamond pinkie ring that she's had a *lot* of experience at listening to guys in bars.

Which is all I want her to do. Cosy up to this bar where I've discovered Clyde sometimes goes after work and let her phenomenal body work its magic. If he's in the habit of hitting on babes then he won't pass on this one. And she'll have a microphone in her purse and get all his shmooze on tape. Or maybe he's a monk and he'll ignore the bait. We'll see.

I went through all this with Bella and showed her Clyde's photo. She held it close to her face as if she were memorising it. Then she turned her wet, toffee eyes on me.

'I love dark men,' she said.

I blushed. I'm a dark-haired guy myself.

I'm not blushing now, though I bet my cheeks are a shade on the red side. Red as in angry. Bella is sashaying into my office in a black cocktail dress cut high on the thigh and low on the chest which looks as if it's spent the evening crumpled up under a bed some place. She gives me a big beam like she knows I'm going to be delighted to see her and throws herself into the chair facing my desk. Having failed to meet me in the Piccadilly Pot Roast parking lot as agreed and not having rung in on the half hour as also agreed, she is approximately two and a half hours late.

I try to control my righteous ire.

'Where the *fuck* have you been, you mindless Italian fruitcake? I've been waiting for you half the night. I'm in deep shit with Marilyn Mountjoy.'

'What you mean "fruitcake"?' she says, an adorable little

wrinkle appearing on the bridge of her nose. Her long long legs stretch carelessly in front of her. The way her thighs gleam hurts my eyes.

'I am seriously pissed off with you, Bella.'

'Are you all right, Mr Raymond?' she says.

'No. I just told you, I'm not all right. I am very displeased. I—'

'Ssh!' she says, jumping up and coming round to my side of the desk. 'I see you are ill. Your head is hurting, yes?'

The next thing is she's leading me to the couch and making me lie down. It's true, I *am* feeling ill. The headache has got worse. The lights are flashing on and off and everything on the edge of my sight is fractured. I feel like I want to pull a big black blanket over my head and bury myself in the dark for ever.

Bella takes off my shoes and lays me out with my head on her lap. It's soft like a pillow yet warm and alive. Her face is suspended over mine, the curtain of her hair falling down to envelop us both, and she's rubbing some kind of lemony lotion into my temples. The effect is instantaneous. Those slender little Italian fingers are smoothing the hurt and anger right out of me.

But not all of it. I have to know what she got up to. Marilyn will be on the phone again at any minute. In fact I'm surprised it isn't ringing right now.

'Bella, please,' I say, 'what happened?'

She smiles down at me. From this angle her breasts are like the Dolomites. 'You are going to be pleased with me, Mr Raymond. I've got your tape.'

'You did?' Somehow I assumed she'd be too much of an airhead to actually record anything.

'Listen,' she says and slips the recorder out of her purse. Then she goes back to massaging my forehead. I am mollified. This, I think, is more like it.

* * *

Voices fill the room through a tinny hiss of background chatter and clatter. The sound is not too good but what the hell, this recording is not destined for public release. A male voice comes through loud and clear.

'Hey, babe, whachoo drinkin?'

'Go away.'

'Say, you're a hell of a looker. Why ain't choo bin in here before?'

'Leave me alone, you don't want to know me—'

'You're wrong there, honey.'

'— because I got a bad sexual disease.'

'Hey, now . . .'

'It's true. I'm here to meet my doctor. Please go, it's not safe to be seen with me. Not if you have other girlfriends.'

'Well, I don't see what harm one little drink—'

'I'm not joking, mister. You stick your penis in me and you'll shoot pus for months.'

I look up at Bella and she's grinning from ear to ear. I already know this isn't Clyde on the tape because I've bugged a few of his conversations already and I know his voice.

'All the guys kept trying it on,' she says. 'I got fed up.'

'Where the fuck is Clyde?' I say, certain she's started a brawl or something and spent the evening being interviewed by the cops. However, it's hard to stay mad at her with those magic fingers massaging my brow and her perfumed thighs cradling my head.

'Ssh,' she says and puts a finger on my lips. 'He comes to buy a drink now.'

'Miller Lite,' says a different man's voice. Sure enough, that's Clyde.

'Put it on my tab.' That's her.

'Do I know you?' he says. He sounds suspicious.

'I'm sorry but I told those guys over there you know me very well.'

'Are they hassling you?'

'They are trying to pick me up. I don't like it.'

'I see.' He sounds friendlier. He's probably got a better look at her by now. 'What did you tell them about me?'

'I said I was meeting my doctor here. You look a bit like a doctor. Handsome, healthy, smart.'

'All the doctors I know look like shit.'

'You don't mind, do you? If we just talk for ten minutes then they'll leave me alone and I won't feel so bad about being stood up.'

'Aha.' It sounds like he's finally sussed things out. The damsel is in distress and fate has selected him to be the knight in shining armour. It strikes me, as the last shreds of my headache are banished by her touch, that the damsel is not as dumb as I'd supposed.

'So who's this person who's stood you up?' says Clyde.

'My ex-fiancé.'

'Ex?'

'We just called it off.'

'Poor you.'

'I don't care now. The thought of settling down with one man – well, I don't know. It's terrible of me, I guess.'

'What's terrible?'

'I can't tell you. I'm embarrassed.'

'Sure you can tell me. I'm your doctor, remember?'

'It's just the thought of making love to only one guy for the rest of my life. I don't think I can do it.'

'If you love someone enough you can.'

'It's not about love. It's lust.'

'Lust?'

'Yes, I have too much lust. I lust after men all the time and sometimes I've just got to have them. Even if I don't know them well. Is that very bad?'

'No. That's how guys feel about women.'

'Is it? Really? I never knew that.'

There's a pause in the conversation. I raise my eyebrows at

Bella and she shrugs, sending a shudder through her delightful superstructure.

'What's your name?' says Clyde.

'Maria.'

'You're some woman, Maria. My name's Jack.'

Bingo, I think, that's lie number one.

'Are you married, Jack?'

'No.'

That's number two. It should be plain sailing from here on.

'Why not?'

'Like you, Maria, I have too much lust. There's too many gorgeous women out there to tie myself to just one. It wouldn't be fair on my wife.'

It's not, you slimeball, I think. Boy, is Marilyn going to throw some kind of shit-fit when she hears this!

'I know what you mean,' says Bella. 'It's like with Tony, my ex. When I first met him I thought he was everything I would ever want in a man. It was funny how I met him. He won me in a fight.'

'What?' That gets his attention. It gets mine too. I look up at Bella and she just gives me her trust-me smile. She's pulled off my necktie by now and loosened my collar so she can massage my neck. I don't trust her one bit but right now I'm not complaining. I settle back to listen.

'I was going with this other guy – Roy. He was a gambler. Sometimes he'd have money and sometimes he'd be broke. He never wanted me around when he went to the track but this one time I went along. I finally nagged him into it, I guess. Well, he lost on the first race and decided I was bad luck so he parked me in the clubhouse restaurant. I didn't mind. I ordered a lobster salad and white wine and I thought I'd play the horses myself. The only thing was, I wasn't sure what to do.'

'Don't tell me,' says Clyde. 'Tony showed up and lent a helping hand.'

'How do you know? That's exactly what happened. Except

it was me who asked him because he was at the window making this bet and I thought he looked, you know, *sympatico*. So when he'd finished I asked him how to do it and he showed me.'

'I bet he did.'

Bella giggles. 'You have a filthy mind, Jack. It wasn't like that at first. Sure, I picked him I suppose because he was tall and looked smart. He had thick black hair like you. I like that. It makes me want to run my fingers through it.'

'You're some sexy witch, aren't you?'

More giggles. 'Don't you want to hear the rest of my story?'

'Sure. Go on.'

'Well, Tony showed me how to do all these funny bets — exactas and trios and things — and I lost most of my money. Then the fifth race came along and I won. I won a lot because, so Tony said, it was a pretty stupid bet. Anyhow it came off and I was holding about five hundred dollars when Roy came storming up. He didn't see Tony, just me and the money. I could tell he'd been losing because his eyes were all beady and hard. He said, "How the hell did a dumb cunt like you pick a winner?" and he took the notes out of my hand. Tony was behind him and said, "Give the lady her money back, mister" and Roy grinned and hit him in the face. Then they went at each other right there in the foyer of the first-class restaurant. By the time the manager rounded up a couple of waiters Roy was laid out on the floor.

'I left with Tony after the manager questioned us. He was going to call the police but all the witnesses said Roy got what he deserved. Anyway, he wasn't hurt that much. The funny thing is, I didn't bother to take my money back. I left it with Roy. I was so hot for Tony I didn't care.'

'It turned you on, huh?'

'It did, Jack. We must have fucked for twenty-four hours straight. I'm sorry.'

'What for?'

'For saying fuck. Now you won't think I'm a lady.'

'I think you're a magnificent horny woman, Maria. I wish half the women I know were as honest about the way they feel. Did you really fuck for twenty-four hours?'

'Well . . . maybe not quite that long. But he had me in his car in the car park during the seventh race.'

'Really?'

'Yes. He had his hand on my ass as he pushed me towards this big Caddy and we were almost running. He just shoved me in the back and pushed my skirt up round my waist.'

'What happened then?'

'Jack! Don't tell me you want the naughty details.'

'You bet I do. Did he jump on you?'

'Well, he wanted to go down on me first. He put his head between my legs and sucked me through my panties but I didn't want that. I undid his trousers and made him put his cock in me.'

'You *made* him?'

'I had to have him at once. I pulled his head up by the hair and tugged him between my legs. He ripped my panties off me and pushed it inside, right up, all in one go. It was wonderful. He had his eyes shut and there was blood on his cheek from the fight and he was going "uh, uh, uh" from deep in his chest as he gave it to me. All the time I was coming I had the taste of his blood in my mouth. It was wild. Have you got an erection, Jack?'

If he's anything like me, I think, he's got a pole in his pants.

'Is any of this true?' I say to Bella but she just shrugs in a kind of who-cares fashion and puts her hand on my trouser buckle and begins to undo it. So help me, she's going to run a flag up my pole and I don't intend doing a damn thing to stop her.

'I've got a little place round the corner,' Clyde is saying on the tape. 'Let's go back there for another drink.' Even as Bella's warm hand is fishing in my fly I'm thinking, what little place?

'Not yet,' says Bella to Clyde, 'it's your turn to tell me a story.'

'I can do that at my place.'

'Here's more fun. I like to sit in a bar while a man with a stiff penis tells me naughty stories. It turns me on.'

'Are you sure you're not just a pricktease?' says Clyde. Suspicion has returned to his voice.

If she is she's damn good at it, I think as she circles my shaft with her fingers and squeezes. She's got my whole tackle, balls and all, outside my pants now and I can tell I'm in the hands of an expert.

'Come on, Jack. Isn't talking sexy to me right here exciting enough for you? Tell me a story. Tell me about a horny time you had.'

'Well, let me think.' He sounds embarrassed, which is a laugh. 'Uh, OK. There's this woman in my office. She heads up the computer support system for the whole building so she's no bimbo. In fact, she's got a department of about a dozen people who maintain and train staff on the computers.'

'What's her name?'

'Francine.'

Now, this is very interesting, I think. Clyde could be making this up but far more likely, given that his brains are currently residing in his pecker, he's about to spill some real juice. In any case, it will be easy to check. I blow Bella a kiss as her fingers ever-so-gently juggle my balls and she bends over and places her lips on mine. I am taken by surprise but, on instant reflection, don't see why I should be. This night has already spiralled off into fantasy. As she and I explore each other's tonsils, we listen to Clyde's little tale.

'Francine's been at the company for years. Longer than me. Sometimes I see her around downtown on the weekends, shopping with her kids. She looks a little different then to how she appears at work. She wears these dark suits to the office, cut tight across the ass and bust. She's big, but in proportion if you know what I mean. She's five nine or ten and wears heels and her hair up. You can't miss her. And the way she comes on to her staff, she's like the wicked governess. Whack! Six of the best and all of that. You can see some of those young assistants almost wetting their pants when she gets going.

'However, she's sweet as pie to me since I'm about two levels up the ladder from her. In fact, the guy she reports to reports to me. About the end of last year he had to go into hospital and she started to come into my office regularly. The more I saw of her the more I liked her. It turned out she had a sense of humour. She knew the impression she created around the place, everybody thinking she was some kind of dragon, but she didn't care. In fact, it was good camouflage for what she was really like. When she told me what she did for a hobby I nearly fell off my chair.'

'What does she do?'

'Invents porno computer games. She told me it had started as a joke but she now had some interest from a software manufacturer and she asked me what the company's attitude would be if she did a deal with them. I said I thought the company wouldn't give a damn what she got up to in her own time. Then she told me about Check Mate – that's her game – and my jaw hit the floor.

'Of course, I wanted to see it. So, one evening after everyone else had gone, I went to her office and she let me give it a whirl. First off, if you're a man playing the game, you have to invent a woman and there's all these choices you've got – long legs/short legs, big ass/small ass etc – but refined to the point where you can specify thirty-four C-cup breasts with pink upturned nipples or a boyish bum with apple cheeks dusted with blonde downy hairs. That precise. But the point of the game is that you have a certain amount of money to spend on seducing your fantasy mate and every little detail costs you. You could end up blowing your stash creating the girl of your dreams but then you wouldn't be able to take her out and buy her dinner. I'm sorry, Maria, this kind of stuff fascinates me so tell me if I'm boring you.'

There's a small silence punctuated by a wet, sticky sound as of two people kissing. A magical sound, I reflect, as Bella and I reproduce it in the here and now.

On the tape, Bella says, 'Just cut to the sexy bits, Jack, before I wet my pants.'

'OK. Francine ran me through the whole set-up and of course asked me if I wanted to play. I said yes and she said it would speed the whole thing up if I had a readymade female to seduce. She tapped in an instruction and, bingo, I got this image of a fabulous naked woman. She was a tall brunette with thick dark hair that fell to just above the most incredible tits – big low-slung melons with pointy brown nipples. The waist was small which made the breasts look even bigger and it flared out into wide rounded hips. The legs were long and solid and there was a strip of chestnut pubic hair that was shaved around the pussy split. And when you chased her round the bedroom her big square ass winked at you. I mean, it wasn't the woman I would have created but she was stupendous.

'"She looks familiar," I said. "She should be," said Francine, "I modelled her on me." She let that thought sink in and then she said, "And I based this guy on you." Up on screen suddenly there was another figure, a naked man, and I looked at it more closely than I've ever looked at anything, I swear. Sure enough, it did look like me: same hair, same eye colour, same build. There was just one thing different.'

There's a pause on the tape. The sound of people ordering drinks and swapping yarns further down the bar can be heard quite clearly.

Then Bella's voice says, 'I think I can guess. Was it his cock?'

'You bet. He had a joint like a baseball bat. It looked like a cannon sticking up from between his legs. I was speechless.

"You're not offended, are you?" she said. "I mean, I know I've probably got a few details wrong." '

'What did you say?'

'I said, "Art improves on life every time, Francine",'

Bella laughs, a real down-and-dirty chuckle, before she says, 'Did you show her the real thing?'

'About two seconds later. We had lust, as you say, all over her office till about midnight. It's about the weirdest bit of fucking I've ever done because she made these two little figures on the screen go at it too. She'd turned off the lights so there was just this flickering from the terminal while we got down to it on her office couch. Every time I'd look up there was me and her screwing hammer and tongs on screen. I give dynamite computer sex, I tell you.'

Back in the real world, as it were, I have my hands on Bella's breasts through the material of her dress. She's not wearing a bra and the tits are hot and heavy. I can feel every ridge and crinkle of the areolae. I pull her bazookas into the open. The nubs are swollen, like someone has been sucking on them already. The thought excites me as I feed a big nipple into my mouth.

'What about Francine? She must have been hot for you.'

'Sure.'

'Was she good?'

'Oh yeah, she's a passionate lady.'

'So you still see her?'

'Do you always ask so many questions, Maria?'

'Only about sex. I like to know what people do. That way you can learn new things. I bet Francine taught you things.'

'Well, I guess.'

'You see? Tell me.'

'Maria, please! We hardly know one another. We just met. We haven't even, you know . . .'

'That's OK, Jack. I'm only joking. You are a nice man not to say everything you do with this Francine with the big titties.

Did she let you put your penis between them? I love it when a man does that to me. Or maybe she let you put it up her ass. That's so dirty but sometimes it's just what a girl feels like – ow!'

There's a sudden yelp and Bella cries, 'Hey Jack, let go of me!'

Clyde's whisper is hoarse and urgent. 'You're leaving with me right now, you little pricktease, or I'll drill you right here, so help me!'

'OK,' says Bella, 'just pass me my purse' and there's a rattling noise and the tape goes dead.

I'm lying across Bella's lap in a state of torment. Above me sway those fantastic breasts now gleaming with my spittle.

'You didn't go with him, did you?' I say. That's the most important rule in the book. No matter how sexy my operatives behave to get the goods, they never, ever, take it further. Even if they want to. It is forbidden. 'You didn't go back with him, did you?' I repeat but I know the answer already. Where else has she been for half the night? It's obvious.

She shrugs her shoulders. Her big titties shrug too, right in my face. You can imagine the effect.

'Why?' I say. 'We've got enough on the bastard to divorce him twice over. You didn't need to go with him.'

'I didn't want to give the wrong impression,' she says. 'People call me many things but nobody calls me a pricktease.'

I laugh and there's a touch of hysteria in it. She shuts me up by pushing her tongue down my throat and speeding up her fingers on my prick. She's been keeping me on the brink for hours it seems and now I can't hold it any longer. My hands close on those creamy globes above me as I'm ravished by her lips and she works me in her hands like putty. Stiff, aching, trembling putty. I spunk over the pair of us like a teenager on a hot date.

Two minutes later we're cleaning up when the office door

crashes open and Marilyn Mountjoy walks in. Her pretty face is drawn in tight ugly despair. My first thought is, thank God I got my handjob before she showed.

'Hey, Marilyn,' I say as casually as I can, 'guess who turned up? This is Bella.'

'So I see,' she says, slamming the door shut behind her with her foot.

'Have a seat. Relax. We've got some great material for you . . .'

'Just tell me,' she says, her eyes like chips of ice, 'has this tramp slept with my husband?'

'Of course not,' I say. 'But I'm afraid we have gathered incriminating evidence about his behaviour which confirms your—'

'Have you?' she hisses, stepping closer and speaking directly to Bella who gazes back at her with wide-eyed innocence.

'Don't get excited, Marilyn,' I say, interposing my body between the two of them. Sometimes clients get a little heated in these situations and take it out on my operatives. 'Bella was only doing her job.'

'Slut!' cries Marilyn.

'Hey, Marilyn,' I say. 'Don't shoot the messenger.' Which is a phrase I often use because it seems to fit the bill, but right now it's a big mistake.

'Why the fuck not?' says Marilyn and takes a pistol out of her purse.

Uh oh! I think as the room goes deathly quiet. Behind me I hear Bella's breath coming in little raggedy gulps. Apart from that you could hear a mouse fart.

'Get out of the way,' says Marilyn to me, 'or I'll plug you.'

'Don't be ridiculous, Marilyn. You don't want to shoot her, she's on your side. We both are.'

'I'll count to three. If you don't move I'll kill you too. *One.*'

Her eyes are full of tears, I can see and her voice is all

wobbly. But the gun is steady. It's a great big mother and she holds it in both hands. She can't miss.

'They got a death penalty in this state, you know,' I say.

'*Two.*'

'You'll fry, Marilyn, and Clyde will be out there screwing around. What good will that do?'

'*Three!*'

I close my eyes. Behind me I hear Bella muttering some kind of prayer beneath her breath. The gun does not go off.

'Shit!' says Marilyn.

I open my eyes and see her knuckles whitening as she squeezes on the trigger. I step forward and take the gun out of her hands.

She looks me in the eye and says, 'The fucking thing doesn't work.'

'Not if you don't take the safety off,' I reply and she falls into my arms and begins to blub into my shoulder.

Bella removes the gun from me and locks it in the top drawer of my desk. Her face is drawn but she's in control. How come I ever thought she was dumb?

She looks up at me and says, over Marilyn's howls, 'She would have shot us dead.'

It's my turn to shrug. 'So much for the death penalty as a deterrent. I always knew it was a crock of shit.'

Marilyn is now inconsolable. The tears have done their work and she's cried all her anger into my shirt. We sit her down and press a glass of Scotch into her hand. Bella wets a handkerchief and swabs Marilyn's throat and forehead. Marilyn clings on to her free hand.

'I'm sorry, I'm sorry,' she says over and over. 'I could have killed you. I'm sorry.'

Bella says it's OK and gives Marilyn a hug that starts the tears up again. She holds her till they stop and then Marilyn looks normal again.

'I want to hear the tape,' she says.

I say I think she should go home and we'll discuss it in the morning.

'Are you crazy?' she says, which is a bit rich since she was the one waving a gun in my face ten minutes back. 'I can't wait till tomorrow. Put it on now.'

I'm prepared to debate this further but Bella is switching on the tape machine. She sits next to Marilyn and takes her hand. I think, What the hell? and take her other hand and sit on the other side of her. Thank God I got a big couch.

'Do you live here all alone?' That's Bella's voice.

'Sure do. It's all a single guy needs.' That's Clyde.

I realise Bella has put on tape two but refrain from explaining the scenario to Marilyn. I doubt she'll need an interpreter.

'Now where were we?' says Clyde and we go into sticky-kissy mode. In the background Mark Knopfler doodles a solo. At least Clyde's got decent taste in humping music.

Marilyn's little pointed jaw is set firm and she's holding it steady. Her fingers are digging into mine though as we digest the slithering sound of clothes being rearranged.

'Man!' breathes Clyde. 'Oh brother, these are the most fabulous titties I've ever . . .' The words tail off as he puts his mouth to other uses. I can picture his lips closing on a puckered brown saucer of areola and a big chocolate-dark nipple filling his mouth. I guess Marilyn can picture it too because her fingernails are about to draw blood.

'Oh Maria, Maria. God, Maria, I love your tits . . .' The words are punctuated by sucking and slobbering as Clyde goes ape over Bella's balcony fittings. And who could blame him? I reflect. It's a silly question, sitting as I am right next to his wife.

'He's always thought mine were too small,' says Marilyn, in a matter-of-fact voice.

'Men are stupid like that,' says Bella.

'God, Maria,' goes Clyde, 'I've just go to, you know . . .'

'Do you think mine are too small?' says Marilyn.

'Don't be ridiculous,' I say, 'they're everything a guy could want.'

'I wasn't talking to you,' she snaps and pulls her hand from mine for which I'm grateful.

'Ooh!' that's Bella squealing on the tape.

'I'm sorry, Maria,' says Clyde, 'but first I've got to fuck your tits.'

To my amazement, Marilyn doesn't turn a hair. She's too busy unbuttoning her blouse.

'What do you think?' she says to Bella, pulling a peach silk camisole up high over two shivering pink-and-cream titties like small perfect pears.

'Oh my,' says Bella. 'They're gorgeous.'

'Uh, uh, uh,' goes Clyde in the background.

Marilyn ignores him. 'Do you really think so?'

'Fabulous,' says Bella and touches one tiny raspberry nipple with her forefinger. I rub my eyes. I can't be seeing this.

'Oh yes, yes!' moans Clyde. 'Lick it, yes – that's it. Oh my God . . .'

'Show me yours,' says Marilyn, tossing the camisole onto the floor on top of her blouse.

I hold my breath as Bella gets her tits out again. The olive-skinned globes dwarf Marilyn's pink pears. The two women look at each other closely as if I'm not there.

'I can see why he liked you,' says Marilyn. 'He's a greedy pig.'

'He's foolish,' says Bella and places Marilyn's hand on her big left breast.

'He's a man,' says Marilyn and lowers her head to Bella's tit.

'Uh, uh, uh,' continues Clyde like a blissed-out soul singer in the background as Bella strokes Marilyn's spun-sugar hair. Her hands rove down the woman's dimpled back, soothing and comforting, like she's trying to smooth out the creases. I can see Marilyn responding to her touch, relaxing into her arms. Just before they kiss, Bella shoots me a glance over Marilyn's shoulder. It says, Leave this to me. As if I were capable of doing anything else.

'Oh God, oh God!' mumbles Clyde, heading into his short strokes from the sound of it.

Marilyn and Bella are mouth to mouth and tit to tit. From the side I can see Marilyn's sharp little nips digging into the smooth enveloping flesh of Bella's round jugs. I'm almost as far gone as Clyde and there's only one thing that stops me coming in my pants. The thought that, for the first time in my career, I've completely lost control of an investigation.

Bella has her hand up Marilyn's skirt as the two of them wrestle around. Marilyn's got great thighs, smooth and slim and silky from years of leg wax, I can tell. She does her bikini line too, that's now clear. The skirt's up to her waist and Bella's walking her fingers all over her little blue panties. The cotton's so wet it's sticking to the cleft. Marilyn's not a natural blonde – I can see that from the dark shadow beneath the blue.

'I gotta put it in – I gotta!' It's a shock to hear Clyde still jabbering. I'm getting carried away with events right here on the couch.

'Oh, you're so big,' says Bella on the tape. 'I don't think I can take all that.'

Who says the guys have a monopoly on the dumb lines? I reflect as I watch Bella yank Mrs Mountjoy's panties to her knees. I lend a hand and whisk them down her legs and off her feet. She's not going to notice – not with Bella's fingers combing out her bush. As I thought, her legs are smooth as silk.

'Oh yes!'

'Put it in!'

'Oh God!'

'Quick, quick!'

I'm getting confused here. Marilyn is muttering out loud as

Bella finds her clit and the on-tape Bella is making with the boudoir dialogue. The room is filled with oohs and aahs and grunt-moan sounds and I can't deny it's having an effect. So much so that I miss what Bella is saying to me. She says it again.

'Have you got a hard-on?' she hisses, kind of impatient like she wants to add 'pay attention, asshole'.

I don't know how to answer this question. There are two half-naked women sitting beside me on the couch, one's got her hand up the other's twat and there's a soundtrack of a man and a woman fucking like they just got out of jail. I haven't just got a hard-on – I've got a prick made out of tempered steel.

I nod my head.

'So take it out and fuck her,' she orders.

Marilyn's eyes bug open.

I stare at Bella like she's a madwoman.

'It's what you need,' says Bella to Marilyn. 'Listen – Clyde's getting his. You deserve it too.'

Marilyn kind of moans. Like she wants to protest and it's stuck in her throat. But her sweet little pelvis is jerking on the seat as Bella handles her pussy and the juice is flowing.

'Get it out,' Bella repeats, this time to me. 'This girl's in distress.'

Who am I to say no? I think as I unbutton my pants. So what if it breaks my sworn vow never to touch a client? This is crazy time. Anyway, this woman held a gun on me. She owes me a piece of her pretty pink pussy.

And Marilyn's not complaining. 'Take off your clothes,' she says. 'Show me what you got.'

I don't want to boast but I know I don't look bad. I keep in shape and I've got muscles. I kick off my shoes and socks and drop my pants to the floor. My cock is straining in my shorts and I drop them too. The women are looking at me with eyes like shiny new quarters.

'Yummy,' says Marilyn and reaches out her hand. I step

between the vee of her legs as she sprawls on the couch and let her explore my cock and balls. She does it with the hand that held the pistol on me. I don't care about that now. She leans forward and looks close at the red head of my dick. She smiles and slips it into her mouth. Jesus, it's hot in that little furnace. Flames lick down my root and up my belly. As she sucks me in and gobbles I thank my stars that Bella brought me off already in her hand. Else I'd be emptying my balls down Marilyn's throat right now.

She lifts her head, her lips are red and moist and very full.

'Please,' she says and I sink to my knees between her legs.

With her on the couch and me on the floor, her cunt's just at the right height for ease of entry. I put my cock at the gate of her pussy and slide right in.

Bella has primed Marilyn for me. She's on the edge, wound up so tight that when I hit bottom, as you might say, she goes off the rails. Her upper body flails and those cute little tits shiver and bounce and she gives out with a string of 'Oh-yes-oh-God-that's-great-you-big-fucker-oh' etc till I shut her up with a kiss. I wrap my arms around her and hold my cock still till she calms a bit. I'm aware that the fucking noises on the tape have come to an end. I'm aware too of Bella, so close to us, watching everything.

I get Marilyn into a proper fucking rhythm, easing my dick in and out of her in a steady pump and she spreads her legs and takes it. She's got her eyes closed and her mouth shut, thank the Lord, and she just lies back in Bella's arms and I fuck her like a doll. This is fantastic.

Now it's a silent serious business. Marilyn's cunt is like a warm glove around my cock, massaging every inch. It's an incredible sensation and I feel like I could go on all night. I'm kneeling up, shafting between her legs, fondling her thighs, watching my dick as it stretches her sweet little puss. For the first time in the whole messy business I'm in control and I'm loving it.

Then Marilyn starts to come. She's lying back across Bella's lap and jerking like a landed fish. Strangled sounds are coming from her throat and she's got her fingers in the dark thatch at the top of her crack, diddling herself. She's got a big clit, a wine-red peg sticking right up and I watch the way she goes at it. She pinches and jabs herself in a way I'd never dare. Whatever she's doing it works, for she's in freefall, way off somewhere else, flopping and moaning and squealing on my cock.

Her orgasm seems to go on forever. I'm not exactly detached about it but I'm wondering what the hell is going through her head as she bounces on my dick. Is this a weird revenge on her two-timing husband? Some kind of hysteria? Or is she always this hot?

There's another noise mixed in with Marilyn's squeals, a long sigh that sends a shiver through me. I look at Bella. She's biting her lip but she can't hold the sound back. Her wonderful tits are shaking and her left arm is half hidden behind Marilyn but I can tell from the way she's sitting that her hand is between her legs.

I think to myself that the moment Marilyn is finished I'm going to push her off my cock and sink it between the luscious olive thighs of my new associate. I look into Bella's big wet eyes and she knows what I'm thinking. She nods her head and smiles.

Then, though I don't want to, the blood starts to rush in my veins and I feel the sap rise in my balls. I grab Marilyn's butter-soft hips and thrust into her. I can't help myself. As I come I hear the sound of Marilyn moaning and Bella sighing and I hear myself shout, 'Oh fuck!'

Bella and I take Marilyn home. She's almost comatose, won't open her eyes and we have to carry her to the car. As we pull up at her house she snaps out of it.

'I'm fine,' she says and vanishes indoors without saying goodnight.

Clyde's car is in the drive so we wait for ructions but all seems peaceful. Lights come on at the bedroom window then go out again.

After half an hour, during which Bella and I say nothing but think plenty, we drive off. I ask Bella to come back to my place but she says she's pooped. So am I to tell the truth.

The next day Marilyn rings to say she and Clyde are solid so forget the whole investigation. She'll put a cheque in the post.

Bella comes in at four in the afternoon. I go to kiss her and she tells me to back off. I go to pay her and she says:

'Put it on my account. I'm hiring you to check out my husband.'

I lift an eyebrow. Is she kidding? This is the first I've heard of a husband.

'I'm serious,' she says. 'I'm married three years and I know my guy is running around with other women.'

'But don't you need the money? I thought you owed the bank.'

'Sure but how else can I afford you?'

I grin and pull some notes out of my wallet.

'Here's your money, sweetheart,' I say. 'You can pay my bill some other way.'

She gives me a look as she picks up her dough. One of the complicated kind.

'Will it be very expensive?' she says.

I just nod my head, my voice frozen in the back of my throat as I watch her fingers undo the pearl buttons on the front of her bulging blouse . . .

The Adventures of a Schoolboy

After the rigours of a term at a Victorian public school, it is not surprising that, come the holidays, a chap tends to let his hair down. Young – but far from immature – Sir Francis and his chum, George, spend their time at George's grandmother's house in the country, formerly an abbey. Though there's much to do in the way of riding and fishing, there's no country pursuit in the world that quite compares to the sport of young ladies. Fortunately for Frank and George, his distant cousins, Maria and Eliza, are only too happy to participate in their games.

Then along comes pretty Fanny Vickars, a new member of the houseparty much put-upon by her infirm aunt and grandmother. Frank is smitten and it seems his interest is returned though it is difficult to separate Fanny from her family obligations. But for all his tender years, Frank is a clever operator. And, like the skilled fisherman he is, he knows it's just a matter of biding his time...

There was to be an archery party given by a gentleman who resided at the distance of about twelve miles from us, and I fancied that in the course of the day I might find some opportunity of detaching Fanny from the rest of the company and accomplishing my object.

Owing to the presence of other visitors, none of the old ladies of the Abbey were able to go; but Mrs and Miss Vickars were to accompany the young people. Fanny was allowed to go with us in the Abbey carriage, which could be thrown open, and Mrs and Miss Vickars went in their own chaise; but I heard Mrs Vickars say to her daughter that she had better arrange to return at night in the Abbey carriage and send Fanny with her. This hint was not lost upon me, and failing all other means I devised a scheme founded upon it.

Despite all my efforts I was unable to make any progress with Fanny all day, beyond giving her a few slight caresses which only tended to inflame and increase my ardour, and I have no doubt they had pretty much the same effect upon her. She either did not or would not understand the hints I gave her to induce her to separate herself from her companions and give me the opportunity I so longed for, and without attracting observation, I was unable to press her.

There was to be a dance in the evening and we prevailed upon the old ladies to remain for it, so that it was quite dark when we started to return home. In the course of the evening I pressed Fanny to drink a few glasses of wine to prepare her for the scene I anticipated; but she would only take a single glass, until shortly before we set out, when she asked me to bring a glass of water. I said it was not good for her to drink cold water while she was overheated, but offered to get what I was drinking myself, a tumbler of soda water with a glass of champagne in it, which she agreed to take. I however reversed the prescription and brought her a tumbler of champagne with a glass of soda water. She drank off about half of it without discovering the deceit, and then laid it down, saying it was too strong. I said that anything she had tasted was too precious to be wasted and finished the tumbler.

In the course of the evening I took an opportunity of saying to Mrs Vickars, that as we should have to return in the dark, she might perhaps like to be accompanied by a gentleman, and that if she wished it, I would take the seat on the box beside the coachman. She said she would be very glad to have my escort; but that there was no occasion for my going outside as there was only to be herself and Fanny in the chaise, and there was plenty of room for me.

This was exactly what I wanted, and accordingly I most willingly agreed to her suggestion. Our carriage came first to the door, I handed Mrs Vickars in, then Fanny, and jumped in myself. It was one of those roomy old-fashioned chaises which could hold three people; but as the old lady was rather of an unusual size, a third seat, projecting forward, had been inserted for Fanny in the middle, which could be raised up or lowered down as required, and which consequently formed a sort of separation between the parties in the two corners.

Fanny had placed herself on this seat, but as it did not suit my purpose that she should remain there, I, without saying a word, removed her to the corner, and took her place. The night had become stormy and wet, and I enveloped Mrs V in a large cloak, ostensibly to protect her from the cold, but in reality to muffle her up and separate her as much as possible from us. Under the same pretext I threw a scarf over Fanny and myself, contriving at the same time to get our knees interlaced together, so as to have one of my legs between hers.

To keep up appearances, I began a conversation with the old lady, which I was convinced would not last long on her part. Under the cover of this, I soon got possession of Fanny's hand, and after some little toying, to divert her attention from my object, I placed it on my thigh, and again made her feel the stiff object which she had previously seen and felt. She resisted a little at first, but I persevered and, as curiosity, or perhaps desire, seemed in the end to prevail, I was convinced I might safely proceed further.

Having thus broken the ice, I removed her hand, and taking off her glove, pressed it to my lips, and threw one arm around her waist, so as to bring her close to me, while with the other hand I unbuttoned my trousers, and throwing them completely open, laid bare my organ of manhood with the adjacent part of my belly and thighs. Then suddenly bringing down her hand, I made her grasp the stiff naked pillar. This proceeding took her quite by surprise, and she allowed her hand to remain encircling the throbbing object for a few seconds, during which I felt a peculiar sort of tremor pass through her frame. But presently, recollecting herself, she attempted to withdraw her hand and remove herself from my embrace. She was, however, so shut up in the corner of the carriage that she was unable to get away from me and I managed to retain hold of her hand, and soon made it resume its position, closing her fingers round the symbol of manhood. Finding that she could not help herself, she ceased to struggle, and in a few minutes she not only made no attempt to withdraw her hand, but even allowed me to make it wander over all the adjacent parts, which I thought were likely to excite her curiosity and afford her pleasure to touch.

Having succeeded so far, I considered it advisable to make a diversion to distract her attention from the main object of which I wished to gain possession. I had ascertained that her dress, which had been changed to a low-breasted one for the dancing party, was fastened by buttons behind. I contrived to unloosen two of them, which made the part in front open and fall down, so as fully to disclose the two voluptuous globes of firm, springy flesh which adorned her bosom. My hand and lips took instant possession of them and revelled in the thorough enjoyment of all their beauties. She moved about uneasily at first under this new attack, but when I slipped one of her nipples into my mouth, and began to suck it, she allowed her head to sink back and left me at liberty to pursue my amorous propensities as I thought fit.

I was perfectly certain now, from the convulsive manner in which her fingers occasionally closed around the staff of life, that her passions had become sufficiently excited and I thought I might venture on an attack in the proper quarter. Stooping down, I inserted my hand beneath her petticoat, and rapidly raised it up along her leg and thigh until it rested on the mount of pleasure. At the same time I advanced my knee between hers, so that it was impossible for her to close her legs, and bent myself over her so as to prevent her from deranging my position by her struggles. It required all my address to maintain my position and calm her first agitation. She struggled so violently at first, on finding her virgin territory thus rudely invaded, than I greatly feared she would disturb the old lady and excite her suspicions. I whispered softly to her to beware of this, adding that I would do nothing but what would give her pleasure.

The precautions I had taken prevented her from being able to offer any effectual resistance to me without making her grandmother aware of what was going on; and she probably felt that after having allowed me to go so far, she had lost the power of checking my further proceedings except at the risk of compromising herself. This, joined with the insidious effect which my voluptuous caresses must have by this time produced upon her senses, soon brought about the state of matters which I desired. Her struggles gradually became weaker, and I was at length left in full possession of the outworks.

As soon as I was satisfied of this, I felt that my object was gained, and I determined not to hurry on too rapidly to the conclusion, but to attempt to bring her by degrees to be as desirous for it as I was myself. I therefore allowed my hand to wander for some time over the soft expanse of her belly and thighs, playing with the silky tresses which surrounded the mount of pleasure and tickling and caressing the tender lips. I then gently separated them, and allowed a finger to insinuate itself a short way within the soft furrow, at the same time covering her mouth and bosom with repeated and burning kisses. When she first felt the intruding finger penetrating into the virgin sanctuary, which had never yet been invaded by the hand of another, she involuntarily drew back as if frightened and hurt.

Anxious to reassure her, I ceased to force it further in, and contented myself with moving it gently backwards and forwards between the lips. When she was somewhat reconciled to this, I sought out the little sensitive object – the titillation of which affords a girl so much pleasure. When I pressed it, she gave a start, but it was accompanied with such a peculiar pressure upon my own organ of pleasure that I felt convinced she was now sensible of the sympathetic feeling which exists between the two, and that she had already begun to experience the foretaste of the lascivious sensations I was desirous of rousing. I continued to press and tickle the little protuberance and occasionally to thrust my finger a little further into the crevice, until I felt her limbs become somewhat relaxed, and her thighs open wider mingled with some indescribable symptoms of the approach of the crisis of pleasure. I redoubled my titillations, now forcing my finger more boldy up and down the narrow entrance, until a few involuntary movements in response to my lascivious proceedings, and a long-drawn half-stifled sigh, announced the access of the voluptuous swoon. Her head sank on my shoulder, her fingers lost the grasp they had for some time firmly maintained upon my burning staff, and I felt a slight moisture oozing out and bedewing my finger as she paid the first tribute to Venus, which had been drawn from her by the hand of another.

When I was convinced the crisis was past, I withdrew my finger, and allowed her to remain quiet for a few minutes, during which I prepared both myself and her for the still more voluptuous encounter I contemplated. She was now quite passive in my hands, and allowed me to raise up her petticoats, and fasten them around her waist, so as not to interfere with the delicious contact of our bodies which I now wished to effect. At the same time I allowed my trousers to fall to my knees, and tucked up my shirt under my waistcoat, so as to be prepared for the encounter.

The conversation between Mrs Vickars and me, which had been very languidly maintained on my part, had now entirely ceased; and the old lady was giving audible tokens that she was not in a condition to pay any attention to our proceedings. I was determined to take advantage of the opportunity to the utmost, and even if I should find myself unable to achieve the victory over the delicious maidenhead in prospect, I wished to make a beginning, by allowing the proper weapon to enter the premises in such a manner as to insure the certainty of his again being allowed to revisit them on any more favourable opportunity. I was, however, at a loss at first how to accomplish this. I was afraid to leave my seat and get upon her, for fear the old lady might suddenly wake and miss me from her side, and I was equally afraid of taking Fanny on my knee.

At length I determined on the following plan: I made her place herself on her left side, bringing her body so far forward that her hip rested on the edge of the cushion of the seat, thus presenting her bottom to me, which, as her clothes were turned up round her waist, was of course quite bare. I placed myself also on my left side, and brought my belly in delicious contact with her charming soft buttocks. The feeling that this produced was so exquisite that I was almost maddened; and it was with the greatest difficulty that, when I found my weapon nestling between the two delicious soft mounts of naked flesh, I could maintain sufficient command over myself to proceed with the moderation necessary to prevent discovery. I then raised up her right leg and inserted my own right leg between her thighs, at the same time drawing her to me, so as to bring the lower part of my belly as far forward between her legs as possible. Then shifting the position of my weapon from its resting place between her lovely buttocks, I lowered my body a little, till I could move forward the champion between her thighs, so that, on my raising myself up again, it reared its proud crest upwards along her belly, rubbing against the soft smooth flesh, almost up to her navel. I remained in this charming position for a few minutes, till she got over the alarm occasioned by the first contact of our naked bodies; and till I had quite satisfied myself that my position was such that I should have no difficulty in effecting the object I had in view.

When I thought she was sufficiently prepared, I lowered the point of the weapon till I brought it to nestle between the soft ringlets which adorned the mouth of the entrance to the grotto of pleasure. Then gently inserting my finger, I distended the lips as far as possible, and pressed the head of my champion forwards against the narrow slit with so much impetuosity that tight as it was, I felt the lips distend, and the point of the weapon penetrate within, until the head was wholly enclosed within the narrow precincts. I found, however, that I was proceeding too rapidly. Whether from the pain or the fright at this novel proceeding, Fanny uttered a cry which she seemed unable to suppress, and put down her hand, trying to remove the intruder from the place which he had so rashly invaded. I succeeded in preventing this and in maintaining my position; but I was sadly afraid she might have awakened the old lady, and I was obliged to remain quiet and not attempt to force myself further in, until I was quite satisfied from her quiet breathing that she still slumbered. I then ventured to whisper to Fanny for heaven's sake to remain quiet, that I would take every care not to hurt her, and that she would soon enjoy the most delicious pleasure.

I presumed that the pain attendant on my first entrance had now somewhat abated, for without speaking she remained quiet and made no objection to my further progress. I tried to manage matters as tenderly as possible, proceeding to improve my position by slow degrees and merely pressing gently forward, without venturing to thrust with force. By this means I succeeded in getting nearly the half of the stiff stake fairly driven into her. But this slow mode of proceeding, though absolutely necessary in the circumstances, was maddening to me. My passions were wrought up to such a pitch by the lascivious manoeuvres I had been indulging in that I hardly knew what I was about; and every moment I was on the point of giving way to the fierce stimulus which urged me on, and endeavouring by one fierce thrust to plunge myself to the bottom and complete my enjoyment. I began also to feel that the struggle could not last much longer, for excited as I was I could no longer ward off the approach of the voluptuous crisis.

I was hesitating whether to run the risk of one final effort and burst through every obstacle at all hazards, or whether to rest contented with the imperfect enjoyment which my present situation could afford us both, when my hesitation was most disagreeably brought to an end by the carriage stopping and by the sound of the coachman's voice calling to someone in the road.

There was not a moment to be lost. I hastily withdrew my palpitating weapon from its delicious abode, pulled down Fanny's clothes, and without waiting to fasten my trousers, leaned forward to one side of the carriage away from the old lady and opened the window to ascertain the cause of the stoppage.

arrived. I told her I should remain with her, for it was no use going to bed to try to sleep as George would be sure to awaken me when he arrived.

We sat for half an hour, talking over the events of the day, until the old lady began to get alarmed at the non-arrival of the other party. I laughed at her fears at first, but as time wore on, I began to think some accident must have occurred, and at last I said that I would take my horse and ride back for a few miles to ascertain what had become of them. She urged me to take the carriage, but I said the horses had had a hard day's work, and that it was a pity to take them out again, unless it was absolutely necessary, but that I would tell the men not to go to bed and to be ready to start if they should be required. I went to the stable and had my horse saddled, and led it quietly out to the turf on the park and then set off at a good speed. I had only gone a mile or two from the park gate when I heard the sound of horses' feet approaching. I drew up, thinking that I would probably ascertain from the rider if any accident had occurred on the road.

He turned out to be a stable boy who had been sent from the place where we had spent the day to announce that our friends would not be able to reach home that night. It appeared that in passing the lodge, the coachman, who had probably been participating too freely in the hospitality of our friends, had run the carriage against a post, and although no one had suffered any injury, one of the wheels had been so much damaged that the carriage was unable to proceed. The ladies had been obliged to walk back to the house, and had got drenched in the rain, so that even if there had been another carriage at hand, which there was not, they could not have travelled in comfort. It had therefore been arranged that they should remain where they were for the night, and the messenger had been dispatched to prevent our being uneasy and to carry back some necessary change of dress, which would be required for them next morning.

I immediately turned my horse's head, and desiring the boy to follow me, returned to the Abbey. As I cantered up the avenue, my thoughts were naturally turned upon the scene which had occurred in the carriage, and the severe disappointment I had sustained in being unable to bring it to a satisfactory conclusion, and I began to consider in what manner I might still contrive to accomplish this.

After two or three schemes had passed through my mind, it occurred to me that I might not again find a combination of circumstances presenting so favourable an opportunity as was then afforded. Her aunt being absent, Fanny would pass the night alone, and George and the girls being also away, there was nothing to prevent me from spending it with her and completing the task I had only half accomplished. I made up my mind at least to make the attempt.

When I reached the house, the old lady's fears were soon allayed. The housekeeper, whom I found sitting with her, said she would get the things which were required for the young ladies without disturbing anyone in the house, and Mrs Vickars said she would go to Fanny's room to get what was wanted for her daughter.

I wished to make certain that she was not to remain for the night with Fanny, and I said I would get a clean shirt for George and bring a carpet bag to put all the things in. When Mrs Vickars returned I said I hoped Fanny had not been alarmed at her aunt's absence.

She replied, 'Oh, no'; that she had found her fast asleep, and not wishing to disturb her, had merely left a note on the table, mentioning what had occurred that she might find it when she awoke in the morning. This information was a great relief to me, for I had feared the possibility of some change of arrangements for the night, or that Fanny, finding she was to be left alone, might bolt the door and prevent me from gaining access to her.

I was not satisfied, however, until I had seen the old lady

proceed to her own room, and even after the housekeeper had retired to her own domain, I watched at the door till I heard the old lady flop into bed and saw that the candle was extinguished.

Considering everything now quite safe, I hastened to my apartment, and stripped off every article of dress, putting on merely a pair of slippers and a dressing gown. Thus equipped, I cautiously made my way to Fanny's room, and softly opened the door, closing it again, and turning the key in the lock. The weather, by this time, had cleared up, and the moon was shining brightly into the room through the upper part of the window, the shutters of which had been left open. The first bed I came to was vacant, but the other presented a most delicious sight.

My movements had been so quiet that Fanny had not been disturbed, and was still fast asleep. But from her situation, it would appear that her slumber had not altogether been unbroken. She lay on her back, with one arm raised up and resting on her head. The bed clothes had been pushed down, nearly as far as her waist, disclosing the form of her bosom, and her chemise being loosely fastened hung down at one side, and gave me a perfect view of one of her lovely bubbies, with its ivory expanse tipped with the purple nipple.

I sat down on the bed beside her, and gazed for a while with delight on her budding charms. But it was impossible long to confine myself merely to their view, delicious as it was. Bending my head down, I imprinted burning kisses on her lovely mouth and exquisite breasts.

This soon roused her from her slumber, but at first she was unconscious of my presence. Moving herself uneasily, but without opening her eyes, she said, 'Is that you, Aunt?'

My first idea had been to jump into bed beside her, and, before she could prevent me, get possession of her person so far as to secure the object I had in view, but I was afraid that, if suddenly awakened in this manner, she might, before recognizing me, call out for assistance, and thus alarm the house. Besides, after what had passed I did not now expect any serious opposition to bring her gradually round to participate with me in all the delight I anticipated, than to attempt to snatch it from her unawares. I therefore repeated my kiss, and whispered gently, 'No, dearest, it is not your aunt, but it is one who loves you a great deal better.'

She started at the sound of my voice, and opened her eyes. At first she seemed scarcely to know who it was, but as soon as she recognised me, she raised herself up, and sitting erect, exclaimed, 'Frank! Is it you? What is the matter? What has brought you here? Good heavens! Something dreadful must have happened! Where is my aunt?' I attempted to soothe her, telling her there was nothing to fear, and explaining the accident that has occurred to the carriage.

She would not believe for some time that I was telling her all the truth, and insisted upon reading the note, which I said her grandmother had left, asking me to light a candle that she might be able to do so.

The bed curtains were drawn back at the head of the bed, and close to it stood a large cheval glass with two wax candles on each side, I saw the good use I might put this to, and lighting one of the candles I gave the note to her to read.

While she did so, I hastily lighted the other candle, and then standing upright by the bedside, I allowed my dressing gown, my only covering, to open out fully in front, and drew it back, so as to expose the whole of the forepart of my naked person.

When Fanny had finished the perusal of the note, she raised up her eyes and the first thing they rested upon was my throbbing priapus, which the sight of her charms had roused up to a brilliant state of erection.

As soon as she caught a glimpse of it, her face and neck became suffused with crimson, and she raised her hands to cover her eyes, exclaiming, 'Oh, Frank! Frank! How could you come here in such a state?'

'You should rather say, my own darling,' was my reply, 'how could I help coming here after what has taken place tonight, and when I found there was such a favourable opportunity of happily completing the work we were so pleasantly engaged in, and which we were obliged to leave unfinished. You cannot yet imagine half the pleasure it will give us to bring it to a successful conclusion.'

It was a considerable time before I was able to soothe her, and to satisfy her that there was no risk to be apprehended for my remaining with her, for a part, at least, of the night. But I succeeded at length in convincing her that the house was closed for the night, and everyone was gone to bed. I told her besides that even in case anyone should come to her door, and wish to get admittance, I could easily escape by the window, and reach my own rooms without discovery.

Even after I had relieved her anxiety on this point, I had some difficulty in persuading her to let me get into bed with her. At length this was conceded on the condition that I was not to take off my dressing gown, and was only to get between the blankets, and not to get under the sheets, or meddle with anything below her bosom, which, with her mouth, was to be given up to my caresses.

I may easily be supported that this being conceded the conditions were not long observed, or even insisted upon. My dressing gown was soon slipped off. During the caresses which I claimed the right to bestow as being within the terms of our agreement, it was very easy for me to remove the coverings which intervened between us, and without much resistance I soon brought our two naked bodies into close contact with each other.

Having now no fear of interruption, I was in no hurry to urge on the completion of my pleasing work. I wished rather by a short delay, and by making use of all the little charming excitements which are so pleasing both to give and to receive, to rouse up her passions to an equal pitch with my own, and to make her as eager as myself for the enjoyment of the coming bliss. I therefore continued for some time the prelude, by the most amorous touches and titillations which I could devise, extending them to every part of her naked body, making her in return perform the same pleasing operations on the corresponding parts of my own person.

This at first she hesitated to do, but she very soon got warmed and excited, and without any hesitation began to put into practice every wanton trick I suggested. I saw that my object was fully attained, and that she was quite ready to co-operate with me in the crowning work. I whispered to her that I was afraid she must still have to submit to a little further pain before we could be perfectly happy, but that I would do all in my power to prevent her suffering and that she would soon be amply rewarded for what she must undergo by the supreme bliss it would enable us to attain.

I then placed her in a proper position to enable me to complete the enterprise. As I was quite aware that I had not yet effected a thorough penetration, and was afraid that there might be some sanguinary tokens of my victory, I arranged her on her back with my dressing gown underneath her, to prevent any stains reaching the sheets. Then separating her legs, and getting on my knees between them, I bent myself forward until I brought the point of the weapon to the mouth of the lovely sheath, into which I wished to plunge it.

When she saw me kneeling before her, with the palpitating weapon fully extended and standing out stiffly before me, she raised one hand to her eyes, as if ashamed to look it fairly in the face. But I seized upon the other hand and made her, not unwillingly, take hold of the extended lance, and maintain it in the proper position, while with my own fingers on each side I gently distended the lips of the cavity, so as to open up an entrance for it. Bending still further forward and leaning down upon her, I pressed the burning weapon into the fiery furnace of love, and as soon as I felt that the point had fairly gained admittance within the gates, I thrust onwards with fierce heaves of my buttocks. But the fortress was not to be gained possession of so easily. I penetrated without much difficulty as far as I had previously reached, but there I was again arrested by an obstacle that seemed almost invincible, without using a degree of force which I was anxious, if possible, to avoid. I soon found, however, that there was no alternative. The closely confined manner in which the point and the upper portion of love's instrument was pent up within the narrow cavity produced such an intense irritation upon its sensitive surface that it drove me almost frantic and, combined with the excitement of my senses occasioned by the lascivious pranks we had been previously indulging in, gave me ample warning that it would be impossible long to refrain from pouring forth the blissful shower.

It would have been too bad to have been condemned a second time to waste all its fragrance on the unplucked flower, and I was determined to spare no endeavours to avoid so dire a calamity. Relaxing my efforts, therefore, for a few moments, I explained to Fanny the necessity for making a vigorous attack, and begged for her to endure it as well as she could, and to try to assist me as far as possible, assuring her that the pain would only be momentary, and would lead to exquisite bliss.

She was now almost as much excited and as eager for the fray as I was, and she readily promised to do her utmost to assist my efforts. Getting my arms around her waist, and making her cross her legs over my buttocks, so as to clasp me round the back, I withdrew the stiff member as far as I could without making it issue from its charming abode, and then with a steady, well-sustained, vigorous thrust, I sent it forward as forcibly as was within my power. I felt at once that I was accomplishing the wished for object. Everything gave way before the energetic manner in which I drove the sturdy champion forward, and I felt him every instant getting engulfed further and further within the narrow channel. This was confirmed by the delicious pressures of the lips which I felt closing round the upper part of the column in the most charming manner possible.

But if all this was delightful to me, it was far otherwise with poor Fanny. She evidently strove hard to keep her word and render me every assistance, but when I first burst through the opposing barrier, the fast hold she had hitherto maintained of me suddenly relaxed, and she uttered a piercing cry of pain. As I continued to force my way in, the pain seemed to increase, and she besought me, in piteous accents, to have compassion upon her and to desist. But I was now far too highly wrought up to be able to comply with her request, even if I had been disposed to do so, which I certainly was not for I was perfectly convinced that it would be the kindest thing I could do, to put an end to her sufferings forever by at once effecting a complete penetration.

There was no time to explain all this to her, so at the risk of appearing cruel, I persevered without any relaxation in my victorious career. Two or three more thrusts sufficed to lodge me within her to the very hilt, and I felt my belly come into delicious contact with her warm flesh, accompanied with the charming tickling sensation of her hair rubbing against me and mingling with mine.

Doubly animated by this exquisite contact, my frantic thrusts were renewed without any regard to poor Fanny's sufferings. But the feelings I endured were too delightful to be of long continuance; the pent-up tide within me could no longer be prevented from bursting forth, and with the most exquisite sensation of gratification and delight, it issued from me and found its way into her inmost cavities. Gasping and breathless with voluptuous joy, I sank down upon her bosom, no longer able even to imprint the amorous kisses on her lovely face with which I had been endeavouring to stifle her tender complaints.

After a few minutes spent in luxuriating in the blissful

annihilation which follows complete fruition, I began to recover my senses a little. I was conscious that, during this period, Fanny had ceased to struggle, and was now lying motionless beneath me. I judged from this that the pain she had been suffering had by this time ceased, and I was anxious, as soon as possible, to make her participate in the delicious pleasure she had afforded me, but of which I was afraid she had as yet hardly had a taste.

The dart of love, though somewhat relaxed and diminished in size from the effects of the charming emission, still retained its position within her delightful grotto with sufficient vigour to assure me that in a short time it would be able to renew its career in the lists of love. I therefore determined to allow it to remain where it was, and thus avoid the difficulty and pain of effecting a new entrance.

Retaining my position upon her, I did all I could to soothe and calm poor Fanny. She was very much agitated, and had been sadly frightened by the impetuosity with which I had rushed on in my triumphant career without regard to the suffering she was enduring. At first she begged and prayed of me to get up, fearing that any renewal of the fierce transports I had indulged in would cause repetition of her agony.

To this, however, I would not agree, assuring her that she had no occasion to be alarmed, and that she had nothing to look forward to but transports of pleasure equal to those I had enjoyed. I soon convinced her of this, by two or three gentle thrusts of the weapon which had caused her so much discomfort, but which now, on the contrary, occasioned the most delightful sensations.

The passage having been fairly opened up and well lubricated by my first discharge, and the unruly member not being quite so fiercely distended as previously, it slipped up and down within her with the greatest of ease. Of course, at first I thrust with great caution, but I soon brought her to acknowledge that the pleasing friction it occasioned to her, so far from being disagreeable, afforded her the greatest delight; and even when our voluptuous movements produced their natural effect and stiffened and hardened the champion of love till it regained it full size and consistency, and again filled up the burning cavity till it was completely gorged and almost ready to burst, its presence within her and the fiercer and more rapid thrusts which I now allowed it to make, so far from being painful, evidently gave her intense delight. Her eyes now sparkled, and her cheeks blazed with voluptuous fires. She clasped her arms round me and drew me fondly to her bosom, while her lips returned the burning kisses which I imprinted upon her lovely mouth. Presently, no longer able to restrain herself, and losing every idea of modesty or bashfulness under the strong excitement produced by the voluptuous titillation which my inflamed organ of manhood exerted over her most sensitive parts, she twisted her legs around mine, she drew her thighs together, and contracted them closely to meet and increase the effect of every lascivious shove I gave her; she heaved her buttocks up and down in charming concert with my motions, so as to insure the most voluptuous and delicious effect from the alternate withdrawal and replacement of the weapon of love, which she took good care not to allow to escape entirely from its delightful prison. Finding her thus charmingly excited and enjoying herself to the utmost, I did all in my power to add to her bliss.

Being now a little calmer than I had been during the first fierce onslaught of her virgin charms, I was able at first to control my own movements and to direct them in such a manner as I thought would afford her the greatest enjoyment – quite satisfied that in doing so, I was only paving the way to still greater bliss for myself. I therefore watched her carefully and moderated or increased my efforts as I fancied would be most agreeable to her, until I saw from her excited gestures that the final crisis was fast approaching with her. Desirous to participate in the bliss, I then gave full vent to my own maddening passions. I heaved and thrust with impetuous fury; I strained her in my arms; and at every thrust, given with more and more force and velocity, I strove to drive myself further and further within her delicious recess.

She responded to every effort I made; her legs clasped me tighter, her bottom heaved up and down with greater velocity and stronger impetus, and the delicious contraction of the lips of her warm moist grotto closed round my excited weapon with still greater and more charming constriction. She sobbed, she panted, her bosom heaved up and down, and she clung to me as if she would incorporate her very existence with mine. Her transports were quite sufficient, without any exertion on my part, to have produced the most delicious effect upon me, and I soon felt that, notwithstanding my previous discharge, I was quite ready to co-operate with her and to enjoy in unison the impending blissful sensation of the final crisis, I had not long to wait.

A few upward heaves, more rapid and impetuous than ever – one last straining of her body to mine – and then the sudden relaxation of her tight grasp, accompanied with a heavy long-drawn sigh of pleasure, announced her participation for the first time in the joys of amorous coition. I was quite ready to join her – two or three active thrusts completed my bliss, and almost before her nectar had begun to flow, my voluptuous effusion was poured into her to mingle with her tide of rapture.

I raised my head to gaze on her lovely countenance, and to watch the gradations of pleasure as they flitted across her beautiful features, while with a few gentle motions of the champion, who had occasioned us so much delight, I spun out and completed the intoxicating bliss, till at length her eyes closed, the colour forsook her cheeks, and unconscious of what was passing around her, she sank into the blissful intoxication of completed desire.

After revelling for a few delightful minutes in the thorough enjoyment of my now perfectly completed victory, I withdrew my valiant champion reeking with the bloody tokens of success, and took up my position, with my head on the pillow beside her, before she had recovered the full possession of her senses.

I was in no hurry to rouse her from the trance of rapture. Although by no means disposed to allow the opportunity to escape me without profiting further by the conquest I had obtained, I felt that after the exertion I had made, I would be all the better for a little repose before attempting fresh exploits. I therefore lay quietly by her side for some time, hardly speaking and merely occasionally pressing her to my bosom and tasting the sweets of her lips and her bosom.

But when she had thoroughly recovered from the effects of her first enjoyment, I found that Fanny was now quite alive to the bliss to be derived from our pleasing conjunction; and that there would be no difficulty on her part at least to an immediate renewal of the amorous struggle. She reciprocated the fond caresses I lavished upon her, and even indulged herself in bestowing fresh ones upon me. I soon found that her curiosity was excited by the difference she found between my person and her own, and as I was quite disposed to gratify such a natural feeling, her hands were presently wandering over those parts of my body with which she was least familiar, but which recent events had taught her were the most attractive. I could perceive her surprise, and I thought her disappointment, when, without any assistance on my part, they reached the spot where the emblem of virility is situated, and when she found in her grasp instead of the hard, stiffly distended object which had penetrated her, causing first so much pain and then so much pleasure by its forcible entrance, a soft, limp mass of flesh which dangled between her fingers, and which she could twist around them in every direction.

I laughed at her surprise, and told her she must not always expect to find the little gentleman in the rampant condition in which she had hitherto seen him; that his present condition was his natural one, and that it was only the power of her charms that could rouse him up to action in his fierce excited state. She was soon able to judge for herself of the truth of my statement, for her wanton caresses were already beginning to produce their usual effect upon the little hero, who speedily erected and uncovered his rosy head, and extended himself at full length, swelling out till the ivory pillar quite filled up her grasp.

She was evidently not more surprised than gratified by this sudden resuscitation, and continued to tickle and play with it till I felt that it was not only in a suitable condition to renew the assault, but even that, if much longer delay, there was a danger of his yielding up his forces under her insidious blandishments before he was fairly ensconced in the citadel. I therefore told her that I could stand her wanton toying no longer, and that she must allow the little plaything again to take possession of the charming abode it had so recently entered, and there again offer up its adoration to her charms.

She readily agreed, though she expressed some fear lest its entrance should again cause a renewal of her sufferings. I told her there was not much fear of this, and that beyond a slight smart at the first penetration, she would in all probability find nothing but pleasure in the renewed encounter.

However, when I applied my hand to the charming spot for the purpose of separating the lips and preparing for the entrance, I found that the sanguine tide which had issued from her on my first withdrawal had now become encrusted on the curly moss which surrounded the entrance. I felt that it was quite necessary that all such traces of the conflict should be removed, and I thought that it would be more agreeable to us both that this should be done before we renewed the game of pleasure.

Turning down the bed-clothes, I proceeded to examine the spot more minutely and was somewhat shocked to find the traces of the ravages I had committed. She was a good deal frightened on seeing her thighs and the lower part of her belly covered with the crimson effusion, but I soon reassured her by explaining how it was occasioned; and the introduction of my finger within the orifice, where it could now penetrate with ease, convinced her that she had not much to fear from again admitting the somewhat larger plaything, which now throbbed under her grasp.

I was pleased to find that the precautions I had taken had prevented any marks which could induce suspicion. All that was necessary was to remove the bloody traces from our persons. This, I thought, would be best affected by means of the bidet. I accordingly made her get up and seat herself upon it. She was at first ashamed and reluctant to expose her naked person so completely to my gaze, for the candles I had lighted, reflected from the mirror; threw a brilliant light over all her secret charms; but my praises of their beauty, joined to the warm caresses I indulged in, at length reconciled her to the novel situation and she soon began to return my caresses.

Taking a sponge, I quickly removed all traces of the fierce combat, but as she seemed to be gratified by the application of the cool refreshing liquid to her heated spring of pleasure, I continued for some time to bathe the entrance to the charming grotto. She had now gained courage to take a fair survey of the wicked monster, as she called it, which had so cruelly ravaged her secret charms, and which now held up its crested head in a haughty manner, as if threatening to commit new devastations in the pleasant country he had so lately passed through. He bore, however, evident tokens of the bloody fray, and she laughingly said that I stood as much in need of the application of the purifying water as she did. I told her that as I had already performed the cleansing operation upon her, it was her turn now to do so upon me, and giving her the sponge, I sat down upon the bidet facing her, and throwing my arms round her neck, began to caress her charming bubbies.

She commenced to apply the sponge to remove the traces

of the combat from my person, and was greatly amused to find the almost instantaneous effect which the sudden application of the cold water had upon the rampant object, which stood upright between my legs. In a few instants its head was lowered, and presently it dangled down, dropping its crest, and hanging over the pendulant globules, till it reached the water in the bidet.

After enjoying her amusement for a while, I told her that it was only her fair hand that could repair the mischief she had occasioned, and that she must take it between her fingers and coax it to hold up its head again. This she willingly did, and her potent charms soon effected a complete resurrection.

She had expressed so much gratification at the effect which the cooling liquid had produced in allaying the irritation of the entrance to her grotto that I proposed to her to try whether we could not manage to pump up some of the soothing fluid within its recesses. She laughed, and asked how this could be done.

I told her I would show her. I made her stand up, and seating myself properly on the bidet I made her get astride upon me, then holding the erected weapon in the proper direction I caused her to sink down upon me until it had fairly penetrated the lovely chink which was thus presented to it. When I felt that it was fully entered, I placed my hands on her buttocks on each side, and leant back so as to enable her to seat herself across the upper part of my thighs, with my weapon still penetrating her. I then told her to move herself gently up and down upon the stiff stake which impaled her, but to take care not to rise so high as to allow it to escape from its confinement.

When I had just made it enter, she winced a little, but I believe it was more from fear than from any actual pain; but as soon as it had reached its fullest extent within her, she seemed relieved from all apprehension and willingly commenced the work of pleasure. Indeed she was so earnest in it and moved up and down so rapidly that I was obliged, in order to carry out my design, to ask her to moderate her transports. Filling the sponge with water, I introduced it between our bellies, and every time she rose up leaving my member exposed I squeezed the sponge so as to cover it with water, and then made her again sink down upon it and engulf it.

It is true that the tight-fitting nature of the sheath which thus received it, prevented much of the water from being forced up into the inner receptacle – still the pleasing coolness which was produced by the constant bathing of the heated member and which was thus in some degree transferred to her burning interior was by her account most agreeable, and certainly I found the effect upon myself equally so. The intermittent action of the hot receptacle into which it was alternately plunged prevented any bad effects from the cold application, and my unruly member, instead of being weakened by it, was rather invigorated and urged on to fresh and more strenuous action. We continued this pleasing amusement for some time till we both got too much excited and too eager for the completion of our final enjoyment to be able to endure the delay between each thrust which this proceeding occasioned.

My buttocks heaved up, and she sank down so rapidly upon the pleasure-giving stake, that I was forced to abandon my occupation. At length roused to a pitch of fury, I made her throw her arms around my neck, and placing my hands under her lovely bottom I rose up carrying her along with me without dislodging my enchanted weapon from its charming abode, and making her bottom rest on the edge of the bed and twisting her legs around my loins, I thrust and drove my vigorous engine into her with the greatest energy and pleasure. She had been as much excited as I had been by our amorous play, and she now responded most willingly and satisfactorily to my lascivious pushes. A few moments of the most exquisite enjoyment followed, which every succeeding thrust brought to a higher pitch of perfection, until our senses, being taxed to the utmost degree of voluptuous pleasure which it is possible to endure, gave way and, pouring out our souls in a delicious mutual effusion, we sank down on the bed in the most extreme delight.

After this charming exploit, we both felt the necessity for some little repose, and ere long we were fast locked in slumber in each other's arms. The rays of the morning sun roused me and warned me of the necessity for taking my departure before any of the servants should get up and observe me returning to my own room.

Fanny was still fast asleep, but the view I had of her naked charms which were exposed half uncovered by the bedclothes, rendered it absolutely impossible for me to leave her without again offering up my homage to them, and the splendid condition in which my little champion, invigorated by a few hours repose, reared up his proud crest along her belly, as she lay clasped in my arms, convinced me that he was quite prepared to do his duty. There was no time to be lost. Without waking Fanny, I lowered the head of the throbbing weapon to the spot of pleasure, and insinuated it within it as gently as possible. I met with no resistance. She made a few uneasy movements as I slowly inserted the weapon; but, overcome with the fatigues and emotion of the previous night she still slept on. I would fain have remained in my delicious quarters, and spun out my pleasure to the utmost; but time pressed, and I was forced to make the most of it. My motions became more and more excited and energetic.

At length, roused by the efforts of the pleasure-stirring instrument within her, Fanny opened her eyes, and for a moment gazed with wonder upon me.

A fond kiss and a home thrust soon brought her to herself. Without a word the kiss was returned and the thrust responded to with hearty good will. A delicious contest ensued, each striving who would first reach the goal of pleasure; and certainly, if her raptures on attaining it equalled mine, she had nothing to complain of.

We had hardly concluded the pleasing enjoyment, when a noise we heard in the house rendered it absolutely necessary I should leave her, and I fortunately reached my own apartment without being observed.

Jazz Baby

Though the heroine of this diverting jazz age tale begins the novel a virgin flower, young Flossie is hardly a shrinking violet. It takes her no time at all to be picked up by an experienced roué with a taste for nubile flesh. Never was a bloom more anxious to be plucked. Though Flossie has the strength to resist her beau's first attempt at seduction – for form's sake – within twenty-four hours she has presented herself sans drawers for a longed-for defloration.

Connoisseurs of the genre may appreciate the language employed by the unknown author to reveal the heightened state of young Flossie's excitement. Her lover's tongue is a 'flaming love dagger', her mouth an 'outpost of my pussy telegraph system', his eager penis a 'pants-shielded cunt-lollypop', her hungry vagina a 'palpitating peter-wanter'. Though these expressions may bring a smile to the reader's own telegraphic outposts they are at least original. In some respects at least, Flossie's first time is indeed unique . . .

I was spending the day window-shopping on Fifth Avenue. As I gazed into a window in which I saw displayed pretty lace lingerie and exquisite open-work stockings, all on seductively shaped forms, I suddenly became aware of someone at my side appraising my girlish contours. His eyes bespoke a man who might be thinking: 'Boy I'll bet she'd make a good fuck! I'd give anything to try it, what an ass – mm – boy! How I'd like to chew on those tits! I'll bet she's got a tight hole. Could I go for her! Think I'll try to make her.' What else could he be thinking about? Yes, what could the thoughts of a man be who tries to pierce the filmy costume and the scanty undies which a daring young miss wears on a warm summer day.

This person sauntered a step here and a step there, running his eyes up and down my shapely calves perhaps trying to imagine what they looked like above my dress, and exactly how I was formed where my legs met.

Modestly, I continued to act as though I wasn't being noticed, but soon I found that I had difficulty in controlling my curiosity. I wanted to know exactly what my new admirer looked like. By slyly glancing through the corners of my eyes I discerned that he was a quite handsome man of middle age. He was still feasting gluttonously on my well-shaped legs, which were garbed in black silk stockings so sheer that the milky whiteness of my virgin calves showed through most alluringly. My gown, which was made with as little material as was possible to cover the female form within the law, molded so clingingly to my figure that it wantonly revealed the tempting fullness and sensuously rounded contours of my pliant maiden torso. Of course, the greatest attraction – my very definitely defined bosom – pointed out teasingly and challengingly. The nipples daringly nosed their way forward and saucily danced at every step I made. My long golden curls flirted with a moderate breeze; some caressed my freely exposed shoulders while others pranced about my large irresistible blue eyes, tickling my nose and stringing in the folds of my cupid's-bow lips. This refreshing zephyr often caught the hem of my skirt and raised it far above my knees, revealing my pink-laced panties, and the charming nudity of my thighs; it also blew my skirt deep into the crevice of my plump, round bottom.

As a whole, I formed the kind of picture that made men say: 'I want to see more,' and the few inches of flabby meat in their pants would suddenly stretch to adult size — at least this man's did, because as I stole another glance I could plainly see his penis bobbing angrily in his pants.

Why I caused this was no mystery to me. In fact, why I attracted most men, particularly this one, who was now so openly and lecherously observing me, was explained to me by my Aunt Stella.

I began to feel uncomfortable under his constant gaze. I sensed that he was measuring and feeling me with his eyes. I felt that his sight had stolen beneath my flimsy attire and was now gloating over the mound of my dainty little white stomach and the curly silk blonde hairs that sprouted on either side of my smiling cunnie. I felt a strange warmth tingling in my veins; my pussy became hot and, as this happened, he began to falteringly approach me, as if he was trying to frame some appropriate phrase. But instead of speaking to me, which I was certain he would, he edged up close to me and glanced down the dark, well-drawn valley between my creamy white bubbies. My very low-necked dress brazenly exposed the tops of these two delicious marble orbs, but apparently he was not satisfied with this abbreviated view. He tilted his towering head so that out of the slits of his eyes he could get a more satisfying picture of my already hardening mounds. I felt his lust-hungry searching gaze! More dewy moisture trickled out of my yet virgin hole.

I was easily made hot by men, but never before had I ever been aroused, as I was, by merely the 'I-want-to-fuck-you' glance of an admiring stranger. Perhaps this was because last night Aunt Stella had explained to me the full use of the female and male sexual organs. Even while she was telling me how to – as she called it – 'straddle a comet,' I felt a strong urge arising within me to try it.

Naturally I knew a few things; that is, I was aware of the fact that it was necessary to have something to do with a man in order to get a baby. I knew how to make myself spend. I did this by frantically rubbing my fingers between the two burning, swollen lips of my twat, and also playing with my clitty at the same time. I always thought though, until my Aunt righted my illusion, that the man rubbed his prick between the lips as I did with my fingers.

Still being 'hot in the pants' from last night's lecture I did not puzzle at my condition then. I had been trying to imagine all during my sleepless night and as I walked, how a man's rigid love lance would feel deeply buried in my itching coozie. In fact, with every man that passed I tried to imagine exactly what the thing between his legs looked like, and I continued repeating to myself, 'I wonder how his thing would feel in me?'

Since I knew exactly what was on this man's mind, who was now alternating his eyes from me to the scanties in the window, I flushed with the rich pigment of a very embarrassed, modest girl. But was it a blush caused by modesty or was it a token of expression worn by a girl who felt that her lustful cravings were being successfully read by this fascinating stranger?

The ardent way he examined me was flattering not because of his attention, but because his general appearance suggested a man who was not only a leader of his kind but also a possessor of amorous skill and physical attractiveness.

Moving still closer to my side, my admirer tipped his hat and in a low, but steady voice said: 'Pardon me, but evidently we have something in common.'

I looked up, hardly daring to speak, because the magnetic charm in his voice seemed to trickle right through my ears, down to my already burning slit, and increase the strength of my throbbings there. I did summon enough aplomb to shyly say: 'I don't understand . . .'

'We both seem to admire pretty things,' he broke in, 'like these dainty thin hose and little flesh-tinted, filmy underwear.'

'Oh, I do,' I exclaimed expectantly. 'I just adore such things!'

'Well,' he continued, 'you are an unusually charming and pretty girl. Surely you would look many times more tempting in those petite silken undies than you do now.'

I felt offended but my scorn melted as I scrutinized this hypnotic-voiced person thoroughly for the first time. I saw a distinguished-looking, elderly gentleman, with handsome streaks of silver running through a well-groomed, once raven, crop of hair.

His dress and mannerisms revealed a man of wealth and culture. The twinkle in his sparkling jet eyes reflected a jocose and witty alertness. The general shape of his head betrayed a person of intellect and power. The upper lip of his sensitive mouth was adorned with a neatly trimmed mustache. His chin confirmed the story his lips spoke: it bore the imprint of a sensuous nature.

He had merely attracted me when I observed him at first but now, since I had studied him more carefully, he fascinated me. Magnetic waves swept through my body and my pulse beat faster as this seemingly perfect representative of the prick-bearing sex nudged still closer to get an even more complete view of my already hard-nippled bubbies. Perhaps he was trying to see if his vision would carry him down to my moss-covered mound?

Busy? Why shouldn't I? It seemed like my throbbing vent was now emitting enough moisture to be seen dripping down on the inner sides of my shapely thighs. At least it felt that way to me. Yes, I blushed like a crimson rose; the mirrored walls in the shop window proved this to me. Oh, I could always blush when the occasion warranted it, that was one of my feminine assets.

Again he spoke, slowly, as if he was trying to strike a happy medium for congenial conversation: 'My dear child, don't you think that at your age you are slightly too young to be thinking of buying such feminine adornments? Why, more mature ladies usually wear those ... well ... er ... to make themselves more enticing,' he finished, anxious not to be offensive.

'Oh pshaw! No!' I replied, shaking my curls and glancing at him mischievously. 'Girls are never too young to dress prettily. That is to try to tempt men – certain men,' I finished, insinuatingly, and by the inviting look in my eyes I hoped he would be able to tell that he was one of those certain men.

We chatted for a few moments. I laid a net of verbal enticement before him. Satisfied that he could fuck me in the proper surroundings he at length bowed curtly and introduced himself; at the same time he handed me his card. It read:

ROLAND PIERCE
SHIPBUILDER
PARIS – LONDON – NEW YORK.

I suppressed a cry of delight! A man of wealth, power and perhaps a connoisseur of women, used to only the best, had gone out of his way to speak to me, a girl far beneath his social stratum. I felt that he was the man who was destined to take my cherry! I shamelessly wished that it would be that way.

When he invited me to lunch I was both surprised, because I thought he would overlook me on account of my class, and embarrassed. I was not properly attired to lunch with him. He finally persuaded me to go by saying:

'Your youth, your refreshing beauty, your figure and your agreeable manner are quite enough to afford you a rousing welcome at Rector's.'

This famous restaurant was a rendezvous for the youths, beauties and the sports of the town. It was my first experience in a place as glamorous as that. I was amazed at the wanton display of feminine charms, yet I was consoled, because I did the same. Profanity and immorality seemed the vogue there.

My friend was most lavish with his courtesy – he dazzled me with flattery. Not once did he remove his lust-hungry eyes from me. Twice he had purposely dropped his handkerchief so that he could feast his blazing eyes on my appetizing, denuded thighs. The second time this occurred I purposely drew my dress clear up to my lace panties, and I spread my legs apart. My! I almost swooned, I was so tantalized by that burning-tingling-itching blood in my hot, prick-hungry pussy. I almost felt his gaze touch my clitoris when he focused his vision – oh, so longingly I could tell – on my swollen-lipped hungry cunnie mouth. I had a very hard time trying to prevent myself from putting my hand firmly over the burning slit. I moved about impetuously in my seat, opening and closing my legs, trying to force myself to come. This inward excitement must have made me look prettier because Roland spoke:

'Flossie, my dear lovely girl, your sweet rosebud mouth was made to be kissed, and the petite girlish charms that you so innocently exposed, and allowed me to gaze upon were created and fashioned for the heavenly enjoyment of some appreciative lover. You are tempting! You are maddening!' Apparently he was in the grip of an overwhelming hard-on, then he continued with more aplomb: 'Your legs, your thighs, your dreamy Venus-like orbs – ' he paused to catch his breath – 'Flossie, I have seen hundreds of girls in my day, a lot of them with shapely legs and attractive torsos but I swear, dear Flossie, none of them were so ravishingly desirable. Oh, if only I could say what I feel! I could eat you! Your figure! Your face! All of you ... you are a tempting, luscious irresistible bon-bon!'

There was a ring of real sincerity in his extravagant compliments. I was afraid at first that what he had begun to say would be just more honey-coated flattery, but as he spoke I could see that he was becoming more serious all along. Yes, he meant every syllable of his speech.

I was careful not to indulge too freely in strong drink – I did not wish to injure the very favorable impression that I had made on Roland – but I had taken enough to set my hot blood afire. That tormenting itch in my pussy continued to burn even more hotly. Very little stimulation was ever needed to make me steam.

Roland must have read my mood:

'Come, my little bon-bon,' he said boyishly, 'let us go to the park. A ride will do you good. You will be revived and your nerves will be soothed.'

What a fool I must have been to try to conceal my real feelings at that time. I was trembling hot. I needed a big, fat, juicy, stiff prick between my legs more badly than anything in the world. I wanted to cultivate an intimate acquaintance with this enrapturing *bon vivant* to accomplish that purpose. Hadn't I felt my nectar dripping from my angrily throbbing womb ever since I met him? And wasn't I in the market for a good time? And hadn't I been dreaming ever since last night how wonderful it must be to have a thick male monster shoved way up into my uterus? And wasn't I always trying to improve my education? Then what in the deuce was I waiting for? As I said, I must have been a fool.

Because the day was very warm, Roland had procured a touring car and a chauffeur. I was deeply distressed, because I knew that it would be impossible to extinguish the devilish heat in my box in a car of this type. I could accomplish very little with a driver in the front seat.

As we rode through the tree-lined mall of the park a feeling of boldness crept into my system. Hang the pedestrians and to hell with the chauffeur, I thought. My pussy was hot and I wanted to get it plugged. Since my desire was driving me crazy, wasn't it better to let a few people witness the fucking scene which I so badly ached for? Was it less desirable to be driven mad by a blood-shot cunnie? Or was it a greater evil to be exposed in the midst of a soul saving, so-much-dreamed-of, sexual act? It was a perplexing problem, but I decided in favor of my lust-seeking maiden cunnie.

I nestled closer to Roland and then I threw my legs carelessly across the top of a half-unfolded auxiliary seat. The wind rushed in and soothingly caressed me beneath my dress on the place which commanded my entire attention. I wantonly moved my thighs further apart to allow the breeze to more freely lick my seething vent. This uncovered my thighs and exposed them clearly, up to my silk-covered, smoldering box. As though I was embarrassed, I quickly covered my denuded parts, each time making some playful and teasing remark. I could tell that I was making progress because of his many short gasps of both surprise and delight. I could sense his steady licentious gaze glutting over the shapeliness of my feminine charms.

We nibbled on everything in general for conversation. After we had disposed of a great deal of this kind of half-interesting chatter, he sat up and looked into my eyes:

'By jove, dear Flossie, never before have I seen such seductiveness in any one pair of legs. What an exquisite figure you have. I can almost picture your nude form silhouetted in the rays of the moon. I would give you a hundred dollars to see you nude!' he cried impulsively then, after pausing for a reaction, he continued, 'Can I tempt you with the offer?'

Gee! Wasn't that a bold beginning, I thought. I was

delighted, and amazed too, at his making such a daring offer after so short an acquaintance. At the same time as I prepared myself to answer him, I let my elbow rest in his lap and with apparent innocence allowed it to press down upon his hidden, bursting member. It felt like a monster. (I even wondered how a woman could get a thing as big as that in her hole. I knew I even had a difficult time last night in getting my finger in!)

'Why Roland!' I pretended, modestly. 'Don't you think you are going a little too far by asking me to undress so soon? You know our acquaintance is very recent.' I paused for a few minutes; I wanted him to gain the impression that I was thinking. Then, turning my head saucily away, I continued, 'Haven't I shown you enough already?' Then I swung my head back to glance at him with a sly, bewitching sparkle in my eyes and puckered my lips poutingly.

It so happened at the time I finished that we were passing through a secluded thickly wooded cove in the park. Roland seemed fully aware of this protection. In a flash he had me twined in his strong but gentle arms, and his lips found mine. He pressed my mouth more firmly to his as the time passed. I almost swooned from the effects of his hot, absorbing, pussy-tickling kiss.

Too weakened by the intoxicating aftermath of the first burning caress, I submissively yielded to another amorous attack. His lips were resilient but firm. His soft, silky, and adorable mustache tickled my face and added to the sensual feeling.

We parted for a few seconds to gaze mutely and dreamily into each other's eyes. Then he clasped me to him again, this time though, he clamped his hand firmly over my left bubbie – gee! What a torrid gust of passion shook my frame. I felt my sensitive pussy shiver with delight. Not satisfied with my reaction to his attack, he again found my lips with his. I was so lust-maddened by this time that I dared anything. With his tongue he pried my lips apart, a favor that I dearly appreciated, and into my mouth he shot his flaming love dagger, and swabbed the walls with his inciting flesh. Boy, did I vibrate! I could feel my red-hot blood racing. I was so damn hot I couldn't even moan! My cunt was so scalding that I was paralyzed by the intense delicious heat there. Oh, why didn't a big prick enter and end my devilish misery?

The frenzied movements of his arms and the quivering of his lips, as they sucked and chewed mine, also revealed very plainly his passion-intoxicated condition.

Since the ice was broken, I yielded to his every advance and even induced him onward, that is, as much as our short acquaintance would allow.

I slipped my tongue into his mouth and there our two molten daggers welded together. I shook even more violently in his arms. He drew a long breath and then added pressure to his hand which was still greedily fingering my heaving bubbies. They protruded plainly through my thin, silk waist.

'Oh, Roland,' I gasped, 'what a perfect lover you are.'

'And, Flossie, dearest,' he returned with more control, 'what a perfect inspiration you are.'

Then we folded into another lingering, soul-scorching kiss.

He bathed and nipped my lips with his; so cunt teasingly, yet so soothingly. His hand stealthily began to creep up my thigh. The sensitive skin there tried to writhe from his feverish touch, but that magnetic intangible something, which the masculine hand near the female nest produces, would not allow me to worm from his, make-you-want-to-fuck, nestling hand. Instead my cunnie involuntarily moved down to meet its approaching visitor. My plump little bottom was bouncing around in agonizing pleasure. Then I clutched his hand as we broke from another embrace.

'Oh, Roland! Please, oh! Please! Don't Roland!' I panted in my cunt-itching delirium. Try as I might, I shall never forgive myself for saying that. What made me say it? I don't know.

'But...' he mumbled as though he wanted to say something and changed his mind. His progress stopped.

'Roland, dear, this is neither the time nor the place for real loving, is it?'

'Well, no, not a very comfortable place,' he half-heartedly agreed.

'Dear, I think you are the most charming man – you are. You are making me forget myself. I really object to your advances.' (I guess, while I said this, if my pussy had the power it would have shot me.) 'Gee, I hardly even know you!'

'That may be true, Flossie, but... take my word for it! Somehow, I can't get the idea into my head that I met you only a few hours ago. I feel like I've known you all my life. Perhaps it's because all my life I've dreamed of meeting a girl like you.' As he spoke, his manner brewed into sincere sentimentality.

'To tell you the truth, Roland dear, I feel the same way. You seem fascinating. Your voice, you – oh, I don't know how to say it. When I look at you, I hear you talk and you touch me with your hand, everything about you makes me ache all over for you. You send warm lustful currents through my whole body.'

'Flossie,' he said, as he patted and fumbled my shaking hand, 'we will get better acquainted in the future. Tomorrow, if you find you are able, I want you to meet me at the ferry in Jersey. I shall have one of my own cars, a town limousine and a chauffeur – you know, the see-nothing, hear-nothing type.

'We will take a long ride through the Jersey countryside and then dine at the Palais D'Coite. It is a place noted for its excellent cuisine. They specialize in the preparation of foods promoting love. All the sporting parties meet there because of the privacy they offer. Of course you'll join me,' he looked at me pleadingly, 'won't you, Flossie?'

I answered him by nestling in his arms, mine entwined his neck. I was always able to do this act with alluring seductiveness, and I kissed him with every bit of unrefined animal passion that I had in my tongue – which in this case spoke for my whole cunt-burning soul.

'Roland, of course I'll be there, I can hardly wait. I know we'll have such a wonderful time.'

He then took me to my train and, after repeating my promise to meet him we parted, ending a day eventful with scorching lascivious wants. These, incidentally, still remained within me unabated. Could I wait for the approaching day, or would I go mad with my desires?

When I reached home, which I shall always call Aunt Stella's Bohemian apartment, I was anxiously greeted by my only relative. Auntie wasn't, as that title suggests, old maidish and conservative. She was a woman generously supplied with charms – that is, she had a coozie that was wedged between two shapely plump thighs and which I think was as anxious for big-pricked visitors as I had now begun to be. Many were the nights when I found comfort and solace by burying my disappointed lust-seeking face between the vales of her two generous titties. Oh, how I used to love to suck and fondle these two enticing lumps of creamy-white flesh! And how beautiful she looked in her passionate ecstasy as I used to perform this oh so-cherishing and and exciting feat; how nice they used to taste.

Stella was only thirty-three, but her face erased more than eight years from her actual age. Her actions and frivolous sexual attitude were all so carefree, comparable to the shaking of her dimpled meaty bottom as she walked. Men oftentimes followed her for miles attempting to either gain her favor or else determine where such a fuckable mass of human flesh might live. This I knew to be a fact.

She was a contrast to me in the color of her hair and skin. Her eyes were the jewel-black passionate kind. She played the role of girlfriend, rather than that of kin.

Stella noticed the new light in my eyes. Naturally I must have looked different for didn't I get a glimpse into a more cunt-full and prick-full life? She exclaimed:

'Hi, hon. My, but you're late. Where – oh, oh, now what have you been up to? Come tell your little Auntie the cause of that shining look in your eyes. You have the same kind of sparkle in them that Sarah had, the first night her husband put his delicious six-shooter in. By the way, I *know* it was delicious.'

'Now, Auntie dear, what are you trying to accuse me of?'

'How did you like it? Wasn't it the grandest feeling. It makes me hot just to think about it.'

'But honestly, Stell, I don't quite get you,' I pretended innocently.

She neared me, then without warning she playfully unbalanced me and I fell upon the soft pillow-padded floor. She picked up my dress and removed my panties, before I could recover from the shock.

'Quit it, Stell. What's the matter?'

'I won't, you sly little dear, not until I get the truth and your pussy's mouth is going to speak it. I kind of thought you would go and do it today. You wouldn't let me sleep last night. You had your legs twined around my bottom all last night, and you should have seen the way you were rolling that can of yours. Why I had to reach for my faithful dildo three times – naughty girl. You lesbian! Now spread your legs . . . wide!'

Her actions and speech had renewed the heat in my box, so I found it a pleasure to obey her command.

'You are disgusting,' she continued, as she opened my lips real wide and kissed my inflamed and swollen cunnie. 'Ah but . . . mmm, your panties are all soiled, now young lady how did that happen?'

Dear Aunt Stell, she seemed to understand me so perfectly. I couldn't resist confessing to her the events of the day.

'And you didn't fuck him yet?' she asked, after I finished telling of my clitty-raising experience.

'But, Stell, I hardly know him,' I argued, modestly.

'And you'll never know him any better unless you let him stretch that cute little twat of yours.'

'Do you really mean that?'

'You poor little fool, what in the hell do you think a twat was made for ... glory? Or the worms? Look at your poor little hole, see how swollen and hot it is.'

'Now quit ribbing me so much. My little cunnie is hurting me enough as it is.'

I waited all night for the dawn to break. I was too peter-thirsty to go to sleep. I didn't want to make myself spend. I wanted to save every drop of my luscious love-dew for the ever approaching moment when I would be gigantically thrilled by that cream-spurting meat stick of Roland's; swabbing every cell of sensitive flesh in my vaginal folds.

I arose about nine o'clock in the morning. Nervous anxiety thundered in my chest, for I was still parched for that juicy meat in Roland's pants.

I clothed myself in an envelope chemise of diaphanous silk. Drawers would have been a hindrance, so I did not put them on. I rolled my sheer black stockings low enough to expose the dimples of my baby-skin knees.

Over all this I wore a flimsy dress with a mild tinting of pink. This plain-cut outfit clung to my form in a skin-on-a-grape fashion. My well-exposed bust gleamed and even sparkled with my virgin freshness. The clothed part of my dancing bubbies protruded saucily and provokingly.

The skirt of my dress hung as if glued to my gracefully swaying, polished round ass. The dimples on either flank were deliciously molded; in fact, I made a picture of what one might call 'The Pinnacle of Feminine Seductiveness.'

As I dared not walk in the street, exposed as I was, I put on an overall of white linen. This coat reached almost to my ankles. It dutifully covered my liberally displayed legs and immaculate apparel. I wore a white tam to blend with the wrap.

After being kissed and wished good luck by my aunt I left the house.

On the way to the ferry, Roland was conjured to my mind! I tried to imagine how his nutritious meat loaf looked, how big it was. And when I tried to imagine how his luscious piece of human, cunt-seeking sausage would behave in my unused eager slit, again I felt that tingling-melting sensation in my sweetly perfumed love nest. There was an instant when I even feared that his divine rod might not contain the vigor of the average male; perhaps this was because I judged him to be past forty. While that tinge of morbidity stained my thoughts, I also imagined that his unsated prick might be the worse and impaired from wear.

Roland had arrived at the appointed place as I entered upon the scene. Apparently he didn't recognize me, dressed as I was, in the chic tam and long coat. He looked about carefully, his eyes rested on me, then his face reflected bitter disappointment. I wanted to see how badly he really wanted me, a scheme impelled by feminine vanity, so I decided to remain incognito and observe his actions.

After watching him grow to the point of acute anxiety I walked over to him and spoke:

'Well, Roland, you don't seem to remember me, do you?'

He demuringly examined me with a wry face.

'Now, Roland, you naughty boy, you have a surprise coming.' I spoke in an unchaste, coy manner, as I hopped into the car in which he was sitting. I raised my bottom so that I could free myself from the long coat and I also discarded the tam. By doing this I revealed the undisguised and tempting Flossie.

He gasped in surprised delight as his eyes in one glance devoured all of my seductiveness.

'Egad, little girl, you are a dream!'

I could plainly see his rising pants-shielded cunt-lollypop. His face glowed and beamed. He was already imagining his approaching carnal meal. And what a meal it was going to be! I hoped so.

He reached for me just as the chauffeur geared the car, but the sudden jerking of the vehicle aided him; it threw me right into his arms.

I too began to notice the clothes he wore. He had on an immaculately pressed white Palm Beach, a very appropriate suit for that warm day. His genuine under-water-woven panama lay on the seat next to him. His hair was carefully groomed. His skin reflected the freshness of youth. I assumed that he was the type who lived by the rules of scrupulous cleanliness and neatness; he would exact the same from his companions.

The automobile in which we were riding was of the town-car type, with a private cabin for the driver. Our cabin was luxuriously equipped with comforts. By raising the auxiliary seats a bed could be made . . . not any less comfortable than mine at home. In fact, we even had one more advantage than the average hotel room, the soothing breeze flowing through, caused by the moving car.

I remained on his lap just long enough to receive a short but twat-burning kiss. He tried to touch my bare knee. I repulsed him, not because I didn't want him to do this, but for one very good reason: I knew that I could not stand much more of his clitty-exciting treatment. I would become so blinded by it that I would give in to my screaming-for-screw swollen-lipped cunnie and bring shame on both of us, by pulling his staff out of his pants and shoving it all the way up into my quivering belly. Therefore I remarked:

'Roland, dear, you must put the shades down if you wish to take such liberties.'

At once he acted upon my suggestion. Even the chauffeur couldn't see after he had completed this task. It was now so comfortable, secluded and nestlike; even nature couldn't have offered a more appropriate trysting place. At last the stage was set!

I hastily threw my arms about his neck and sought his mouth with my lips. How wonderful and thrilling that kiss was! I caressed him, wildly tonguing and lipping his fire-emitting mouth. By this fierce and soul-stirring attack I tried to suggest to him what could be expected if he properly directed his erotic talents.

Between body-inflamed kisses, as we rode, Roland outlined a brief history of his life. He had been married once and as a result he had a son who was now twenty-two. He lived in the sporting center of the Occidental World, Paris. His wife died while giving birth. His boy was at this time managing his European industries. From the way he spoke about his son I judged that he loved him very dearly. The conversation then drifted to matters such as his analyzing his personality and other confidential topics. All this, I realized, was done by him to make me trust him implicitly as well as to increase my longing and lustful desire. If he had noticed my very suggestive attitude, or had he even tried to pierce my flimsy gown and saw that I wore no drawers on this occasion, he would have known that I would have been an easy sacrifice on the altar of Venus. His romantic phrases and his soft, full voice had almost as much effect upon my pussy as his coddling hands.

'Now, Flossie,' he continued after outlining his character and his attitude towards morals, etc., 'I want you to know exactly how I feel about you . . . and my strongly passionate nature.

'All my life I have been, you might say, a ladies' man. I am very fond of feminine charms and the soulful bliss they afford me. In fact, I am a very discriminating sensualist, meaning of course, that I have an abnormal lustful appetite. My particular appetite craves girls of your age and type. I like your charms, that baby-like softness, yet tender firmness and vigor. Angelic innocence such as you alone possess is so deliciously satisfying to a man of my nature and age.

'I have had intercourse and have indulged in every type of passion's embraces with every kind of female loveliness.' He paused to moisten his lips, like a dog who thinks about the swell bone he just had, then continued. 'I can truthfully say, Flossie dear, that I have never met a girl as desirable as you.' He finished gloating over my half-concealed titties and my partially exposed thighs.

'You, every bit of you, suggests to me, you dainty little devil . . .' he nipped my cheek, 'such sensual delights – so deliciously seductive.

'You are intelligent, I presume, well read and very conscious of your bewitching charms, but somehow you seem to display the pureness and innocence of a child. It makes you so much more . . . I can't explain!' He quivered and squeezed his bursting prick in his hand. He was almost overcome with emotion.

Suddenly he released his giant stiff from his hand and made a wild, but successful lunge at me. He drew me so firmly to his breast that I shuddered in delightful pain. A fire had shot from the rock-hard tips of my titties down into my palpitating peter-wanter. He drew my head down to his broad bosom; I was hot! But this was only a mild beginning, as I afterwards found out. I tilted my imprisoned head upwards and looked into his eyes with a glance that was bedimmed by a filmy coat of passion's moisture. I was dazed by my inflaming needs. Even my lips, which were sopped by the excessive salivation of my mouth, quivered, screaming my inward cuntful emotions. Then – oh it was so glorious – he poured an avalanche of sensuous kisses upon my awaiting lips. He did this tenderly and effectively; at the same time he sucked and chewed, oh so deliciously, upon this outpost of my pussy telegraph system. He laid his free hand over my waiting milky orbs. First he played with these through the thin covering of my semi-transparent waist and then he fondled them after they bounced out of their very inefficient hiding place. Each time he rubbed my cute little nipples with his warm and hypnotic fingers a more rabid wave of wanting-to-make-me-fuck emotion shook my prick-greedy frame. Oh, how I longed for something between my lust-sweated and cunt-dewed thighs! How I squeezed my legs together, and how I wormed and wiggled my burning meaty bottom! Yes, that fleshy little spot where my legs come together pined for Roland's visitor. I knew it would slide in and out. I dared not imagine more for fear that I would go mad.

I moved my legs apart, then together, opening and closing my cunnie's mouth! I twisted and moved around like an eel! In my libidinous excitement my dress worked up and exposed me nearly to the waist. My plump, dimpled knees, my round full thighs were now an added incentive for my lover's searching eyes. His vision even found some of the longer silk hairs of my golden-framed puss.

For a moment he could only pant, he was too paralyzed by desire to even speak. I imagined this exposure would produce this reaction. In a trembling voice he gave vent to his feelings:

'Flossie, dear, can I kiss your sweet little legs? God! I never dreamed a woman's legs could be so beautiful, so exciting!'

'Oh, Roland, darling,' I panted, 'can't you see? I need you! Everything! Everything you have! I am yours. Do what you wish with me! I'm—'

I couldn't finish. The overwhelming heat in my pussy caused by his thorough caressing of my legs with his lips and hands almost choked me with mad desire. From my slender ankle to mid-thigh he ran his hand, nipping and squeezing as it went along.

'Lord! What exquisite flesh!' he exclaimed while he glided his hand amorously and lightly over my smooth, powdered skin.

My cunt, my clitoris, my tits and my lips, ached more strongly as the time flew by for more and greater thrills! If ever there was a woman aflame, I was her. Yet Roland hesitated. No doubt he was afraid he might invite some remonstration or incur some resistance. He just didn't know his own power! Nor did he know the state of Flossie's cunt.

Then I said in fluttering words:

'Oh dear, don't stop! Please! Oh darling, fondle me, everywhere!'

I stretched my legs far apart, praying that he would soon find my helpless slit.

With an expression that was more akin to a moan he uttered:

'I will, darling . . . oh, you angel, I will! At last, at last you are going to be mine.'

He shook very noticeably in his anxiety. A virgin was his! He plunged his open hand between my parted legs and clamped it hard up against my pussy's mouth.

'Oh, God,' I prayed, 'is this heaven?'

I moved my bottom around so that his hand would irritate my lips, but he sensed my desire. He removed my soft silk-curled heated pussy from his hand. With an upward sweep, a delicate and tender finger found my bobbing clitty. No man had ever made me feel that way before! He stroked my legs and thighs, squeezed my full-meated bottom and then – then he almost drove me crazy. He kissed me, beginning at the dimples in my knee, and worked his way up to the perfume-douched cavity of my soul. Would he ever put the real thing in? God, I was dying! I was going blind! I couldn't hear a thing, save the thundering of my heart! My pussy was screaming!

'Put it in! *Put it in!*'

At last he worked himself between my widely spread legs. I swooned when I saw him pull out a rampant tool from his fallen trousers. Somehow I managed to slip my dress and chemise completely off. He too removed his shorts. I stretched my legs from window to window. I grasped his monster. I wanted to feel it nude. It almost burned my hand. Gosh, it was hot! It bobbed from my hold!

Everything blurred. I felt my eyes roll wildly in their sockets! Even the lips in my coozie seemed to stretch forward toward their intended visitor. The object of my lustful desires was by this time directly over my seething vent.

'Please! Oh, please! Quick!' I rambled, deliriously.

'I will guide it in, girlie,' he said with more reserve.

He parted the curly tuft and opened the tortured mouth of my mellowed cunnie. At last he was astride my moist, burning slit! He pulled me over to him and he slipped forward to get in a convenient position. God, would he ever put it in? At last! His hand deftly guided his magnificent, but angry, ruby-headed one-eyed tool to my red hot, fleshy, steaming, boiler-like cunt. He worked the head in until it was buried in my tight, puckering, prick-sucking orifice.

'Oh, dearest,' I mumbled faintly; 'it's going to hurt me dreadfully, I know. I don't care! Oh, ow-woo-oo-oo-oh!'

The first partial insertion thrilled me so, but I held my breath and I grabbed his ass and drew him closer to me. The turgid knob stretched me and slowly began to worm its way into my juicy tube. How my heart fluttered, both from fear of the first cherry-breaking pain and the electrified thrills of this pulsating burning rod.

Little by little it poked its way into my quivering belly. The pain was not as great as I feared it would be. Gosh, oh gee, it was swell!

Roland increased my fires by playing and sucking on my denuded bubbies; he also nipped and plucked my ass. I reacted to this by my cunnie's sucking his prick with harder and ever-increasing zeal.

Under the influence of his emotions, Roland swore and cried out in unrestrained, lecherous language. He rose to the heights of obscene eloquence. I was both influenced and delighted by his outcries, perhaps this was because I had never heard such passionate, smutty expressions. I reasoned that Roland would invite an excess of voluptuous outbursts which might emphasize his erotic feelings during the screwing act. I soon accustomed myself to this habit, also, for soon I was wantonly using lewd language to express my feelings as he mustered his big prick in and out of my tickling, itching, flaming cunt.

My painfully stretched hole was already beginning to get accustomed to this turgid, monster-cock, which it was struggling to swallow. Now that turgid throbbing mass began to feel so wonderful! It imbued in me such pleasureable, soul-reeking sensations. Never before had I felt like this.

Until now, Roland's organ was only partially inserted. A little at a time I felt more of it struggling to enter! My coozie tried to aid by sucking it in. I began to feel my spend approaching! I did so badly want to prolong that moment. Merciful God! I thought my heart would explode! Oh how my vaginal tube squeezed together – so tight! A wonderful, unexplainable, ecstatic bolt suddenly electrified me. Then something seemed to snap in my vaginal tube and a flood of pasty liquid poured forth. At the same time my cuntie's neck expanded and contracted several times. Each time it did this a new thrill shot through my body. I could plainly feel it nipping the head of Roland's inward-traveling monster. I found the sensations overwhelmingly blissful. I wish I could describe it so one could feel it. All I can say, there is no word that can be equal to the joyful cunt-throbbings of a splendid come! It is the one thing that I know which defies description.

This happened just as my cuntie was beginning to get used to the tremendous joint it was sucking in. I really wanted to prolong the climax. Only about three inches of his turgid, throbbing mass was in me when this ecstatic wave made my whole body quiver in delight. Never before had I experienced such rapturous emotions. Oh, but they were glorious!

Even now, as I sit and write my memoirs, and in spite of the hundreds of all kinds of fuckings since, I can plainly hear my frenzied shouts, cries, and moans of my first prick-caused spend!

'Oh – oo – ooo – oh – oo – ooo – ah... Roland! Oh dear... I... ooo – oo – Oh, how lovely! More! Push it in more... ah – h – h! Roland, you sure can fuck! Please! Oh fuck me to death! Oh, how wonderful! Mmm – mm – mmm – ah – h – h!' Then everything became blurred and my body trembled convulsively with pleasure. Then my legs gave away and I came down full weight upon his prying peter. Another series of delightful moans escaped my lips.

Then it was Roland's turn to moan: 'Keep it up, you beauty. Oh, you wonderful piece of ass! Come give my cock a bath in your girlish virgin juice. Enjoy it again, pet, I haven't come yet!'

His eight inches of palpitating stiffness was now into me to its very roots. His hard, hairy balls tickled my bottom and my cunnie lips. I was ravished by sensual delirium. I almost feared that I was dreaming. Could real pleasure be so great?

I heard Roland speak again, in an excited, but mellow voice:

'Oh you, oh darling! You peachy little cunt!'

He began increasing his speed. He pulled his big cock in and out so fast that the friction singed the walls of my pricklover.

'You, my delicious – your cunt, it's wonderful!' he continued, as his speed still increased! 'My hot little mistress. My lovely little sweet fuckable baby girl! I'm – I'm coming! Flossie! Uh – uh – h... mmm – mm... Flossie, quick! Fuck me off! Hurry! How wonderful!'

I came out of my trance when I heard Roland say: 'Fuck me off.' That expression somehow rejuvenates my passions and makes me fiercely erotic. My feet were touching the floor. I braced myself on my toes and reared up to meet his gorgeous tool more intimately. I strained every muscle in my legs and back, but in and out his rammer went. I could feel the head of his dick begin to swell. My cunt began to stretch with it.

I answered his erotic outburst:

'I am so glad you think me fuckable, beloved. I am going to do my best to make you feel good too. You made me feel so grand when I came. Oh – ooo – I think I'm going to come again.'

'Hold your dress up, girlie. I want to see your cuntie sucking! How delicious it sucks my prick! What a pretty white belly! What nice hairs around your cuntie. Oh how I'd like to suck and kiss your silky hairs!'

I continued moving up and down on his splendid affair. Each time I arose I almost let his tool completely out. I could appreciate the gigantic size of it this way. I could tell how tight I was because I had great difficulty in moving up and down. The friction caused by the barbed disc of his swollen penis was maddeningly thrilling. No woman knows the titillating and exciting feeling of a big, hard, bulbous knobbed penis with little ticklers or 'grabbers' on the end of it. No, not until she had one, it cannot be described!

While working, I noticed that I was the possessor of a rare gift: the art of twisting a man's cock. With every down motion I circled my bottom. This movement set a strange apparatus in my cunnie to work, that nipped and hugged the end of his dick and when I came completely down on his big prick my nippers would hold it so tight it would twist as I spiraled my bottom. Roland howled with delight:

'Oh, baby! *How you can fuck* – I'm . . . I'm coming! Girlie it's the hot juice coming! Oh, God, keep it up! Oh – ah – h – uh!'

My lover grunted as he was spending. He acted like a maniac. He closed his eyes. Each time a spasmodic jet of hot white spew shot into me, he groaned and cried in delight. Did I feel those lava-like loads of juice steaming in and splashing against my uterus walls? I'll say I did. They continued to splash against my walls until I went off again.

In my paraoxysms of pleasure my cunnie sucked and pumped every drop of that thrill-containing juice from him.

My coozie seemed dreadfully thirsty for that rich creamy effusion that my lover so generously sprayed me with. I screamed from sheer ecstasy. Lord, but it felt good!

Like mad, I began to heave, shove and roll my fat bottom with lightning-like rapidity. My ever lustful cunnie circled and rubbed his cunt-crazy prick until I had many luscious spends. I brought my lover to another point of coming. How he heaved and trembled as he neared his second spewing goal! How he uttered, swore, and moaned during our long, pleasurable frigging orgy. Roland's tool lost none of its power during this time, but continued with its task as big, fat, and turgid as ever. I continually jerked and pumped it; soon I knew I would feel those precious drops of hypnotic spew sending spasms through my whole system. His balls had begun to get hard once more. I took them in my hands playfully and squeezed. I wanted it all! Yes, every drop that my lover's bag contained. His balls got harder and harder! Would they break?

His dick's head swelled and sent forth another creamy supply of love's dearest juice into my drinking cunnie. Gee, my pussy loved that stuff.

He fell on me limply. I felt more – oh double the pleasure, for my performance. I had made a man past the age of youthful vigor spend twice – two wonderful cunt-flooding times! I gloated over his utter abandon and his expressions of lascivious satisfaction. Never since have I seen a face so distorted by lust. His eyes rolled deliriously as he lay prostrate on me after the climax of this long-drawn-out feast of the flesh. What a ravishing spend he must have had!

I gazed with carnal satiation upon this wealthy, amorous man as he lay helpless and spent upon me. He was completely at my mercy. I still insisted upon tightly holding the remnants of this once prodigious hard-on, now soft but thick, within my steaming slit. The very thought of it in my cunnie and the pleasure that it had afforded me made me come. For the seventh time I gave him my dew! Then I slumped backwards in a semi-swoon, hugging Roland mightily. At the same time I allowed his shrunken tool to slip from my inundated and passion-charred pussy. What heavenly bliss!

We reclined there on the seat too exhausted to move. I was entrapped in his arms. We were both enjoying the afterglow and the soothing dying-away, as we sped on through the countryside.

I emerged from my trance as dear Roland began to wipe my sensitive crack with his soft silken handkerchief. He also offered me a sip of brandy which he said would help me regain my strength.

Believe me, my friends, that was some auto ride!

He too, soon recovered his aplomb. He lavished me with extravagant praises. In a voice faint and tender he spoke:

'Flossie, dear, I am a fortunate man. I am more than that, for I have possessed a creature so lovely and so tempting. You are absolutely the most skillful and the most perfect little fucker that I have ever humped. Oh, how you can screw! I have had women in every land but you excel them all, not only in your ability to out-fuck them, but also in beauty, shape, and girlish charms. When we dine, Flossie, darling, I will drink to the most perfect woman in the world.'

We made many plans for the future. As he talked he fondled my legs and bubbies. Suddenly he raised my skirt above my waist. He drew me closer to him so that he could pet and feel my lily-white, soft bottom. As he molded the cheeks with his hands he spoke:

'What a handsome bottom you have, baby girl. I know it is beautiful.' He patted and squeezed the tender, pliant halves.

'Now, Roland,' I billed sweetly, 'how can you know? You haven't had a real good look at it yet.'

'Girlie, I don't have to see it. I *just know!* After performing so well, you know the old saying, "What works beautifully must be beautiful." You've heard of it?'

I kissed him furiously again, and ran my tongue far into his mouth. It was my turn to do the complimenting:

'Now, Roland, darling, I don't wonder why you have women and girls galore. Anyone with a cock like yours could win an entrance to any cunt. It doesn't make any difference whether the pussy is a part of the juicy body of a fifteen year old anxious-to-fuck maiden or the worn and particular cunt of the old maid of fifty.

'Your prick is a darling. It's the kind that I have always dreamed of having ever since I learned the use of the male stiffness. That's been I guess since I was sixteen.' I lied, because I knew that the night before last was my first lesson of its real use.

'Not that it makes any difference, but tell me, Flossie, dear, how did you lose your maidenhead? I don't think I took it.'

'Honestly, Roland, you are the first man I ever fucked. Do trust me!'

Then I told him how it happened, how a girl friend of mine at school used to rub my twat with hers and one day she got so excited that she jammed her whole hand in between my lips and I felt something break. I grew very scared because blood flowed from the punctured place. I was very cautious never to allow my hand to slip in the region again for fear of rupturing some blood vessel.

All this I told him in my usual innocent girlish way. The tale caused him to become so passionate that his cock grew very stiff and big again. I too became hot. We thought that we were going to have another round of frigging but we neared instead the famous Palais D'Coite, the place where we intended to dine. We postponed the promised tryst and rearranged our attire. A mad impulse seemed to sway Roland. He picked up my dress and kissed my belly, clitty, and sucked my lips with all his cunt-satisfying might. Then he combed my curly pussy hairs through his teeth.

Hooligans! All this made me feel hotter than hell! I cannot keep cool when a person kisses me that way, for I do love it so! I almost went off again, but the car pulling into the driveway of our destination prevented any furtherance of Roland's operations.

We straightened our clothes again and stepped from the car. We looked as respectable as anyone else.

The Devil's Advocate

She's quite a looker. Pretty face, good breasts, great legs – even if her clothes and hair-do are strictly from Hicksville. Exactly the kind of diversion a busy criminal lawyer needs on a boring afternoon at the office.

And soon celebrated defence attorney Conrad Garnett – 'the devil's advocate' – is helping innocent young Clara solve the mystery of her vanishing elder sister. All Rita left behind was a ring with a scorpion on it, a collection of lurid erotica – and a diary of sexual confessions. Clara is convinced her disappearance is mixed up with the terrible new friends Rita has made and the horrible goings-on at their weekend houseparties. She'll do anything to get Rita back. Anything. She'll even accompany Garnett to one of those weekend parties herself...

It was half an hour later by Garnett's watch when the doorknob turned and the door opened very, very slowly.

He looked up. 'Good Lord!' he exclaimed. 'What happened to you?'

Clara leaned against the door. Her make-up was smeared, her clothing rumpled and her hair dishevelled. Her eyes were red from crying, and the tears were still wet on her cheeks. 'They whipped me,' she said hoarsely. 'They whipped me.'

She staggered across the room. Garnett met her halfway and carried her to bed. As he laid her down, she rolled over on her stomach, burying her face in the pillows and sobbing unrestrainedly.

Garnett very cautiously lifted her dress over the back of her thighs. The flesh was pinkly striped, but not raw. He raised her dress higher and then gently pulled down her panties, sliding one hand under her waist to raise her from the bed as he did so. Her buttocks, like her thighs, were not raw, but they were bright red. 'Who did this to you?' he demanded.

'The people in that room. Three men and a girl.'

He moved her head off the pillow and onto his lap. He stroked her hair and said: 'You know, your buttocks look very pretty like that. All pink and red. But they probably don't feel very nice. Have you got any cream or salve? That might take the sting down a little.'

'There's suntan lotion on the little table right next to your hand.'

He found the bottle and scrutinised the label for several seconds. 'This should do it. Now just lie still and I'll put some on. It'll have to be rubbed in well, but I'll try not to hurt you.' He moved his fingers lightly over the smooth flesh, working the oil into it with just the tips, not pressing at all. He rubbed the lotion into the horizontal lines where her buttocks joined her legs and also, extraneously, between her thighs. 'Tell me how it happened,' he said.

She was silent for a moment. Then she said in a small, colourless voice: 'I just knocked on the door. It seemed like such a wonderfully simple solution. It was simple, all right, and so am I! When I knocked at the door, it was opened at once and a man took my arm. There was only a dim light and I couldn't see anything for a moment. Then, when my eyes adjusted to the light, I saw three men and a naked woman lying on the bed.'

'Tell me more,' prodded Garnett eagerly.

'At first I thought I had been right about the drugs, because she was lying limp, with one arm and her head dangling over the edge of the bed. But then she raised her head and one of the men went to the bed. For the first time I noticed that her ankles were strapped to the bed posts. Then there was a knock on the door and the man who had taken me by the arm let go and went to let in the girl who had knocked.'

'Did you recognise her?'

'I think I've seen her around. It was pretty dark in there, but she looked like someone Alice Burton was talking to the other night. The girl came over to me and said: "May I watch you before my turn comes?" I was terribly confused. I didn't know what to say. But I was afraid to let them know I had no idea of what was going on, so I said yes. Then the girl said: "I'd like to help, if it won't spoil it for you. It always makes it better for me if another girl helps." '

'What did she mean by "help"?'

'I didn't have the vaguest idea. But is seemed rude to say no to someone who offers to help you – or so I thought then – so I thanked her and said of course she could help. In the meantime, the other woman was being unstrapped and helped off the bed by two of the men. "That was beautiful," she said.

"I'm sure to have a fabulous evening, feeling the way I do now." '

'What happened then?'

'I began to wonder if perhaps these people gave seances, which would account for the darkness. Or perhaps they were physical therapists, which would account for the woman's nudity and her comment. Then the girl said: "I always try to imagine how other people will act. You like to pretend that you hate it, don't you? Girls as young and feminine as you usually do." She didn't seem to notice that I didn't answer, or maybe she took my silence for assent. Anyway, she rattled right on. The woman who had just got off the bed now spoke up. "I think I'll stay and watch too," she said.

'Suddenly one of the men said: "Well, let's get on with it. Take off your clothes."

"Oh, no," I said. "I couldn't."

'The man standing beside me laughed and said: "If that's the way you like it, we'll take them off for you!"

'He picked me up and carried me to the bed. I was kicking and screaming. I tried to tell him that it was all a mistake, that I had knocked on the wrong door, but he just laughed harder. Then the other two men came over, and I realised that I didn't have a chance, so I let them strip me.'

Garnett glanced at her buttocks and saw that all the oil had been soaked up and that the skin was again dry – even slightly parched. He poured more oil onto her succulent spheres and began to rub it in.

She resumed: 'Two of the men held my arms while the third went to get something – a whip, it turned out. When I saw it, I began to cry and plead with them to let me go. I promised that I wouldn't say anything to anyone. But that only made them laugh, and the woman who had just been on the bed said. "You know, that's the most convincing performance I've ever seen." '

'How gauche.'

'Yes. Anyway, one of the men began to beat me. It was just horrible! All those people were watching me, and I didn't have any clothes on. The men had made me turn over with my face down and had strapped my ankles to the bed posts just like they'd done with the other woman. It was awful.'

'I can imagine.'

'At first I felt more shame than pain but then the lashes got harder and harder. I began to squirm around, and, the more I moved, the more my tormentor beat me. Oh, God, it was awful!'

Clara appeared lost in her narrative and didn't seem to notice that Garnett had spread her legs quite far apart in his efforts to thoroughly grease every inch of the injured area. Now completely open to his vision – and to his fingers, which crept ever nearer – were all of Clara's feminine goodies, enticingly displayed between her lovely, marble-white thighs. Carefully, Garnett rubbed and rubbed, working his way into the crease of her thighs. If he noticed that the oil had dried on his fingertips long ago, he did not let on.

Clara continued. 'The girl stood beside the bed the whole time watching. Then, after what seemed like hours, the man stopped and she raised her hand. I saw that she too had a switch. It was smaller than the one the man used. She began to switch me on the backs of my thighs and between them. She beat me much more quickly than the man had and more viciously. I begged her to stop but she just laughed and said that she'd known that I'd pretend to hate it. I told her over and over that I wasn't pretending, but she kept on switching and finally said, rather nastily: "All right, kid, don't overdo it." She was whipping me between my legs and I was sure I was bleeding, because I was all wet down there. I could feel the liquid all on my thighs.'

'Very interesting,' Garnett observed.

'The other woman was also watching. She seemed to be getting very excited, and she kept saying over and over:

"Don't tease the poor girl, satisfy her." Finally the girl stopped. She had taken off her skirt when she first came in, and now she ripped off her blouse and threw herself down on her stomach across the foot of the bed. "Do it to me while I watch her," she told one of the men, handing him her switch.

'He began to switch her buttocks while another man began to beat me with a bundle of three or four switches all tied together. The man who was switching the girl began hitting her very hard. I could hear the lashes whistling in the air. I don't know too much about what was happening to her because by now I was not thinking very clearly. Mostly I was just feeling the pain. But I do know that she suddenly rolled over next to me and put her arms around me. She pressed her stomach against me and pushed her thighs between mine. "Whip us," she cried. "Whip us both."

'Someone produced a whip, and one of the men began. I wouldn't have believed that anything could hurt more than the lash had but this seemed to hurt a hundred times more. I screamed and screamed – as though, if I didn't, I would lose all contact with the little reality I had left.

' "Harder," cried the girl. "Oh, much harder!" She wiggled and squirmed, but she never once screamed. I could feel the liquid running out from between her legs and over mine. Finally she whispered in my ear: "Haven't you had enough?"

'I could hardly stop screaming to answer her and my voice wouldn't seem to form the words at first, but I finally managed to say "yes." She sat up and said to the man: "I think our little friend here has had enough to keep her bottom warm tonight." I could hardly believe it, but he stopped immediately and began unfastening my ankles.

'I was so weak I could hardly put my clothes on, but somehow I managed. While I was dressing, they strapped the girl down. She told them to strap her ankles, too, because she wanted them to beat her hard and she didn't know if she'd be able to stand it. Then, just as I was leaving, she said to me:

"Don't you want to stay and watch? You can lie down in front of me and I'll suck you while I'm getting whipped – if you want me to."

'I said no, I had to meet someone, which made them laugh, and I finished dressing as quickly as I could and came right back here.'

While Clara had been finishing her account of her adventure, Garnett's fingers had not been idle and, by this time, one of them had worked its way between her buttocks and was moving gently in and out of the rosette opening. Now, for the first time, the girl seemed to notice what was being done to her.

'Stop it!' she cried. 'What are you trying to do?'

Garnett poured a drop of lotion on the opening, which he had been so assiduously rubbing. He said: 'You said the girl switched you here, didn't you?'

'You know very well that she couldn't have switched me there,' replied Clara, in an acid tone. 'Between my legs, I said.'

'Oh, here,' he said, gently caressing the petals of her rosebush.

'Yes, there. But it doesn't hurt any more. Not at all.'

'Oh, but it will if it isn't properly taken care of. Stop wiggling and let me rub some more of this oil on it.'

'I don't want you to. I don't care if it hurts a little. She didn't really switch me there very hard. Hardly at all, honestly. Now stop. I don't want you to massage me there!'

Garnett pushed her shoulders down firmly as she tried to sit up. 'But I'm going to anyway,' he told her. 'And, furthermore, I'm going to use what ought to be used for rubbing you there.'

He bent forward, undid his trousers and slid out his shaft. It came between her legs in one quick movement. 'Now don't try to struggle,' he said, 'because if you do, you might excite me so much that I won't be able to control myself and my member will slip all the way inside of you.' She said nothing and he proceeded to tickle several sensitive places between her legs with the end of his big pointer.

After a while, he moved slightly forward. The oil-smeared tip of his hard organ touched the slit between her buttocks and rubbed at the orifice. He ran the tool back and forth over the opening for some minutes before moving it back to her Mount of Venus. Finally, he positioned himself so that he could rub her tiny petals with the base of his shaft while he nuzzled at her rear with its tip. He smiled down at her as he fancied he felt some movement in response to his efforts.

'Poor little girl,' he said with all the sympathetic commiseration of a hungry crocodile about to swallow a small fish. 'It must hurt terribly when I do this.'

'No, it doesn't hurt – much.'

'Does it make you feel better?'

'Oh, no! This never – uh, well, yes, it does, frankly. The oil, you know—'

'Of course. The oil. Certainly. Shall I rub harder?'

'No. It feels fine just like that.'

'Hold your legs tighter together.'

She did, and he rubbed more persistently until a spasm shook her body and she cried out, gripping his shoulders and bucking her whole body up and down. Then the spasm passed and she fell back, limp.

Garnett watched as Clara came out the small bathroom adjacent to her room and gingerly let herself down into a pink plus armchair. 'Is it painful?' he asked, smiling sardonically.

'No. It just feels awfully feverish, really. It makes me quite restless.'

'All that's wrong with you is a literal case of "hot pants". You know, Clara, I'm afraid you're simply incurably unfortunate. Wherever you turn, you seem to find yourself in the middle of an indelicate situation.'

'Don't make fun of me. You know very well that at least

half the "indelicate situations" I get into are of your making. And, whatever I've done, I've done because I thought it would help you in your investigation.'

'I know,' said the devil's advocate soothingly. 'I was just teasing you. As a matter of fact, I don't think your efforts to help me have been in vain. Everything we learn about these people and this place will ultimately form a composite picture, which we can then study and analyse in terms of the causal factors of your sister's disappearance. And from this analysis we should be able to ascertain her current whereabouts.'

'That sounds like a lot more legalistic double-talk to me. And how can I help but be pessimistic when I see the horrible things that go on here? All those women going into a room to be whipped – wanting to be beaten, just like Rita said she wanted to be.' She sat up with a start. 'Oh! Were you trying to suggest that because Rita does seem to enjoy whipping, no matter how ghastly it seems to me, that we might find her in that horrible little room?'

'Well, it'd be a good idea for one of us to spot-check the corridor every once in a while, just to see who goes in and out. There's no point in posting a perpetual guard, because that would ultimately draw attention to ourselves – and besides, it would waste time we can better use exploring the rest of this ever-fascinating entertainment palace.' He paused, then went on: 'But you know, Clara, you must be more tolerant of the things you see here. Who are you to say what's right or wrong, pleasant or horrible? If there people enjoy being whipped and it doesn't disfigure them in any way, or mar their health, why should you think of them as perverts? Why, you yourself admitted that the whipping made you feel quite "restless". What you meant was sexually excited, didn't you? Well, that's why these people go to be lashed. To stir up their sexual appetites.'

'I don't want to hear such talk,' cried Clara. 'What I did just now, you made me do. You're just talking to hear yourself talk. You seem to forget that we're here to find my sister, not to see what dirty things you can make me do or like doing.'

'I haven't forgotten. You're the one who's delayed our investigation. What with getting yourself whipped, and then distracting, or should I say seducing, the investigator...'

'Oh... I never... how can you...?' Clara's apparent outrage at this suggestion left her seemingly unable to complete a coherent sentence.

Garnett, taking advantage of her spluttering, went on: 'I suggest we begin immediately to "case the joint", as I understand the saying goes, and waste no further time in this useless bickering.'

'And I suggest,' said Clara, who seemed to have recovered her powers of speech, 'that we ought to meet as many people as we can. We won't get anywhere staying in corners by ourselves.'

'Excellent,' said Garnett. 'And I'd especially like to meet your lesbian friend with the brand on her belly.'

They left the room and started down the stairs.

'Shall we begin with wine or something stronger?' he asked.

When she looked at him with apparent bewilderment, he explained: 'It's my theory that the people you meet at parties are determined by what you drink. So, shall we begin with wine or something else?'

'But if we start with such a mild drink, we're bound to meet mild people. And it seems to me that the people who were instrumental in Rita's disappearance are more forceful than wine drinkers – more the Scotch or Bourbon type.'

'Theoretically, yes, but wine is a mocker. Red wine is especially deceitful.' By now they were standing near a large sideboard, and he poured them two glasses of Burgundy from one of the decanters among the vast assortment arrayed there. Then he took Clara by the elbow and propelled her through the crowd, keeping up a running commentary as they walked.

'Here, for instance,' he said, indicating the object of his attention with a nod of his head, 'is an excellent example of what I mean. The sizzling brunette in the red velvet gown. She looks pretty forceful to me. And she's sipping a good red wine. And here—'

'Is something even better,' interjected Clara. 'The lady with the tattoo on her stomach.'

Alice Burton smiled and stood up as they crossed the room to join her. 'I'm so glad to see you, my dear,' she told Clara. 'I've missed you this evening.'

'Oh,' said Clara. 'I've just been showing my friend around the grounds. Mrs Burton, this is Mr Douglas.'

Alice smiled at Garnett and extended her hand. 'I'm very pleased to meet you. Your name is familiar to me, you know. I'm sure I know Douglasses somewhere ... Oh, yes, the aeroplane people. That wouldn't be you, would it?'

Garnett smiled and said no, that wouldn't be him. He did not say what line he was in and she did not press him. Instead, she asked: 'How do you like it here, Mr Douglas?'

'Very much, so far. Of course, we've just arrived, you know, but the grounds are lovely. Miss Morrow and I were speculating on the possibility of some formal entertainment.'

'What did you have in mind? A poetry recital? A pantomine? A record concert?'

'Something on the order of a Roman circus. Our minds have been stimulated for too long; right now we're looking for something to tickle the libido.'

'I believe they're throwing some male poets to the lesbians,' quipped Alice. 'But are you serious?'

'Completely.'

'Then we go this way,' she said, linking one arm through Garnett's, the other through Clara's.

As they walked towards the north wing of the house, Mrs Burton said to Garnett, *sotto voce*: 'I hope I'm doing the right thing. This is no puppet show, you know.'

'We've seen the puppets at Coney Island,' Garnett replied. 'Very silly and squeaky, with people batting each other about for no apparent reason... Dash it all...' He stopped. 'We must have some more wine. You wait here, I'll get some. Clara, give me your glass. Mrs Burton, we're drinking Burgundy. What's your brand of poison?'

'Burgundy will be fine,' smiled Alice. Then, as Garnett hastened off, she said to Clara: 'Your friend is charming. I suppose he's your lover.' She sat down on a nearby settee and drew Clara to her. 'Quick,' she whispered loudly, 'raise your dress!'

'Not here,' cried Clara. 'You can't.'

'I must!' She lifted Clara's skirts to her thighs. 'Just for one moment. It'll taste so nice with the wine.'

'He'll be right back,' warned Clara.

'He will be if you keep arguing about it.' She drew Clara's skirt all the way up and laid her hand against the bare stomach. 'No panties,' she said. 'You *are* progressing! Or is this in honour of your friend? If that's the way it is, then you must let me know, for he'll have you all night and I'll have to be content with only the memory of a stolen moment. Don't begrudge me such a small pleasure, Clara.' As she spoke, she pushed the younger girl's legs apart and kissed the soft moss that grew between them. The tip of her tongue curled around and down into the slit. Clara shuddered. 'Rub against my tongue,' Alice whispered. 'I won't get off my knees until you do, not if everyone in the house comes by.'

Clara spread her knees, sunk her hips into a semi-squat and rubbed herself back and forth against the woman's mouth. Soon, Alice's lips and Clara's little flower-patch were both as wet and slippery as a peeled plum. 'Please let me stop,' begged Clara, continuing to rub. 'He'll be back any second... listen, someone's coming now!'

Alice ducked her head and brought her nose up through the petals of Clara's rosebud in a gesture of farewell.

When Garnett entered the room moments later, the older woman was primly seated on the settee while Clara languidly reclined on a nearby sofa. But the roseate hue of Clara's cheeks and the heavy feminine odour which hung in the air were enough to enlighten Garnett as to how the two women had occupied themselves in his absence. He pinched Clara's fingertips as he handed her a glass and smiled knowingly at her before extending the other glass to Mrs Burton.

Alice smiled her thanks as she accepted the wine. 'This way,' she said as she rose. She led Clara and Garnett through a door in a shadowy corner of the alcove in which they had been waiting and up a tiny, twisting flight of stairs. At the top of the stairs they turned sharply through another door and down a narrow, unlighted hall which led to another tiny flight of stairs. At the top of these stairs, Alice opened a door and shepherded the attorney and the younger girl into a small private theatre.

At one time there had been two rooms here, one above the other, but the flooring between them had been broken through and had been replaced by a narrow balcony with a low railing. The balcony ran around the entire room and was furnished with chairs, couches, hassocks and countless, multi-coloured cushions, all of which were drawn close to the railing for the convenience of the spectators. At each corner of the balcony was a stairway leading down to the stage, and the hanging pillars that supported the balcony divided it into facsimiles of theatre boxes.

The balcony was submerged in darkness. One could see only by the soft glow of the lights underneath it which focused on the oval dais in the centre of the stage. Blue and diffused, this illumination was sufficient to light everything onstage with detailed clarity but soft enough to create an atmosphere of compelling intimacy, an atmosphere which was reinforced by the delicate romantic strains of a Chopin 'Impromptu' flowing through the theatre from hidden amplifiers.

The dais was covered with a huge, diamond-shaped, white angora rug. On the rug were over-sized satin cushions, some blue, some green, some black and some white, and a heavily smoking incense-burner set into a dull brass stand.

The entrance of Alice, Clara and Garnett evoked no interest among the persons who were already in the theatre. Smoking and conversing in intimate tones, no person among the score or so of spectators so much as glanced up at the two women and the man who now stood near the entrance, adjusting their eyes to the dim light.

'We can still leave,' murmured Alice, glancing towards Clara and then looking intently at Garnett. But, if Garnett heard her, he gave no sign of having done so, for he said: 'Let's be seated, shall we?' He then sat on a small couch in an unoccupied loge, and motioned to Clara and Mrs Burton to take places on either side of him. They did so as he observed: 'Our hosts provide handsomely for their guests' entertainment, I must say.'

'The guests provide for one another,' Mrs Burton corrected. 'The hosts merely supply the opportunity.'

The throaty tone of an unseen gong, melting into the liquid quaver of a vibraharp, now cast a hush over the audience, putting an end to all conversation. Suddenly a girl materialised out of the darkness. She ran lightly to the centre of the stage and up onto the dais, flinging herself down on the cushions. Her red hair glowed like flame in the semi-darkness, providing a vivid contrast to the stark whiteness of her naked body. There was a pause, while the audience absorbed the picture before them. Then two men in their early twenties entered the stage. They approached the dais from opposite sides.

'The artistic touch,' whispered Alice Burton. 'Colour combinations: a blond, a brunette and a redhead.'

The two men mounted the dais at the same moment, and the audience was now able to perceive that one was blond, deeply tanned and muscular, while the other was black-haired, sallow and angular. Together they approached the cushions over which the girl sprawled.

Clara bowed her head and covered her eyes as the men sank down on the pillows surrounding the girl. Garnett leaned towards Clara and stroked the hair on the back of her neck, murmuring into her ear: 'Don't look away!' She pulled her head away from his grasp, but he persisted. 'I want you to look,' he hissed, taking her hand and holding it tightly in his.

The two men were sharing the girl, caressing her thighs and her belly, exploring between her legs with their fingers. Her clenched fists dug into the cushions around her, and she arched her body, rubbing her thighs against the men. Then she turned and rubbed her breasts – the nipples grown sharply erect – against the shoulder of the muscular blond, at the same time rotating her buttocks against the crotch of the brunette.

Next, she bent over the blond, swaying her shoulders and brushing her nipples against his chest. Then, jutting her breasts forward, she rubbed them against his chest and belly, at the same time slipping her hands under the waistband of his trousers. He turned her over on her stomach, and she lay between his legs, probing inside his pants with frantic fingers as he began rubbing his hand between her thighs. She began to slide one hand up his trouser leg as Clara whispered: 'Please, let's go now.'

'No. Drink your wine.' Garnett pulled her hand across his lap and pressed it against the bulge in his trousers. He held it there, curling her fingers around his shaft as the girl on the dais opened the fly of the blond man.

Now the girl pulled the trousers down over the man's smoothly tanned hips and along his strong, muscular legs. She ran her fingers through the blond curls over his already erect organ, bending over him and taking the organ itself wholly into her mouth. While she did so, the other man stripped off his bathing trunks and lay down at her side, stroking her breasts and her belly. She removed the shaft from her mouth and turned towards the dark-haired man, arching her body as she did so. She licked his member for a short while, then rolled over on her back and began to rub the testicles and organs of both men simultaneously.

Almost immediately, the blond mounted her. Supporting himself with one hand, he held his shaft with the other and pressed it between her legs, rubbing it back and forth for a moment before pushing it upward into her gaping love nest. He drew it back and then pushed it forward again, and the girl exclaimed loudly: 'Harder.'

The thrust that followed seemed to knock the breath out of her, but a moment later she murmured the word again. She fell silent as he began pumping rhythmically in and out of her, then once again cried: 'Harder!' She drew up her legs, bicycling them up and down in the air, lifting them higher and higher until at last they were practically straight up and down.

She now worked her hips violently against her partner's slow but unremitting strokes. After a moment, she turned her head and stretched out her hand towards the sallow man. He approached her and she took his organ in her hand and moved it towards her mouth.

Clara, her hand trembling, gulped down the last of her wine. Garnett quickly refilled her glass with some wine from his own. Then he removed her hand from his lap and put his own hand on her thigh, underneath her dress. He stroked the smooth flesh for a moment, then allowed his fingers to stray between her legs, gently probing and tickling the soft, fleshy lips of her nether-mouth.

Clara slid forward in her seat, allowing his hand more freedom to roam, as the girl on the dais rubbed the organ of the darker man against her lips. Suddenly, she took the whole rigid shaft into her mouth. The blond man shuddered convulsively, then lay motionless atop her. She clawed the thighs of the sallow man, and the blond rolled off her to be replaced almost instantaneously by the other.

'Here,' whispered Garnett, 'give me your hand.' When Clara did not respond, he reached for her hand and placed it on his member, which protruded boldly from his trousers. He put his hand over hers and showed her how to move the skin of his shaft up and down. Then he put his hand back between her legs. He slid one finger into her now-warm oven and rubbed his thumb around the oven door.

The men on the dais were taking turns with the redhead, the sallow one making love to her while the other one allowed her to gratify him orally.

'Are you enjoying yourself?' whispered Garnett.

'No!' hissed Clara. 'This is horrible! Filthy! I don't see how she can let herself do such things. And with all these people watching!'

'Friends and enemies,' said Alice Burton's voice out of the darkness. 'Which do you think would be more trying?'

Clara did not reply and the voice continued casually: 'And there's her husband. On the other side of the balcony.'

'She must be a monster,' whispered Clara, 'to do this with her husband watching.'

'Oh, he doesn't mind,' laughed Alice. 'He knows she married him for his money and not his sexual prowess. It gives him great pleasure to watch her sex workouts. You see, he loves her, and he wants to see her satisfied in every respect. And she has come to love him because of his understanding and tolerance.'

The subject of their discussion was now lying on her stomach between the two men, each of her legs thrown over one of each man's legs. She took the blond's sex in her hand, placed the other's member in her mouth and wriggled her toes as though she were in ecstasy.

Garnett gently removed Clara's hand from his shaft, which she had been pumping vigorously up and down. 'Oh . . .' she whispered. 'I didn't realise . . . that is, I didn't notice . . .'

' . . . that you were about to bring my organ to a state of

erection which it would be impossible to sustain for any lengthy period of time – say, no more than fifty seconds?' Garnett's words seemed to add to her confusion, and she wrung her hands together in her lap, whispering over and over: 'I'm so ashamed . . . so ashamed.'

She quirmed and wriggled away from his fingers, but they would not release their hold. 'My bottom is starting to burn again,' she informed him suddenly. 'From the switching, you know. Strange, how restless it makes me feel. Or maybe it's the wine that's making me so restless. And you, too. With your finger wiggling up and down. That makes me restless. Do stop, Conrad. Or I'll make you stop. If I press my legs together hard enough, your hand won't be able to move and then you'll have to stop!'

She seemed very pleased with herself for having figured this out, but she did not suit the deed to the word. Perhaps she thought she did. Perhaps the unaccustomed amount of wine she had consumed so confused her that she thought she was pressing her legs together when, in reality, she allowed them to relax and spread even farther apart. Perhaps.

'It's cold in here,' she said suddenly. She began chafing her wrists, imitating the up and down motion Garnett had taught her to use to stimulate his love instrument.

On the dais, the darker man removed his organ from the girl's mouth and stood up. She turned to him on her knees and he thrust the shaft back into her mouth. She threw her arms around his legs and began sucking his member passionately and in such a way that it was apparent that she meant to bring him to a climax. Clara leaned forward in her seat.

Suddenly, the girl on the dais jerked the man's knees to her breasts with all her strength. He thrust forward with a savagery which almost sent her toppling backwards with him on top of her. He staggered and Clara pressed clenched knuckled against her lips.

The man recovered his balance. He then moved away from

the redhead, who began to crawl on her knees towards the blond. She approached him and tried to take his member in her mouth but he made her lick it instead.

'More wine?' asked Garnett. He handed Clara his glass, and she downed the contents with one gulp. 'Slowly, slowly, or you'll get dizzy,' cautioned the attorney, raising her dress over her hips.

'Oh! Stop!' whispered Clara. 'I feel as though everyone is watching me – as though it's me on my knees down there . . .' Her voice faded as the redhead arched her torso and stretched, cupping one of her breasts in her hand and lustfully smearing the roseate nipple with the dark and fevered tip of the love instrument she had been licking.

Clara stiffened. Slowly she raised her hand to her own breasts and touched the nipples through the silk of her dress. 'Perhaps I should have worn a brassiere,' she said aloud, swaying her own hips in what seemed to be an unconscious imitation of the motions the girl on the dais was now making as she bent her head towards the blond's manhood.

He drew sharply away from her. The theatre was totally silent – the music had stopped when the gong sounded – and the girl's heavy breathing could be heard in every corner of the balcony.

The man began to move away. The girl held onto his member and crept after him on her knees, following him as he stepped backward across the furry rug. She stretched her neck forward, trying desperately to reach the object of her desire with her lips. 'Please . . .' she whispered loudly. 'Please . . .'

'Oh!' gasped Clara, 'I'm so ashamed . . . so ashamed . . . for her . . . to lower herself like that . . .'

The redhead bent forward again, and Clara's lips silently formed the word as the girl repeated: 'Please.'

The tanned, sleekly muscular body stopped its backward progress, and the blond Adonis allowed the supplicant to touch his organ with her lips. Soon she had thrust the length of the coveted shaft into her mouth and was sucking it even more passionately than she had sucked that of the sallow man. She tossed her head from side to side as she moved the love instrument in and almost out of her mouth. Her hair fell over her face, but she didn't even stop to fling it back, only brushing away the strands that strayed between her lips.

Clara ran her hand through her own hair and pressed forward against Garnett's hand. Her thighs tensed, her belly shuddered, her breath came quickly and her fingers clenched tightly. Garnett moved his hand faster and faster, harder and harder.

The redhead drew back, then savagely plunged forward again. The blond grasped her shoulders, digging his fingers into her flesh. He threw back his head, his face ecstatically convulsed, as his splendid body bucked uncontrollably. The redhead sucked and swallowed.

Clara gasped: 'Oh... I'm... I'm... going to... I'm... *Ahhhhhhh!*' Her own body jerked spasmodically for several seconds before relaxing into limpness, and she murmured: 'Oh... what gorgeous fireworks!' Her eyes were tightly closed, and her lips smiled dreamily. 'So bright and green. And such interesting shapes... Oh! They're fading now. What a pity.' She slumped back against the couch cushions and opened her eyes.

A match flared suddenly in the darkness, revealing Alice Burton with her face buried in Garnett's lap while his hand worked vigorously under her skirt, which was pushed high above her thighs. The brief illumination flickered out just as the attorney threw back his head, his face contorted. Tiny sucking sounds pierced the newly-fallen darkness.

Clara sprang out of her seat. She yanked down her skirt and adjusted the waistline. Almost immediately, Garnett was standing also, calmly buttoning his fly and taking Clara's arm.

'Shall we leave now?' he asked. He turned to Alice, who was lying back in her seat limply, licking her lips and working her hand violently up and down under her dress. 'Later,' she said.

Garnett took Clara's arm and escorted her out of the theatre. As they reached the bottom of the little staircase, Clara suddenly exclaimed, 'Oh, darn! I've left my purse upstairs.' She turned and Garnett prepared to follow her.

'You needn't bother,' she said. 'I can see very well in the dark. I'll find it myself.'

Garnett chuckled. 'In other words, you didn't need that lighted match to tell you what was happening.'

'I have nothing to say to you,' retorted Clara.

'You understand, of course, that I was merely trying to find the mark on her stomach.'

'Of course,' echoed Clara. 'And she was merely trying to bite the same mark into yours.'

'What she did was her own idea. I didn't ask her to, but I didn't see any reason to stop her either. You hadn't made a better offer.'

'Oh!' gasped Clara. She turned on her heel and ran quickly back up the stairs.

Three minutes later she reappeared. Her face was white and she looked as though she had just had a terrible shock.

'Is something wrong?' asked Garnett as she pelted down the stairs towards him. Clara nodded dumbly. He took her by the shoulders and shook her lightly. 'Pull yourself together,' he said, 'and tell me.'

Clara raised her head. 'On the stage,' she whispered breathlessly. 'Rita . . . my sister!'

Clara crumpled against Garnett's chest. She swayed against him, and he clasped her tightly in his arms to keep her from falling. 'Pull yourself together,' he repeated. 'Now that you know she's alive and safe, there's no reason to fall apart.'

These words seemed to produce a steadying effect on Clara, for she lifted her head and pulled it slightly away from the attorney. 'I guess you're right,' she said, 'It's just the shock . . .'

'Yes, I know,' said Garnett quickly. 'But if you want to see Rita again, you'd better get hold of yourself. I'm not going to carry you up those stairs, you know.'

She nodded assent and took his arm. 'All right,' she said. 'I'm ready.'

When they were back inside the theatre, Garnett steered Clara towards their former seats. Alice had vanished, and they now had the couch to themselves. Garnett peered over the railing of the balcony into blackness. The blue light had dimmed and nothing could be seen on the stage but the red, unwinking eye of the incense burner. Then a greenish light suffused the dais and two girls were revealed, lying languorously among the pillows with their heads nestled between each other's legs. Clara leaned forward.

'Which one is Rita?' whispered Garnett.

'Neither.' Clara sounded bemused. 'I . . . I . . . never saw either one of them before in my life. But she was there — honestly she was. I tell you I saw her . . .'

'I think we'd better leave and go someplace where we can talk privately.'

'But what about Rita? Maybe she's behind stage. Or maybe we could find someone who knows her — and knows where she is now.'

'Okay.' Garnett stood up. 'I'll go and ask around. Does she look like you?'

'Oh, yes. She's a little taller and she wears her hair in a very sophisticated upsweep but we do look a lot alike. In fact, people sometimes ask if we're twins.'

'Then I shouldn't have any trouble recognising her. Or describing her, either. You sit here and don't move until I come back, no matter what happens. Even if you should see Rita again. I don't want to have to investigate your disappearance too.'

'All right. I won't move, I promise.'

Garnett turned and disappeared into the blackness. Clara

sighed, leaned back against the sofa cushions and closed her eyes.

She was still reclining, eyes closed, when Garnett returned some five minutes later. 'Come on,' he hissed, 'let's get out of here.' He took her roughly by the arm and propelled her down the narrow stairway. Clara tried to ask what had happened, but he silenced her. 'Wait till we get back to your room,' he said. 'Then we'll talk.'

When they arrived, Garnett shoved the girl gently down into the pink plush armchair. Then he stood in front of her, his arms folded across his chest. 'Well?' he said, his annoyance obvious.

'Well, what?' queried the girl innocently.

'Look here, Clara,' he asked, 'exactly how much do you feel the wine you had? Are you drunk?'

She looked startled. 'I suppose I'm pretty high,' she admitted. 'On the edge, you know? But I'm sober enough to go anywhere we've got to go – or to take any bad news you have to give me.'

'There's no bad news and we're not going anywhere. Just tell me: are you certain you saw your sister on the stage?'

Clara sprang from the chair, eyes wide, mouth agape. Garnett pushed her back down. 'Now take it easy,' he said. 'You say you saw Rita, and I'm sure you believe you did. You *saw* Rita but she wasn't there. She certainly wasn't there when I looked.'

'But the time lapse . . . It was several minutes before we went back upstairs. She had plenty of time to leave.'

'Yes. And it was several minutes between the time we left the theatre and the time you went back for your purse. Several minutes, Clara. Maybe five in all. Do you really think Rita would have remained on the dais for only five minutes? And alone. She was alone, wasn't she?'

'Oh, yes. There was no one else. I would have told you if there had been.'

'So. She performed a five minute solo. Do you honestly imagine that that audience wants to watch a woman playing with herself, even for five minutes? Why, if they want that, they can go to a burlesque show. Practically the same thing . . . No Clara, it just won't wash.'

'You're being ridiculous! I wasn't having an hallucination, if that's what you're implying.'

'How can you be sure? An hallucination has all the appearance of reality. That's what makes it an hallucination. You were in a state of mental excitement. You'd been drinking an abnormal amount of wine on an empty stomach. Rita's on your mind constantly. What could be more natural than for you to imagine that you saw her?'

'And I suppose this conversation is an hallucination too, perhaps this whole party is an hallucination.'

'Now you're being irrational. Please try to calm down. You know, I haven't told you yet what happened when I went down to the stage.'

'No. You didn't. What did happen?'

'Nothing. Nothing at all. There was no sign of your sister, or anyone who looked like you or who answered to the name of Rita Morrow. And I couldn't find a single soul who could tell me exactly what did happen in the interval between the end of the act which we watched and the beginning of the lesbians' performance. Everyone I spoke to had either just gone out for a smoke, or hadn't been paying attention, or had just arrived, or something! No one saw anything, no one knew anything, no one had ever heard of your sister. I even tried checking with the man who works the lights. I was sure he'd be able to tell me who had been on the dais during the interim . . .'

'What did he say?'

'Not a thing! There is no man who works the lights. They're automatically rigged to go on and off at timed intervals.'

'Oh.' Clara seemed deflated. 'But you didn't prove that I

didn't see her . . . that she wasn't there . . . And I was so sure . . .'

'Yes, Clara, I know you were sure. We won't argue about it, any more. Let's suppose for a moment that you did see Rita. What could you do about it?'

'You should know about that better than I do. You're the lawyer! We should go to the district attorney and have him arrest Mrs Mason for kidnapping, and have the police search for this mysterious husband of hers. I wouldn't be in the least surprised to find out that he's the "Scorpion".'

'In the first place,' said Garnett, 'if I went to the police now and asked them to arrest Mrs Mason, I'd be the laughing stock of the Bar Association. Even the greenest law student knows you can't accuse a party of any crime without having evidence to back up your accusation. Sure, you can prove, with the bookplates, that your sister had some association, either with the Scorpion or with some unknown third party who had an association with the Scorpion. But that's all you can prove. You don't even have the ring any more. You have absolutely no way of knowing for certain that Rita is here. And, in the second place, even if you swear up and down that you saw Rita on the dais, you'll have a pretty tough time convincing the DA that she wasn't in there of her own free will. Which brings us to another point. You don't suppose that if she was on the stage she was there against her will, do you? She could have screamed and tried to get away. And remember, she was alone there — so you said. I just don't understand your sudden hysteria, Clara. If you did see Rita, you know she's safe. If you didn't see her, then you have no reason to be any more concerned about her than you have been all along. I think that rather than talking nonsense about arresting Mrs Mason you should be much more interested in continuing to track down Rita.'

'Well,' said Clara, 'perhaps you're right. Perhaps I'm just overwrought. What do you think we should do now?'

'I think I should do a little more investigating. And the best place to start would be with your Mrs Burton. After all, she did remain in the theatre after we left. Perhaps she can tell us who, if anyone, was on the dais during that interval. Was she there when you went back?'

'Why, yes, she was!' answered Clara. 'How convenient for you!'

Garnett grinned. 'Don't be catty, little girl. It doesn't become you.' He pulled her to her feet. 'Come on, it's time for you to get some sleep. You've had quite a day.'

'That may be, but I have no intention of going to sleep. While you're having your little *tete-a-tete* with Alice Burton, I'm going to find my sister.

'Do I have to put you to bed by force?' asked Garnett wearily.

'You don't have to put me to bed at all. And it's time you understood that I don't like this overbearing attitude of yours!'

'Disgusting, isn't it?' He chuckled. 'Nevertheless, you are going to bed.'

He picked her up and carried her to the bed. The instant he put her down, she rolled over to the edge and would have gone off the side if he had not caught her around the waist and dragged her back. Silently he pulled her dress over her head, imprisoning her arms. Then he slipped her shoes off and removed her stockings. Bare-legged, Clara writhed inside the confinement of her dress and spat out unintelligible insults.

'If you aren't quiet,' said Garnett, 'I am going to give your beswitched little bottom a spanking.' He turned her over and tapped her bare buttocks oh-so-lightly with his hand. Then he unfastened her garter belt. 'You don't want me to do that, do you?' he asked, gently stroking her thigh.

'What are you doing?' asked Clara's voice, muffled by the folds of the dress.

'Looking at you,' Garnett replied. 'What else would I be doing?' He let his hand fall on her hip and slither between her legs.

'Don't!' said Clara. 'Let me sit up! I don't like you to look at me when I can't see you. Let me up!'

'Not yet. I like you this way.' Garnett took a tuft of pubic hair in his fingers and gently tugged it. 'Very soft and nice,' he said.

'I can't breathe,' Clara objected. 'I'm smothering.'

'I'll let you up,' promised Garnett. 'But not just yet.' He moved his hand forward, spreading her legs farther apart. His eyes widened appreciatively. 'If you were any riper, you'd burst and spill all over my fingers, wouldn't you?'

There was a muffled protest from inside the dress, indicating, Garnett assumed, that the young lady did not agree with his estimate of her condition. Unruffled by his lack of encouragement, he asked: 'Can you guess what I'm looking at now?'

Clara jerked her legs together and squeezed the fleshy parts of her thighs against each other.

'You're clairvoyant,' Garnett told her, 'but I can still see it. In fact . . .'

'What did you do?' exclaimed Clara suddenly. She rolled away from him and thrashed about wildly inside her improvised prison.

Garnett pulled the dress over her soft white shoulders.

'What did you do?' she repeated.

'I kissed it,' he said coolly. 'Here, lie back and let me do it again from the front. It's easier that way.'

'I think I'll sleep now,' she replied hurriedly, slipping away from him.

'You change your mind so quickly!' Garnett clutched her around the waist and hips with one arm. 'I'm beginning to believe that you have absolutely no convictions.' He smiled. 'You don't really want to go to sleep, Clara. You want to lie here on the bed and let me play with you for a little while and kiss you . . . all over.' He arranged the pillows under her in such a manner that her shoulders were raised and she could look down at him as he bent his head towards her thighs.

'Why can't you leave me alone?' she whispered feebly. 'Just for a little while – until I get my bearings and—'

'Your mirror will tell you why I don't leave you alone,' he answered softly, brushing his lips across the hair which shielded her love-nest.

Immediately she placed her hands between her legs, guarding her treasure against further intrusion. 'Please don't do that again,' she begged.

Garnett propped himself up on one elbow and gently but firmly pulled one of her sweet dimpled knees away from its mate. 'Didn't you like it when Alice Burton did it?' he asked, reaching between her thighs and plucking at the hair which grew over the lips of her love-mouth. The little lips parted with a tiny, audible kiss. Garnett went on: 'I won't insist that you answer that question, but I do insist on the same privilege you allowed Alice.' He kissed her just above the knee and squeezed the flesh tenderly.

'Don't – please don't!' Clara murmured. She put her hand on his head to push him away, but the strength seemed to ebb from her fingers as his breath stirred the hair on her Mount of Venus. Her fingers curled in his hair as his lips slipped up over her thighs. 'No – no further,' she whispered.

With his ear pressed against her thigh, Garnett peered over her belly and the points of her heaving breasts. He took a bit of the flesh of her thigh between his teeth and nipped, evoking a surprised 'eep' from her. He spread her legs further and further apart, and carefully examined the glowing ruby treasure which now lay completely exposed to his sight and touch.

'Don't look at me down there,' the girl whispered. 'It makes me feel like an animal.'

'And what a lovely animal you are!' He kept his eyes fixed between her legs. 'And what a wonderful little treasure you carry with you!'

Clara slipped one hand between her legs to cover the object of his interest. 'Don't come any nearer,' she pleaded.

He brushed the hand away. 'Only near enough to kiss it,' he said. He stroked upward towards her crotch with his lips, dragging the inside of his lower lip over her now-warm thighs, leaving a wet and moist trail along the upper part of her leg.

Clara twisted and writhed as though the bed had suddenly turned into a briar patch. 'No nearer,' she begged, 'Oh – no! Conrad! The room is spinning! The bed is going around and around – like a—' She tangled her fingers in his hair and clutched the strands tightly. 'Ohhhhh' she moaned. 'My bones feel so heavy!'

Garnett's lips now touched her dark crown of pubic hair. She shivered.

'I'm so ashamed—' she whispered. 'So ashamed of myself for lying here without any clothes on and letting you do anything you want to me. For letting you look at me like this. I know what you want. I can feel it in your fingers. I can feel it in my own legs, in my thighs, even . . . down there, inside me . . . And now,' she continued, her voice barely audible, 'I'm ashamed because I can't control my body . . . because my body wants your mouth to press against me as much as my mind wants it to stop.'

Garnett kissed her welted slit, urging the lips open by turning his head from side to side. The tiny, fleshy lips pressed and swelled against the lips of his mouth. They were hotly wet and brightly flushed. He kissed them with a loud sound, then kissed them again, moving his mouth across the wet open area towards her buttocks.

Clara moaned. 'I can't move,' she whispered. 'I want to but I can't move.'

He slid his arms under her hips and raised them so that he could kiss her solidly between the legs. He shut his eyes as he pressed his face into the thick tangle of her pubic hair and the soft mound of her flesh. He flicked his tongue across the throbbing lips of her sex. Clara shut her eyes and rolled her head from side to side on the pillow.

She began to press herself against him, spreading her thighs and drawing up her knees, allowing his tongue access to every part of her. 'How can you?' she murmured. 'How ... can ... you ... do ... that ... oh ... *do that!*' She rubbed vigorously against his chin, and he licked harder, curling his tongue, probing the extra-sensitive head with the very tip of his tongue.

Suddenly, he stabbed his tongue into her now-gaping lovewell. She cried out, and pressed her hips forward, driving the welcome intruder further inside her. She appeared to be completely consumed with passion, and she stretched out blindly to touch his hard male body. Her hands encountered his trouser buttons, and she began fumbling with them wildly, seemingly desperate to open them and to unsheath the manhood which the cloth kept from her grasping fingers. At last she succeeded and was able to clutch triumphantly at his love instrument. Her hands slipped down to the sides of his crotch. She raked her fingers through the sweaty warmth of his pubic hair, then slipped them into the incredibly soft grooves of his thighs. She kept them there for a short while, just stroking the flesh and making small moaning noises in her throat. Then she moved them back up to cover his swollen organ.

In response to her touch, Garnett pulled his hips back and manoeuvred his organ out of his trousers as she began rubbing her hands up and down on it. He then made a muffled, glubbery sound – by which he meant that he wished her to unsheath the rest of his maleness. She plunged her hands back into his trousers and fished out the fleshy sacs. He ran his fingers slowly along the crease between her buttocks and into her love cavern alongside his busily working tongue.

She hugged his body to her, pressing her breasts against the swollen organ she was holding. He inched his hips around towards her shoulders. Suddenly, her body went rigid. 'No,' she whispered. 'Oh . . . *no!!!*' Her hands froze around the shaft which she had been rubbing against her nipple. 'I'm doing the same thing that . . . that . . . redhead in the theatre . . . was doing. Oh! No more . . . please . . .'

She pushed him away from her, but to no avail. He took his shaft in one hand and rubbed it across her face. 'Kiss it,' he said, pulling his mouth away from its task. 'Lick it if you want me to go on licking you.'

Clara grimaced as the hot bud seared her lips. 'But . . . I don't want . . . I told you I'm afraid to . . . Ohhh.' She moaned as his tongue curled back against that least-resistant part of her. She kissed the tip of the member and began to rub it with the flat of her tongue. She licked its length and breadth, taking it into her own hands and pushing his away. She licked it from top to bottom and back again, letting her tongue lap up the moisture that sprang from the tip. Her hips rocked back and forth under the gentle guidance of his hands.

It was not long before he took his organ out of her hands again. Her tongue lapped over his fingers in an effort to reclaim the newfound treasure she had so recently begun to lick. She probed between his fingers and under them and around them. 'No,' he chuckled, 'you can't have it. Not unless you're ready to suck it.' He pushed the spongy gland against her lips. She turned her head away sharply. 'Suck it, Clara,' he demanded. 'Suck it!'

She shook her head and whispered. 'Let's just go on as we were . . .' He did not reply.

She was silent for a moment. Then she said. 'You know, I feel as though I'm watching myself, lying there on the bed . . . naked . . . squirming around in the arms of a man . . . doing unspeakable, unthinkable things. And she horrified me . . . that girl on the bed . . . she's lascivious and disgusting . . .'

Garnett was not at all interested in the horrified and shocked Clara; only in the lascivious, squirming one to whose lips he now held his warm, ripely swelling engine. 'You must do it to me,' he whispered as he caressed her warm, succulent buttocks. 'Before you do it to someone else,' he added.

'I won't ever do it to someone else. Or to you, either.'

'I think you will.' He touched her mouth with the tip of the shaft. 'Lick it. Go on. You like to lick it, don't you?'

In response, her tongue slipped out and lightly brushed the tight-skinned organ. It was as though she didn't want to, but somehow couldn't help herself. She rubbed her tongue over it, and when it pressed into her lips, she did not stop. She kept licking it until it had pressed so deeply between her lips that she could no longer deny the fact that she had the tip inside her mouth.

But when Garnett slowly pushed the totality of the shaft into her mouth, she did protest. Pushing him away with all her strength, she said in a quavering voice: 'I can hear the voice of that girl – the redheaded one – pleading to those men to let her do what I'm doing to you. If I give in now, someday, maybe, I'll be on my knees, pleading... like that... please... please.' Somehow, a note of supplication crept into her voice, and she bent her head to take the erect member back into her mouth. Garnett moved forward until it met her lips and slid easily between them.

She flung her arms around his back and hugged him close. He slid his tongue back into her slit and began lapping at her savagely, shaking his head wildly from side to side and licking fiercely. His hips pumped passionately as he drew his stout weapon in and out of her mouth, and she curled her tongue around the tip and licked each time he drew it outward. His movements grew faster and faster.

She tensed her body and rubbed wildly against his tongue. Her body began bucking uncontrollably as her mouth filled with hot liquid. His lips held her head on one side and the pillow held it on the other side. There was nothing she could do but swallow.

Betsy Thoughtless

Taken from the infamous collection of Victorian debauchery, *Venus School Mistress*, here is a young lady's account of how she lost her virginity. It should be of no surprise that the catalyst of Betsy's fall from grace is a birching, for *Venus School Mistress* is a volume dedicated to the celebration of 'birchen sports'.

'Many persons,' states the Preface, 'not sufficiently acquainted with human nature and the ways of the world are apt to imagine that the lech for flagellation must be confined either to the aged or to those who are exhausted through too great a devotion to venery. But such is not the fact, for there are quite as many young men who are influenced by this passion.'

One such is Betsy's 'brother' Tom. And after the pair of them have enjoyed the spectacle of pretty Sally Meadow's bare white buttocks reddening under the birch, he seizes his opportunity . . .

I became acquainted with this lovely girl during my visit to Cheltenham. She was the daughter of a rich commoner in the West of England, and we soon formed an intimacy of the sweetest and most agreeable kind. She was in her eighteenth year, with a form and face seldom equalled: her hair was of a lively brown, her skin perfectly white, and her face full of ardour and beauty. I discovered her secrets very soon after my introduction; by the recital of a warm and very libidinous story, which I had read in the French, and which I pretended to have witnessed. This won her confidence, and she confessed that she had been seduced by a young gentleman, a *protégé* of her father's.

I lent the beautiful creature some luscious prints, tastily executed, and which made her almost mad, as she had never seen anything of the kind before. In return for these, which I afterwards gave her, she promised me, in writing, a memoir of the circumstances and causes of her seduction, and I cannot do better than give it in her own words:

To Miss Wilson

My dear friend,

'Tis well that I am alone, for I blush to the ears in making a confession, even to you, of the wanton and naughty scenes which led to the first indulgence of my passions, passions the most ardent and glowing but which, I am happy to say, have met with a corresponding feeling in those of my lover, but to my tale.

A youth had been brought up by my father from infancy. He was called my brother and though we frequently remarked the want of likeness between us, and other circumstances, no suspicion that he was not my brother ever entered our minds until a few months since. This youth bore our family name; was called Tom Thoughtless; was educated by my father liberally, and a midshipman's berth was obtained for him. In progress of time he became a lieutenant, and in that capacity, full of life, full of health and beauty, and at the glowing and impetuous age of nineteen, returned from a long station and came to see us.

Whether Tom had had any intimation of our non-relationship, I know not, but when he took me in his arms, his embrace was boisterous, though tender: he dwelt upon my lips with a fervour that made me thrill all over. He sucked my lips, he grasped my form to his, sighed, breathed short and seemed full of emotion. Lord! what a tremor and flutter I was in, so new was the character of this embrace.

'Oh Betsy,' said he, full of agitation, 'you are the first woman I have held in my arms for five years.'

'Am I indeed?' I replied, scarcely knowing what I said.

I fluttered dreadfully and felt quite overpowered, so new was all this and so much awakened my passions. I lay back in his arms, he put my ringlets away from my forehead and kissed my brow, my eyes, and my mouth. Oh! what unhallowed kisses I then thought them. Flames wantoned through me and seemed to centre in one spot – that *spot* which we keep so sacred and which had scarcely been visited by my curious touch.

'Oh! Betsy,' said he, 'that we were not related. Let me at least for a moment indulge the sweet, the blissful idea.'

I knew not what he purposed, but he thrust his tongue between my lips – it was in my teeth – upon my tongue. This motion so strange, so unexpected, almost took away my breath. I tried to speak – to cry out. Alas! I could not, my feelings choked me. His right hand had been round my waist; he dropped it to my posteriors; he felt them three or four times through my dress, then carried me to the side of the room, against which he placed me. His body was now against mine, his knee separated my limbs; he stood between them as far as my garments would allow and began heaving by short tilts his body against mine.

I cannot describe what I felt. I thought I should faint through excess of delight. This heaving motion continued; it made me mad. I – how shall I confess it? – I followed his example and met his bobs with eager activity, sighing and crying out all the time, 'Oh! Tom, Tom, my dear fellow, what are you doing?' But he evidently knew not; he was completely absorbed and kept wriggling the middle of his person against mine, and I intuitively followed his example – so seductive is passion.

In the midst of this I felt him gradually lifting up my clothes; a cold shudder communicated this to me. The next moment a looking-glass that stood in a recess opposite to where we stood, revealed to me our shaking clothes and agitated persons. In this I saw that my legs were uncovered and part of my thighs!

This alarmed me dreadfully and I immediately seized his hands, full of blushes and confusion, and burning with passion, exclaimed: 'Tom, what are you doing? The servants will come in, we shall be discovered.' I slipped from before him and at the same moment heard my father's voice, giving some directions. He very shortly after entered the apartment.

I will pass over the emotions this interview occasioned, though I dreamt that Tom was my husband, and was happy in my arms. My waking thoughts were of this dear fellow and, so impassioned were they, that I kicked down the bedclothes, and pulling up my shift, all the lower beauties of my limbs lay open.

I said to myself, 'Ah! here is a pair of legs handsome enough, and a couple of round plump thighs; there is a good sprinkling of curl about this mount; but what an unmeaning thing is this slit! Can this be what the men hunt us poor women for? I can easily imagine that man has something divine for us: something delightful to feel, to grasp, to handle, to look at? Oh! that I had it now – that it was just dividing these glowing but opening lips. Tom, look at me – you want to deflower me – I know you do. Come then, I am ready to receive you – put it in – there, I feel it (and I pushed in my finger). Now it entered – Oh! how delicious – push, push – Tom, my dear fellow – Oh! I feel it – there, there.'

With such expressions as these, and in working my fingers upon that susceptible spot we all possess, I soon dissolved in a flood of lascivious joy.

I dressed myself with peculiar care, and was complimented by my dear Tom on my good looks and beauty. After breakfast he proposed a walk, and I eagerly put on my bonnet, and taking his arm, proceeded through the park, in which my father's house stands. We were both in high spirits, and enjoyed each other's society.

In passing a cottage which belonged to the estate, we heard bustle and cries and, through the broken palings, discovered the cottager's wife in pursuit of her daughter, a full grown girl. She caught her near where we were peeping and, putting her left foot on a washing tub, which was reversed, she pulled the girl across her knee and drew from under her apron a birch rod. In a moment the girl's clothes were all gathered up, and her legs and limbs sprawling in the air. Her person was beautifully formed and her skin particularly white and rendered more so by her having on black worsted stockings.

Not a moment was lost by the enraged mother, who began to flog away at the girl's posteriors like a fury, the violence of which might be seen by the redness which followed the strokes. The girl twisted and kicked about but was obstinately silent and, after having received about twenty severe strokes, her petticoats were put down by her mother, who exclaimed, 'There, that will teach you to stay on your errands and them tell lies to excuse it.'

She left the girl but, chancing to turn her head before entering the cottage, she observed the girl making faces at her. Roused by this, she darted at the girl, who was in a moment on her knee, and her clothes again flung up. The eagerness of the mother made her drop the rod and we had time to inspect the glowing bottom of the girl, the cheeks of which were red with the recent punishment.

The mother, mad with passion, now began to switch away at the thighs and buttocks of the girl; and it was evident that she made more impression, for the girl began to entreat for forgiveness. But the mother was inexorable: she kept rattling away without mercy and, after whipping her for I am sure full a minute, till her bottom was the colour of crimson, flung her down and quitted her, saying, 'You'll make faces at your mother again, you young harlot, I dare say.'

Oh! how this scene affected me; it roused my passions to a pitch of frenzy, and had we at that moment been in a place of greater privacy, and I had been solicited, I should have fallen a victim to the excitement. I walked with my impassioned companion who, after some artful interrogatives, drew from me an avowal, that I had not only enjoyed the whole of the scene we had witnessed together, but should dearly like to have been the administrator of the punishment if it had been inflicted on a girl so pretty as Sally Meadows.

We returned home. My father was out and Tom asked me to show him my boudoir, which my father had praised for its taste the evening before. Ah! how pleased was I to do anything to give the dear fellow amusement or delight. He praised my taste in the disposition of the furniture and general arrangement; spoke of my drawings, the beautiful shrubs which adorned the large balcony of the only window in the room.

'How beautiful,' he exclaimed, 'how elegantly planned! What ample admirable chairs for courting and what a voluptuous sofa.'

He came to me, and kneeling close by me, pressed me in his arms. A voluptuous languor crept over me; he saw it, and drew down my face to his. He rapturously kissed my mouth, and when I least expected it, his impassioned tongue burst between my lips.

What an electric thrill did this produce! I was absolutely filled with passion; but think, my dear Miss Wilson, what was my surprise when he produced from under his coat the identical rod with which the cottager's wife had whipped Sally Meadows. The sight of it made me giddy. I knew not what I did. I felt him lay his body across my thighs, his coat-flaps were thrown up, his trousers were entirely down, and nothing covered his naked posteriors but his shirt. His putting the rod into my hand had brought me to my senses.

'Oh! Tom,' said I, 'it must not be – I dare not proceed – do not ask me.'

He canted up his shirt, so as to leave his naked flesh entirely exposed to my view.

'My dear Betsy,' said he, 'don't baulk your wishes, you said you should have been glad to change places with the flogger this morning – gratify me – indulge yourself – we are alone – treat me as a truant – think me an idle boy that deserves chastisement.'

'Don't look at me then,' I said.

He promised. I took the rod and began to exercise it gently on his white buttocks. Oh! the delightful sawing through the air, the whisking sound as it met his flesh, the knowledge that his breeches were down, that the secret staff of life was lying on my limbs – kept from my naked flesh only by my garments. All this conspired to fill me full of the most unchaste wishes.

'Do I hurt you, my sweet fellow?' said I, in a voice of extreme tenderness.

'No, my love; use more strength – strike with more nerve – Ah! there – that's it – that's it, my sweet Betsy.' He now laid more in front of me, and I felt him falling in between my opening knees. As my clothes were down I did not heed this; indeed, my active strokes of the birch had changed the colour of the flesh cushions and I entered fully into the spirit of the adventure. He kept jolting his person in front of mine, at every motion of the rod and I, to hold him more secure, had worked myself nearer to him, and close to the edge of the sofa.

One of his arms was round my waist, the other grasped me lower down. My clothes, by his working gradually, got higher, which he seemed to be aware of, for his workings increased, and his long strokes pushed them higher at every heave of his body. My strokes upon his bottom continued and I found myself cutting him without mercy.

Oh! what a delirium I was in: he was now entirely between my open thighs – they expanded to admit him – Oh! I shall never forget the moment – new, intoxicating and delirious.

Something hard pressed against my thighs, then against my belly; it kept repeatedly bobbing against the most sensitive part of my body. I thought he was debauching me. I seemed to feel that he was really entering my – I had not power to prevent him; indeed, I found that I was spreading myself out, jutting up my body, and doing everything that I thought would facilitate his purpose.

I lost all sense of shame and of propriety. I urged him not to delay my happiness, that I was ready, and would bear anything for his sake. This I accompanied by an eager imitation of his motions. I met his thrusts; we went on in regular cadence; the rod fell from my nerveless grasp; my arms intuitively embraced his naked back. I cried, sighed, and fell back in a state of insensibility. I recovered. He was just in the act of getting from off my body. I now felt confused indeed and jumped up and made my escape in the greatest disorder into my bedroom.

Ignorant as I then was of man, I really believed that my virginity had been taken, and having bolted the door, I sat in a chair facing the looking-glass. I pulled up my clothes, and was surprised to find a very large portion of my shift completely wetted in front. This indeed, had saved me.

I looked at the wet – with amazement, and exclaimed, 'What a quantity – I am quite flooded – what an inundation – Heavens! if this had been deposited within my person!'

This thought, which at first alarmed me, inflamed me more on consideration and, amid a thousand extravagances, I eagerly proceeded to obtain all the gratification within my own reach.

When my intoxication had ceased, I found it necessary to change my linen. I accordingly dressed for dinner, taking as much pains with my person as possible, for which I was again rewarded by the extravagant encomiums of the young sailor. When we were alone, he took occasion to remark that my father had informed him that he wished to have a conference with him before dinner on the morrow, as he had something of importance to communicate.

The morrow arrived. My dear fellow was at my side and he again led me blushing and trembling to the boudoir. I had reassured myself into the supposition that he would not proceed to extremities with me from fear of consequence, our fancied relationship and from his pausing yesterday on the very threshold of happiness. This made me bold, though excess of passion kept me weak and trembling.

He again produced the rod; I tried to persuade him not to proceed. He heeded me not, but put down his trousers. He was kneeling on the sopha where I was sitting. He brought both my legs upon the sopha, against which proceeding I remonstrated, but could not prevent him. He now drew off his trousers, and kneeling between my legs, leaned forward to kiss me.

It was impossible for me not to see his shirt bolstering out in front of him, and my imagination was instantly at work. His soul-thrilling kiss set me in a blaze. He seemed to wish to uncover my neck; the removal of my neckerchief and half-a-dozen buttons undone behind, not only enabled him to lay my bosom entirely bare but my shoulders also. He made the most wanton observations on their whiteness, size and beauty; called them a most charming pair of pouting bubbies, and said he had no doubt my hidden beauties were equally voluptuous and desirable but what could exceed my surprise and admiration, when he pulled up his shirt, and discovered to me that monstrous things, about which I had so often dreamt and agitated myself, of a thickness and length perfectly frightful, as it stood in all its pride and stiffness.

I devoured its shape, head and appendages, as it started in convulsive throbs before me. He then tumbled me backwards – I had not the power to resist him, though I felt that he was lifting up all my garments and exposing my most secret parts. An exclamation of joyful surprise broke from him, as he caught a view of my person. My native modesty had made me close my limbs, which were now perfectly naked, but his hands opened them to their fullest extent, in spite of entreaties.

'How can you now, Tom, use me so! It's quite a shame to expose my person in this way.'

'I must, my dear, dear sister,' said he. 'What a bright, transparent skin! What beautiful legs! What round, white, soft, fleshy and voluptuous thighs! What a rough and hairy concern you have got here!'

'Really, Tom, you are too bad. You make my face burn like scarlet,' and I put both my hands over the *spot* he had named. They were soon, however, pulled off, and I found his fingers busily opening the hot and fiery cell of my virginity.

I could not prevent him – I lay fluttering like a wounded partridge – the victim of lust. If I looked up, the truncheon of love was throbbing before me and rendered me perfectly reckless of any consequences. Enjoyment I wanted and I facilitated all his endeavours for that purpose.

He placed a cushion under me – I was completely exposed to his touch – he opened the lips of the virgin slit; he touched the sensitive nerve; he laid down upon my body, and dividing the lips of my *moss-rose*, lodged the head of his capacious instrument between them. I still thought he meant to go no further. He put his arms round me – I clung eagerly to him, and abandoned myself to the transports of the moment. We kissed each other with fervour unceasingly.

'Have you ever been enjoyed, my sweet girl?' said he.

'Oh! never,' said I.

'Why cannot we give each other pleasure? You are ready for the amorous conflict – I am maddening for it. My instrument is throbbing against your eager avenue. Let me enter, my sweet girl – let me push it in but a short way.'

'Ah, no, no,' I exclaimed, 'cannot you be satisfied to do as yesterday?'

'Oh! Betsy,' said he, 'can I witness your impassioned look? Can I look at these throbbing breasts heaving with desire and not feel emotion? Can I know that I am now standing stiffly, ready for the encounter, placed at the very entrance of the portal of love, and that portal a virginity? No, no, impossible. I must – I must, by heavens – I must put it in!'

A gentle movement of his bottom sent the instrument lip deep; another, and the head was in; a third, I found opening the rose leaves of my pucelage. He was on the high way to happiness; I felt him every instant making more way, penetrating by inches. He hurt me, but I heeded it not – I was maddened, intoxicated and felt ready for sacrifice.

He had placed me so advantageously for his purposes that his most trifling movement told. I felt distinctly the fibres of his instrument as he advanced and drew back. He kept up a short and steady rocking motion, which provoked passion and made me, in spite of myself, reply to his movements. Oh! with what rapture did I meet his thrusts! How loud were my sighs! How ardent my expressions of delight!

'Oh, heavens!' I exclaimed, 'what pleasure. This is beyond my hopes – beyond my expectations. Oh! Tom, my dearest Tom, I will ever love you; do you love me, are you gratified?'

Kisses long and ardent followed these expressions, whilst the mighty engine kept working its way within me. I felt that the narrow limit was filled; I felt the head of the instrument distinctly. I still kept up, working my loins to meet him, and had flung my head back and shut my eyes, to enjoy the full swing of the imagination.

'Are you fainting, my sweet?' said he, 'are you dissolving?'

'No, my dear Tom,' I returned, hiding my face in his shoulder, 'but I think I soon shall.'

He began to move faster – I kept pace with him – our movements were violent. I cried, laughed and sighed by turns as I felt the intoxicating moment coming with furious haste upon me.

'Oh!' said he. 'My love – Betsy – my queen – sister – love – I am coming – I am coming – Oh! there!'

At this instant I found shot into my very vitals that hot liquid, so maddening to the female – so exquisite in its administration but so fatal in its consequences to the unmarried. I shrieked as the boiling juice was spouted into me; another followed; but before I had received a third, I had lost all remembrance of the scene in an hysterie.

Upon my recovering, I found myself sitting upright in the arms of Tom. My clothes were down certainly but my bosom was entirely bare and my hair, having got loose from the comb, hung over my naked shoulders, and I was in dreadful disorder. I threw my arms round the dear fellow's neck and sobbed upon his bosom, for my heart was full of the tenderest love for him. I wished him to leave me alone and he kindly complied, kissing me with a fervour that rekindled my desires. Had he pressed it, I should again have yielded – I felt I could refuse him nothing.

I went to my bedroom, and there found it would be necessary to change my chemise – Lord! Lord! how it was marked – the whole story of my virginity might be read upon its tail.

When I had dressed I went down to dinner and learned with sorrow that Tom had been sent by my father to a neighbouring town, to bring some papers from his lawyer. This evening I passed in a feverish impatience for he came not. He returned to breakfast in the morning. We met like lovers after a long separation.

During the morning I was in my boudoir, when my father entered, leading in my sweet ravisher. I could perceive from the countenance of each that something of importance had passed between them, and my father undertook to explain the cause to me.

'My sweet child,' said he, 'you are now come to years of discretion and I ought to explain a secret which, for motives not now necessary to give you, I have kept from your knowledge. Tom is not my son but the child of an old college friend whose finances were exhausted by play. You have hitherto looked upon him as your brother. Perhaps, in a year or two you could prevail upon yourself to accept him as a husband, for I mean to share my fortune between you.'

I could hear no more – I sank into the extended arms of Tom, who kissed me again to life. When I came to myself, I turned my eyes on my fascinating seducer.

'Did I hear aright? Are we, indeed, strangers in blood?'

A long kiss that half recovered me was the reply. We reeled to the couch – we both sank upon it. I drew up my clothes (think how shocking that was!) to be ready. He was in the act of unbuttoning his trousers when it occurred to me that the door was not fastened and that Papa might return.

I told Tom of it; he hastened to bolt it when he luckily heard someone coming. He gave me the signal. I jumped up. Adjusted my clothes and with a pair of old scissors began to trim the flowers in the balcony. My father entered and was delighted to see me so completely recovered. The rest of the day he spent with us.

What need I say more, my dear Miss Wilson? But during

the happy fortnight of Tom's stay, every moment we could pass in secret was devoted to passion. He left me only for a short time. He is to return next month, when I am to be a bride, and Tom is to go to sea no more. Think, my dear friend, how my young heart beats for that moment. Think of my impassioned dreams. I go over repeatedly all we have done together and feel that I must love this dear fellow for ever.

I remain, my dear friend,
Yours very faithfully,

ELIZABETH THOUGHTLESS

March, 1839

With Open Mouth

With Open Mouth has well-defined characters, a compelling plot and underlying themes that belong in the literary mainstream — and there's plenty of hot fucking too. What more could a discerning reader ask for?

Avelino, a handsome Spanish peasant, is seduced by Janice, a sophisticated older woman, and she takes him home with her to Barcelona. But he is out of place in the city and shocked by the lax sexual habits of Janice's circle. When he discovers that Janice and her aristocratic friend, Count Alvarez, live off the proceeds of brothels which exploit underage girls, he decides to inform the police. Instead he finds himself pursued by hired killers and flees the city driven by Janice, who has thrown in her lot with her honest peasant lover. In the mountains the killers catch up with them, shots are exchanged, Janice is killed and the car plunges over a ravine. Now, as they say, read on . . .

He was warm – comfortable and warm. That was the only thought for a long time. And then there was no thought. And again, much later there was the warmth and the comfort again.

Avelino opened his eyes and gazed at gloomy flickering rock above. The rock was flickering because near him there was a wood fire, fierce and warm. He was in a cave.

There was a movement somewhere near and an old woman's face was there looking at him, unsmiling but not unkind. They stared at each other for some seconds and then the woman called out; 'Maria, bring the soup; he's come to.'

Avelino understood nothing. He could see the entrance to the cave. It was slightly lighter than the inside. It must be night. He was lying on his back on some soft substance and he was covered with a blanket. When he tried to move a pain shot up his right leg and he was unable to move it.

The old woman knelt down beside him.

'Lie still,' she said quietly. 'You will feel better after the soup.'

Avelino lay back, relaxed and looked at the woman again. He felt he should know her, but he didn't. She was a big woman with a strong, lined face. Her clothes seemed to be a mixture of odds and ends. He was going to speak but then, somehow, the effort seemed too great and he didn't bother.

And then there was another woman beside the first, but much younger, a girl in fact. She was holding some sort of army mess tin with steam coming from it. She knelt down beside Avelino and her blue eyes were soft and a little shy as she looked at him. Avelino was aware that she was beautiful, but his mind wouldn't focus on the thought. He could think consistently only of the smell of the soup.

The old woman propped some logs and an old haversack behind him so that he could half sit up without moving his legs and the girl put the mess tin on his lap and raised a ladleful of the soup to his mouth.

Avelino sipped the soup as she fed it to him and although he said nothing, his eyes told how wonderful it was. The girl smiled.

'Would you like some bread and cheese?' she asked. 'It is not a proper meal; just something to restore your strength a little.'

He nodded and his eyes followed her without any clarity of thought. She was wearing a loose, fawn-coloured skirt with a white, cotton blouse. Her body was compact and she had the look of health which a lot of time spent in the sun gives to fair skin. To Avelino she seemed sweet and refreshing – and then he began to remember why she seemed refreshing.

He remembered the headlights chasing them, the spatter of shots, the hoping to reach the bend in time, the shattering of the back window, the blood trickling down Janice's head. He remembered but without any acute feeling. It seemed long ago and it seemed unreal. He hadn't been able to believe in it at the time and now all he felt was a certain curiosity and relief that it was over.

'What happened?' he asked, speaking, with effort, for the first time.

Nobody answered while the girl handed him a tin plate with bread and cheese on it. She retreated again into the shadows of the cave and the old woman looked down at Avelino. She had the strong face of a woman who had lived through and dominated herself through a great deal of unhappiness. She would sympathise in a practical way. She would be there to be relied on – but she wouldn't hide things in an effort to be kind.

'We found the car you were in at the bottom of a ravine,' she said. 'There was a woman in the car and she was dead. We brought you up here unconscious and you've been here for two days. You have a broken leg.'

Avelino automatically tried to move his leg – and winced at the pain.

'The car is smashed up. It's incredible that you're alive. Was the woman your wife?'

'No. She was just a friend.'

The old woman gazed at him reflectively for some moments. She seemed about to ask another question, but changed her mind instead and said simply:

'You'd better sleep again after you've eaten. Your leg will mend.'

Avelino slipped his hand under the blanket to feel his leg. He touched cloth and wood around his leg. They had made a rough splint for his leg.

'You are being very kind,' he said.

'Then you have been used to unkindness,' she replied. 'We are doing no more than human beings should do for one another.'

Avelino slept again and occasionally drowsily reawakened and then slept once more. During his waking moments he was aware of several people in the cave against the background of the fire always flickering.

When he awoke fully again a stocky, bearded man with a rifle was coming from the bright patch of light which indicated day at the entrance of the cave.

The man flung down a bunch of four rabbits on the rocky floor and there was a general movement towards them.

'Best catch in a long time,' the stocky man said, grinning in self-satisfaction. 'And there may be some more in the traps.'

As his grinning companions gathered round, Avelino was able to see that there was a third woman – youngish, but rough-looking from experience – and two other men, both wiry and apparently in their thirties. It was only now that he realised that this must be the band of gypsies Janice had spoken of.

The rabbits were gathered up by the women, taken to a roughly constructed wooden table, which by craning his neck Avelino could see deeper in the cave, and the work of skinning was deftly begun.

The stocky little man surveyed Avelino, lowered his rifle against a wall of the cave and advanced towards him.

'Well, you've had enough sleep to last for a lifetime, my boy,' he declared. His eyes were smiling and honest.

Avelino smiled back.

'Not long ago I expected to be put to sleep for a lifetime,' he replied.

The man looked at him for a moment.

'Sure. You were having a bit of trouble,' he said. 'But you're all right now. You're among friends and if you're still in trouble then you can let us know about it in your own time. There's no hurry.'

He called the other two men over.

'Rafael and Antonio,' he said, indicating each in turn. 'And I'm Emilio.'

Avelino reached up an arm – noticing, for the first time, that he was in his underclothes and that his arm was covered in scratches and bruises – and shook hands, telling his name.

'How long do you think it will take for my leg to mend?' he asked, addressing Emilio who appeared to be the leader of the band.

'A couple of months should set it right.'

Then seeing the look of consternation on Avelino's face, he added: 'But we'll make you some crutches in a day or two so that you can hop about to your heart's content.'

During the days that followed, Avelino slept and ate and talked with the gypsies; leaving out his peasant origin, he told them how he had become aware of the wide-scale vice in Barcelona and how he had been hounded for trying to expose it.

Emilio shook his head sadly when he had heard the story.

'Sure, whenever you get big masses of people together, trying to outdo one another you get trouble,' he said philosophically.

'And don't you get trouble often enough in a little group living in the mountains?' That was the elderly woman, Eva, his wife.

Everyone laughed. It was obvious their troubles were seldom directed against one another.

'Oh, we have our squabbles – but it's only because you're such a tyrant.' And everyone laughed again while Eva stood, arms akimbo in mock severity.

Soon Avelino was hobbling about on the crutches they made him. It was wonderful after so many days of confinement in semi-darkness to be able to move about in the sunlight. They were some distance from the point where the car had crashed over the ravine and he accepted the fact that he would have to remain with the gypsies until his leg had completely recovered. They had no transport and were more or less out of touch with the outside world. Their food consisted of the game they were able to kill, the wild fruit they picked, wine and an occasional liqueur which they brewed themselves from a sweet-smelling plant which grew in the mountains. Every so often they would make a trip into the nearest villages with their little carvings from wood and stone and gay trinkets. Then they would return with a few luxuries in the way of eatables and, perhaps, some fresh clothes and shoes – although their garments gave evidence of lasting them for ever.

They were a happy band who sang, sometimes danced with the instruments they made themselves and talked merrily all the time. To Avelino they seemed the happiest people he'd ever known. With them he began to feel at home. He learned to carve so that he could add his share to the supply of knick-knacks which went out into the world beyond, he gathered wood for the fires and did everything his handicap would allow.

As he hobbled, the girl Maria would often help him, catching hold of his arm or taking his hand to guide him. Although they had spoken very little, he became increasingly aware of her as a woman: the lithe swing of her buttocks and thighs beneath her skirt, the way her nipples jutted, slightly visible, on the summits of her impudent breasts.

She, too, would return the extra pressure of his hand and their eyes would meet in a smile.

All this did not pass unnoticed by Eva, who had summed Avelino up and decided she would give them every opportunity of getting to know each other.

When Avelino suggested one day that he should collect the rabbit traps – a long job as they were spread over the mountains, Eva demurred at first as he still had to walk with a stick, but then she thought better of it, telling Maria to go with him to show the way and help on the rough stretches.

On the way, it was Maria who slipped on some loose stones and fell against Avelino. He caught her in both arms and in the moment they were pressed together she looked up at him and he kissed her. It was a sweet, innocent kiss, behind which, when they drew apart, her eyes were laughing and happy.

'How often have you been kissed before?' Avelino asked with a grin.

'Oh often – when I was young, by my father.' Her blue eyes twinkled.

'Emilio is not your father?' It was a rhetorical question. Avelino was sure he was not.

Her eyes clouded.

'No. My father was killed fighting with the Republicans in the war – and my mother also. We have all been here, in the mountains, since the last days of the war. We are happy here and nobody bothers us.'

'What happened to you when your parents were killed.'

For some time she looked at him and he thought she was not going to answer.

'Some soldiers – Fascist soldiers took me away . . . I have been kissed before. There were three of them and they fought over me in a field near the town. They tore my clothes off and were going to rape me . . . but then they started fighting . . .'

A tear welled out of an eye and rolled slowly down her cheek and Avelino drew her to him, kissing her hair.

'Then Emilio came. He had known my father in the town. And he shot them all and brought me into the mountains with Eva and the rest. He was wonderfully kind. I shall never forget . . .'

Her voice broke off and she cried quietly against his chest.

Avelino felt a slow, strong rage simmering up inside him against the Fascist beasts who were going to rape Maria. He was astonished. He who had killed jealousy – to feel this passion boiling inside him again.

He kissed her forehead, her eyes, her wet cheeks and at last her lips again.

'I love you,' he whispered.

She clung to him, tightly, pressing her face against his chest, and then she looked up slowly and her eyes, glistening with tears, had a radiance. She pulled his head down and kissed him hard on the lips and then buried her face again in his chest.

When they returned to the cave, later, hand in hand, the bag of rabbits flung over Avelino's shoulder, Eva stood in the entrance watching their approach.

'Looks as if you made a good catch today,' she said, without looking at the rabbits. There was a deep smile in her eyes.

Time seemed to race by on the old calendar on which Emilio scratched off every day with a piece of charcoal as it passed. Eventually Avelino was able to walk without the stick, but he stayed on, 'convalescing', and nobody mentioned his departure.

During this time Avelino and Maria seldom had any time

alone. Their lovemaking took the form of looks, small gestures and a kiss during their short walks. Eva was aware of the relationship growing between them, but nobody else appeared to notice.

Avelino would watch Maria moving about the cave and the stifling of the desire that was in him – even to kiss her or put his arm around her grew steadily. Her slim back and waist as she bent over the cooking; the tightening of her skirt around her compact buttocks as she reached for something and the thrust of her breasts through the blouse – everything charged him with a great longing. Often, too, her eyes when they looked at him would change slowly from a laugh to a strong, almost glittering gaze and then would smile again slowly.

One day at supper Emilio announced that tomorrow they should take their wares and sell them in the markets of the villages. They needed to buy more ammunition and a new frying pan would be a good idea.

After some discussion it was agreed that everyone should go except Eva and Maria to look after the cave and Avelino to collect traps and provide a masculine element in case of any unforeseen emergency.

At the first twilight of dawn the little group started off with its bags and baskets on the long track from the mountains.

Avelino was glad he had not gone with them. He was quite content with the mountains. He could not gauge what his reaction would be to get back to the verge of civilisation again. When he thought of Count Alvarez and the others he was not even sure what was meant by civilisation. And above all he was happy to stay with Maria in the greater intimacy which was left.

During the morning, Avelino collected the traps while the two women gathered wood for the fire and washed some clothes in a stream not far from the cave.

After lunch, Eva, her face unemotional as always, regarded Avelino and Maria for a few seconds.

'Avelino, why don't you take Emilio's line and try to catch

us some fish for supper? There's a still part of the stream a couple of miles from here where he fishes.'

Avelino hesitated. He had hoped to spend more time with Maria.

'Of course, Maria will have to go with you to show you the way,' Eva added. 'Perhaps she might not want to do that.'

There was a slight smile on her face as they both raised their eyes to her uncertainly.

'Off you go,' she laughed, 'and be sure to bring back some good fish.'

They left a little later, Avelino shouldering Emilio's strong, home-made rod.

'Which way do we go to the fishing ground?' he asked.

'I don't know,' Maria said with a laugh. 'I've never been there before.'

Avelino stared at her for some moments, uncomprehending. Then he chuckled.

'Well, well,' he said. 'She really is on our side.'

'She's the sweetest person in spite of her austere appearance,' Maria said.

They walked for a mile or two, arms linked, into the mountains. Avelino had very little trouble with his leg now except for an automatic limp – a habit which would gradually die.

'Let's climb down to the stream and find somewhere to fish, now,' Maria suggested after a while. 'Will your leg stand it?'

'My leg will stand anything today,' Avelino replied.

She glanced up at him quickly with a look that was both shy and knowledgeable. She took his hand and they began to clamber and grope their way down the steep side of the ravine to the slim stream which frothed over the rocks below. On either side of the stream was a little border of red sand strewn with boulders and it was along one of these that they walked, Indian file.

They followed the stream for about another mile, searching all the time for a pool. The sun shone down from a cloudless sky, cut off only occasionally by a jutting crag above. Maria walked ahead and the slim, brown length of her calves seemed to gleam in the sunlight.

They found a pool at last, a broadening of the stream, an overflowing onto the sandy borders caused by a partial damming with boulders. A few weeds grew here and the water in places was deep and opaque. The rock side of the ravine was also scooped away forming a shadowed hollow overlooking the pool. A few shrubs and small trees even grew from the sand.

'How wonderful!' Maria exclaimed, looking around her and then up to the sun in delight. 'I've never been here before. It's a perfect spot.'

Avelino swung his small shoulder bag down to the sand and began to assemble Emilio's rod.

'I hope there are fish here,' he said. 'It looks a likely place.'

Maria stretched herself out happily on the sand and watched Avelino throw out the line and then wedge the rod firmly between two rocks.

'Now we'll see what happens,' he said coming back to where she was and lying down beside her.

'I'm sure you should take more interest in the line,' she smiled as he turned to look at her.

'There's much more future in looking at you,' he said.

Her slim fingers caressed his cheek. Her eyes were shining.

'I've never felt so happy,' she said softly. 'I would like this little fishing trip to go on forever.'

'Why shouldn't it go on forever?'

Her eyes clouded for a moment.

'Don't tease me, please. I had managed to forget for the moment. I know you will have to go away soon.'

Avelino pressed his cheek against hers. Her cheek was smooth and warm. He could feel the firm bones beneath the skin.

'I want you to marry me, Maria.'

For several seconds her breathing seemed to have stopped. Avelino caught her face in his hands and held it away from him. Tears were slipping down her cheeks. He pulled her body against his on the sand and held her close against him.

'What's the matter?' he asked. A horde of questions whirled in his mind. Questions that preceded a vision of happiness slipping away.

But her voice when it came up, small and muffled, from his chest was warm and doubt-dispelling.

'It's only because I'm so happy,' she whispered.

For a long time they lay together on the hot sand, the drifting line forgotten. Her body lay along Avelino's, clamped against him. Her head was buried in his neck, feeling secure there, not wanting to move away from the little aura of happiness which seemed to have surrounded them. As he ran his fingers gently over her hair, Avelino felt a purpose for living which seemed all at once better and simpler than his confused existence in Barcelona with its complications and lack of order.

Her hair was like sand running through his fingers, her body both that of a child happy in its protection and of a woman wanting to be a woman. And the happiness in him grew in the passing minutes as she moved slightly against him to a desire for the physical peak of the happiness, a desire that flushed his whole body with passion and tenderness at the same time.

He pressed hard against her and her breasts heaved against him with her rapid breathing. He ran his hands over her shoulders, down her back and strained the compact buttocks against him, feeling her firmness under the skirt.

Her face looked up to him, the eyes intense, lips parted and he kissed her on a mouth which crushed his and then opened in yielding.

'Can you forget the Fascists – or does this remind you?' he whispered, drawing his lips a centimetre from hers.

'I can forget,' she whispered back. 'But it would not be rape because I love you.'

A thrill twirled in Avelino's stomach and a tenderness pervaded him like a blush at her words. She wanted him to make love to her.

He kissed her again and an intuitional fire drove her body hard against his, wrapping one of her legs around his. She was completely ready.

Kissing her, running his lips over her face while her hands traced the contours of his head, Avelino moved a quivering hand up to her breasts. Then one of them was under his hand. His first really intimate touch of her body. He caressed it gently, a butterfly touch. It was firm and bulbous under his fingers. She wore no brassiere; she needed none and the sharp outline of her nipple hardened under his searching fingers.

His hand sought the buttons of the blouse, eased them gently undone and her hands squeezed his back tightly as he did so. She was half afraid now. But then his hand was tenderly fondling her bare breasts and she relaxed again, only her breathing betraying her anxious yearning.

The skin of her breasts was taut, like stretched tissue. Only around the nipples did it pucker into a little roughness of pattern.

She lay back now on the sand, under the hot sun, with Avelino leaning over her, his lips running down her neck, her neck stretched in longing, mouth slightly open. Her blouse flapped out on either side leaving her breasts exposed to the sun and Avelino's eyes.

He moved his mouth voraciously down her shoulders, sucking in the hollows until the flesh reddened and then his lips were on the hills of her breasts, drawing the nipples into his mouth, sucking them in like a whirlpool so that she whimpered slightly in her passion.

Her hands clasped his head, crushing him into the yielding

mounds of flesh. Her legs moved together as he sucked and then relaxed again in rhythm.

The smooth texture of her breasts – a magnet with his lips – created a sensual trembling in Avelino. His penis had jerked up into a violent rampancy of which he was hardly aware until her stirring thigh brushed against it so that he could feel the warmth of her leg through the skirt.

Avelino placed one of his hands on her abdomen, rubbing it gently, savouring the springy firmness of the flesh beneath. His fingers roamed over her hips, exploring the well-covered bones on which he would soon be lying.

Maria lay half beneath him, breathing heavily, but mainly passive, waiting to be led.

He slid his hand away down her skirt-covered thighs, aware of their roundness, down to her knees and below. Then his fingers met the flesh of her calf and were moving up again, this time under the skirt. He lingered around the knees, stroking the backs of them and then he was advancing up her thigh, up the light suppleness of the outside muscle.

Waiting, Maria was tensed, each breath seemed to fall over the other from her parted lips.

The thigh was smooth, glassily smooth until suddenly the fingers had reached the glossy silk of her briefs – the last covering of that desired area of her body.

She tensed a little more as the fingers probed under the leg of the briefs and the hand followed to hold, flesh to flesh, her buttocks.

Avelino felt that the buttons of his trousers would fly off. His belly was jerking furiously from his shortness of breath. The buttock was as smooth as the thigh: a lovely rounded, firm lobe of flesh which relaxed at last into his hand as he squeezed it gently and stroked it. His hand moved on relentlessly, curving in with the incurving of the buttock, gently rubbing that provocative canyon and then bridging it to fondle both buttocks together as Maria rolled slightly towards him.

Every breath Maria uttered now seemed to be a whispered exclamation, a whispered *oooooh!*

Avelino caressed her bottom for a long time, revelling in its texture. He felt in no hurry. The end was sure. He did not want to rush her. Did not want to rush himself.

At last he slid his hands round from her behind, under the briefs until his fingers were tickling her groin. He slipped his hand down, brushing the inside of her thigh until she was wriggling under him. And then he advanced upward again, under the tiny scrap of material which covered her vagina, until he was at the lips and could feel the moisture of her passion at his fingertips.

Maria snapped her thighs together – a sheer involuntary action – at the sensation of his fingers there at the place nobody had ever touched her before.

Avelino relaxed. He just tickled her thighs gently at their very summits until slowly she opened her legs again.

'Be gentle, Avelino,' she said softly.

He lowered his head and kissed her lips in answer and then his finger had entered the long moist groove of flesh and was searching for the deep well hidden there, while Maria gasped against the pressure of his mouth.

She made no further effort to close her legs against him. Her arms went around his neck and clung there. Her legs were apart. From this point she was giving without question.

She gasped again and gave a jerk as Avelino's probing fingers found the tight cavity and pushed in. The flesh was warm against his middle finger. After a while he felt the channel expanding and contracting around his finger as she waggled her hips in agitation, breathing his name as if she were going to repeat it for ever.

Avelino withdrew his finger gently from the passage and found the firm little clitoris. Maria jumped and gasped as he rubbed it, catching it between his thumb and index finger. He played with it for a long time, kissing her mouth, neck and breasts all the time.

As her breathing began to grow thick, he thrust two fingers up into her belly, pushing against the confining pressure so that she uttered a little scream.

'Am I hurting you?' he breathed.

She shook her head from side to side in answer. Her face was screwed up in passion.

Avelino worked with his fingers widening the passage, accustoming it to what was to follow. His penis seemed to be bursting; he was afraid he would have an orgasm without entering her. At last, as her gasps changed to a gentle moaning, he slipped his hand from her vagina and pulled her briefs down her hips.

Maria lay there, quivering all over while he took off her skirt. Her hips were rounded, compact like her buttocks; the hair was golden.

Avelino bent and kissed her belly and she pressed his face to her navel. He moved his head up to her breasts again while his fingers plucked at the buttons of his trousers. He could stand it no longer. He must have her now.

He kicked off his trousers and pants and his penis was hot, so hot and rigid along her thigh. The sun burned his buttocks and his legs felt mobile and free, licentious.

He slipped his fingers back to her vagina and she began to squirm. The skin had drawn back on him and his knob seemed to have bloated like a drowned animal and become as moist. A little trail of seminal fluid made a snail's path across her thigh.

Maria's hand slipped under his shirt and stroked his chest, moving around his muscular back as she moaned her passion.

He took her hand at last and drew it down to the massive swelling of his rod. Veins were standing out on his penis, not violently, but visible – blue and some almost red.

Her hand felt cool as she touched him, cool enough to make him jump and grit his teeth with the sensation.

She ran her fingertips tentatively over the top surface back to where the tube disappeared into his body as if she were measuring it. Then she drew them back on the underside.

Avelino's loins were flaming with heat as he pulled her hand now to his testicles so that she could stroke their hairy expanse. She stroked his genitals tenderly, lovingly, almost without embarrassment. She clasped his organ in her hand as if to feel how it would be inside her – and all the time her gasps were growing as Avelino flicked her clitoris and thrust his fingers into the soft wet channel.

She began to breathe his name again as if she were reading a poem with all her emotion and Avelino swung his body gently onto hers, his hips on her half-parted thighs.

'Oh darling!' she breathed.

She opened her eyes; her whole face proclaimed that she was his for as long as he wanted her, and she kept her eyes on him as she gently drew her thighs apart and he guided his penis to the spot.

His great, swollen, pulsating knob moved into her, hesitated at the brim of the cavity and then pushed gently but firmly into her, forcing through the ring of flesh, then tightly enclosed as if in a quicksand.

Maria had cried out as he drove into her and her eyes had screwed up, her thighs flattened to the hot sand.

Avelino felt a great, indescribable relief sweep over him, a gorgeous, sensual, blood-sucking relief as if here was home after a terrible day.

Maria twined her arms around his neck, burying her face in his, abandoning the rest of her body to the delirium of the union.

Avelino thrust in, drew out, thrust in, farther, farther in a deep burying of himself into her. Her passage clasped his penis in an embrace that became almost painful as he lost more and more of it between her legs. She writhed, brushing her buttocks in the sand as he rammed in. Her nipples were taut on his chest as he squirmed against her uplifted thighs, worming in with a grinning pressure which contorted his face and made a vein stand out in his neck.

Maria was there, naked beneath him, receiving his stiff pinion like a sword embedding itself in her vagina. She was sweet and virginal, but not ashamed of her passion, gasping and panting in the fury of moving to the climax.

'I love you,' he whispered as his penis slid solidly inwards.

Her thighs clasped his hips momentarily in response and then flung open again in complete giving, complete cooperation.

Avelino slipped his hands down her sides and dug through the sand to hold a smooth buttock in each. He slipped his hands forward and drew her thighs up farther, feeling the moist staff of entry, wondering at this incredible sensation which took up his whole being and yet found its physical quality only down there in that dovetailing. His hands went back under her buttocks, straining them up to him with each deep insertion and her panting took on a fury, like the steady puffing of a train.

Avelino, his head swaying on his shoulders, eyes dilating as he looked at Maria's impassioned face, felt the throbbing of his penis, becoming a heavy drone of sensation, catching in his stomach as the excitement skewered there.

Maria's tortured eyes were open now as he bobbed on her and they looked into each other's anguished eyes as their breath became uncontrollable. Avelino felt the twisting and churning in his loins, the desperate excruciating moment before the deluge. Maria's legs were flailing wildly, her hips sliding in the sand. Her panting became a long groan and, as Avelino felt restraint slipping away, her eyes dilated and she clutched him like a dying woman, the groan choked in her throat and her hips locked into his in a furious pressure. The flood of climax swept from her loins as Avelino felt himself lost . . . lost . . . and then the unbearable bursting into her, the shooting and shooting and shooting again of his hot cascades of sperm way up into her belly.

* * *

Few fish were caught that day, but that was not important. Maria and Avelino, both happy, she a little shy after the moment of passion, returned to the cave where Eva's knowing eyes would have, perhaps, embarrassed them if they had been able to think of anything but each other.

It was not until the return of the rest of the band the next day that Avelino announced that he and Maria were going to be married and then there was a general celebration with the wine and a couple of chickens that Emilio had brought back from the village. Everyone got very merry in the flickering light of the camp fire, but as the hours passed Eva looked sadly at Avelino.

'We're very happy for you,' she said softly. 'But there are some things an old woman thinks of at these times other than that she had good times in her youth.'

'What's the matter?' asked Avelino.

'I'm just thinking that you'll be taking Maria back to the city with you, or maybe to find some work in a town far from here and we'll see neither of you again.'

'No. You're wrong, Eva,' Avelino replied quietly. 'This life is too good. I've made my decision and Maria is happy. We're getting married in the nearest church, we're taking a tent and going to tour the mountain for a few days and then we're coming back here to you. This is the sort of simple life that needs no analysing. You accept it. You work to no pointless, soul-destroying end, you grow or capture your food, you make your clothes, you fish, you sing, you walk in the mountains. Your relations are clear and simple and honest because there's nothing to make them otherwise, nothing to corrupt them. We're here amongst our few good, trustworthy friends for our lives. Don't worry.'

Emilio leaned round the fire from where he had listened, as everyone else had listened.

'We'll drink to that, Avelino. We'll drink to that.'

Maria's hand covered Avelino's on the floor of the cave as the mugs were raised and Avelino felt a warm glow of love and friendship all around him. Everyone here a friend he could trust.

Later that night, lying on his bed, with the other humps around him with were Emilio, Rafael, Antonio and, farther back in the cave, the women, Avelino thought of Barcelona. He thought of the vice going on there. He thought of the chateau. He thought of the luxury he'd had, of Juanita, Theresia, of everything. All he wanted now was peace. Those who wanted anything else could have it. But he had found his peace and he was staying with it. He loved Maria. He had nothing to leave the mountains for.

He looked at the stars through the lighter patch of darkness which was the cave entrance. He supposed idly that he could after a time go back to Barcelona if he really wanted to. Juanita would be happy to see him and willing to go anywhere. A little luxury would certainly seem fantastic after living in a cave. Yes, he could go back to Barcelona, to luxury.

The fire flickered still, throwing fluid patterns into the darkness. Somebody stirred in his sleep.

And Avelino, lying awake in the dim firelight, wondered if he ever would.

The Carefree Courtesan

In the canon of erotica, sometimes it seems all paths lead to Paris. 'Seated here in afternoon leisure in my luxurious boudoir on the Boulevard Haussmann, a feeling of exuberant self-satisfaction overwhelms me. Last night, in this very room, I entertained no less than a president . . .' writes the elegant Madeleine, heroine of all that follows. But the road that leads to lucrative assignations with wealthy dignitaries is a long one. It winds from Plattsburg, USA and a life of farm-girl drudgery as plain Louise Smith, to New York and the grisly realities of medical school.

The horrors of the dissecting room are not the only ones Louise must experience. She has a rich lover, Charley, who worships the ground she walks on – or so she believes. Then she returns home unexpectedly from an unpleasant day at the hospital and learns a different kind of lesson . . .

Riding home in the cab, I revolved the horrors of the past few minutes in my mind. I was sick to death of the whole ill-smelling graveyard of medical science. I had wanted to learn from life but not from corpses. Rather would I pry with my bare hands in the bowels of a living person than touch my scalpel to the empty mockery of a dead person's shell. One thing was now certain: I could not go back to that dissecting room, to that table, and work under that same cruel leering light.

Wearily I climbed up the stairs to our apartment, unwilling to be seen even by the elevator boy in my present disturbed condition. I had to rest my head against the doorpost to collect sufficient strength and steadiness to insert my key in the lock. I entered the sitting room. There was no one there. The lights were out. I was just about to call Clementine to help me off with my things when her voice, coming from my boudoir, arrested me.

'No – please sir – not here – not now! Mistress may return at any moment and catch us. Won't you wait and come around in the afternoon sometime again when mistress is at school? It would mean my discharge if she found us here.'

'Discharge, hell! Who do you think pays the bills around here?' I blanched. Was this another hallucination? It was Charley's voice.

He went on. 'Come on, kid. Let's knock it off now. Your mistress won't be back for hours yet. Here, have some champagne. Now, to the bed with you, and do your stuff!'

I could not believe my ears. If Charley had been lying to me every time he told me so earnestly that I was the only woman on earth that he wanted, I would simply – well, I would simply lose all faith in men.

Silently I trod over the heavily rugged floors and approached my room, to disclose myself and sever all relations with him immediately. With no intention of eavesdropping, I stood boldly in the open doorway; but unable to master any words to express my indignation, I merely remained stationed there, waiting for them to see me. Clementine was on her back on the bed – my bed – her eyes closed and her hips wriggling expectantly, or perhaps in preliminary practice. Charley had his back toward me, and was so busy uncovering the mulatto wench that even if he had been facing my way he would not have seen me. Up went her white apron and skirt, disclosing her lithe but substantial thighs, encased in black silk stockings up to the garter, and above that bare flesh that would easily pass for white.

Not satisfied with unveiling her to the waist (the little hussy wore no underwear) he rolled up her dress to her very chin. Reluctantly, I had to admit to myself that her figure was not bad. Her breasts, if anything, appeared firmer and more outstanding than mine, more conical than round, coming to two sharp pointed peaks that lent her a sort of fetching impertinence. Except for the region around her nipples, which was of a coffee shade, her skin was only a trifle more tanned than that of the average white woman. Her pubic hair, too, seemed thicker and darker and less silky than that of a Caucasian.

But my faithful Charley does not give me much time for either reflection or observation. Drawing his weapon forthwith, not wasting time fondling or kissing (somewhat to my relief), he takes up his position at the breach. Then, with a tremendous shove, as if thinking perhaps of the difficulty he had with my maidenhead, he charges fiercely inward. But if he flattered himself that there were obstacles to overcome, he must have been sadly disappointed – for he falls in as suddenly and completely as if he had stepped into a bear pit. Generous as was the size of his engine, yet it was not comparable to those that the members of her own race are credited to possess — and it was no doubt with huskier and more gigantic devices that her cavern had been explored and exploited — and now he is floundering helplessly about inside her, seeking no doubt in vain to reach bottom or touch sides.

To offset this overspaciousness however, Clementine launches upon a campaign of concentrated movement that I watch with growing envy. Wrapping her legs tightly about his back and throwing her arms wildly about his neck — a familiarity which I hoped he would resent with a 'Here now! This fuck is off!' but which brought no such interruption — she thus suspends herself entirely from his body. When, with his knees and hands upon the bed, he raises himself for another dive into the abyss, she comes up clinging to him, much like an agile ape hanging to the bottom of a strong bough. With her whole underside thus unimpeded by pressure upon the bed, she proceeds to perform a series of furious gyrations with her buttocks and the hollow vaginal cylinder that surrounds her visitor's piston, which actually sets me dizzy. With quick circular and spiral motions, she manages to keep all sides of her mortar in rapid successive contact with his pestle, thus compensating with artful vaginal counterfeits what she lacks in snugness and tightness and overcoming the disparity of size.

I cannot imagine myself performing the love act with such unabashed eagerness and furious activity as she. At best, I can be responsive or abandoned but rarely so aggressive in movement. But witness the effect on Charley, who is soon gasping in admiration, 'God! But you can do it!' His own attempts at movement are ridiculously futile alongside the mad grinding and pumping of the female wildcat hanging onto him.

Now, the climax of her efforts approaching, she suddenly changes from her rotating centrifugal tactics to a quick direct up-and-down motion, rubbing her joy button upon his member with a frank directness that must have exceeded in effectiveness anything that man's blundering motion could do in dispensing pleasure.

'Fuck me hot!' she pants in ecstatic elation, but Charley's ensuing efforts are an insignificant sideshow compared with the circus of rapid acrobatics that she performs.

Soon she brings on for him that divine discharge which without her active help he could not have engineered for himself in less than a quarter of an hour. Gasping with the supreme paroxysm of pleasure, he collapses upon her and, as he shoots his sperm into her body, he murmurs, perhaps from habit, perhaps irresistibly, 'I love you!'

Since that dark moment, dear reader, I have heard these words spoken on so many frivolous occasions that they have become meaningless to me. What a man or a woman says at the moment of sexual orgasm is no more to be held against him or her than what is said when one is drunk. I have had men gasp to me at such times everything from 'God!' 'Mother!' 'My sister!' 'My wife!' to 'Oh! You darling bitch!' or 'I will love you forever!' or 'I could rip you apart!' every form of endearment, the wildest promises, the most murderous threats – all to be forgotten immediately. Perhaps Charley had his eyes closed and was thinking of me at the time. Who knows? But at that moment, his words added insult to injury.

Blind with rage, I wanted to rush upon him and strike him with my fists, to break furniture and mirrors, to denounce him and tell him I had seen all. But suddenly it occurred to me that to do so would be to admit that I had been eavesdropping. I backed away from the open door. I was stifling with hate and anger, with the heat of the lustful scene I had just witnessed, with the still lingering malodor of my earlier miserable experience. I had to get into the air and think! I left the apartment quietly.

It was after ten o'clock. I sat on a bench in the nearby park and tried to straighten out the tangle of my thoughts and emotions. I was not jealous. If I had been in love with Charley no doubt I would now have been bent on murder; but I had looked too objectively upon him – upon all of life, for that matter. Faithfulness? Well, he had never hidden the fact that there had been many women before me. I could scarcely read an agreement for chastity into our relations. Vanity? Yes, that was it. Hurt pride. That he should resort to a little wench, so far beneath him in every way, when I was available to him. That my favors should be of insufficient strength to bind him to me, if not forever, at least for the duration of our affair. The piquancy that a man finds in a change of cunt was a principle that I would not recognize. I knew only that, in all modesty, I was more attractive than Clementine and a better piece all around. Consequently his action was an insult that merited punishment or vengeance.

Revenge – to throw myself into the arms of the first man that came along! That would be the only way to even accounts. It did not occur to me at the time that Charley had paid generously for my virginity and chastity, not I for his. I was just a woman whose vanity had been hurt. Too much reason could not be expected of me under the circumstances. Yet, even as I revolved my plan for vengeance in my mind, I decided that it might be best, after all, to postpone action for a while. I was in no mood for men anyway.

I walked down to Broadway and found a public telephone, called Nanette and asked her to meet me downtown at midnight, called Charley and told him hurriedly that I would work late and he needn't wait for me. I did not return to the apartment at all that evening. Nanette and I spent a delicious solacing night together at a hotel for women only. I told her everything. We agreed that men were detestable.

When I saw Charley next day, I gave him no inkling that I knew of his escapade and, of course, he volunteered no information. There was, however, in his appearance, or at least so it seemed to my knowing eye, something remorseful and chastened. He even seemed a bit ashamed of himself and, as if to make amends, treated me more tenderly; but as a woman I could not quite forgive him. When in the evening he took me to bed earlier than was his practice, I could not help but feel that he did this deliberately to avert suspicion of his recent infidelity. When he had entered me, I cooperated with him to bring on his own ecstasy but I held myself back entirely. I might lend him my body but I could not give myself to him.

There was a deep reproach in his eyes as he finished alone. This had never happened before. It hurt his male vanity. Not to wound him too deeply however, I took up my movement anew for the sole purpose of bringing on my own discharge. He remained still within me. Like the Grecian women of old, who would spit themselves on the artificial phallus of a statue of Iachus their satyr god, I worked myself up and down with an economical maximum of movement and thus brought on my own critical orgasm. He didn't like my impersonality. It flattered him so little. And it wasn't much fun for him, having me wriggling on his sensitive penis just after he had come and when a little intermission is generally necessary before a man can enjoy further friction.

With such little subtleties did I vent my woman's wrath upon him – indirectly, without committing myself. Our affair, which till recently had filled me only with a conviction of its permanence, now seemed a thing drawing to a close. Charley was pained. He guessed that some intuition had made me wise to his little interlude. He tried to bribe my forgiveness with prodigious gifts of clothes and jewels. I did not discourage him. Jewels had an easy money value. Looming in the offing was the time when I would be on my own again. With the disappearance of love, a woman becomes as shrewd and calculating as before she has been naive and sincere.

'I don't think I'll go back to school this year,' I told him offhandedly toward the end of the holiday recess. 'I just don't feel like it.' He was surprised but pleased. Perhaps with the burden of my work lifted, we could once more become the blithesome companions we had been.

I tendered my resignation and the ensuing days were idle days. And the devil finds work for idle hands to do. There was a handsome page boy of about sixteen who was employed by the house to render odd services to the occupants. He was from upstate, just as I, and his fresh, rosy-cheeked brightness reminded me of the days preceding my own loss of innocence. Lots of times I would call him to get me some postage stamps or some toilet article from the drugstore and he would gaze at me with that open worshipful admiration that so eloquently proved that women were to him a still unfathomed mystery. It was just this clean, wide-eyed innocence that captured my interest. Sometimes I would send for him on some pretext, just to see how prettily he blushed when I complimented him on his light golden hair, his perfect complexion, or his graceful gentlemanly bearing.

On one such idle afternoon, I was lying about in a negligee, reading a copy of *The Memoirs of Fanny Hill* which a bookseller had just picked up for me at rather a preposterous price. Charley was at the races. It was Clementine's afternoon off. It was indeed an inflaming situation. I, a young lady of healthy erotic tastes – alone – with the greatest pornographic masterpiece of all time – and my imagination. Soon I found myself writhing about voluptuously as the vividly drawn erotic pictures writhed before my mind. My hand unconsciously caressed my body and came to rest in that sensitive slough whither most things gravitate in a woman's life. I would have thrilled myself with my hand, something I hadn't had occasion to do in ever so long a time, had not the passionate scene I was following come suddenly to an end – as such things will.

Hurriedly, I read on, anxious to join in on the very next arousing passage. Fanny comes home one day unexpectedly to find her worthy master betraying her with a slovenly servant wench – the similarity between her and my own recent misfortune – and I suppose something like this happens in every woman's life, whether she discovers it or not – awoke all my former resentment. I read on. Yes, Fanny seeks revenge – as what woman would not? She seduces a handsome young boy who is in her master's service. What could be more logical? Apart from that tremendous oversized penis that the page, despite his youth, possesses – and that is merely part of the author's dramatic scheme of making every prick she encounters larger than the one before (and even the first one is the largest of all when she meet it again toward the end of her career). My own adventures showed no such perfect architectural design. But I am ahead of myself. My amorous state, my aroused resentment against Charley, and most of all the utterly delicious wickedness of seducing a spotless virginal boy, of giving him first glimpse of heaven and his first knowledge of the wonder of woman – all this appealed to some deep submerged desire within and set my pulse beating wildly.

The book fell from my lap – its insidious work done. The young page, Tommy, was just the thing. Desire alone would never have brought me to what I was about – nor would revenge alone; but the two motives together were irresistible.

I rang for the page. He was not long in making his appearance. I received him as I was, in my intoxicating dishabille, lying on the bed.

'Tommy,' I said, 'come closer. You see, your friend is ill.'

'You look fine to me, ma'am.'

'Oh ho! What a cavalier! Come here. What do you know about women?'

'Nothing much, ma'am – except you are the prettiest woman I've ever seen.'

'Thank you, Tommy. Already I feel better. I was going to send you for some headache powders but perhaps if you keep me company a bit, I'll get well without. Here, sit by me on the bed.' And in settling him beside me, I made as if carelessly to give him a little glimpse of my luscious breasts. His eyes were riveted upon my bosom and he was blushing furiously. I took his hands.

'Oh, how nice and cool your hands are, Tommy. Do you mind if I put them to my forehead?'

He was as in a trance, still gazing at my bosom, where the flimsy half-transparent lace and silk of my negligee drooped down to allow a tantalizing view of part of two round swelling globes, with a soft valley between leading the eye and the imagination down and down.

'What are you staring at so?' I went on. 'Don't you know what these are?' and I led his hands to the soft-contoured objects of his inspection. 'Don't be afraid. Your mama had these, did she not? And your sister? Now tell me, are mine as nice?'

Timidly he handled the exquisite flesh of my breasts but at every attempt to speak he choked in his throat, so overcome was he. The innocence of his touch served only to inflame me doubly. Was I experiencing the incestuous desire of a mother to take her child into her and so perpetuate herself by the seed of her own body? Or was it just a lasciviousness to which innocence lent a stirring fillip? I only knew that my own countenance was beginning to burn as hotly as the boy's.

I drew his face down to my scented bosom. His soft hot lips kissed me there. 'Do you like to play with me, Tommy?' I murmured. 'Then go and lock that door.'

He sprang up, turned the key and came back at once. While he was away, I quickly opened my negligee a little in front, leaving uncovered all of my legs and part of my thighs. He was by my side now, torn between the two sets of views open to him.

'Will you remove my slippers, Tommy, please?' I asked, extending my bare legs.

He hastened to obey – gently removed them – and kissed the arches of my feet with uncontrolled ardor. Encouragingly,

I played with his hair, then, reaching for one of his hands, placed it high up on my bare thigh.

'Oh, how nice and smooth you are!' he gasped, 'and so beautiful!' His fingers moved tremulously back and forth above my knee.

'Am I smooth all over?' I asked, my voice a little cracked by the intensity and diabolical lasciviousness of my feelings. He looked into my eyes worshipfully, questioning. I nodded my head.

'I don't mind a bit, Tommy – you're such a dear boy. Go ahead.'

More boldly his hands now wove their caressing way around and upward. The suspense became unendurable as he approached my burning center spot, and to bring the moment of contact nearer, I wriggled my whole body downward to meet his blundering hand. At last his fingers reached the tangled silky outposts. Startled, he quickly glided over the hill of love and caressed my lower abdomen, looking extremely abashed. I sighed with disappointment, but I could easily forgive this further proof of the innocence which I so longed to destroy.

'Tommy,' I said softly, 'am I so hideous that you refuse to look at me?'

'Oh no!' he expostulated, and guardedly, he let his hand run down my body to that mysteriously shaded meeting place that, when all is said, remained the region of greatest fascination for him.

'If you're afraid to look at it,' I laughed, 'you might hide it with your hand.' With a combination of anxiety and hesitancy he did so – finally mustering enough courage to insert a finger in the slit as I slowly edged my thighs apart to aid him.

I drew him up beside me on the bed and, with my lips slightly parted, invited his awkward but ardent kisses. Then, opening my negligee all the way down the front, I brought him in close to my naked, glowing form. As his hands caressed blindly about my bosom and belly, my own fingers went softly to his trousers where a bulge, not too phenomenal but yet interesting, merited my investigation. Undetected by him, I opened all his buttons – then softly inserted a finger. He sprung back in fright, then, seeing that my entire front was nude, he buried his face for shame between my breasts.

I laughed delightedly at this youthful compliment. 'Have you ever had a woman before?' I asked. He did not seem to comprehend. 'Have you ever played this way with a girl or a woman before?'

'Oh no!' he reassured me earnestly, blushing anew.

'Well then, since you are in love with me, Tommy, and since I'm very fond of you, we're going to do something very nice—' I was beginning to breathe heavily with the weight of gathering desire, 'and you mustn't fear anything I do.'

With these words, unable to brook further delay, I reached into his trousers and brought out his part. It was scarcely half as large as Charley's, dear reader, but when will people abandon the fallacy that size is the only criterion of pleasure? It was only about four inches long and an inch thick – all that could be expected of the untried and unused plaything of a boy; but it was stiff – and that is what counts most to a woman.

His eyes closed in grateful pleasure as I gently stroked his white pulsating part. Hugging him close to me, I slowly turned onto my back, bringing him over me. Then, with our bodies in the proper position relative to each other, I spread wide my thighs, and myself coupled his throbbing pego to my anxious, hungry cunt. His utter awkwardness made this process not an easy one but, at the same time, it delighted me, for it was yet further evidence of his innocence. With the little muscle that guards the entrance to my cunny, I clasped the head of his penis. Then, giving him the motion by the rhythmic rise and fall of my hips, I asked him to copy me. Fitfully and irregularly he did so, but on his first really vigorous move, his member was torn from my cunny's grasp.

Once more I placed it in position. This time however, bringing my thighs together and clasping his penis tightly between the lips of my vulva which, moist and overflowing with the excretions of my own unbearable excitement, gave him sufficient play without danger of losing him again.

So tensed was I for pleasure, so maddening was this wicked situation and so delicious his irregular, unexpected little motions within me, that my climax came on almost immediately. As I began writhing and moaning in the extremity of my ecstasy, Tommy suddenly stopped and asked solicitously 'Do I hurt you, ma'am?'

'Oh no, dear boy!' I gasped, crushing him closer to me. 'Keep on! I love it! Only faster!'

He complied. At once I was bathed in bliss. He kept on with his delightful pressures and titillations of my clitoris and vulva. I had expected him to go off almost immediately and here he was outlasting me.

'Do you like it, Tommy?' I asked, as with my motions I now regulated the rhythm. His speechlessness was the most eloquent possible answer. His pretty blue eyes were clouding over, dim and misty with pleasure. For a moment I felt like a goddess bestowing beneficences; but then my rearoused clitty demanded my attention. As if my life depended on it, I squirmed and strained to get the utmost from every contact, to myself join in the boy's approaching orgasm. My efforts, as all such dear attempts, were crowned with success. Just as he collapsed upon my soft generous body, quivering and pouring a remarkable torrent of hot sperm into my vulva, I brought myself up to him with a last thrust, sending down my corresponding internal secretions and causing my drenched cunt to twitch spasmodically around his organ.

Voluptuously we lay thus for a time, then, drying and replacing his part, I pledged him to secrecy, promising to let him come and see me again. So overwhelmingly grateful was he to me for his initiation into the secret rites of Venus that I had difficulty wresting his arms from about my neck and sending him away.

Charley, of course, suspected nothing that evening when he entered into possession of what he still deemed his exclusive private territory.

'Ah,' I thought to myself as he fucked me, 'if you think that yours alone is the delight of possessing many, of comparing partners, and the satisfaction of concealing a wicked secret, you are wrong.' And stimulated by such thoughts, I enjoyed the connection much more than I would show.

In the following weeks, I saw increasingly more of Nanette. Freezing out Charley as I was, yielding but not often giving myself, I had need of some reliable satisfaction, and there is nothing so dependable in this respect as a delicious mouth to cunt *soixante-neuf*. As for Tommy, I lost interest as quickly as he lost his innocence. Handsome as he was, his unsophisticated mentality could not long bear me company. I was very kind to him and tipped him generously at every opportunity but, as for the rest, I told him that what we had done was very wicked and could not be repeated. Imagine! Nanette, on the other hand, was always ready with some intriguing story of the goings-on at her place, and with such stimulations our practices were made ever more enjoyable.

More important still was the data I was avidly gathering from her on Paris – for, dear reader, with the waning of the last bond that held me to crude Yankee-land, my intention of moving to France became definitely crystallized. I confided my intentions to her. Though sorry to lose me, she was glad for my sake. Perhaps she would be able to join me there some day soon. Meanwhile, she aided me with information of every conceivable sort, with concentrated lessons in her language, and with numerous references and addresses of friends. Before long, I felt as if I could find my way about Paris blindfolded.

Secretly, I made reservations for a future trip to Europe. In those days, a first-class passage on the Cunard liners was only about eighty dollars – and of course, this amount was an insignificant part of the few thousand I was able to realize on my jewels. Unknown to any but Nanette, I bought a trunk which I filled with such of my gowns and possessions as I wished to take with me, and stored it at the steamship company's piers. There remained only to affect a satisfactory final break with my protector – and that was not difficult.

As the springtime approached, with its renewal of sexual urges in mankind, I made no effort to come up to Charley's requirements. I never told him nay – and yet at the same time I managed things so that he rarely asked for another. Soon he made no attempt to conceal his dissatisfaction, though he was still unwilling to give me up.

After starving him as much as possible, I set the stage for my finale. To Clementine, from whose attitude I gathered there had been resumption of engagements, I made a gift of a number of my dresses, stockings and unmentionables, insisting that she appear at all times clothed only in the most alluring manner. From the standpoint of flaunting, outright provocativeness, she soon had me far outdistanced.

At length my day arrived. Charley was spending the afternoon with me. I kept Clementine much in evidence. My clothes and her natural attractiveness did the rest. Soon most of his glances were for her alone. He watched the lascivious motions of her hips in a manner that I would have resented ordinarily, but which now made me quite glad.

When I felt sufficiently assured of his interest in her, I pretended suddenly to remember that I had some important shopping to do. Charley made no effort to dissuade me. In fact, he could scarcely conceal his eagerness to have me go.

'How long will you be gone?' he asked.

'Oh, for quite a long time,' I said.

I left, but went only as far as the street, then, timing before my mind's eye the procedure for overcoming the chaste objections of even the most bashful maid, of leading her to the bedroom and maneuvering her unwilling fall – allowing even time for engineering the entrance into the tightest conceivable cunt – I returned to the apartment, admitting myself quietly.

'Fuck me hot!' were the first, now familiar words that met my ears. I presumed that things were nearing the proper crisis. Humming aloud, I walked ostentatiously into the boudoir. This time Charley was at the bottom of the amorous heap, lying on his back, his trousers down. Upon him, her clothes high above her hips, uncovering her splendid thighs and buttocks, rode Clementine, with a fury equalled only by the charioteers in the days of Ben Hur.

He saw me enter and made as if to rise. But Clementine in the complete savagery of her lust would not let him up, but glancing around for a moment, continued her passionate pumping contortions. Hers was the right idea after all. As long as she was caught, she might as well get the full benefit of her misdemeanor.

'Don't mind me' – I made my speech clearly, indifferently – 'and don't stop on my account by any means. I have merely returned for my traveling bag and some clothes. I am sailing for Europe this very evening. Now, children, just go ahead and have a nice time while I get my things.' And playfully, I slapped Clementine's heaving posterior.

By the time I had hurriedly thrown my remaining possessions into my valise, Charley stood before me, nervously readjusting his trousers. Whether he had finished or not, I did not know.

'What does this mean, Louise?' he demanded piteously.

'A fine question for you to ask me, indeed – while you stand there buttoning yourself! It means merely that I have known all along what you two were doing. I don't blame you a bit. But you can't expect me to enjoy it. I have my pride, you know – and rather than wait till you cast me out into the gutter, I am leaving you. My ship sails tonight, and all my arrangements have been made. No ill feelings, I want you to understand. Just good common sense. I'm grateful for everything you've done for me, Charley – and if ever you think of me in the future, you will concede that you have had your money's worth. Now let's shake hands and part as good friends as we met.'

Tears came to his eyes. He fell to his knees abjectly, kissing my hand again and again. In a broken voice he succeeded in murmuring, 'I've acted like a cad, Louise. I deserve the worst, I know. But won't you give me another chance?'

My heart went out to him. Our delicious months of intimacy could not pass, surely, without leaving some residue, no matter how small, of genuine affection. For a moment I was tempted to abandon all my plans and stay. But a greater wisdom reminded me of the futility of trying to revive dying embers. The end must come sooner or later.

Gently I released myself from his embrace. 'Good-bye, Charley,' I whispered. 'Best of luck to you! I'll write you from Paris.' And then, ashamed of the utter sentimentality of this tearful leave-taking, I allowed my beastly cynicism to come to the fore.

'Oh, by the way, Clementine,' I addressed the cowering girl, as I made my exit, 'your master needs cheering up. Be sure to fuck him hot.'

Madeleine,
a Lady of Quality

The Carefree Courtesan's adventures run to two volumes and this extract from the second follows hard on the heels of her flight from New York and the treacherous Charley. As yet the lady has not arrived on the Boulevard de la Madeleine to rechristen herself. On board ship she is still Louise Smith and keen to learn the lessons of love that will equip her for a life of whoredom.

In these circumstances she is fortunate to meet a new tutor in the unlikely shape of a British naval captain. Here is a sea dog with forty years experience of life afloat, not all of it confined to the pursuit of sea-faring . . .

My trip across from New York was by no means uneventful, as indeed, how can any fairly attractive and not too icy a lady travel alone without some interesting adventure?

On the very second day out I was presented to the captain – a handsome old rake of about fifty, retired from the British Navy and occupying his present sinecure in a social rather than a nautical capacity. His main duty seemed to be to make himself pleasant to the wives of rich travelers and thus make them partial to his company's liners. He accosted one on deck as I stood alone at the rail, watching the wake of the ship, a vanishing trail over which I would never travel again. Seeing he was the captain, I could not very well ignore him. With pointed directness he complimented me on my beauty, then asked if I was married. No. Going to meet a fiancé? – No. Traveling with parents? – No. Friends? – No. Alone then? Ah! It was not the custom for conventional young ladies to cross the ocean alone, he reminded me. Conventions did not faze me, I told him. It was not long before the old dog was inviting me to share his suite for the rest of the voyage. I refused him coldly.

'But you must have some company,' he insisted, 'else your trip will be blooming tiresome – and I'm here to see that it is not. Would you prefer that I introduced you to some younger men than I?' I did not dare accept his offer – as I could not without hurting his feelings. He misunderstood me. 'Ah, I see. You don't care for male company. Oh well, I have just the thing: a very charming and interesting woman whom you ought to get along with very well.'

That same afternoon he presented me to Madame Mona Lugini, a mysterious and beautiful Italian woman of about thirty, an opera singer by vocation, returning from an engagement in the United States to meet her husband at Cherbourg.

'Call me Mona,' she insisted as soon as we were alone.

'It must be nice to be going home with a husband waiting for you,' I said inanely, just to make conversation.'

'Oh, men!' She snapped her fingers contemptuously. 'I have to keep one just for appearances. But they do not understand us... say, as you and I could understand each other, *carissima* Louise.' She took my arm in a most unjustifiedly affectionate manner. 'Take this hairy old sea-ape who just introduced us,' she went on. 'From the moment the ship left New York, he has been making love to me, asking me to sleep with him. But men do not love women as women can love each other. They are just arrogant fools, out to add another conquest to their experiences. Don't mistake me. I don't mind men when there is something to be had for it, as when I favor my managers, or a critic now and then. But to go through all that mess, and pretend to enjoy it – ugh!' Her fine breasts quivered under her black satin bodice with the violence of her disgust, her breath causing her luscious bosom to fill out like sails before a wind. I had considerable difficulty getting away, so assiduous was she in her attentions.

Late that same evening, after I had retired and lay abed reading in my stateroom, the door quietly opened, and there stood Mona in a most intoxicating negligee.

'Can I come in for a few minutes, Louise?' she asked. I could not refuse her. She approached, shivering with a strange intense excitement, and sat on my bed. Her thin decolleté nightdress, falling away from her bosom, disclosed two full, glorious spheres of flesh as only the well-developed woman of the Latin races can boast. She was so lonesome, she told me, and couldn't sleep, and just had to come in to see me. Her teeth chattered audibly as she spoke. There was a rather cool ocean breeze coming in through the open stateroom window, but nonetheless the violence of her shivering could not be explained by it alone, for she was a magnificent full-blooded woman.

'I am so cold,' she confessed pitifully. 'If only you would let me get into bed beside you, Louise.' I am naturally too aloof a creature to relish such intimacies with a stranger, but humanity compelled me to grant her request. She joined me under the covers. Instantly her shivering ceased. She took me in her arms, fondling and kissing my breasts with a hotness that belied entirely her recent shivering.

'What on earth does this mean?' I demanded in confusion.

'It means that I love you!' she replied intensely, 'with a love that transcends the mere lust of men – and yet a love that is persistently misunderstood.'

I was considerably perturbed. It was all too sudden for me to reconcile myself with. But soon the pleasant, titillating warmth of her caresses overpowered my undecided objections. Soon her hands sought the hem of my nightdress and gently raised it, caressing my thighs as she went along. Then, slipping entirely out of her own light negligee, she pressed her burning body close to mine. Our breasts glided over each other with a strange, ineffably smooth and soft sensation, till they came to rest dovetailed together, one of my bubbies nested deliciously between her two gorgeous globes of flesh. At the same time, her belly began writhing softly about, bestowing a glorious satiny caress with which nothing can compare. The passionate heaving of her bosom, too, kept our titties in a continual palpitating turmoil against each other.

For a time she continued thus, caressing me only with her wondrous body, her hands employed all the time at my buttocks to hold me closer to her.

To this point, our embrace might have been excused as the harmless mutual admiration of any two women similarly situated. But suddenly she threw the covers from off the bed, extinguished the light, returned, and forcibly separated my thighs. There was something so hypnotic in the intensity of her ardor that I could not resist her. Her desire was so palpably real, and my resistance was so tentative and weak, that it would have seemed a kind of blasphemy, a revolt against divine authority, for little me to try and stop her.

Her panting breath ran before her moist kisses up my thighs like a hot windstorm before rain. The sirocco reached my cunny, now some days without visitation. A moment later her tongue entered, her arms embraced my posteriors and raised my entire love-groove to her hungry mouth, and she launched upon a divine single gamahuching that, so far as mad intensity had real passion was concerned, has never been equaled in my whole lifetime of similar experiences.

The strangest thing of all was that she desired no reciprocal stimulation. Her sole joy was to devour my cunt with her delicious tonguings and bitings. While thus unselfishly bestowing delight upon me, she raised her own hips up and down, writhing about as if experiencing ecstasies again and again. I have never met another such exclusively active cunnilinguist. Most women will lap another only out of gratefulness for the same thing, or in exchange, or perhaps to bribe execution of the reciprocal favor. Again and again I came. She would not let up until I was screaming out with the unbearable sensitivity of my repeatedly stimulated cunt. We slept together that night.

Next morning the captain accosted us after breakfast with a knowing satyr's smile.

'I was searching for you two ladies late last night, don't you know? There was an extempore little party in my suite. The stewardess whom I sent reported *you*, Signora Lugini, as not in your room – and as for you, Miss Louise, sounds so jolly strange were heard at your door that the stewardess was afraid to disturb you. Putting one blooming thing and another together I needn't ask you two whether you slept well last night. Now what I'm aiming at is this: I'm the law on board ship, I suppose you know, and I'm not allowed to countenance such goings on. Now, tut, tut – I'm not proposing to put you two in the brig, but you might at least, out of common decency, ahem – declare me in on your party. What say, ladies?'

Angrily I walked away. I would have slapped him, had I not been restrained by the silly thought that to do so might constitute mutiny or *lesé majesté* of a sort. Mona remained behind to give him a piece of her mind – though it was a piece of another nature that he sought.

When she rejoined me, it was to report that he had continued his indecent proposals in all seriousness, urging that he could give either or both of us a much better time than we could bestow upon each other. What British bluntness! After thinking it over, I decided it was all quite funny: 'Let him pant,' I said, but at the same time, I made Mona promise not to join me again that night, in case there should be any further eavesdropping.

Night came. Once more I lay abed reading. Again the door opened and there stood Mona, despite the promise I had exacted from her. I was very angry with her and told her so; but so convincingly did she picture for me the tortures she suffered when sleeping alone, the nightmares and phantasms that beset her highly strung imagination that once again I had to grant her admission to my bed. Immediately she took up her subtle caressing and mad rubbing. Soon she had stripped, doused the lights, and was between my thighs, quieting my fears with a repetition of the delights of the preceding night.

I was just on the verge of my orgasm when I was frozen with horror by a sound at the door. It opened. Someone entered quickly. The door shut again. By the partial light that sifted in through the transom-ventilator from the corridors, I made out the glistening uniform of the captain. Mona had her back to the door and was too absorbed in her task to note his entrance.

'Heave ho, my hearties!' he spoke in a voice full of insolent assurance – too easy success with other women no doubt made him this way. 'I was making my evening round of inspection and just stopped in to see how my two young charges are coming along. Ripping nice, I should say, from what I can make out in the dark. A pretty picture you do make – but what say to my finishing it up for you in the grand way intended by the good Lord Almighty?'

Mona raised her mouth from its delicious occupation only long enough to snarl these words in a low tone: 'Get out of here! We don't need your help, you beef-eating British bastard!' – and like a tigress that cannot be lured off its prey, her mouth seized again upon my cunt, sucking and nibbling as if there had been no interruption.

The intruder whistled softly and came closer. 'All right! All right! Come now, Mona – I shan't interfere. But you might be a little more hospitable . . .'

He was silent for a while. Mona continued her mad tonguing but now I had some difficulty in catching up to where we had been with that masculine form looming in the darkness.

He approached still closer. As what dim light there was came from behind him, I could make out his every move – which I marked with an unearthly fear that was quite absurd, considering that neither of us had either maidenhead or chastity to lose.

His hand went down and felt the white heaving posteriors that projected over the foot of the bed.

'How nice! How nice!' he said. 'Is this Mona or Louise?' Neither of us made answer; both of us were speechless, though from differing causes. There was a moment's silence, during which I could hear, above the slight pulsating of the ship's engines, the soft liquid lapping of Mona's tongue, the heavy breathing of the horrid intruder, and the slight rasp of his coarse hands upon the ivory smooth buttocks that met his caress. He spoke again, now very nervously: 'I say . . . if no one is going to claim this, I'll take it myself.'

I expected Mona to fly up and scratch his eyes out; but whether in consideration for me, or in oblivion to all but her sweet task, or perhaps from plain indifference, she said not a word, confining herself more closely to the conversation in that dear language of love which held her so spellbound to my cunt.

In dim silhouette I could see the captain whip out a huge truncheon of a member. Then, raising Mona's entire lower body with his easy strength, he forced her legs wide apart and held her up by the thighs so he could position himself between them. Mona groaned with rage; but like a leech would not let her mouth be torn from me. Her hands clasping my buttocks more fiercely, she dug her nails into me as if to anchor herself against all the forces in the world.

What a mad scene to transcend the imagination of the most fargone erotomaniac! Within the inverted angle of Mona's luscious thighs, white and almost phosphorescent in the semi-darkness, I caught another momentary glimpse of his glistening bar as it slipped down between those widespread thighs till it found the narrow place of origin.

I could hear his stentorious breathing; I could picture his amorous fumbling as he sought the breach and lodged lip-deep in this ingenious position. I could not help but feel the fierce plunge that sent him gliding home into Mona's most intimate inners, and brought him up with a dull fleshy thud as his belly met her upturned arse in this provocative upside-down connection.

'Louise! Mona!' he was gasping as he lunged in and out, his quavering accents testifying at once to the extreme delight he was experiencing and to the fact that, my face in complete shadow, he still did not know which of us he was plugging! It was a situation to court madness. The worst having been accomplished, I yielded myself completely to Mona's titillations, to the whole unutterable lewdness and salacity of the scene. He was fucking me, for all he knew, and though his prick was in Mona's cunt, I was experiencing all the exquisite stimulations of that heavenly act. By substitution, by transference – oh, how can I explain it, dear reader, so involved, so diabolical, so divine was it, I felt as if he were really doing it to me. More – since his very thrust forced Mona's whole mouth closer into my cunt, I shared the identical rhythm of the act.

What a delicious complexity of movements, as I joined in with the other two, my hips screwing downward to Mona's mouth as he shoved her firmly toward me! It was his thrust that I was meeting. If his monster organ had torn its way clear through her passion-tossed frame till, through her mouth, it had met my cunt, I could not have been fucked more effectively. To top this lascivious thought was the realization that I was being both fucked and cunt-lapped at the same time. At one moment Mona was a mere impersonal agency to my connection with that fierce fucking man which we crushed and tore apart between us. At another moment she was my dear, tender female lover, allowing herself to be plundered rather than suffer my pleasure to be interrupted.

Add to this indescribable commotion of our senses and bodies the vibrations of the ship and the incessant rocking contributed by the waves, which now, whether in sympathy or by coincidence, or perhaps because I was just becoming aware of them, seemed to increase in wildness with the strong surge of our passions.

With such sights and sounds and thoughts and feelings lashing on my lustful senses, it did not take long for that earlier fear-frozen discharge still stored within me to melt and gain release through the tingling of all my fibers and the ecstatic quivering of my limbs. Down to Mona's avid mouth, my twitching womb and vagina poured a flow of love's secretions that a man could not outdo, so increased was it by the delay and by the unusual lasciviousness of our triple union.

But Mona, gurgling in her throat with joy for my joy, did

not stop at administering a single stroke of love's exquisite dying fit, but went right on – and soon my pleasures began anew. As for herself, she seemed to be coming continuously in a ceaseless spasm of spending. There are such women, who, at times of sexual excitement, can bring themselves on at will again and again – and so it was with her.

The captain, not for one moment inactive during all this, but slow in reaching his climax because of his advanced years, now gasped, 'Jove! What pleasure! Mona – Louise – whichever you are – I am coming! Push, closer to me! Now! Ah! Ah! Gods! Ahhh!' And with the furious short plunge that accompanied each violent exhalation, I could almost see and feel the great hot jets of sperm that were sent into Mona's cunt which, as I found later, overflowed bounteously her belly and buttocks and dripped in great gobs, like tallow, on the floor at the foot of the bed.

Mona, as if nothing had happened, kept up the delicious caresses of her tireless tongue and the wild writhing of her hips.

'Stop! Stop!' the captain groaned. 'Are you trying to pump my life's blood out of me? Or do you want to wrench my part off? Stop, I say, you insatiable siren, until I pull out at least?'

It chanced just then that the motion of the ship changed perceptibly and it seemed that the engines had gone dead from some cause or another. The captain withdrew his dripping rammer hurriedly, replaced Mona's thighs on the bed and dried himself.

'Sorry. Must leave you ladies. Navigation requires my attention,' he muttered as he stumbled out of the dark stateroom.

When Mona had finished me a second time, she arose and turned on the light. Thick, creamy fluid was trickling down her thighs. She made a move of distaste.

'Do you have a douching syringe, Louise?' she asked. 'It would be funny if I became pregnant by that beast. I guess he thinks I enjoyed that swollen piece of meat crammed into me. If I came, Louise, it wasn't due to his efforts, but to that delicious cunt of yours.' So she hadn't enjoyed his wonderful fuck after all!

Next day the captain accosted me once more while I stood alone on deck. I had intended ignoring him completely but, somehow, my dreams of the night before had been entirely of being loved in that erotic wheelbarrow fashion by a vigorous, slow-coming, fully matured man.

'I say, tell me,' he asked, 'was it you or Mona that I had so deliciously last night?' In fairness to my friend, I could not claim credit for it, so I refused to say. He took it as an admission and there was no use telling him otherwise.

'By Jove, you were great,' he said, 'but we could do much better if we two were by ourselves, don't you know. Tonight at my suite, aye what? And I'll have some bloomin' fine champagne; two bottles of Heidsick Monopole '89.' Something compelled me to play up to his impression of me.

'Supposing I did meet you – what's in it for me?' I queried provocatively. I decided that I might as well start right in to learning how to handle men if I was to make a success of my life.

'Ho! ho!' he laughed in his rough John Bull manner. 'What's in it for you? I say that's quite funny. What's in it for you, eh? Why, if you don't mind my telling you, there'll be a fine stiff John Thomas and a good copious injection of the sap of life, by Jove!'

'By Jove!' I angrily mimicked his detestable self-assurance. 'Your employers may pay you to amuse the old ladies on board in that way, but I'm attractive enough to take my pick of the youngest and handsomest men on board – if that's all I wanted.'

'Oh, I see,' he muttered, hurt in his vanity for all his thick skin, 'you want to be paid. Well, I've never done this before, but I suppose your kind have to live too. How much do you want me to pay you?'

'I don't want you to pay me anything,' I answered, confused by the strangeness of being asked my price, and utterly unprepared in the methods of bargaining, 'but I don't like the idea of flattering you by being just another woman who has given you what you want. So let's not say anything more about it.' And I walked away.

In my stateroom, I found a note to report at the purser's office. 'You haven't turned over your passport for inspection yet, miss—'

'Passport?' I put in fearfully, 'I have no passport. I intend becoming naturalized in France.'

'But have you a permit of the French immigration bureau? Without one or the other, I'm afraid you won't be able to get by the port officials at Cherbourg. Perhaps you'd better speak to the captain.'

In a frenzy I sought out the old satyr. As I entered his office, he came out of a corner where he had been squeezing a young Irish stewardess. She left hurriedly, leaving her neckerchief behind her. I told him my predicament. In his best official manner he told me that I would be deported immediately upon landing and that he would probably have the pleasure of my company on the return voyage. I burst into tears.

'Well, well,' he put in, human once more, 'if you were a good friend of mine, I could vouch for you personally to the immigration authorities and everything would be spiffy. Only you've just refused to be nice to me, and so I suppose you'll have to ship for another voyage till we do become acquainted.'

I was sport enough to admit myself fairly beaten. My tears evaporated, and my prettiest smile adorned my features. 'Dear Captain! Tonight then, in your suite?'

'No!' he roared. 'Not tonight, and not in my suite, but right here and now, by Jove!'

'By Jove, Captain, you are a dear boy!'

He locked the office door. After that we got along wonderfully. Of course there was a fine sofa in the room, but when the preliminaries and stripping had been accomplished, I shamelessly confessed that I wanted it done wheelbarrow fashion.

'So you liked it after all last night, aye what?'

'No. It wasn't me.'

That put an extra edge on his appetite.

'I'll be able to tell in a minute. John Thomas has a better memory than I. He can always scent the difference where I can't.' And he presented to my touch an instrument that completely defied my grasp and blasted all my misconceptions of sexual vigor being exclusively youth's monopoly.

A sofa cushion was placed on the richly rugged floor. Upon this I positioned my folded arms. With scarcely an effort, my gallant grasped my thighs and placed them about his hips where I locked them firmly for the time. In a moment I became accustomed to the slight strain of the upside-down position. My breasts, though not naturally pendulous, now swung back and caressed my chin. Looking backward between them, and under my belly, I could see what was being done. The strange topsy-turviness of the lewd pose served only to inflame me with impatient desires; to have the barrow hitched to the rider in that equivocal cart-before-the-horse gallop we were about to set out on.

His belaying pin lay ready, pressed up against my belly by its own tension. Loosening my thighs a little to allow himself to draw back somewhat from the breach which lay so fairly before him downside-up, he lodged the thick swollen knob between the outer lips. Then, the proper direction determined, and his hands no longer needed for steering, he grasped my thighs and slowly drew my buttocks to him, as at the same time he steadily pushed down and inward to the crimson velvet-lined cavern of love. Moist and well prepared as that part was for his reception, however, never had it entertained so bulky a visitor. And as he drew the sheath up over his majestically disproportionate weapon, I received so violent and painful a stretching that I burst into sobbing, regretting my over-adventurousness. I would have been split apart, had I not been favored by the generous lubrication afforded by my excitement and by the natural elasticity and adaptability that healthy young women are blessed with in those parts.

'Don't cry, child,' the captain comforted me. 'You'll be all right in just a minute. No ... it wasn't you last night. We, Thomas and I, haven't been in one so nice for as long as we both can remember.' And he held still for a time, savoring and enjoying the unusual constriction of the moist hot sheath.

Then, as the wet juicy folds adjusted themselves to the huge object that engorged them, he slowly withdrew to allow my blood to resume circulation at the parts from which his bulk had forced it out, and then he slid all the way home to the hilt the luscious flesh cylinder. I gripped him deliciously. His succeeding motions gave him no more difficulty than what served to increase his enjoyment.

What strain there might have been in sustaining our rather acrobatic positions merely served to increase the lubricity of the act and the violence of the contrast when the final downpouring relief came. But between the beginning and the delicious end, there was an infinity of sensations that defy description. Firmly, back and forth, the captain drew and plunged his broad satisfying instrument, like the wielder of a bow on a bass-viol, never once losing contact with those strings that sent reverberating chords and harmonies of pleasure through me.

Soon my eyes glazed over and became dim with the approaching ecstasy. I could no longer discern that red blood-gorged joy-dispenser as it plunged in and out up there between my thighs. Then suddenly I went stone blind. The rich, hot, climactic flood of sensation went eddying and sizzling through my veins, contracting all my visceral organs and causing me to faint away momentarily with the glowing overpowering sensations that inundated my brain.

I collapsed upon the cushion but the captain continued to sustain me, slowing up his motion to a gentle massage of my inner vagina until I should recover. The entrance muscle of my cunt was so rigidly clamped about his member that he could scarcely move at all. But as the last waves of agonized pleasure passed away, my organ relaxed once more from its attempt to hug its delicious intruder to death.

Now gradually letting out sail and picking up speed, the captain rode along at a spanking clip before the full blast of his own desires. But before his majestic ship entered the harbor of ecstasy, the seas of delight rose again to floodtide within me. We shared the stormy motions of pleasure together, give and take, back and forth, his pumps working furiously, and finally inundating me even further with his hot effusion as I drowned in bliss.

As he took a last farewell plunge into my flooded hold, his creamy sacrifice, suddenly displaced, frothed over my outer cunt and hairs, sending a warm trickle across my arse and down the small of my back.

When I was dressed and taking my leave, he again assured me that everything would be arranged with the French officials.

'Now that there's no longer any need of hypocrisy between us, shall you come here tonight?' he asked.

'Mona might be suspicious,' I told him. Jealous, is what I meant.

'Well, let's make it tomorrow afternoon again – between luncheon and tea.'

I agreed.

Dear reader, a cunt may be a snob when some strange cock is concerned, but when once the first introduction is effected, all social distinctions and barriers are down, the better she likes it. Forty years of the captain's service in His Majesty's Navy hadn't been for nothing. In the five days that remained

Madeleine, a Lady of Quality

to our voyage, the captain demonstrated upon me the essence of this forty years of experience. And when he had tried everything from the Argentinean to the Zulu method, geographically and alphabetically inclusive, his fingers still fondled my tiny rear entrance rather longingly. A sailor will always be a sailor, I thought, but paid no further heed.

Our last afternoon together arrived. He was quite fatherly and most solicitous of my future welfare. I confessed my purpose of becoming an exclusive *vendeuse de l'amour* in Paris – in blunt language, of living by my cunt. He laughed and promised to give me letters of introduction to some wealthy prospects. 'But,' he went on, 'not to seem discouraging, cunt is now *tout passé* – out of fashion – in Paris.'

'What do you mean?' I asked anxiously, not believing him, but yet disturbed at the implied threat to my plans.

'They are a sophisticated people, the French. Naturally, with time and excess a whole populace may become relatively jaded and blasé toward the conventional sexual refinements – or "perversions," as the Anglo-Saxon mind is apt to consider them. But don't be frightened. There's nothing that a bright girl can't learn in time.'

'Oh! So you haven't taught me everything?'

'I'm afraid not. But there's still time for one more lesson, the pupil willing. You understand French? *Votre prochaine leçon, c'est faire l'amour en cul.*'

If I hadn't understood his words, his hands, creeping from my thigh where it had been resting, around to my coveted bum-hole, was explicit enough. I blushed.

'Oh, Captain!' I exclaimed, 'do you mean that this huge thing' (indicating the weapon that was generally in evidence whenever I was about) 'can be introduced into that tiny place where I cannot even insinuate a finger? Oh no! It would kill me.'

'Darling child, you little understand the wonderful

possibilities of the human body – especially of a woman's body. It is only at the very entrance that it is so tight – and even that is very stretchable. Beyond that there is nothing to hurt.'

His knowledge of anatomy was correct. It is only the sphincter or anus muscle that seems so impenetrable. Within is the wide mucus-lined rectum, in size and shape very much like the vagina. He prevailed upon me to let him try it. I might more wisely have waited for a less monstrously sized lover to take this, my second maidenhead; but somehow it seemed to me especially appropriate to have this operation, smacking as it does of male homosexuality, performed by an authoritative naval man. My literary and dramatic sense has betrayed me again and again, but all through life I have acted and chosen situations as if for a projected autobiography. And sure enough, here it is.

Dotingly, as usual, the captain removed each article of my clothing, pausing to admire my disarray at each stage. When he could remove no more from me, he proceeded to doff his own clothes. Then, having me kneel on a soft cushion at the side of the couch, with my body leaning over it and my buttocks projecting at right angles, he went in search of some pomade – to ease his entrance, as he explained.

Like one condemned, with head upon the block, I awaited the executioner. I entertained but little expectation of pleasure – rather indeed, expectation of great pain; but a sort of wicked curiosity, the wish to see whether this unnatural thing could be done, kept me – as yet – from relenting. Anyhow, I told myself, I wanted to savor to the dregs every experience that life had to offer – and since I would be persuaded to do this sooner or later, why not at once?

He returned with a jar of scented vaseline. Kneeling on the cushion behind me, he gently applied the soothing lubricant to the pink, puckered little exit that he so enterprisingly meant to employ as an entrance – the needle's eye through which he

Madeleine, a Lady of Quality

hoped to pass a camel – patiently dilating the exclusive little muscle with his middle finger and working in the vaseline. At first I was miserably embarrassed by his intimate handling of that most personal part of me. (I say 'personal' because, unlike my cunny, I could not think that it was meant for two.) But soon, the caressing of that zone more sensitive and erogenous that I had ever dreamt, became so pleasing that I was wriggling my hips with anxiety for him to get started, though the Lord only knows what pleasure I expected to derive from it.

At last, satisfied with these preliminaries, the captain oils his own part, from head to root, which, as I glance across my shoulder to watch the procedure, seems, unless I am really seeing it for the first time, almost twice as large as it has been before. I bury my face in the sofa cushions to see no more.

Now he brings the weapon to bear upon the tiny, crinkled crevice. Two or three times it slips down the groove of my buttocks toward that other cavity where it more rightfully belongs. He brings it into position once more. But this time it flies upward at his earliest pressure. Guiding it with his hand then, so as to restrain its merest slip, he brings just the tip of his huge arrow to the tiny aperture and slowly, firmly presses inward. This time he succeeds in gaining the entry of half the head – as I know soon enough by the horrible, unendurable agony I suffer as that narrow passage is so cruelly distended. At the same time, the muscles of that part contract rigidly – to force out the terrible foreign object that is being crammed into its disproportionately small entrance. But the captain, expecting this, counteracts it with the pressure of his body, fully holding his own.

'You must relax, Louise,' he tells me, 'and not try to force it out.'

'Oh no! I can't stand it! Captain, you hurt me dreadfully! Oh! How you are torturing me!' I cry tearfully. 'Please, please

– stop! Oh, you are tearing me open! I'll do anything; but not this! Oh! Oh!'

'Now, now!' he comforts me. 'As soon as the head gets by, the distention will not be so great. Come now, relax and press toward me. Take it in as slowly as you like – or as quickly as you can endure it.' And at the same time, to divert me from the local agony which has me writhing and beating the cushions with pain, he puts his arms about my waist, and slips a finger into the top of my cunt. The dear clitty does not fail as a universal anaesthetic. As the pleasure from his light, quick massaging increases, the pain fades, and soon my motions change to a back and forth movement which, with his gentle pressure from behind, soon has his whole tool sheathed in my rectum to the very root.

The vaseline it is that allows its huge bulk to slide all the way in without bruising or further pain. I feel a most peculiar sensation of being full up . . . and a slight desire to evacuate – which, however, quickly changes to a desire to hold that great bar of flesh within me indefinitely.

Now he withdraws halfway and presses in again, his movement easy and unobstructed. The caress to my soft inside passage is anything but unpleasant; only the entrance is still somewhat sore.

Very slowly, he relishes each stroke.

'Oh, how close and hot – and soft – and moist it is in there!' he says. 'I confess, though, it takes me half an hour to come in a cunt but when I do this, I come almost immediately.' And he stops his motion again to keep the climax from overtaking him too soon. 'Tell me when you are ready, Louise,' he whispers, and, with his arms drawing me closer to him, he continues the rapid digital stimulation of my cunt.

'I am coming, soon, Captain!' I gasp, as the divine dissolution approaches. He resumes fiercely the full plunge and draw and thrust into my behind – the swelling, fleshy curves of my buttocks alone protecting me against the violence of his contacts.

'Now! Now!' I cry. 'Oh! Oh!'

As the exquisite climax enthralls me, I feel innumerable jets of hot sperm shooting out from his thick vibrating member, seeming to flood all the secret recesses of my body.

We have come off simultaneously and I kneel there bathed in thankful bliss as well as in his generous effusion, till the exquisite turmoil subsides.

His member is still hard and stiff. He begins moving back and forth within me again.

'If I pulled it out now,' he explains, 'the greater size of the head over that of the shaft would hurt you again – like drawing an arrow from a wound. It would be better to wait till I get soft. It won't take me long to come a second time.'

And he continues, more easily than ever now, what with the additional lubrication of his part by his own generous ejaculation. True to his word, in scarcely more than twenty of his strokes, pleasant to me, divine to him, I feel another, though less prolific injection of his warm, tingling love juices. Almost immediately his terrible engine begins shrinking, permitting the relaxation of my own dilated part until, with no difficulty at all, he draws it out of my cream-gorged bottom.

And so the deed was done – and I was the proud possessor of two separate and distinct bodily cavities, each for the full and complete celebration of the rites of Venus. My newer cunt I even felt some predilection for, insofar as its use entailed no fear of pregnancy and no contraceptive precaution. As for after effects, there were none. After bathing, I found my rear just as prettily puckered and chastely closed as ever. No sacrifice to love is long regretted.

Lust at Large

Eroticon Fever

It's Midsummer's eve in the vale of Blisswood, an idyllic valley in the north of England known only to local people and discerning visitors. But the veil of secrecy is soon to be lifted, for Blisswood harbours the hottest criminal in the land – Bra-less Brenda, the topless robber whose exploits have turned her into a national heroine. Inspector Monk of the Metropolitan Police is all set to crack the case, assisted by his youthful sidekick Stephen Fantail. Their movements are dogged by a pair of competing tabloid journalists – Maxwell Shaftesbury of the *Daily Dog*; and Robyn Chestnut of the *Daily Rabbit*, abetted by Josie Twist, a young woman in search of her errant fiancé, Gavin, who is on a personal quest to confront Bra-less Brenda. Since this is an excerpt from a Noel Amos novel, there's also the entire sales team of an underwear company and a gold-digging French girl with a unique method of organising a company takeover. If kitchen sinks could copulate, they'd be in here too.

As night falls and the annual Midsummer orgy gets underway *Lust at Large* moves to a climax . . .

It was a hot and broody summer evening. On the village green the local youth, dressed in their finery, mingled with middle-aged tourists clutching cameras. Half a dozen venerable donkeys chomped listlessly at the grass and laid horsey turds. The air was thick with the smell of beast.

'This is hardly sin city,' said Josie, wrinkling her nose. 'Are you sure this is where the action is?'

'Have patience,' replied Robyn. 'You've got to realise that this is a traditional event. It starts slow and builds to a frenzy.'

'We hope.'

'First of all, the young married women who want to conceive ride to the barn on donkeys.'

'What's the point of that? If that's how they've been doing it all these years I'm surprised the community has survived.'

'It's tradition, Josie. Don't knock it till you've tried it — and you're going to. Miriam!'

Miriam Jarvis, looking eager for the fray in a well-filled peasant blouse, answered the call.

'Miriam's been giving me some background to this affair,' said Robyn, 'and she promised a ride on a donkey to the *Bunny*'s special reporter. That's you.'

'What!' cried Josie.

'Come on, honey, you promised you'd help me out. You can't go wrong on a cute little fellow like this.'

Robyn was indicating the small grey donkey that Miriam was holding by a rope halter. The beast fluttered a dark-lashed eye at Joise and swished its tail. It *was* cute.

'This isn't a boy,' said Miriam, 'this is Josephine. She's the tamest of my little lovelies.'

'OK, then,' Josie heard herself say and then yelped in

surprise as the woman suddenly thrust her hand up her frock.

'I'm sorry,' said Miriam, her hand exploring without embarrassment, 'but I must check to see if you are properly dressed. It's just as well I did, isn't it?'

Josie stood stock-still in shock as her panties were slipped down her legs, leaving her naked beneath the thin cotton.

'That's better,' said Miriam, tucking the knickers into her pocket. 'Now, on you get.'

Josie did not protest; given what she hoped to be doing later, underwear would doubtless prove an encumbrance. It was not until her leg was half over the donkey that she noticed that its hairy grey back was bare — and covered in a creamy ointment.

'Hey!' she cried as she realised that her private parts were about to sink into an unsavoury mixture of fur and goo. But it was too late to back off, for Miriam had placed her hands on her shoulders and firmly plunged her downwards. Her bare bottom met the soggy mat beneath her and stuck.

'Yuk,' she said. 'That feels disgusting. What the hell is it?'

But Miriam was gone, leaving the rope halter in Robyn's hands, and Josie became aware that she was now part of a group of mounted women.

'I've got gunge all over my fanny,' she hissed at Robyn. 'Did you know about this?'

The tall American grinned. 'No one else is complaining.'

That was true. A pretty redhead with a freckled cleavage was squealing with glee as she rubbed herself backwards and forwards on the donkey next to Josie. The chubby blonde beside her had her eyes closed and a dreamy smile on her face.

'Besides,' said Robyn, 'you'll find someone to lick it all off later.'

'You bitch.'

'Just don't forget to give the *Daily Rabbit* all the juicy details.'

* * *

It was not much more than half a mile to the barn but the donkeys took their time. The group set off from the green at a sedate pace, the spectators falling in behind the riders. Cameras clicked and voices were raised in boisterous cheer. Bottles began to be passed from hand to hand.

Josie found the sensation of riding very pleasant. Unlike those around her, she suspected, she was no horsewoman but Josephine was a kindly mount, solid and sure-footed. Suddenly, as she swayed along, her eyes fixed on the back of the blonde girl in front, she became aware of the heat rising from between her legs. She pictured the rough hairs abrading the tender skin of her bum cheeks and the pouting lips of her pussy slicking back and forth in that white ooze. This time the thought did not repulse her. Her mind revolved around primal images. Coarse hair. Hot skin. Honeyed body fluids.

'Oooh!' She sucked in her breath. She was fiercely on heat.

The girl in front turned and grinned over her shoulder.

'It's got to you now, has it?'

'God, yes!'

'Set your clock ticking, I bet. Look under the trees – see anyone you fancy?'

Josie was puzzled at first. She was so absorbed in her own feelings that she couldn't grasp what was said to her. Then she noticed the men. They lined the route under the trees along the river bank. They looked like farm lads, most of them, young and bronzed and strong. Some were dressed up, with jackets and ties, but most wore jeans and open-necked shirts; others were in shorts and many were stripped to the waist, their muscles gleaming in the low slanting light. They looked delicious.

'I want one,' said Josie to the blonde who had dropped back to ride beside her.

'Take your pick. They're all available.'

'But I don't know which one. It's like opening a big box of chocolates – you don't know where to start.'

'I do,' said her companion. 'I want that big fellow there in the cut-off jeans with the earring.'

'Good choice,' said Josie as her new friend waved at the boy. 'I bet he's no soft centre.'

The lad needed no encouragement. He approached the blonde with a white-toothed grin, brown eyes flashing. He took hold of the donkey's halter and led it out of the parade, his other hand in the girl's golden hair. As they disappeared out of sight into the woods Josie saw the girl pulling the boy's shirt from his waistband.

She noticed other couples embracing on the parched grass. Two boys lay on either side of a girl, her body almost obscured by their attentions. Only her long bare legs were visible, scissoring open beneath their prying hands.

Without realising it, Josie had steered Josephine towards the verge and a black-haired youth in a starched white shirt and faded blue jeans had hold of the donkey's head.

'Whoa there,' he said, 'you're running out of control.'

'I'm not,' she cried, mesmerised by his muscular forearms and the cut of the tight denim on his thigh. She hadn't intended to stop. She knew if she joined this youth beneath the trees she may never get to the dance at all. But a tide of lust was rising in her belly and a fire was raging in her pussy. Out of control scarcely covered it.

'My name's Martin,' he said as he led her off the road to the knowing cheers of the pack of spectators.

'Have you got a big cock, Martin?' she whispered.

'Enormous,' he replied, hurrying her away, one hand already high up on her thigh under her skirt.

'And is it stiff?'

His fingers had found their way into her groin. The motion of the donkey seemed to wedge them into the opening of her vagina.

'Rock hard, I promise.'

They had passed under the fringe of trees now and he was

hurrying them along fast. Josephine responded happily, as if she recognised the urgency.

He picked her up in one movement, holding her up in the air as he pressed his mouth to hers. She devoured him, hooking her legs around his waist and bearing him to the ground, her tongue halfway down his throat.

He pulled her dress to her waist and palmed and squeezed the firm flesh of her buttocks in a fever. Kneeling like that, with the evening air fresh on the wet mouth of her empty vagina, she felt ablaze. She scrabbled at his fly with both hands and had his cock out in a flash.

'Thank God you weren't lying,' she whispered, clasping it in both hands. 'You're huge.'

He said nothing as he pushed her onto her back and knelt between her thighs.

'You're hung like a horse,' she continued, weighing his big balls in one hand and skinning his satiny knob with the other. She placed the broad red head of his glans between the slippery lips of her pussy. 'Or like a donkey. That's more appropriate given the circ—'

He drove his outsized member home in one relentless thrust, cutting off her words.

Josie cried out with pleasure and clasped his tight buttocks digging her nails in to spur him on.

'Come on, stuff me then,' she yelled. 'Stuff me as hard as you can! Fuck me with that big thing! Oh yes! Oh yes! OH!'

He thrust his pile-driver into her without finesse, as if she were a block of wood and he were hammering home a nail with thunderous strokes. And at each blow she cried out until the woods around her echoed with her squeals of pleasure. It was the most brutal fucking she had ever had and when it was done she felt as if she had been run over by a truck.

As she caught her breath, lying on her back with him sprawled across her, she caught sight of Josephine calmly munching at a bush.

She mustn't forget she was on an assignment. There was a lot more riding ahead of her on this Midsummer's night.

The barn dance was not a sophisticated affair, yet, to her surprise, Mitzi Bluitt was enjoying herself. There was sawdust on the floor and the band was a rustic ensemble of banjo and squeezebox and country fiddle. Nevertheless the dancers swung into complicated routines with gusto. The large barn was already as hot as a furnace and outside it was hardly any cooler. The evening sun was sinking but the heat was fierce and the atmosphere airless.

'You're looking pretty spiffing tonight,' said Tony from Wales.

Mitzi took the compliment as no more that her due for she *was* looking pretty damn good in a lightweight cream jacket and black culottes. Her rich chestnut hair was pinned up, exposing the elegant sweep of her long neck. The jacket was held in place by one button and beneath it she wore a Louche Lingerie classic bra which lifted and separated her big brown melons to considerable effect.

'I thought I'd make an effort,' she said. 'The competition's pretty hot.'

'You're not kidding.' Tony stared at the knot of dancers with their whirling skirts and flashing thighs. Mandy was prominent amongst them, her breasts fighting to escape from her low-cut blouse as she wiggled to the music. Tony tore his eyes from the tempting sight and gazed at the no-less-delicious vista of flesh exposed in Mitzi's gaping cleavage. 'Fancy a dance?'

Mitzi would have said no but she had just spotted Don the Marketing Director jumping about on the floor with a buxom blonde. Sod him. She sank her gin in one gulp and gave Tony her sexiest smile. 'I'm game,' she replied.

Max Shaftesbury was feeling far from game but he wasn't

going to yield exclusive coverage of a genuine pagan fertility festival to Robyn Chestnut and the *Bunny*. Not that it looked much more than a bucolic knees-up to him. He was feeling exhausted and the reason was right by his side, clinging to his arm, her big liquid eyes blazing with excitement.

'Ooh, Maxwell, isn't this fabulous? I love dancing.'

'Well, you'll have to find someone else to do it with, Marilyn. I'm one of life's observers at this kind of shindig.'

'Yer what?'

'Go and find a man your own age. Just fetch me a decent glass of claret first.'

'They have beer, cider, whisky and gin.'

'I might have known. Get me something strong. A lot of it.'

And he slumped into a chair leaving Marilyn to battle her way to the bar. As she retreated he watched her capacious bottom, like two plump cushions squeezed into red velvet hotpants a size too small, and his penis gave a reflexive twitch in his trousers. *No more big women*, he said to himself. In this one day he'd had enough outsized loving to last him a lifetime. He needed a tall slim girl with less violent desires.

'Hiya, Max, you look pooped.'

He lifted his eyes to a woman in a peacock-blue silk shirt and black leggings that seemed to go on forever. They didn't come much taller or slimmer than Robyn Chestnut.

'Have a seat, Robyn. I haven't the energy to stand.'

'That's a shame. I thought we might bury the hatchet with a ceremonial dance.'

'"The *Bunny* and the *Dog* trip the light fantastic at rustic love rite" – it has a certain ring to it, I admit.'

'Here you are, Maxwell,' said a shrill voice and Marilyn thrust a dripping pint glass in his direction. She took one look at Robyn and retreated with a sniff.

Robyn watched her depart. 'Isn't that the tender-hearted nurse who ministered to my photographer this morning?'

'Poor fellow.'

'She got him back on his feet. Thanks to her, the swelling went down.'

'Really? She had quite the opposite effect on me.' Maxwell had drained the rancid brown liquid to the dregs and was suddenly feeling much better. 'Come on then, Robyn, let's boogie.'

Inspector Monk had emptied the mini-bar in his room of Scotch and was considering the vodka. No, what he needed was company, friendly faces and jollity – and more whisky, of course. Wasn't tonight meant to be some local celebration?

He left his room and wandered along the corridor. He descended the stairs and found himself outside Julia Jarvis's office. He knocked. There was no reply. He went in.

Though the room was empty it was full of her. Of her scent and her presence and the memory of her upturned face as she boldly defied him that morning. And the feel of her soft lips on his and the warm weight of her bare breasts in his hands as she lay down on the desk for him. It was funny to think he had turned his face steadfastly from sex for fifteen years and all it took was one embrace and his abstinence meant nothing – except a string of missed opportunities, of course.

He closed the door behind him and descended to the lobby. It was deserted. A lone barman read the paper behind the counter. Monk went out onto the terrace in the hot evening sunshine and heard the sound of laughter and music from across the fields. He began to walk towards it, turning his predicament over in his mind.

His job was to assemble the evidence to convict Julia of the Brenda robberies. It was a serious crime and she faced serious punishment but he couldn't help that. One intense and passionate encounter meant nothing. It was his duty to arrest her.

He was close to the barn now. He could see the clearing outside where people milled around a barbecue. He smelt smoke and charcoal and hamburger and realised he was famished. The music was loud and tuneful. He couldn't remember when he had last had a dance.

As he opened the gate which led to the field by the barn there was a flurry of movement to his left and a gurgle of laughter, smartly cut off. A couple lay in the grass, their mouths glued together. Their hands were tussling while she fought to hold her dress down over a slim brown thigh.

As Monk closed the gate behind him he had a vision of a new future. One free from cynicism and distrust, from police politics and self-serving fools like Hatter, from forever seeking the worst in his fellow man. It was a vision with a warm curvaceous body in his bed every night. *Dream on, Archie*, he said to himself. It was a dream that would haunt him, he knew, if he arrested Julia Jarvis.

He bought a sausage and ate it, dripping grease down his front. He bought another and a can of warm lemonade. As the last sweet and sticky mouthful disappeared down his throat he felt a sudden glow of happiness and found himself grinning stupidly at the people around.

One of them returned his gaze.

'Hello, inspector.'

'Ms Jarvis!' He spoke the name with reverence. 'I've been looking for you.' It was true, he realised.

She looked startled. 'Surely you aren't going to subject me to further interrogation here?'

'Just one question.'

'Yes?' Her lower lip was trembling, her clear blue eyes were enormous.

'Will you dance with me?'

Stephen Fantail watched with admiration as his boss led Julia Jarvis onto the dance floor. By God, Monk was a cunning bugger. All that stuff about resigning had to be his idea of a joke. Poetry indeed! Mad Monk was obviously going in for the kill.

A hand took hold of his upper arm, just above the rolled sleeve of his pale blue shirt.

'Excuse me, officer.' A tall blonde with a kiss-me mouth looked at him out of sky-blue eyes.

'We'd like your assistance.' The voice came from his other side, from a second blonde with cloudless eyes and pouting pink lips. He looked from one to the other. They were beautiful, stunning – and identical.

'How do you know I'm a policeman?' he said.

'We work at the hotel,' said one. 'You're DC Fantail, aren't you? Room 31.'

'And we need help. I've lost a ring.'

'Has it been stolen?'

'I don't think so but I might need to report its loss officially. For the insurance.'

'It's over here in the bushes,' said the other. 'Please come and help us.'

What else could he do? Police officer or not, a red-blooded young man with no current attachments does not refuse to go into the bushes with two horny-looking blondes. And they were decidedly horny-looking . . .

One walked beside him, her hand now burning a hole in his shirt. The other strode ahead, the pert halves of her bottom swelling the skintight denim of her jeans. Her hips swivelled as she walked and the cleft between her cheeks winked and tightened with each step.

'She's a peach, isn't she?' said the girl by his side.

'You both are.'

Twin peaches ripe for plucking, he said to himself and wished he could adjust his trousers without attracting attention.

They led him into the next field and the first girl turned and pointed to the far corner. 'Over there,' she said.

They searched for fifteen minutes. Fifteen minutes in which Stephen was treated to their lithe and nubile bodies bending and leaning and rubbing against his in a cock-stretching selection of poses. The girl in jeans doubled over before him, thrusting her rear into his crotch as she meticulously searched the grass. Her twin leant on his shoulder as he looked for the ring, her long blonde hair brushing against the side of his face in a golden curtain. She turned to face him on her knees and he found himself gazing down the front of her blouse into a deep ravine of creamy breast flesh.

'You won't find it down there,' she said, making no attempt to cover herself. He blushed to the tips of his ears.

'You know,' said the first girl, 'maybe I never put it on at all. Maybe it's still at home.'

'Oh dear,' said the other, 'now we're in trouble. He'll have us for wasting police time.'

'Will you?' said girl number one, putting her hand on Stephen's knee as he squatted on his haunches among the weeds. 'I think it's all her fault, she suggested we ask you to help. You should smack her bottom.'

'I, er . . .' Stephen gulped, bewildered by the turn of events.

'Go on,' the girl said. 'Take her jeans down and smack her bum. She deserves it.'

'Yes, it's true,' said the other, unbuckling her belt and hooking the flaps of her denims over her hip.

'Turn around,' commanded her twin. 'Take them down slowly and show him your arse.'

Stephen's eyes bulged from his head as the girl did as she was told, thrusting her bum back almost into his face as she lowered her jeans. Her bottom glowed white in the thickening light. Her panties, caught in the divide between the cheeks, provided little protection from his prurient gaze. Without being asked, she peeled the scarlet scrap of material down her legs as well and tossed it aside.

'How do you want me?' she asked over her shoulder, her pale satiny behind fully revealed beneath the hem of her pink T-shirt.

Stephen was struck dumb. He had the urge to plunge forward and bury his head between those plump curvaceous cushions, to lick her from the golden beard of her pussy, right up the crease of her arse to the base of her spine.

'Get over his lap, of course,' said her sister, pushing the half-naked girl towards Stephen.

He sat in rigid disbelief as she arranged her nude loins across his lap, compressing his mighty erection into his belly. She wriggled her warm weight against it. 'Ooh, officer,' she said, 'I can feel your truncheon.'

'Go on,' said the other girl, kneeling by his side, her eyes big with excitement. 'Slap her arse hard. Make her cheeks wobble. You're dying to do it, I bet.'

Stephen didn't believe in physical violence and he didn't believe in corporal punishment. He was revolted by the thought of sadistic practices and repulsed by masochism. That was the theory. But he discovered, as he brought his hand down hard on the firm rounded bum flesh spread across his lap, that theory and practice were two different things. Before he had laid on two solid smacks and set the smooth white flesh in motion he knew that he believed in spanking a girl's naked bottom when she asked for it.

And this one was asking for it all right.

'Harder,' she cried. 'Do it harder! Oh yes, please! Do it again!'

The sounds of the spanking and the moans and squeals of the spankee echoed across the fields. There were whoops and coarse shouts from the barbecue as connoisseurs of the art recognised what was taking place.

'That's enough,' said the first sister, 'any more and you'll have to fuck her straight away.'

'What!'

'Don't worry, you can fuck her soon enough but you've got to spank me first. It's my turn now.'

She was serious. She was stepping out of her black miniskirt, revealing long slim thighs in stockings and suspenders. She wore no knickers and a blonde bush sprang from the base of her belly, the pink stripe of her slit fully revealed beneath. She laid herself across his thighs in place of her sister, her glorious white bum cheeks framed by the black silk of her suspenders and stockings.

'Go on, smack me. Take your revenge.'

'I don't understand.'

'Melanie,' said the other blonde in worried tones.

'Don't worry, sis, he'd never tell. Besides I'm sure he's already worked out who tied him to the garden roller this morning.'

'You!' exclaimed Stephen.

'Well done, Sherlock. Why don't you warm my bum and even the score?'

'It's a deal,' said DC Fantail and set her pretty buttocks dancing.

In the barn, the action was hotting up. The local girls had cleared a space on the sawdust-strewn floor and were performing a dance unknown to outsiders. It involved a lot of hand-clapping and whooping and skirt-flipping – an action that soon turned the male revellers into bug-eyed spectators.

'Did I see what I thought I saw?' said Tony from Wales.

'You did,' replied Mitzi. 'None of these sluts are wearing knickers.'

'Good Lord,' muttered Ray from Humberside as a small brunette lifted her frock to her waist and, for a split second, bared brown thighs and a triangle of black pussy curls.

'Fantastic!' cried Barry from Scotland who had his eye on a strapping blonde pirouetting in front of him. He could not be certain but he'd bet money she had a shaven fanny. Any second now he'd find out . . .

'Hey!' he cried in protest as a small but determind hand spun him round.

'That's enough,' said Mitzi, pushing and pummelling her Gartertex colleagues into a line with their backs to the dance. 'If you guys want to keep me company then you can take your eyes off other women. Don't I look good enough for you?'

Certainly she looked good enough, they agreed. She looked quite splendid. In fact, they had never seen her look so mouth-watering. Particularly in that brassiere.

'Would that be a Raquel you're wearing?' asked Tony as he gazed with fascination at the inner curve of her golden left breast, enticingly exposed in the deep vee of her jacket.

'Looks like a Cleopatra to me,' said Ray. 'Lifts and separates as if by magic. My year-in, year-out stock line.'

Mitzi smiled. This was more like it. 'What's your guess, Barry?' She leaned towards him and gave him the benefit of both barrels, as it were.

He considered the problem. His professional judgement was on the line. 'It's a Samantha,' he pronounced. 'Enhances as it entrances. Only the biggest and the best can get away with it.'

'Correct,' said Mitzi and undid the button holding her jacket over the glories of her chest. 'Look,' she said, and they did.

The big beautiful balloons of her breasts were supported by the flimsiest of scalloped black brassieres. A transparent veil moulded her bosom into twin thrusting peaks whose upper curves were completely bare. The dark brown thimbles of her nipples pointed at them, just begging to be thumbed and tickled and sucked.

'I think Barry deserves a prize,' said Tony.

'Too right,' said Ray. 'Let him take it off.'

Mitzi hesitated. Over Ray's broad shoulder she saw Don. He was dancing in a clinch with that fat blonde and he had his tongue down her throat.

'OK,' she said hoarsely, wondering where this might lead. 'Take my tits out, Barry. You can all have a good look.'

* * *

'Which one do you fancy most?'

Max gave Robyn a surprised glance. The pair of them were sitting on a wooden bench watching the dancers.

'What makes you think I fancy any of them? This set-up is rather too provincial for my taste.'

'Come off it, Max. You're known as the horniest newshound on the *Dog*. Which one of those birds would you like to flush into the open?'

Max surveyed the swirling crowd of girls cheerfully showing off their plump thighs and pouting pussies. A flash of light drew his eye to a slim figure in cool silk whose copper-coloured hair was pushed back off her face as she aimed her camera. Adriana was taking the sensational shots which, suitably censored, would soon adorn Max's shock-horror exposé of naughty nights in the North Grinding.

'Robyn, even if I did fancy one of those fair maids do you think I'd tell you? You'd claim I was about to sell her into white slavery in tomorrow's *Bunny*.'

Robyn smiled. Something of the sort had crossed her mind.

'More to the point,' Max continued, 'why don't you tell me which one you fancy? What about that small dark one with the brown legs who looks Spanish? I understand you have a penchant for Latin girls.'

Robyn forced a laugh but couldn't keep the shock off her face. How the hell did he know about Mercedes?

'It's OK, Robyn, I won't say a word in print. Alistair told me in strictest confidence.'

'He's a bastard. You don't want to believe anything he tells you about me.'

'Quite.' Max appreciated the unobtrusive way Adriana skirted the leering lurching crowd, crouching gracefully to get her shots. 'Did you know that they mix specially prepared seeds and grasses with sawdust and spread it on the floor? That's why the girls leave their knickers off. The seeds fly up and stick to their pubic hair and sexual parts creating in them a furious desire to copulate.'

Adriana was down on one knee in front of him, the thin peach of her loose trousers pulled taut across the full rounds of her buttocks. Max admired her professionalism. He reminded himself that he did not lust after her in the least.

'So?' said Robyn.

'So if you slipped your panties down your delectable legs and stamped around on the floor for a bit we might be able to verify the existence of this aphrodisiacal phenomenon.'

'Are you saying that you want to screw me, Max?'

'You bet. DOG SHAFTS RABBIT – it would make a great headline. Let's go for it.'

'OK but I don't fancy getting a load of grass and seeds up my snatch, thanks very much.'

'Don't worry. I can provide something much more satisfactory.' And he grabbed her hand and led her out of the door, making sure not to catch his photographer's eye on the way.

Julia Jarvis did not feel a part of the hysteria all around her. She observed the girls in their ritual dance as if from afar – to think she had been part of the obscene exhibition last year! She saw her mother cavorting in the crowd, her eyes alight with happiness and lust. Somehow, cocooned in Archie Monk's arms, it did not seem real.

The pair of them swayed together on the fringe of the festivities, like a pair of waltzing pensioners. Julia loved the firm shackle of his arms around her, his lean body pressing into hers, the soft burr of his voice in her ear.

'You've led me a fine dance,' he said. 'You've fooled the entire country, you cunning witch.'

Julia's heart was thumping – surely he wasn't going to arrest her like this? She had the security of Rodney's alibi now, but it was still a frightening prospect.

As if guessing her thoughts, he said, 'Don't worry, I'm no threat to you any longer. I've resigned.'

'I've resigned too,' she blurted.

'I should hope so, you've done enough damage.'

'From the hotel, I mean. I've had enough of it all.'

'What are you going to do?'

'I don't know yet. Find another hotel job, I suppose.'

'How about Scotland? Come with me and we'll open a place in the Highlands. Somewhere miles away where I can keep an eye on you.'

It was an extraordinary thought.

Bedlam erupted around them as one lad threw himself on the small dark dancer who had been taunting him by wiggling her bare belly under his nose. The boy hoisted her over his shoulder and carried her off through the throng, her pert brown buttocks uppermost, a black wedge of hair clearly visible in the crevice between. It was the cue for a free-for-all, as men and women made a grab for one another, some falling to the floor, others surging for the door and the fields outside.

Julia watched her mother exit into the open air, her arms locked fast around a tall blond youth half her age.

The soft Scots voice was still purring into her ear. 'Come on, Brenda, what do you say? Give up your life of crime and come away with me. I'll make an honest citizen of you.'

Julia giggled. 'What if you don't succeed?'

'I've got a very firm hand. I'll teach you some real discipline.'

'Ooh.' Julia snuggled tighter, pushing her full bosom into his chest. 'I like the sound of that.'

They kissed, a deep-throated clinch that sucked the breath from their bodies. His fingers found the hard bud of a nipple through her clothes and she swooned against him.

'What makes you think I'm Brenda?' she asked.

'I examined you, didn't I? I'm sure you're the one.'

'No doubts at all?'

'Well...'

'I think you'd better make certain, Inspector. Take me outside and examine me again.'

The sun had gone down but it was no cooler despite a wind that gusted from the south. The breeze blew hot, like dog's breath, propelling big low clouds across the face of the moon. A storm was approaching and the pressure was rising – particularly in the fields surrounding the barn.

In the weird blue light cast by the moon, Stephen Fantail examined every inch of the two glorious sisters who cradled him between their naked bodies.

'We're not absolutely identical, you know,' said one, running her finger along the rigid barrel of his tool.

'But only our very best friends can tell us apart,' said the other, grazing the tips of her breasts across his chest.

Stephen licked a patch of tender skin high on one girl's inner thigh. He knew, at least he thought he knew, where he would find the mark that would distinguish one from the other. He advanced his tongue and teased open the outer lips of the girl's pouting honeypot. Above him, he heard the hiss of indrawn breath; below, between his legs, he felt the lap of a prying tongue on his balls. Gently he began to suck. He was in no hurry.

Mitzi Bluitt was in the dark in every sense. With one of Ray's big red handkerchiefs tied across her eyes, she could not see a thing. But she could feel and that was the name of the game. From titty-ogling and nipple-pinching and three-way snogging, Mitzi and her admirers had progressed to cock-fondling in the field. As she knelt in the grass, naked to the waist, the men were grouped around her. Their erections were bared to the night air and Mitzi was trying to identify their owners. It was a new diversion for her and she was taking it seriously.

'Circumcised,' she said as she examined the cock on her right. 'Big broad head, fat shaft and – mmm – I can hardly get my lips round it. That's got to be Ray.'

'By gum, she's good,' said a thick northern voice.

'Don't put it away, Ray. I'm going to need it in a moment. Now, this one . . .'

From across the meadow came a harsh, bull-like grunting. Mitzi recognised it at once. It was Don reaching his short strokes with the over-endowed blonde. For a fleeting second she felt sorry for the girl, Don always came too soon. With three men of her own at hand, for once Mitzi was confident she was not going to go short of cock.

'This one's very long. Sweet, too. It's like a stick of rock. I bet it says "Barry" all the way through it.'

'Fantastic!' they cried.

'So this big juicy prick must belong to Tony. It's so smooth, like hot velvet. Let me just rub along here and suck this—'

'Mitzi, be careful! I don't think I can – OH!'

'Wow, Tony, you've gone off like a fire extinguisher! Look, boys, he shot a gallon all over me.' She pulled the blindfold from her face and grinned at them in triumph. Then she began to rub the come into her tits. The sleek rounds of flesh glistened in the moonlight, the nipples shining like wet pebbles.

'God, Mitzi, you're the sexiest woman I've ever met,' said Barry, awestruck. The others murmured hoarse agreement.

Mitzi smiled and took hold of the two remaining erections that pulsed and throbbed inches from her face.

'Thanks, boys, you say the sweetest things. Now who's going to have my mouth and who's going to fuck my cunt? You choose.'

Outside the barn, with the sticky sounds of love and breathless cries of pleasure echoing all around, an earnest conversation was taking place.

'What are you doing here, Chantal? I though my father had you under lock and key.' Graham knew he sounded callow and petulant but he couldn't help himself.

'I came to find you, Graham, though I don't intend to spoil your fun. You should go with that Mandy, I can see you are longing to play with her tits.'

'Don't be ridiculous. I only want you.'

'Maybe, but I saw you watching Mandy dancing just now and your penis was sticking out like a salami. Of course, now you have missed your chance. You will have to wait your turn with her.'

'Chantal, please!'

'She won't mind, I promise you. She's built like a cow, that one, she just loves having her udders squeezed. The man with her will be finished soon.'

'Shut up, Chantal.'

'Don't mind me, Graham. Go and join the queue. I'll wait until—'

He silenced her by placing his lips on hers. He invaded her small sweet mouth with his tongue and held her so tight she thought he would squeeze the life out of her. The kiss went on for a long time. When they came up for air, they were lying full length on a bank of grass and her hand was inside his shirt, toying with the tangle of hair on his chest.

'You mustn't tease me, Chantal,' he said.

'OK,' she said, moving her hand down his body, inside his waistband, to take hold of his rigid tool. 'I came to tell you I'm going to marry your father.'

'That's not funny, Chantal.'

'This is no joke.'

'I don't believe it. You can't do this to me!' He struggled to push her away but she was doing such delicious things to his cock that all resistance soon ceased. Her thumb and forefinger ringed his thick penis, sending waves of sensation down that unthinking limb.

'You're a tart,' he sobbed. 'A cruel gold-digger. You know I love you!'

'Don't be silly, Graham. I'm just the first woman you've slept with who knows how to please a man. You're too young to look further than between my legs.'

'We're the same age!'

'Maybe, but you're a provincial English boy who carries his rich daddy's bags. I'm a French peasant who's never had anything she hasn't earned for herself. There's a world between us.'

'You're a heartless bitch.'

'Drop the self-pity, Graham, and listen to me.' She slowed down the rhythm on his tool and ran her thumbnail gently across the head. The big organ leapt at her touch. He was well under control. She whispered into his ear.

'I'm offering you a deal, Graham. I want us to be friends while I learn about your father's business. A firm like Louche Lingerie is made for me. I know about sex. I know what makes women desirable and I know just how to sell it to them. But all those other deadbeats won't see it that way. They'll hate me. That's why I need you on my side.'

There was a silence. Chantal undid Graham's trousers and pulled his throbbing member into the open.

'What's in it for me?' he said at last. 'The firm will be mine anyway.'

'When? If GG dropped dead tomorrow you wouldn't have a clue what to do. And if he lasts ten years he'll have run it into the ground and you'll have been pushed around for all that time for no reward.'

She pulled her top over her head and threw it into the darkness. Her little breasts jiggled with the movement and she leaned over him to brush their stiff points across his cheek.

'I can manage your father, Graham, and I can manage the business. I'll cut out the dead wood. All those clots like Jason Quiff will be out of work by Christmas. There will be plenty for you and me to do. Apart from the kinky sex, that is.'

She had pulled off her wrap-round skirt and now she was nude. The moonlight gleamed on her pale perfection. She knelt up over him and held the stiff pole of his penis between her thighs.

'What do you mean, kinky sex?' he said, panting.

She spat daintily on her fingers and began to rub the juice into the swollen head of his cock.

'You know, Graham. Sex. Fucking and sucking and wanking whenever your father's back is turned. He's too old, he'll never satisfy me. I need a young cock. Yours.'

'You said kinky sex.'

'You don't think fucking your mother is kinky?'

She surveyed his glistening tool with satisfaction. She could barely contain it in her two small hands.

'Your father is marrying my arsehole, Graham, did you know that? Would you like to bugger me too? Would that be kinky enough for you?'

'Chantal, I—'

'Go on, Graham, admit it. You'd like to stick your big cock in my special place. Of course you would.'

'Oh, Chantal—'

'Mmm, I'd better let you right now, I can see. I like it in my *derrière*. I'll need it regularly once I'm running Louche Lingerie. Suppose I bend down and stick my bottom up like this?'

'Chantal, you're so beautiful!'

'Before you put it in, Graham—'

'Yes?'

'Tell me I can count on your support.'

'I'll do anything you want, Chantal, I promise.'

'Then hurry up and fuck my arse.'

Robyn had a mouth full of cock or she would have said something to Josie as she passed by in the half dark. The

Bunny's special reporter looked as if she had spent a week in the undergrowth with an Under-21 football team. She was naked but for the tattered remains of a torn T-shirt and her buttocks gleamed in the fitful light of the moon. There were leaves and dust on her back, her hair was wild and a river of spunk ran down her legs. For all that, there was a spring in her step as she picked her way between the writhing bodies in search of further conquests. Obviously she was taking her assignment seriously.

Robyn watched her go with half an eye. Her hands were wrapped round Max Shaftesbury's mighty genitals and she was pumping on his shaft as she gummed and sucked the big, mushroom-shaped knob. Between her legs a rasping tongue reamed her dripping honeypot and a lurch in her stomach told her she was approaching orgasm again.

This epic clash of the tabloids might be going the *Dog*'s way – so far he'd brought her off four times and she'd milked him dry only twice – but there were some battles well worth losing. What's more, she felt a remarkable appetite for the fray. After this episode of *soixante-neuf* had run its course, she resolved to get down on her hands and knees and put him through his paces – the thought was amusing – doggie-fashion.

A finger found her clit and she pressed her hungry vagina against his lips. He might be winning a few battles, she told herself, but at the final shot he'd discover he'd lost this particular circulation war.

The storm clouds were racing in fast and the moonlight flickered across the field of heaving bodies. In the distance could be heard the rumble of thunder.

Miriam cried out in ecstasy as Gavin emptied his balls into her with a shout that matched her own. Plunging forward onto the soft cushions of her chest, he fastened his lips around a big ridged nipple. She let him toy with her sumptuous breasts for a moment then impatiently turned him onto his back.

Slithering down his lean body, she buried her face in the hair of his belly and sucked his limp cock into the warmth of her mouth.

Gavin lay on his back and allowed Miriam to do as she wished. He heard a whisper behind him and reached his hands above his head. There he encountered flesh – soft female flesh that answered his curiosity with explorations of its own. An unknown mouth descended on his in the dark. A sly tongue slipped between his lips. He found the curve of a firm buttock and squeezed. Between his legs Miriam had no trouble in restoring his erection.

Across the fields, hands traversed and prospected, mouths solicited and tongues probed, thighs opened and legs entwined. Couples parted and reformed in more interesting configurations, exclusive friendships were shared out, groups evolved and were reshaped afresh. Rampant and naked men and women set about fucking as if the world was due to end the next morning.

The annual Blisswood Midsummer's orgy was approaching its climax.

Josie picked her way across the field by flashes of lightning, the sudden light illuminating lustful tableaux at every step. A woman rode, squealing, on a prone male, her gargantuan breasts rolling on her chest like medicine balls. A man's broad hairy buttocks were frozen before Josie's eyes, the dark plums of his testes dangling in the vee of his thighs. Two girls sat giggling on one lover, one on his stomach, the other rubbing the gash of her pussy across his face.

Josie walked on, stepping carefully between the groups of naked people, avoiding the hands that reached out to detain her.

Her adventures of the evening had been torrid. As she had guessed, her games with the boys in the wood had not been easy to conclude. First had been Martin with his donkey-sized cock, then a thin and beautiful youth who had played on the guitar and then on her clit with a similar dexterity. He had introduced her to two hippies with long hair, enthusiastic tools and inventive minds. She had missed the dance in the barn. She had lost her clothes. And still, despite being ravaged in every orifice big enough to welcome a penis or a tongue or a finger, there was an itch inside her she had still not satisfied.

She stumbled against a soft form on the ground and fell. Hands caught her and she found herself held fast against a broad and hairy chest. He smelt like seasoned wood and felt hard like teak. Without thinking she cuddled into his arms and pushed her soft belly against his groin. He was hard there too. How satisfactory.

Gavin cupped the big breasts in his hands, fondling and stroking their satiny mass. If only he could see!

A flash of lightning answered his prayers and for a split second he held in his hands the object of his quest – the fabulous tits of Bra-less Brenda. Then the girl was pried from his grasp by another man and borne to the ground in front of him where, in another flash, he saw her spreading her legs for her new admirer. He sat on his haunches and listened to them, just a few feet away, as the man drove into her with a grunt and they began the steady see-saw of a fuck.

'Come on, baby,' whispered a soft voice in his ear and a slender arm curled around his neck, pulling him into a perfumed embrace that was impossible to resist. He answered her kiss and ran his hands over a pneumatic form as perfect as any he had ever embraced. On a rising tide of lust he dipped his head to her bosom and the lightning cracked again.

It was only then that he realised his search was over, his crazy and ridiculous quest to find the woman who had robbed him at breast-point and sent his life spinning off the rails. By God, he was grateful to her for rescuing him from his former existence. But now, as he kissed and fondled these new breasts in the darkness, he knew he must call a halt to his journey. For these tits, too, were the pair he sought – the warm and weighty, strawberry-tipped globes of the Topless Raider. To be sure, it was a wonderful way to be driven mad but unless he returned to reality they'd be locking him up for good.

There was a collective cry of joy as the first drops of rain fell on the parched earth and on the sweating bodies locked in their lewd embraces. The sky opened with the roll and crash of thunder and the water fell like waves breaking on a beach.

The photographer Cliff Rush, the only abstainer at the feast, leapt like a demented leprechaun to take the weird and wonderful shots of the orgy in the storm that were to make his name. His uncanny eye led him to capture remarkable scenes of sexual licence lit by lightning. Of Marilyn the former nurse, hosing two ejaculating cocks over her vast wet breasts. Of Mario the waiter, holding Lucy Salmon back to front on his shoulders, his nose in her muff, her face upturned in ecstasy to the turbulent sky. Of Mandy, the would-be model, taking it simultaneously in her bum and in her mouth from two Gartertex salesmen while kneeling in a puddle the size of a small duckpond.

But Cliff failed to capture the one encounter that Robyn Chestnut really wanted – even if it was only suitable for her private scrapbook . . .

At the first drop of rain Gavin stood up and ran, his arms held high, his face turned to the storm. He collided with a woman and they stuck together, arm in arm, shouting and laughing. She was smaller than him and he bent to kiss her unseen face. She gave him her lips and flung her arms round his neck. It felt wonderful.

Gavin was tired but the rain was rejuvenating, like this girl. He hoisted her up and her legs curled around his waist. He held her by the buttocks. They were firm yet full and fitted into his hands as if made to measure. He slipped his little finger into the soft folds of her cunt and she mewed with pleasure, sinking her teeth into his neck.

As if by magic, the swollen head of his penis butted against the spread mouth of her vagina and lodged there.

'Oh yes,' she breathed into his ear. 'Do it to me please! Fuck me standing up in the rain, whoever you are.'

Gavin froze, the voice as familiar yet unexpected as bad news. But this, he realised as she wriggled the tight sheath of her pussy over the head of his trembling tool, was the most miraculous news he had ever heard.

The lightning flashed again and confirmed his happy fate.

'Josie!' he cried and drove his cock up into the depths of her.

My Secret Life

My Secret Life is a monument to one man's obsession with sex and his daunting literary urge to record a lifetime spent in its pursuit. This unknown Victorian's unique confession runs to eleven volumes, chronicling his erotic life in unrelenting detail. Despite research, the identity of the author, 'Walter', remains as mysterious as that of Jack the Ripper.

The following excerpts are taken from the end of the author's account when it evidently took something out of the ordinary to keep his fires burning. Walter's consuming interest in whores and their tricks-of-the-trade, in watching others and glorying in the physical evidence of their excitement is, as he acknowledges, a consequence of his advancing years. The book is a treasure-trove of information on Victorian sexual customs, in particular these passages shed light on the activities of the Englishman abroad. It is no surprise that the language of sexual engagement transcends all barriers – especially where easy women and ready money are concerned . . .

In early autumn I was at the baths of ******. At seven o'clock a.m. I was on the promenade near the brunnen, and saw a woman looking about twenty-five years old, with whom in form, height, features and complexion, few could compare. She was one of the most beautiful women I ever saw, and unmistakably a whore, tho she neither looked right or left or at any man. I followed her up and down discreetly till I caught her eye, gave her a significant look, and followed her to her lodgings. At the foot of the staircase told her that after breakfast I would be with her at half past ten that morning.

There at the time was she expecting me, in a loose peignoir which thrown off, left her but a chemise of finest cambric, and that removed left her nude, all but blue silk stockings and kid boots. She was one of the finest, most beautiful perfect creatures, that God ever created, yet she was but a Paphian, facile to a degree, and without any nonsense about showing it. Soon she was on the bed, and between a pair of thighs and buttocks perfect in form, smoothness and color, opened a smallish, delicate aperture, fringed sufficiently with chestnut hair. It was of the most enticing description, was indeed one of the loveliest cunts I ever saw. – Neither clitoris, nymphae, vagina or lips, were too large or too small, – ample crisp and fine hair was around it, and shadowed the mons, but not a hair was on her buttocks, nor near a little tight anus looking too small and close to let a straw through it. The oval buttocks with their gradual elongation into the loveliest tapering thighs were exquisite. In fact, buttocks, belly, thighs, fringe, gap, clitoris, nymphae, color, all were perfectly beautiful.

Tearing my clothes off rapidly in lustful impetuosity, throwing myself upon her greedy of her charms, hurrying to pierce her, to fill that diving gap with my spunk, with a plunge up went my prick into her. It was a bottomless cunt, my tip found no obstacle, all was divinely soft, lubricious, elastic, compressive. In a thrust or two it found its place, no thrusts were needed more, it was in a fleshy paradise, needing no exertion to enjoy it, and where it loved for a minute to remain quiet. But the lovely sheath had its own desires, its own way of acting, of evoking pleasure, of getting out from my testicles the emulsion which was to soothe its heat. – With the gentlest heaves, with imperceptible compressions, it received my equally gentle movements, constricted, pinched my pego more and more, and yet with exquisite delicacy, till at length from out of my reservoirs, spurted my spermatic mucilage, and I died off in her arms faint with pleasure, sleepy almost with sensuous fatigue, clasping her buttocks, sucking her sweet tongue as I lay quietly up her; whilst her thighs gradually sank lower, her belly ceased its heavings, her cunt its grips, and wallowing in my sperm, both prick and cunt lay joined in blessed quietude.

How I wish I'd been younger and at liberty, I think I should have had her night and day till exhausted, but that was physically and for other reasons impossible. But I enjoyed looking at her, and as she appeared in handsome clothing at the various places, sat and looked, or followed and looked at her, and in my mind's eye saw those lovely thighs and belly, that exquisite cunt, as well as if she'd been undressed. Then I began to wonder what other man had enjoyed those charms, and longed to see a man as handsome as she was, giving her pleasure, injecting his semen into her.

Of this divine creature I can say no more than that for some weeks I saw her often. I could have loved her, big woman, sausage eating, beer drinking woman, harlot tho she was. I could have loved her, for she was for sexual pleasures absolute perfection. She loved her profession, yet was not greedy of money. 'I can have as many men as I want, I expect a friend at

half past eleven,' said she, on the first day, 'and you must go.'
— How many scores of women I have had, whose cunts never seemed to give me such complete physical pleasure as this woman's did. — To be happy with any woman the cunt must fit the man's prick. — A subtle refinement of sexuality this, but such is my belief, and then in conjugal life all is happiness.

One afternoon on a blazing hot day, I called without notice, and had not been in her room five minutes, was not undressed nor she, and I had placed her on the bed with her clothes negligently thrown up so that her magnificent backside and cunt were visible. I sat in a chair opposite the bed enjoying the luscious spectacle, when a knock came. 'Oh' said she, 'I'm so sorry, I'd forgotten. I was to see a man at this time, and he's here, go into the other room for a minute, it's Mein Schwester's room, till I've sent him away.' Quick as lightning came the letch. — 'No, I'll wait. Let him fuck you, let me see him fuck you, then come into your sister's room, with all his sperm in your cunt and let me see it full of it, make him quite naked, you be so too, and I'll pay you well.' In polyglot language, in half whispers, all this was said, but I was understood. — 'Yah, yah, — but you cannot see — the sparm yes — schnell, — go — he is outside.' — More knocks were heard, and in a few seconds I had passed through the door into the sister's room, locked it, peeped, and Oh joy! found I could see the lower half of the bed, and a tall handsome fair haired young man standing there, talking to my woman.

Until that moment I did not know my charmer had a sister — I had seen her walking about with a shorter and younger woman and this was Mein Schwester who began her blandishments in a very quiet way and spoke in a quiet voice. — Did I mind her dressing? — certainly not — whereupon she stripped to her waist and began washing a lovely youthful breast. But I wanted to see a fine couple fucking, and could not take my eye from the keyhole. Finding that, — 'If you get on a chair you'll see better' — said the Fraulein pointing to the door;

and sure enough thro a natural crack high up in an ill made door, I now saw the whole bed.

He was caressing her, feeling her cunt, sitting on the bedside with her. She had got his prick out which looked like a rolling pin, its tip uncovered, red as crimson, and ready for insertion. They spoke in a foreign language of which I understood little, but from occasional words and from her movements, knew that she was urging him to undress. A blazing hot day it was. All at once he began undressing in haste till in his shirt. 'All, all,' said she, and off that went whilst she threw off her chemise. There they stood naked, a splendid couple, he nearly six feet high with clean white flesh without hair, with a stalwart prick full seven inches long, and thick as well. On the bed quickly she laid, her exquisite thighs apart. I could see her adorable gap which he licked for a minute as he stood, then laid down beside her for a second only, she handling his splendid organ whilst he felt for hers. But all was too quick, his prick must have been standing whilst waiting outside her rooms for me to escape, it was rigid when he undressed, and the next second he was on her fucking. Then I could only see his back and a bit of his balls at times, at he thrust and withdrew, which he did with such energy, that in a minute I saw by the movement of his arse and his pressure on her, that the libation was given. Then they lay languid and quiet.

Wild with lust, not willing to lose any of the spectacle, I beckoned the sister to me, and pulled off coat and waistcoat as I stood and gave them to her whilst looking still thro the aperture. – Soon I heard her say something, which I knew was that she'd go into her sister's room and wash. Down I got, pulled off every thing I had on but shirt and socks, and just as I'd finished doing so in she came, holding her finger to her mouth for my silence, holding her cunt to prevent the sperm from dropping, but speaking aloud to her sister. – At once she, knowing my letch, laid at the bed side and opened her thighs.

Oh accomplished Paphian! and how they like their trade when they succeed.

There was the lovely cunt, its red surface well nigh hidden by white thick sperm. The sperm hung to the fringe, it lay thick low down on the orifice of the avenue into which the libation had been poured. – My brain whirled with sensuous excitement. I scarcely knew what I did. – Intending only to have seen the copulation and the results, now the desire to have her just as she was, to cover my prick with his sperm, overwhelmed me. Motioning her on to the bed, I threw off my shirt, mounted her, and plunged my prick into the soft semenalized vagina, revelling in baudy delight as I felt the grateful lubricity on my prick, then felt all round the stem where her cunt lips touched it, and rubbed my balls against her bum furrow, so that all his spendings might be on and about me. Then not so young now, or so full as my predecessor, I lingered quietly up her, thinking with salacious delight of what I'd seen and where I was. – 'Have you spent with him?' 'No he was so quick,' was all that was said. then at the idea of giving *her* pleasure, of fetching out *her* juices I began my thrusts, my prick squashing the sperm as I moved it up and down. My beauty's passions were roused, I know that this fucking in another's sperm excites women; murmurs of fuck, prick, cunt, sperm, ejaculated in three languages were given, and with our tongues exchanging and mingling their salivas, we spent together, and the essence of two males and her own spendings mixed together in her cunt.

Before my stiffness had gone she uncunted me, washed, and went back to him. I with prick still moist mounted again the chair. There he laid naked on the bed (it was a scorching hot day) feeling his prick. 'Have you washed?' said she. – 'No, I'll fuck you again,' and pulling her on to the bed he began feeling her cunt.

Tho tired and reeking with perspiration, I wished to see more, but got down and washed. Silently. Mein Schwester held the washhand basin for me. Then I mounted the chair again and watched them at their amorous dalliance. Soon after on looking round, I saw the sister was stark naked sponging herself all over. Was it to wash herself, or to show me her charms?

He did only what I have done hundreds of times, and described many times in this narrative of my secret life, but how fresh, ever fresh and voluptuously exciting are such scenes, such amatory amusements. To me this was exquisite. There were these superb creatures in the fullness of youth and beauty, feeling each other's genitals, feeling all over their bodies, and kissing almost in silence, for speech is useless almost in such delights. Then his mouth settled on her cunt and he gamahuched her. How I envied him, for I have already sucked and tongue titillated that lovely gap. Soon her lovely backside writhed, her belly heaved, and as he kneeled I could see sideways his prick, still and nodding as his lust got stronger with his delicious amusement. Why did they not consummate? I was impatient to see the termination, to see her thighs around his — his buttocks oscillating with the thrusts of his prick up her cunt, I longed to be feeling his buttocks whilst at the exercise. But he was now in no hurry, wisely delaying the lust destroying crisis. — There I stood peeping, stark naked, sweating now with excitement, every now and then looking down at the sister leisurely washing herself from head to foot. Soon she had put on chemise and slippers, and looked up smilingly at me. Another peep, they were talking side by side, his prick lolling on his thigh not now quite stiff. The glorious finale would not be yet, and down I got, for my companion began to rivet my attention.

Questioning her, she declared that she was the sister, was twenty-one, her sister twenty-six. Her eyes and face showed family likeness. 'Is your cunt like your sister's?' — 'I don't know.' 'Show it to me, take off your chemise.' — Without reply she took it off, and laid on the bed. I saw that potential almost omnipotent charm of the woman, that red, central, hairy framed furrow, that scented, red lipped, division of her belly, that orifice which subjugates the male whether emperor or beggar. The gamahuche of her sister was in my mind, she was perhaps being gamahuched at that moment. The letch seized me, and applying my tongue to the Fraulein's cunt, I licked it rapidly, thinking of her sister's gamahuching, wishing we were all in the same room, and gamahuching side by side.

When the Fraulein had enjoyed my lingual treat, when the twitching of her thighs and bum gave warning of her coming crisis, she pushed me off. 'Nein, nein, fuck me.' – I stood up, prick stiffening, and looked at her rosy flesh. Much younger, neither so tall nor so stout as her sister, but plump and fine in form, with solid bubbies was she. She'd such a pretty mouth, that I cried, 'Suck me.' – 'Wash it then.' – Rapidly I sluiced my injector, heard speaking in the adjoining room, ceased frigging the Fraulein, mounted the chair again, and saw her sister opening wide her thighs for the entry of that grand love staff. – 'He's fucking' – I cried, and then with rapid multiplication of desires in my brain, wishing for all things voluptuous, to be fucking both the sisters at once, to be frigging him, cried out, 'Suck me, suck me, mein lieben.' Without a word or any hesitation, she took my penis in her pretty mouth, and so I stood, her tongue and palate ministering to my pleasure, whilst I saw the other two joined into one body, heaving, thrusting, writhing, as he plunged his pego up and down, till one long cry of pleasure, told that his sperm was shooting into her.

Then getting down, furious for similar pleasure, I mounted Mein Schwester, fucked hard and quickly, and just as my pleasure was increasing, in came the elder stark naked as before. I stopped for a second. 'Come to the bed,' I cried and moved my beauty and myself close to the wall to make room. The elder laid down, I buried my fingers in her lubricious cunt, put my prick again in the younger, and fucked out my sperm into her in a delirium of baudy desires, and visions of what I had just seen.

The man went away, the two washed their cunts, I spent another hour with them, they and myself naked, for it was a day on which nudity was alone tolerable, and then fucked my favorite after putting my prick first into her sister, then into her. The elder said she didn't know of that natural crack in the door: perhaps not, but perhaps thro that crack some one had seen *me*, fucking *her* — what matters?

I could not for health's sake fuck her as often as I desired, but visited her at times solely to see her naked and to gamahuche her, for now I love gamahuching a pretty cunt whether quite a young one or not — love to give a woman that pleasure which few whether harlot or modest can refuse.

She told me she was born at ***** and had four sisters. — One was kept by an Austrian nobleman. — Another was a gay lady at ****. She and her sister there made the fourth. They were a harlotting family evidently, *all* beautiful and open to all the male sex. — Thank beneficent providence for that.

A month after being in the mountains I went to the lapunar at Paris already mentioned. At various periods, many of the Paphians there knew my tastes — I usually saw the salon when full of women, and each was anxious for my selection, for I was liberal.

I went to the bordel early, the women had only just left the coiffeur's hands, few had been fucked that night, tho some no doubt had during the day. — About twenty of them were in the salon, some quite naked, stockings and shoes excepted, others with diaphanous gauze around them, thro which all their charms were visible. Some sitting, others half reclining, one or two standing. — Breasts, arms, fat thighs and backsides nude — mottes shewing like charcoal set in ivory, some women exhibiting hairy armpits — an indescribably voluptuous scene.

'Salon mesdames,' said the *sous-maitresse* opening the door. – For a second the chatter ceased, then recommenced, limbs moved, eyes flashed, many spoke and all at once. – 'Ici, Monsieur.' – 'Monsieur c'est moi.' – 'Moi Marguerite.' – 'Ohé.' – 'Ah cochon.' – 'Vous ne vous souvenez pas du moi.' – etc. etc. – Some put out their tongues lasciviously. – Some opened wide their thighs. – Some put fingers on their clitorises with frigging movements, – others pulled their cunt lips open. – It is one of the most marvellous sights in the world, but the excitement renders selection of a woman difficult. My eyes roved from one to another of the Paphians, dazzled, bewildered by sight, sound, and lewed suggestions.

I selected a woman, who went upstairs naked, stepping up daintily, I following just so low behind her, that I could see the dark furrow between her buttocks, which moved with a wriggle as she went prancing up step by step – a cock standing sight, but mine didn't stand – 'Marie, est ce que la jaune est occupée?' Her hand was on the handle – I had asked for that room. – 'Si, si, Mademoiselle, pas la, – ici donc, – ici.' We entered another room, rich looking and hot – they are all kept hot, so that the women who are naked for hours should not catch cold, and can strip themselves. In fact, a fucking atmosphere is kept up.

I did not like my choice, she was thinner than I'd thought, but was beautifully made, had dark brown hair on her cunt and not too much of it, – a pretty cunt. Her face was Southern, her head dressed in Oriental fashion was hung with sequins, large gold bracelets were on her arms, gold coins round her neck. She was she said twenty-two. 'I'll make my toilet,' quoth she. I don't know what made me say it or what passed thro my mind, for I had come to be gamahuched, and on those occasions like to feel a *quite clean cunt* – for all that I objected. 'Have you been fucked tonight?' – 'Not yet.' – 'Don't wash, I don't like a dry cunt.' 'Tres bien, je le rafraichirai seulement.' Out she went, in a minute returned, I put my fingers up her cunt and felt its natural state, it had not been washed inside. – Then I wished it had been but did not say so, looked at it well but was confused, saw a cunt and nothing particular about it, and had no desire to fuck.

I had travelled much two days previously, felt tired – and worse – that I should not like *her*. I had felt my cock whilst she was washing and there was no stiffness in it. – 'I shall give you trouble, am old, may not be able to fuck you.' – 'Old? not so old – I'll make you do it.' – 'No, I am old.' – 'How old then?' – I told. 'Quel mensonge – what shall we do – faite l'amour?' – 'Let me see your cunt more.' She threw herself on the bed, her legs invitingly apart – It was a pretty and fresh cunt but it did not stir me. – When I had done amusing myself with it, 'Suck my prick,' I said. – 'Tres bien.' – Taking a wet towel she washed the top, pulling down the prepuce and looking carefully at it – I took off my clothes and laid on the bed, she began running her nimble tongue all round the roots, over the balls, and finally taking the tip into her mouth, gave a preliminary lick, spat out, and then went on quickly rolling her tongue over the tip, moving her head up and down. One moment the tip came into sight the next it was hidden to the roots.

For a moment it stood stiff under her delicate tongue friction. – She gave it a gentle frig, and down my prick sunk again, – to my shame – 'I told you I was tired.' 'Never mind, I'll make it come up' – and she recommenced.

I turned her about in many attitudes, her lithe form twisted any way. I felt her cunt deeply whilst she gamahuched, then put her over me kneeling and looked at her cunt, but all was useless. – Ashamed, 'I told you so.' – 'You are fatigued' – I was glad of the excuse which was true tho. – 'Let me feel your finger.' – Finding the nails short, – 'Put one up my bum, gently, oh, gently.' – 'Open your legs wide.' Wetting her finger with spittle she gently drove it up me, irritating my fundament, sucking my cock all the time, giving me voluptuous sensations – but no cockstand came. Then she ticked my bum hole with her tongue, then up went her finger again – but it remained limp.

'It's of no use,' she said, – 'Shall I get you another girl?' – 'Have you a dear, dear friend?' 'Yes, a fine woman – superb – dark – oh dark, such black hair on her cunt, – You'll like her.' – 'Will you play at minette with her, voulez, vous faire la tribade avec elle?' – 'Oh yes, we often do it, shall I get her?' – I wanted some excuse, yet for some intangible reason said, 'No.' – 'Do, – you have made me randy,' – said Sappho. 'Whilst she minettes *me*, you can fuck *her*.' – 'What's her name?' – I did not want a woman who knew me. – 'Raffaella – so lovely, – the finest woman in the house – and si chic, si polissonne, je l'aime la petite cochonne' – and she kissed the air and wriggled her backside. – 'She is si fraiche, only been galante deux mois – ah! je l'aime.'

I did not want Raffaella, had come to be gamahuched, wanted to feel my prick tip rubbing in a pretty mouth, my sperm gushing into it, to feel the peculiar sensation which gamahuching can alone give the prick when it spends – to feel it shrinking – yet retained and sucked – no cunt can do *that* quite, tho, it does much better. I felt angry and ashamed. 'Suppose your friend won't.' – 'But certainly she will, let me fetch her, she will minette you, and so will I her.'

Just then I heard a woman coming up stairs singing, and the tread of a man following. They went into the adjoining room, and we could hear them indistinctly through the partition. – Lewed thoughts now came. I had many times seen the cunt of my handsome H*1*n M***w**d covered with the sperm of her lover, had gloried in its viscid glistening, had seen and heard her in her throes of pleasure, whilst a magnificent prick was jetting out its essence into her, and afterwards had put my own prick up and added to the libation; but had then no desire to see any other cunt in similar state. Yet now the letch seized me. 'Fetch *her* directly she's been fucked, and before she washes.' – Out went Sappho, knocked at the next door, there was a low toned conversation, and she came back. 'It is *she, she* who is my friend, she will come, you shall see she is the finest woman in the house. – Yes, she'll come with foutre in her cunt.'

Laying half naked, thinking and frigging my prick, a voluptuous sensation ran from its tip thro my balls, but no stiffness came. I heard laughter in the adjoining room, and a screech like that which a randy woman sometimes gives when a man baudily assaults her. Sappho was standing by the door. 'Why stand there?' – She wanted Raffaella to come in quickly without being seen she said, to bilk the landlady by not letting her know she had had two men. All was quiet now. 'They are making love,' said Sappho shutting the door and beginning to play with my cock, which had shrunk to the size of a walnut again.

A door slammed, mine opened, and in came a fine tall young woman. – Jet black she looked in hair and eyes as she entered, one hand on her cunt, pinching the lips to prevent the spunk dropping on her legs. On the bedside she laid at once and opened her thighs, shewing a cunt surrounded with hair black as charcoal from motte to arsehole, where the thick growth hid the buttock furrow. The lips opening, shewed a dark crimson lining where thick sperm did not cover it; the bright light fell on her cunt. Sappho soon leant over her, sucking her nipples, muttering I know not what in an endearing manner.

Raffaella pulled open her cunt lips with both hands. It was dark crimson colored, shining and with little lumps of opaque sperm laying near the prick hole. – 'Do you like looking at a cunt so?' she asked. – 'Yes.' – 'Fuck me cheri, fuck then.' – My prick stood now. – 'Has he spent much?' – 'Oh! yes, much – look.' – raising her thighs and buttocks but keeping them wide apart, she then gave a tightening, and a mass of gruelly sperm rolled out slowly towards her bum furrow, till caught by the crisp black, curly, hairs. – 'Did *you* spend?' – 'Nearly, I want it now, fuck me and I shall.' – My cock stood stiffly, but I did not insert it. 'I am frightened,' I said.

She moved sideways on to the bed, closing her thighs, grabbing my prick as she did so. – 'It's quite safe, he is a friend, and I often see him, a blond with a fine beard, his foutre is good, fuck me cheri, put it in.' Again she distended her thighs and frigged my prick hard. Her thighs had now got spermy thro her moving. There I stood I looking at her, Sappho recommenced kissing her, and every now and then feeling my balls, whilst Raffaella sometimes twiddled the tip gently.

Tho this was yesterday, I am confused about my thoughts and sayings at this juncture, then all is clear again. Raffaella looked lovely, her body was gloriously formed, large globes with small nipples, black armpits, large creamy colored thighs, joining her belly in a thicket of black hair. The cunt slightly open and fuckingly aromatic, smelling like the cunt of a woman, soothed by male sperm which had not mingled with her own. I wanted her, yet did not accept the invitation of, 'Baisez moi donc!' But fear and disgust at the male sperm came over me – my nature is so curious.

All at once I thought of H*l*n's cunt. 'Faite la minette,' – Sappho dropped on to her knees and began. I laid my head on Raffaella's thighs and smelt the sperm, my bum began to oscillate as I fucked in Sappho's mouth. She held my balls in one hand, whilst her finger penetrated gently my bum hole till I spent. Raffaella was frigging herself when my pleasure came on.

Raffaella saying she must go back to her friend, left, but she would soon return. I laid on the bed tired, Sappho sponged and wiped my prick, and wanted to know if I always was gamahuched. 'No.' – 'Why not fuck now?' – I did not want the man's spunk on my prick. It was all right, *she* knew also the man, besides Raffaella had wanted me to fuck her. –

'Nonsense,' I remarked. Sappho was sure she did. Then we heard laughing in the next room, the door opened and champagne ordered. – 'Ah mon Dieu, they will be some time, he will fuck her again.' I would wait, and Sappho remarking that I should have to pay the house for her, I consented, was now indeed ready to pay anything to see that fine black hair cunted, woman naked, and her semenalized cunt again.

I laid on the bed fatigued, languid with voluptuous anticipations. Sappho chatting and playing with my cock, at times sucking it. At times it stood, but fell when she ceased. I played with her bubbies and cunt, then noticed that her clitoris projected much, tho not very large nor ugly. I frigged it till her bum wriggled and she pinched my prick hard. 'Do you like gamahuching a woman?' she asked. I had done such a thing. – 'Do it to me' – I declined, was too old. – 'You look better than half the young ones,' said she.

I told her I'd had many women in that house. – Had I seen women flat fucking each other? – I mentioned women I'd had, some were there still, others had left. – Said she, 'I never had a man who wanted a woman just when she has been kissed, and I thought you wanted to fuck her so.' – I replied that when the desire seized me I scarcely knew quite what I wanted, but now wished to see them two flat fucking together. 'What will you give us?' – 'A napoleon each if you flat fuck properly, spend together, – faites la tribade.' – Laughing in the adjoining room ceased. 'He's fucking again,' I said. She went outside the door again. – 'The chambermaid's there and says you must pay the house as well.' – 'I have already said I will!' – Sappho again went out and coming back, 'She will be here directly – he is going.' – 'Let me see him.' – 'No.' – Gentlemen did not like to be looked at and it was the chambermaid's business to prevent it. – I heard, 'Monsieur descend.' The next instant Raffaella came again into the room smiling and with fingers on her cunt as before and at once threw herself on the bed and opened her charms to my gaze, the cunt looked much as before, but less wet. The spunk was in the roots of the hair and on one of her thighs, but her cunt was less inviting.

'Did you spend with him?' — 'Ah yes, *now* I had my pleasure.' — I stood enjoying the sight, and again she pressed me to have her. — We kissed, she shoved her tongue in my mouth, used all her incitements. 'Kiss me cheri. — Ah? fookee moi donc, c'est anglais, n'est ce pas? fookee me — fookee me, n'est ce pas. — Ah polisson.'

I wanted to feel her cunt, yet could not bear to touch the man's sperm — strange inconsistency — but amused myself by squeezing the lips together and letting them go, they opened with a slight noise. She every now and then heaving her rump, sighing, and asking me to poke her, took hold of my prick. Sappho then began sucking Raffaella's bubbies, and cooing her in an affectionate way. — Raff got more energetic, grasped and licked my prick, begged me to do it — it was delicious with the sperm of another. 'Mais que c'est donc delicieux.' — 'Faites la minette avec Sappho.' — 'No do me — fookee me donc.' — 'Don't you like Sappho?' — 'Perfectly, yes' — I, weary of begging them to flat fuck ceased my entreaties. — Sappho had been tippling my champagne, and suddenly sprang on the bed, put her legs across and knelt over the mouth of the other, the dark one put her hands round Sappho's buttocks and licked Sappho's cunt. I saw her tongue go up and on it, saw Sappho's arsehole. The dark one's legs closed up now. I only saw the wriggling of Sappho's buttocks — and in the large looking glass on the wall against which the bed was placed — the movement of her breasts and belly. The sequins on her head shook as she moved, she sighed, murmured, her buttocks wriggled, and Raffaella's fingers buried themselves in bum furrow. Then Sappho crying, 'Suck then, suck quick — quick,' — and jogging her backside on Raff's mouth rapidly — leant forward over her head, then reeled off by her side, and lay panting — legs slightly apart — the hair of her cunt drenched with spittle.

Sappho soon got up, gave champagne to her friend, drank herself and asked for another bottle, then pissed. The two were getting noisy. French women soon get lively under champagne. They rarely piss before a man unless asked, most of their arseholes I expect have been stretched a little, and farts then escape easily I have been told.

More champagne was brought. – They questioned me. – Raffaella asked me to lie down – I did. – She moved more on her side to let me, then began frigging my cock, which was quite limp. – Sappho again stood by the side of the bed, and told Raffaella she had put her finger up my bum hole. Raffaella laughing asked if I liked *that*, and why I wanted, to see her without having 'made her toilette.' – French women don't use the strong expressions, unless lascivious with desire and really wanting a fuck.

The room was very hot. – There I lay on the outer edge of the bed – the dark one by my side – Sappho standing by the bed. I slipped one hand on to Raffaella's cunt, and the other on to Sappho's, which was still wet with her friend's saliva and her own spend. Raffaella's was moist and I longed to feel up it, yet had the dislike to put my fingers into the man's sperm. Raffaella went on handling my doodle. – 'Kiss me' – she said. 'Let Sappho kiss you.' – 'I'll wash first,' said she. – 'No – no – just as you are.' – 'I can't.' – 'Yes, I don't mean minette, but tribadez – rub your cunts together – clitoris to clitoris – till you both spend.'

Both laughed long and loud. – 'We never do *that* – jamais.' – 'You lie, – Sappho said you did.' – 'Oh, but isn't he a villainous old pig.' – 'Oh the old rogue,' said one. 'He has lived, hasn't he?' said the other. – 'Do English women do it? – tell us then' – said Sappho. – I told them all I knew, and how I had had my thumb up one woman's cunt, and finger up the other's whilst they lay flat fucking.

'My God! – he is fit for a school teacher or a professor,' said Sappho. – 'I'll wash – yes, – it's not healthy,' said Raff. –

But I pushed her back – 'I wish not that, but with the sperm.' – I had got off the bed, was pulling wide open the dark one's thighs again, and now the sperm attracted me. – It made me stiffen as I saw the still glazed cunt. – I was longing, yet disliking it. Then Sappho laid herself down by the side of the black haired and kissed her, began sucking her bubbies, put one hand to her cunt and frigged it. 'Was it the German?' asked she. 'Yes.' – 'Which?' – 'The tall one – he is coming tomorrow, he likes me,' – this all said in a low confidential tone. – The other slightly then turned round, quite closing her thighs as a woman sometimes does, when a voluptuous randy thrill goes thro her. Sappho put her tongue into Raff's mouth then turned on to Raffaella's belly, who opened her thighs, and lay on her back.

Sappho nestled her belly to her friend's, put her hand between them, seemed to be feeling their cunts, then withdrawing it again squeezed her quim down, and clutching Raffaella's backside, wriggled – Raffaella raised her thighs and crossed her legs high up over Sappho's loins, then they both wriggled, sighed and kissed, their tongues were joined, I heard the slobber of their salivas. – Then furiously Sappho began to move somewhat like a man fucking, Raffaella's hands slid up and down Sappho's back, then clutched her bum. – 'Ah! quicker! – Ah! God!' – cried she. Again their mouths slobbered and smacked whilst their arses heaved, their bodies moved all over, both sighed, then gently subsiding lay quiet in each other's arms.

I saw every movement of their arses, their heads, their eyes and mouths – not one escaped me – they were reflected in every direction, and every wriggle, twist, thrust, grip and thrill was visible. – I stood by the bed feeling Sappho's bum, then got my fingers between the cheeks till they were buried in wet hair, and then my fingers slipped further into a mass of wet cunt – for both cunts were close together – I could not touch one without touching the other. I thought they had done, when

Sappho again began wriggling, and for a quarter of an hour was more kissing and wriggling, then murmuring their delight, and at last loudly, they again lay tranquil, but with bodies palpitating, their limbs straight, the red silks of Sappho between the white silks of Raffaella. Again I pushed my fingers between the cheeks of Sappho's arse. She distended her thighs to let them thro as if she liked my groping. Their cunts were still touching each other.

'Sappho,' said a shrill voice outside, and a knock came at the door – Sappho went out quickly. I looked at Raff's cunt, as Sappho got off from it. It was wet, the hairs were sticking on her mount. – She caught hold of my prick. 'Foutez moi donc, chéri – fookee me – c'est anglais n'est ce pas chéri? ah! que vous êtes méchant.' – She liked a fuck after a flat fuck she said. [Some women do I find.]

My prick was stiff now and I was about to put into her, when the dislike and fear of the male spunk again overtook me. 'No, suck me.' – She wriggled to the bedside pulled me to her till my prick touched her thigh, but I got away from her and wouldn't fuck. – Sappho returned, and I put her on the bed with knees up, and one leg so that her foot rested on the pillow, thus her thighs opened, and I saw sperm on *her* cunt, she'd been fucked when out of my room. Raff put her head on Sappho's leg which lay nearest, turned on to her side, her face close to my belly, and raising herself on her arm took my prick in her mouth. 'Put up *your* leg, let's see *your* cunt.' – Up one went, and there in front of me was the brown haired cunt of Sappho open, and glistening with spunk, her clitoris jutting out, and the large white thighs of Raffaella distended, her black haired cunt, gaping and shining.

Then I fucked between Raff's beautiful red lips – glancing first at one cunt, then the other. – 'Aha – aha – I'm coming. – Je décharge.' – Withdrawing my pego – I thrust one hand's fingers up Sappho's cunt, the other up Raffaella's, forgetting now the male spunk, both cunts wet with it and their own spendings. My hands outspread were covered with it, my fingers glided in and out of the prick holes, and then I felt the whole of their cunts at the same time. Suddenly the sperm which I had disliked excited me, made me lewed, I wanted to fuck in it, one hand was wet to my knuckles, the sperm squeezed between my fingers, it was the outcome of the spending of two lewed women and two men. – 'Oh you hurt,' said Sappho. – The idea of that fetched me. – 'Christ! I'm coming.' Putting my pego again into Raffaella's mouth, I spent, half fainted with pleasure, – my body drooped over her – and still I kept my fingers in the cunts. – When I came to, Raff was still gently sucking. Oh! the delight as it drew the last drop of semen in a way that no cunt can, – dragging it out from the roots of my balls, my anus tightening with the throbs. – I almost dropped down with voluptuous enervation.

Then I staggered to the sofa, half stupefied. In a few minutes came to, my hands still sticky, and I lay feeling my fingers with eyes closed, and thinking of the voluptuous delights. There was movement, sighs, a sob of pleasure. Opening my eyes, there was Sappho on the top of Raffaella again. – They were cunt rubbing hard, sucking each other's tongues, backsides agitating, they moaned, kissed, sobbed, then shrieked, their thighs and buttocks moved so fast together, that the spring mattress heaved them up, they were almost glued together. Then all was silent.

Sappho rolled off, her backside towards the looking glass. Raffaella's cunt had every hair of it soddened, Sappho's was the same – I opened Raff's thighs, she still panting. Sappho opened her eyes. – 'Have we done well, vieux cochon?'

Sappho's head dress which she had begged me at first to take care of during our frolics was now in disorder, gold sequins had tumbled off. Raffaella's hair lay loose about her neck. – Both mechanically put a hand under their cunts as they got off the bed. Both took up the champagne bottle. – It was empty – I'll order another. – 'My God! if I have more, there will be a row' – said Raff. – 'Never mind I have you both for the night.' – '*Are* you going to stay? – do – sleep between us naked.'

I was done up – my long journey – the heat, excitement, and spends had finished me; had a violent pain in my head, my eye sight seemed to be going – it was exhaustion. – But I could not bear to leave the naked women, sat feeling my prick without desire, yet in a state of baudy pleasure looking at them. – Sappho went out to wash and came back. – 'Let's see your cunt again Raffaella before you wash.' – 'Look at him feeling his old prick.' – Saying that she put one of her feet upon my knees, and pulled open her cunt lips. – 'Tchec,' said she with her tongue. – 'Is not he a baudy one?'

Both then sucked my cock, and got it stiff again – but throbbings in my temple warned me, just as I was about to put my prick into the thicket of Raff, so I left. Ten years ago, I would have fucked each of them twice.

In the month of September I was at the little village of **** in Switzerland. There was [then] a little building called a casino – to which people went to read the journals – situated in small grounds filled with trees and large shrubs. – It was a dull, muggy afternoon, and had been raining hard when I wandered there just before the table d'hôte. Few people were out, and walking by herself, quite on the outskirts of the grounds, was a well-grown woman seemingly about twenty-five or more years old, dressed very nicely in dark silk. She never approached the building and I got curious about her, passed and repassed her looking in her face, wondering whether she was of easy virtue or not. She looked at me in return but quite in a casual way, without the least indication of the demirep about her. For all that, as I passed a desire for the woman came over me, and a voluptuous thrill passed through my pego. I had been some days at the place and had never noticed the lady there before, tho I must have seen nearly all the visitors there.

My Secret Life 329

I dined, not thinking any more about her. Soon after, it being quite dark, going towards the casino to read I saw her somewhat nearer the casino than before, but well away from all light and still walking alone. — At once I guessed she was a free lover. My dinner had warmed, my pego began to get rebellious for it had not touched strange cunt for nearly two months, and I went towards her. Seeing that, she went further off quite into the dark under some trees and stopped. — Next minute I was by her side and heard I could go home with her. We spoke in French, but I don't think she was a Frenchwoman.

She had told me where her lodging was and I agreed to follow her. She went away by a path I'd not traversed, crossed a wooden trembling bridge over the roaring rushing river, and was soon away from all street lights and human habitation as far as I could see. The road lay alongside the river, it was pitch dark, and at first I kept her just in sight, but as it was much further than I'd expected I got uncomfortable, as it was a spot where a knock on the head could very easily be given, and a body pitched into the river within a few yards of our path would have been thirty miles off before next morning, and had I screamed, the roar of the torrent would have drowned my voice, so I went up to her and said I could go no further. She said we were close by her dwelling and again we walked on.

When I first followed her I wanted to grope her, but she refused it. I got however one hand upon her thigh, the crisp hair of her quim touched my finger, and the feel of her tho slight and but for an instant only, made me thoroughly randy. As I followed her, I thought of her make and possible perfections, as I usually do when I follow a woman. From her walk I guessed she'd good limbs and a fat bum, my cock stood rigidly, pleasurably, and directly I'd crossed the bridge, with one of my old erotic whims I pulled it out of my trowsers, and went along with it sticking out naked. The lewdness of the act pleased me much, absurd as it seems. Hearing someone or something approaching, hastily I tucked it in, but it was only a donkey, I fancy tethered. Then as the distance increased and I grew anxious, my John Thomas drooped, and remained so till she stopped, when desire rose again. There was a huge piece of rock close by there, and I suggested an uprighter against it, but she wouldn't hear of such a thing.

On we went now side by side. I was about to refuse going further, when a building of Swiss type appeared on a little eminence about a hundred feet from the river. The light in two windows gladdened me, tho I didn't like to be in that lonely spot with a stranger at that time of night. There was seemingly a balcony all round it as is customary in those chalets. A big man, who was, as well as I could see in the darkness, sitting against the steps leading up to it, was smoking a pipe, and apparently took no notice of us, yet I didn't like his being there. Up the steps she went, I following on to the balcony, from which she opened a door into a large bedroom, meanly and coarsely furnished, tho there was everything needed for convenience, and a large common lamp alight. I complained that the light was not enough, whereon without reply she sought and lighted a candle. It was an angle room with windows on two sides, on one side only were short white curtains. The gaunt, naked look of the place, and the noise made by our feet on the naked wooden floor, the complete silence she observed, the gloom seen thro the uncurtained windows, and the roar of the river, I confess made me most uncomfortable – I wished I hadn't come and resolved to pay her and leave.

'What shall I do?' said she, taking off her bonnet. They were the first words she'd uttered in the room. 'Let me feel your cunt and then I'll go,' said I. – 'I'll take off my things first,' and she began to undress herself quickly. – Her face was very handsome, she had dark hair and luminous dark eyes, and as she pulled off her gown she showed such a fine pair of arms that I forgot my fears, touched them, and then let her strip to her chemise. – She sat down and piddled, then washed her quim, then pulled her stockings well up under her garters, and disclosed a very handsome form with thick bushes of dark hair in her armpits. Then to my question she said she was twenty-five.

Then I wanted to see her quim more plainly, but she resisted that a little, nor would she let me bring the light to it. — She didn't like to be looked at 'in that vulgar way.' She'd unbuttoned my trowsers and got my prick out, and as soon as it was in her hand said, — 'Aha — baisez moi, cheri' — and laid down on the bed, but somehow a feeling came over me, that I'd better not have her, said I wouldn't, put down her money, and said I'd leave. — 'Oh! come all this way without kissing me? that you shan't' — Getting off the bed she came to me, put the money first into a drawer, then throwing an arm round me kissed me and felt my cock. 'Are you quite well? if you're not quite sure, if there are any of your monthlies about, tell me, you've got the money, and I am quite content.'

She was perfectly well, she replied. 'Kiss me — come — you've paid me — is it likely I'd let you do it if I wasn't well? — Oh — kiss me, come take off your things, you're a fine man, you've made me want it so, baisez moi cheri' — and laying down she lifted her chemise to her armpits. I saw a fine bust, large thighs, a dark haired motte, desire returned, I threw off coat and waistcoat, with my trowsers on mounted her and in a few minutes had filled her quim with sperm. She enjoyed the embrace as much as I had.

She wanted to keep me in her, but I rose and washed, she washing directly afterwards, then she laid hold of my prick, looked at it, kissed it, and invited me to have her again. I didn't want that, and asked her a few questions. She was so pressing for me to have her that it surprised me. — 'You're fucked every day, I suppose.' — 'No' — she wasn't a gay woman. 'Tho you may think I am.' — Indeed I did, and do yet, tho she hadn't quite the manner of a Paphian. — I insisted on going. — She said I shouldn't — 'What! refuse a lady when she asks you? – oh fie.' – Yielding a little I said, 'Let me see you quite naked.' – 'You shall.' Off went her chemise and she laid down naked, but it was chilly and I let her put in on again. – I went to the side of the bed with my prick hanging. – 'See, I can't.' – 'You will in a minute.' – 'You will have to suck it then.' – For a minute she looked me full in the face without speaking, then took it in her mouth, I put my fingers on her cunt, and the joint effect was instantaneous – it stiffened. – 'There,' she said triumphantly. 'Baisez moi.' She laid down opening her thighs wide at once, hurriedly, as if her cunt was longing. – In another minute her cunt lips were round my propagator, and soon after we were blissfully spending. She seemed to have intense pleasure in the fuck, more than in the first.

She wanted me to stay all night – then to fuck her again, – it should cost me nothing more, – but away I went along the lonely road to my hotel, and was glad to get there. – Two days after I had a clap. – Incensed, I was fool enough to go to the chalet. – A man there – I suppose the proprietor – said that Mrs **** had left the day after I'd been there.

I stopped a week or two at Paris and then again visited the lapunar. The personnel of the house was the same, and the chambermaid seemed delighted to see me – I had a long conversation with her, and tipped her a napoleon – a nap well spent for me and on the sly of course – for I believe that employees in these bordellos are supposed to hand over gratuities – I think so from the secrecy I've been asked to observe by the recipients when I've given them – the door-keepers excepted, who openly expect, ask at times, and take. – Whether they put that into the hands of the *sous-maitresse*, or *patronne*, or not, I can't say, nor do I know if Frenchmen who have the women at the tariff *(prix-fixé)* give the servants anything – certainly they give presents to the women they stroke, but not as much as foreigners do. – Garter money the

Paphians call it, and if it be gold or silver always slip it under their garters into their stockings. What English and Americans give I can't say, having seen but few there – and expect that for good reasons those nationalities were rarely shown into the room with the peephole when I was peeping.

The chambermaid was called up to, who asked me, 'Which is it to be?' and making a circle with finger and thumb put it to her eye – I understood – she implied *peephole* by that. – 'No, foutre,' said I. – Then altering my mind. – 'No – chambre jaune.' – and there I was soon installed, and in a well lubricated quim or two had my pleasure. – I saw couples fucking when at the peephole directly afterwards, and then the ladies with cunts washed or unwashed – I paid for each woman I saw come in, but nothing was worth retaining in my narrative till I saw Diane the following evening.

It is singular, seems contradictory, but I write what occurred, that I rarely seemed to have the same excitement, pleasure, or even desire, in tailing the women whom I had seen fucked, as I did those who came in to me from other rooms. – More often than otherwise, I didn't even put my pego up them. – Sometimes I only looked at their quims without separating the covers of the vulva, when I did not like the look of the man who'd had them. Often times this was so. – But *I always desired those who'd been stroked in other parts of the house* – I always fancied the sperm was that of handsome very young men tho often it was not so – I rejected those directly if the suspicion of their having been fucked by seniors occurred to me.

I was at the peephole when I saw Diane, a little devil who had a very fine man with her. He stripped, she was naked, he was playful and she gratified him. – I never saw a woman put herself into more varied postures. She licked and sucked his prick from all sides, laid on him, sat on his prick, put it in her quim this way, that way, stood him up, laid him down on the bedside, turned over on to his belly, licked his arsehole, put his cock between her breasts, bum cheeks, thighs, and knees, and then taking off her stockings, caught hold of his pego between the soles of her feet, and twiddled, a thing I never saw being done before, tho I'd had it done to me. He had a noble prick, which stood without drooping much for half an hour. – Every now and then when they had a new pose, she looked at my door. – Once when lying over him, he licking her clitoris, she minetting his cock, her head being towards me, she lifted her head, looked at the door and winked, shaking his red-headed poker at me as she did so. – Never did I see such variety of attitudes in so short a space of time – most of them studiously posed that I might see both prick and cunt. He got impatient at last and fucked her, only thrusting about twice before he was over. – He got off the bed directly with prick dripping, and naked, looked at his watch, then hurried on his clothes. She went out as if to wash, – they all do that to avoid notice – when she came back he was at the door, – next minute her thighs were opened to me, the sperm was running over furrow and thighs – Alexandrine had told me she was the most salacious one of the harem, and would let men bugger her – she said that cautiously.

She was a sweetly made, brown-haired, lewed-eyed creature. – I enjoyed the sight of her lubricated quim, rushed my staff up it and spent rapidly. When she had washed, she began to play with me, wouldn't let me dress, began to gamahuche. 'Lie down and let me play with you, darling.' – When my pego was in her mouth, she put her finger up my bum. – I returned the compliment slightly. 'Put it up' said she – 'put your prick in it.' – 'What! bugger?' – 'Yes, if you like' – I declined. – 'You are stiff, why not try, put the tip in a little.' – She pulled open her buttocks, shewing her arsehole, elevating her thighs high. 'Another night perhaps, what do you want for that?' – 'Fifty francs.' – 'All right, I won't tell any one.' – 'I don't care if you do, many of the women do it.' – 'I won't believe they do.' – 'Ask them then. I shewed the man to you well didn't I?' – 'Yes.' – 'I've made myself lewed.' – 'Does *he* bugger you?' – 'Sometimes, should you like to see him, if so come next week this day and time, and I'll make him do it to me.' – 'Perhaps I will,' said I, having no intention of the sort. – 'She is a most lascivious little devil,' said I to Alexandrine afterwards. – 'Yes, she is woman or man, it's all the same with her, she'll go mad like Sappho.'

Sappho was a lovely woman whom for three years I had at times. She flat fucked a girl before me one night without my desiring her to do so, became a slave to erotic passion, had nymphomania which drove her at last mad. Her voice was like that of a man's the last time I had her. – Many French harlots get that sort of voice in time. – Sappho's history was well known in the house, and to me.

[I have an impression that cases of erotic madness are not infrequent in these lapunars. It is perhaps attributable to natural concupiscence in the particular woman, encouraged by facilities for every form of erotic pleasure. – Some years ago at another lapunar, I had a woman named Wanda who two or three years after I heard had gone mad concupiscently. Both the Sappho now alluded to – I've had several Sapphos – and also Wanda – were well sized – absolutely perfect in form – beautiful in face – delicious in coition – and both had hoarse voices. Each must have been from about twenty-three to twenty-eight years old when last I had them – but I'm not clear about their ages. – This is written many years after the events.]

One evening, a week or two after being at the spyhole, in came a well-grown man looking about eight and twenty, and with him a lovely, dark-haired, dark-eyed little creature named Raymonde, whom I'd stroked and a more willing, voluptuous little devil never knew. – She gave a glance at the peephole door, and a smile, then disappeared to sluice her quim before beginning her gambols.

He undressed quickly, his prick – a very full-sized one – was already stiff. I longed to handle it. – His shirt dropped over it, Raymonde raised it and rolled up the shirt, and then laid hold of his stiff tool with a laugh. – 'Take your shirt off' – Alexandrine had instructed all the women to let me see the pricks well. – He wouldn't, took her to the bedside, and kneeling began gamahuching her. Playfully she raised herself. 'Take it off, I like you naked' – and she began to pull it off as he knelt. He then complied and again knelt, titillating her cunt with his tongue, his tool standing with utmost rigidity and with a very unusual curve – like a bent bow it was. – I've never seen one so curved before, tho I've seen a hundred and fifty stiff.

He only licked her split for a minute, then rose up, and she getting off the bed handled his prick to show it me – I found by their conversation that they were acquaintances. – 'Mon Dieu! how stiff it is – why you've actually not seen me for a week.' – Bending forward she took the red tip between her pretty lips, then removing it she handled his balls – I never saw a prick with such a strongly defined curve, I think it was much greater than the curve of any vagina.

All was done quicker than I write this, for he was impatient. Standing then by the bedside he turned her about in all directions, kissing her all over, then mounted the bed, laid on his back, and putting her kneeling over his head, began licking her cunt. His face was then hidden by her lovely buttocks which his hands clasped. Then moving away she took his prick in her mouth, then taking it out gave it a shake, looked at the peephole, and laughed at me whilst she exhibited his tool. But soon she dropped her head on his thigh by the side of it, and her buttocks began to writhe under the delicious titillation of his tongue on her clitoris.

Then he moved her onto her back, mounted her belly and began fucking. In a dozen thrusts I saw *his* backside and thighs quiver and squeeze up to her – one very loud prolonged cry – almost a groan – escaped him, and all was over. – I knew he would be quick from the state of his pego when he took his trowsers off, saw clearly that he was filled with semen and lust.

He did not enjoy laying up her long, but came to the bidet and washed his prick which was still quite stiff. – 'Aha! – mon Dieu – what sperm,' – said she quite loudly, not moving off the bed as they usually do, but lying with thighs wide apart, – pulling open the lips, as she spoke, and turning partly round more towards the gaslight, to show me his overflowing libation. – Never before had I seen at that distance a cunt more plainly whilst the male was present. The light was turned on strongly, and I saw a mass of sperm, which made her cunt look almost as white as her thighs. She looked towards him and to my door, smiled and nodded, pulled the lips of her cunt further apart for a second, and then went out. He had his back towards her whilst washing his tool and she thus exhibited. – How easily we men are cheated.

He laid himself in her absence on the bed, his prick stiff still. How I envied him. She returned, began to suck it and it disappeared in her mouth. – Sometimes her hand grasped the balls, sometimes the stem. Full of sperm as he had been, now he needed a rest. For full ten minutes did she labour with her mouth, he laying motionless, speechless, in voluptuous tranquillity looking up at the glass in the bed top. He never turned his head to see her ivory backside, and breasts and movements. He didn't lay even a hand upon her.

I thought he never would spend, yet his prick whenever she removed it from her mouth was rigid as iron, and red tipped. Gradually came slight movements in his thighs, then his belly heaved a little, his eyes closed. She ceased minetting, knowing that a change was coming. Then again he placed her above him, her cunt to his mouth, hers to his prick, and they sucked each other till *she* gave a jog or two of her buttocks, relinquished his tool, and laid her head again on his thigh – his machine standing up against her face.

Then he placed her and himself in positions which I don't

recollect a couple fucking in before, tho I have seen perhaps every possible posture — indeed now recollect having had a woman in that position myself. — How deliciously varied may be the postures of a willing man and woman, what inexhaustible pleasures they can get together, what idiots are they who refuse them, — if any do.

He put two pillows for her head and back against the looking glass which covered the wall against which the side of the bed was placed. She then put herself leaning back and reclining anglewise along the bed, and he laid across her. They were like two sticks crossing each other. His head was nearly at the edge of the bed, his feet against the looking glass. *His* legs lay *over* her left leg, and *under her* right which she put up *over* his left hip. In that position he got his prick up her cunt. — No one with a little prick, or with a limp one, could manage it in that awkward position.

Then moving with a short jogging, rather than the long stroke belly to belly fucking, her right leg keeping him to her and both of her hands placed over and clasping his rump, they fucked. Then he stopped, then went on, and not a word was said. The back of his head and rump were towards me, and I saw the length of his fine white body from head to heel. At last Raymonde who at the beginning of the play in this position had looked at my door and smiled more than once, began to close her eyes, her right hand seemed to be feeling his arsehole or the back of his balls, then both her hands clutched his bum convulsively. She was spending and lovely she looked. Her hands stopped, her breasts heaved, his buttocks gave some strong quick jerks, another loud cry escaped him, and he was quiet.

Then he washed, she remained on the bed as if quite fatigued, then went out, returned, and shortly he went away. She hadn't washed her cunt this time, which was full of his second libation. Excited by the sight I plunged my prick into it, and spent before Raymonde had a chance of spending with me. He came to see her once a week she said, and always made her spend. 'Who could help spending with such a man, and such a prick up her for ten minutes?' she asked. Certainly at the second poke it was in her a very long time, a quarter of an hour perhaps before he spent.

In winter I went again to **** for a longish stay and the lapunar saw me frequently, much more than before or since. – I have notes of about forty or fifty couples fucking, and perhaps of a hundred and fifty spermatized cunts – but they were brief notes. Half a dozen incidents spread over two years alone I retain almost word for word as I wrote them. I have never departed from my habit of writing accounts of my erotic pleasures.

On my first visit to the lapunar I went to the saloon. As I entered the outer room, there were three girls standing naked like the three graces, and talking together. – Looking thro the open door at a looking glass, I saw reflected a dozen nudities in the saloon itself. The rump of one of the graces attracted me, and in a minute she was with me in the room on the *entresol* – a favorite room of mine.

She was a shortish well-formed woman of five and twenty, judging from the dark hair on her quim, which spread widening out halfway to her navel, then with a diminishing line running up towards her navel. I have seen hair growing like that up from a man's motte, but rarely in a woman. I didn't like it, and it set me for a minute a little against her. But her face was pretty, she was talkative, obliging, and by the time I had laid on the bed and she had gamahuched me a little, I was contented. – We talked about women I had known in that house, at intervals she sucked my cock, shewed me her cunt, and we indulged in other fornicating preliminaries.

This room is at the end of a passage, at the other end is a lavabo and a little room by its side, where the ladies prepare themselves for and after love-making. I have seen dozens there slopping and syringing, naked almost as born. They retreat into the room when they hear a stranger. – If the door of the room where I was be ajar, one can see these operations, and I select it for this, if my companion for the time allows me. They prevent this as a rule – but I am known, and permitted.

I heard water drawn. – 'A woman's washing' said I to Isabel. – 'Yes.' – 'Let me see.' Isabel did not object, I peeped, and saw a fine woman sluicing her cunt over a basin. Isabel said I could look at others but she had better always look out first. Another splash – with a sudden rush of baudy desires, one to see the woman's cunt before she washed the sperm out, I told Isabel – half ashamed as I did so of my wish. – 'I'll call her,' said she, as if it was a usual and natural thing. – 'You have washed?' she cried. – 'Comment?' – said a voice. 'Have you the foutre, still?' – 'Mais non.' – 'She has washed. I will tell the chamberwoman to tell them to come here first, do you like browns or blondes?' – 'Browns.' – Isabel disappeared, and returning said there were several girls 'en société' and one would soon come.

In voluptuous expectation I sat on the sofa feeling Isabel all over. Soon up she jumped, opened the door, and a well-grown, dark-haired girl holding her cunt lips together came in. 'Is the sperm in your cunt?' I asked. – 'Comment?' – In my excitement my French was not perfect. – 'Vous avez la, la foutre,' – said Isabel in baudiest French. 'Ah yes, I'll wash.' said Zora – not understanding my object and turning towards the door. – 'No, no, I want the sperm,' – I laid hold of her and led her to the bed. – She understood, and laying backwards opened wide her thighs.

What a sight. A lovely creature, with a well-fledged, ebony-haired cunt, the sperm thick and thin lying on it. Opaque masses just inside the outer lips, and on her thighs – shining yet milky looked her vulva. – 'He has spent much. – Baisez moi,' said she. – 'Suck my prick.' – Isabel knelt and complied. I put Zora's thighs wider and wider apart, she stretched open her cunt lips, her fingers in the sperm. I kissed her thighs, smelt the male, and with a spasm of baudy delight instantly gave Isabel's mouth a libation.

'I must go, my friend is waiting,' said Zora and left. My prick was still in Isabel's mouth, she was finishing me divinely. – Then she left the room. I laid on the bed till the two women came back. Then looked at Zora's fresh-washed privates, paid her and she left, Isabel remaining.

Stupidly, I felt ashamed. – 'You will think me a beast,' said I. 'Not at all, it often happens – there is a Monsieur who comes to this room by himself, he will stay *all* the evening and see us *all* – they *all* come in before they wash, he looks at *all*, stays hours. There are one or two Messieurs who lick the cunts and swallow the sperm – yes of strangers. – It's not good, is it? but it is true. Two gentlemen come here together and have two girls, I have been with them – they stay all night sometimes, and each has the same girl and fucks without their washing – and more.' – She stopped short. 'What more?' – 'They bugger each other.' – 'Not the girls.' – 'Ah my God, no – but sometimes one fucks a lady whilst his friend arseholes him.' – 'Why not the girl?' – 'Did *you* ever do it to a girl?' she asked. 'Yes' – 'Who with?' – 'I *never* tell' – I said this lie to try her. We talked of such matters and of the girls I had known, until what with talking and feeling her quim, and her pulling me about, I was randy again – then she gamahuched me until nearly finished, when hearing the water tap going, I said I should see another lady.

To help me – tho there were two gas lights – she got candles and set them on the mantelshelf, so that I could see the cunts well. She would tell them to get rid of their friends if they could before they came in, so as not to be in a hurry with me, but most would see the ladies after they'd washed, and a girl must not displease a friend 'vous savez donc.' – She named some women just then engaged, I told her those whom I did not want. – A gentle rap. – 'Entrez.' – In came Theo, a dark-haired girl who placed herself on to the bed and opened her thighs, the sperm was oozing clear and thin, both thighs wet with it, plenty of it. – Isabel held a candle to it whilst I questioned. He'd not spent so much as many she replied. 'Fuck me, – you, I want it and shall spend then.' – 'Monsieur does not fuck,' said Isabel, 'he likes minette.' – The other repeated, 'Fuck me.' – 'No gamahuche *me*.' She turned round lengthways on the bed and put my prick into her mouth – I could not keep my fingers from her cunt, pushed them up her thro the sperm but instantly withdrew them, wiping them, for a fit of squeamishness came on. – Another knock. Isabel let in a shortish, plump woman with thick legs and large thighs; ginger-coloured hair curled round her cunt.

I treated her like the other. the spunk was thinnish, much of it lay above the clitoris in the thicket, as if the man had spent outside. 'Baisez moi, cheri.' – She was dazzlingly white in flesh – I looked at her cunt and then at the other's – enchanted – on the highest state of salacity.

'Fuck me, darling' said Eugenie putting her tongue out, agitating it like a serpent. – Isabel repeated. – 'The gentleman does not fuck.' – Making the pair hold up their legs I went to the end of the room to contemplate – Isabel stood by the bed with a candle, – 'Isn't his prick stiff?' said one. The other took up the towel which was under her bum and was going to wipe her cunt. Isabel cried, 'Don't.' The girl laughed. – Knock – knock. – 'Come in.' – 'I don't want any others,' said I, but Isabel opened the door. – 'Oh, she's come purposely – it's Leda – the biggest woman in the house, a fine woman, tall, superb.' – 'Let her come.' – In came a splendid woman five feet ten high, stood still, looked at the two girls, laughed, then looked at me.

I was delighted with her ample form, could see the black hair peeping from her armpits, the jet black mass on her mons – 'lay on the bed.' – 'Monsieur wants to see the sperm,' said Isabel – I took her round her bum, feeling it as she moved towards the bed between the others. – Up went her legs – open her thighs – and Ah Dieu! What a sight. Sperm lay all over her cunt from above her clitoris to the furrow of her buttocks, the entry of her sex was full, was covered with it, the prick hole hidden. – Between the outer and the inner lips it lay in a thick white mass – the nymphae peeping through a milky glaze. It lay thick in the roots of the hair all round the lips – lay thick and shiny on both thighs some inches down from her cunt, not all transparent gumminess but some opaque, alternating with thin shiny essence, that must have just issued from strong, healthy, full ballocks. I pulled apart the beautiful buttocks which closed together under her cunt. 'Let me see your arsehole darling.' – The sperm had run down even to there. – All round her bum hole for a space of three or four inches, her buttocks were covered with short dark hairs, seeming to grow out of the sperm like grass out of ice. I stood with prick throbbing, Isabel holding the candle in front of Leda's cunt. I glanced at the other shiny cunts, and the darkeyed, smiling, baudy faces of their owners on each side of Leda, till I felt mad with lust.

'Do the nutcracker,' said I. Leda raised up her knees towards her breasts, her belly had a muscular motion, the cunt slightly closed and out rolled more viscosity down towards the bum furrow. 'Fuck me,' said she. – Again Isabel, 'Mais monsieur, ne baise pas.' – 'What sort of man was he?' – I asked. 'Ah! an old friend, sees me every week regularly, every Monday, a grand man – beau garçon – never sees any other girl. Look at his sperm – he only kisses me.' – 'He spends much?' I said. 'Mais oui, beaucoup, toujours beaucoup, never a man more – jamais. – He visits me alone – moi seule.' – 'Are you sure?' – 'Mais oui, bien sure – si si – si – je vous le dis qu'il m'aime. – Il me baise seule et chaque lundi toujours, toujours.' She seemed angry at my doubts.

All this whilst Leda was laying on the bedside, thighs apart, cunt slightly open, arms back under her head to raise it, shewing thickly haired armpits. I standing in front of her with stiff prick within a few inches of her split, glancing rapidly from hers to the quims of the two on either side of her, Isabel holding the candle, the two side women frigging their quims, putting out their tongues, a maddening lascivious sight. In my youth I should have spent at once without my prick being touched by cunt, mouth, or fingers.

Still I did not fuck, didn't know which to select for my homage, the variety of charms made me greedy of all and uncertain, I looked closer and closer at each woman, my eyes ran up and down them from head to knees, closer I looked at the three cunts, feeling the thighs of each in turn, kissed their bellies and the smell of cunt and semen rose into my nostrils. The room was reeking hot, a pervading odour of fresh young female flesh, cunt, armpits, sweat and spunk mingling with the perfumes in their hair, intoxicated me – I was choked, excited with it, madly erotic, but still lingered, looked, smelt and kissed, not knowing which to have, longing to fuck all three at once.

'Baisez moi,' said Leda, giving a bum waggle, opening her thighs wider, delicately distending the hirsute entrance to her warm red avenue, her finger tips in the sperm. Then I put my pego's knob against her bum furrow, catching a globe of thick sperm lying there, and drawing it up along the division or furrow to the mouth of her sheath, drove it up closing balls and belly onto her with a shiver of pleasure. Then up and down it went, now drawing out covered with male essence, then squashing into her again, till my pleasure increased and I stopped, holding her lovely buttocks, resting my head upon her superb breasts, wild with voluptuous thoughts. 'I shall spend in his sperm. – My pego's in it now – his prick rubbed where mine is rubbing, it has throbbed and swelled where mine is.' – Ah summit of baudiness – sublimity of voluptuousness – heaven of sexuality, physical and mental – mind stimulating body – body exciting mind – to maddening erotic delight.

So flew my thoughts, as I wriggled my belly and thighs to hers – this way, that way – with one hand dabbed my balls against her buttocks to get the sperm on to them, pushed high and rubbed my motte against her motte, that my fringe might get the sperm from hers – anything, any way, every way, so that I might be saturated with it. – It rubbed into the roots of my prick – it stuck to my balls – yet still her cunt seemed full of it – my prick seemed moving in butter – I cried out 'foutre – foutre' – and drew out my prick. – 'The candle, Isabel.' – She held the light, I gloried in my pego's moisture, in the spermy spottiness and sheen. It chilled when it left its warm companion and up into her I plunged it again. – 'Come nearer dear – lower down – nearer the edge of the bed – put up your thighs – higher – draw me to you.' – Her thighs came on my hips, her legs clutched me, and I could then only wriggle my prick up her, leant over her fucking thus – now smelling her flesh, now sucking her bubbies – smoothing her buttocks, – now feeling round the junction of prick and cunt, whilst with her heels on my arse she still drew me tightly up to her, and on each side of her lay a woman with her cunt gaping.

Spunk, spunk, more spunk, I was mad for it. My hands left her bum, and spreading out felt the two girls' vulvas, covered them with fingers and palms, then thrust my fingers up their gluey vaginas. – How hot, how soft and slippery, how large they felt, I was furious for spunk, could have sucked it, swallowed it, had any been on Leda's ivory breast – Leda heaved up. 'Push,' said she closing her eyes. – 'Say spunk, Leda.' – 'Aha, le foutre, foutre, foutez moi – baisez moi donc chéri – foutre – pousse.' – 'Say foutre, cheris.' – Both girls wriggled their buttocks crying out 'foutre, fuck.' Then with prick ramming against Leda's womb, fingers groping in two cunts, all four crying out baudily in a chorus of lewedness – 'Fuck, spunk, balls' in French and English – I spent – Isabel who'd put down the candle holding my balls, and gently pushing one finger up my anus without request from me. – Ah the ideal! the kaleidoscope of rapid lewed visions, as they flashed thro and grouped in my brain.

My head on Leda's breasts I reposed – Leda did not. 'Push, push chéri,' said she. 'Don't stop' and kept up a vigorous wriggling – her heels still over my hips, she pulled my body closer to hers, and pulled by face to hers. – 'Push' – I did my best with half-standing cock. A long sigh, her limbs fell down by my side, her eyes closed, she was still. I felt a rapid movement of a hand on the clitoris of one of the women up whose cunt my fingers still were – she was frigging herself – Leda gave me a hearty kiss, the girl on the left was quiet.

Out came my prick. – A glance at Leda's quim. – Sperm lay on the notch, it was mine. My thighs, prick, and balls were covered with her lover's. – Her thighs and hair still wet and shiny, but the opaque masses had gone, were distributed – dried up. – She sat up, so did the others. 'Quel bougre de cochon,' said one. – 'Ah Polisson – ah sale cochon,' said Leda – and the four women burst out laughing. I called for champagne, and we drank it.

I cared no longer for cunts, and paid the ladies. Isabel held the basin for my ablutions. Did I like Leda? – yes, I did. – 'What spunk she had!' – Leda had gone out of the room to wash. 'Did you ever see so much spunk on a cunt?' I asked Isabel. – 'Not often from one man.' I did not think of the reply till I came to write this – what did she mean?

And to think, that formerly I made a woman wash her quim before I took to it, for fear a drop of sperm should be there! – Every age brings its pleasures and tastes. – Five cunts and four with sperm in them in three hours, besides one woman as show woman and introducer! – an orgy.